A couple of mudlarks were stripping a corpse near the barricades at the southern corner of the Heaps. Riot cops guarding the gibbets where the bodies of a dozen felons hung watched impassively, eyes masked by the visors of their helmets, Uzis slung casually at their sides. They stirred the usual little frisson of adrenaline in Cameron's blood, a reflex that was all that was left of his days on the run, a student revolutionary with an *in absentia* sentence of treason on his head. But he was beyond the law now. He was one of the uncountable citizens of the invisible country, for whom there were only the gangs and posses and the arbitrary justice of the New Families. Law was reserved for the rich, and fortress suburbia, and the prison camps where at least a quarter of the population was locked away, camps Cameron had avoided by the skin of his teeth.

Also by Paul J. McAuley in paperback

SECRET HARMONIES

RED DUST

PASQUALE'S ANGEL

FAIRYLAND

PAUL J. McAULEY
THE INVISIBLE COUNTRY

VISTA

First published in Great Britain 1996
by Victor Gollancz

This Vista edition published 1997
Vista is an imprint of the Cassell Group
Wellington House, 125 Strand, London WC2R 0BB

A catalogue record for this book is
available from the British Library.

ISBN 0 575 60189 2

Printed and bound in Great Britain
by Cox & Wyman Ltd, Reading, Berks

97 98 99   10 9 8 7 6 5 4 3 2 1

Contents

With thanks to my editors: Greg Bear,
Ellen Datlow, Ed Ferman, David Garnett,
Stephen Jones, David Pringle, Sue Shaw
and Lewis Shiner.

We should not be surprised that life, having subjugated the bulk of inert matter on Earth, would go on to subjugate technology, and bring it also under its reign of constant evolution, perpetual novelty, and an agenda out of our control.

Out of Control,
Kevin Kelly

Introduction: McAuley Moments

In the summer of 1993, Paul McAuley and I travelled separately to California, mostly to attend the World Science Fiction Convention in San Francisco, but also to remind ourselves of that frayed edge of reality lapped by the Pacific. We hooked up in Los Angeles, where I staked out in an anonymous motel and he stayed with an academic couple who keep a remarkable cactus garden. Paul had lived and taught in LA for a couple of years before he got started as a writer, and knew his way around the grids of endless streets and neighbourhoods. I'd been there before, but was more familiar with the fantasized city projected through popular culture. Between us, we had adventures, coped with things and picked up story ideas.*

At that time, Paul's latest novel was *Red Dust*, in which Elvis Presley is a mythological figure to Chinese cowboys on Mars. In America, Paul was on the scout for E-Moments, those tiny incidents in which Elvis touches your life, whether as a stained-glass window or through a telecine sample on a tape loop in a retro-diner. As we travelled around two cities, and took a long drive between them that brought us to San Simeon and the kelp-beds of Morro Bay (Paul has a thing about kelp), I realized we were more likely to be struck by McAuley Moments. These are chance encounters with a person, building, cultural event or phenomenon that convince you Paul J. McAuley is the only writer in the science fiction field whose future is already here.

The cumulative effect of three weeks of McAuley Moments is that you come to believe Paul is the only man in the

* At least, Kim did – see for instance, his novella 'Out of the Night, When the Full Moon is Bright'. *I* got a guy with a crusty head wound. [PJM]

universe capable of dealing with it, if only by wearing mirror-shades ironically (not as easy as it sounds) and sniggering like some post-modern Muttley. Actually, the cool shades he is seen to be sporting in some photographs are old-fashioned granny-takes-a-trip black sunglasses: Paul has the knack of tilting his head so the photographer's flash catches the lenses *just so* and makes mirrors of them. Confronted with an impossibility, he will mull it over for a few quiet moments as if considering accepting it, and then chortle 'fuck off'.

A wino came up to us outside Book Soup on Sunset Boulevard and claimed he had just triaged his head with a bottle of cleaning fluid. He had the bloody marks to prove it. In Los Angeles, down-and-outs can form sentences using the word 'triage', probably some fall-out from battlefield medical jargon in one of the USA's odd little pseudo-colonial embarrassments. That bum reappears in Paul's novel *Fairyland*, which is essential reading, and not only because it is the largest component of a loose cycle of near-future stories represented here by 'Prison Dreams', 'Dr Luther's Assistant', 'Children of the Revolution' and 'Slaves'. You don't need to know the novel to enjoy the stories – a throwaway line in 'Slaves' unfairly sums up its entire plot as bad fiction – but each shard illuminates the others. It's a fallacy to subdivide Paul's work into cycles (the story clusters that accrue to *Fairyland*, the alternate world of *Pasquale's Angel* or the far future setting of *Eternal Light*), since his ideas cross the barriers between them, and stories with apparently the same background sometimes cut different ways.

The triage bum was a McAuley Moment, revealing a truth about the way the world is going that runs through McAuley's humane but sardonic commentaries: you don't have to be ignorant to lose the place. Science fiction used to give us technocrats as heroes, visionary spacemen and thinkers who would expand mankind's (America's, they meant) manifest destiny to the stars. Paul's science fiction, which is as involved with the magic and romance of *realwelt* science as anyone else's, gives us the marginals: workers, artists, hustlers, ex-revolutionaries, criminals, losers, eternal students. For a long time, he has taught at various academic institutes: his characters are the types who drift around the edges of any university, never quite getting round to taking or teaching classes but often spinning elaborate and pleasing theories in common rooms or hall of residence kitchens.

While Cyberpunk™ replaces the old-style Dan Dares with supercool drop-outs, the Fonz with a plug in his skull, Paul knows what life in squats and collectives is really like. His outlaws spend most of their time in the cold, glimpsing the ripples of history that pass them by, sensing the great changes overtaking the universe, struggling sometimes to do the right thing in extreme circumstances, never entertaining fantasies of omnipotence or martyrdom, as deeply surrounded by naff cultural debris as by anything which might be categorized as trendy pop reference. Like any English writer (he has Irish ancestry and lives in Scotland, but he's English), McAuley often pinpoints the exact rituals of tea-making and snack-sharing that underly his characters' circular arguments.

Through it all, wonderfully in two stories here that (following *Pasquale's Angel*) embroider the character and legend of Dr Pretorius (the waspish mad scientist played by Ernest Thesiger in James Whale's 1935 film, *Bride of Frankenstein*), there's a sense of the sheer looniness of those hidden masters who have tapped into the way the world works and manipulate it for their amusement. Dr Luther is also an avatar of Pretorius, taking this creature of hidden history into the future.

Later in our Los Angeles trip, Paul and I visited the La Brea Tar Pits, where the Japanese-style wing of the LA County Museum of Art offered another vision of a future that is already here, and happened into an exhibition of huge pictures by the artist Mark Tansey, which turned out to be another McAuley Moment. Among Tansey's most impressive works is 'Derrida Queries de Man', a parodic recreation of Sherlock Holmes's struggle with Professor Moriarty above the Reichenbach Falls in which the French philosophers Jacques Derrida and Paul de Man dance close to a precipice on a turquoise mountain-top etched with words.

The mix of complex allusion, wry humour, minute detail, populist form, serious content and figurative-narrative elements strikes me as the canvas equivalent of a McAuley novel or story. Also in that exhibition was 'The Innocent Eye Test', in which a cow in an art gallery is shown a seventeenth-century canvas of a bull by dignified experts, which a passing American child told his parents was his favourite picture in the exhibition. Why? 'I just like the cow.' Similarly, though there's an exhausting amount of content in a story as brief as 'Gene Wars', it could also be read and loved by that kid who just liked the cow.

Paul is of that post-New Wave generation of sf writers who have rediscovered the pleasure of the gosh-wow (witness the far future kaleidoscope of 'Recording Angel') and of stories with plots and characters as well as big ideas and unusual structures. In many ways, his strength is that approachable narrative allows you to get closer to the white heat of Idea than you might think. And, with Paul, ideas always proliferate, rushing like the dizzying waters of that fall which claimed (but didn't) Holmes, throwing up patterns and resonances.

In San Francisco, crammed in the back of a wild taxi with Ellen Datlow, Paul got into a conversation with the driver about Theory. If you have to ask 'theory of what?' you wouldn't have been able to get into the conversation. As he debated the finer points of de Man's arguments with the cabbie, I realized this was another McAuley Moment, drawing out of the woodwork yet another surprise. The philosophical taxi driver has yet to show up in Paul's fiction, but he would fit in, exchanging Theory with random fares, delighted to find someone capable of talking on his level. Ellen was annoyed because the guy couldn't find our restaurant, but I think that was a small price to pay. As Paul reminds me, the guy blurted 'Oops, I forgot I was a taxi driver,' killed the meter and did get us to our meal only half an hour late.

Pay attention to these stories. There are things in them that you need to know.

Kim Newman, 1996

The Invisible Country

Cameron was discharged from the black clinic with nothing more than his incubation fee and a tab of painkiller so cut with chalk it might as well have been aspirin. Emptied of the totipotent marrow that had been growing there, the long bones of his thighs ached with fierce fire, and he blew twenty pounds on a pedicab that took him to the former department store on Oxford Street where he rented a cubicle.

The building's pusher, a slender Bengali called Lost In Space, was lounging in his deckchair near the broken glass doors, and Cameron bought a hit of something called Epheridrin from him.

'Enkephalin-specific,' Lost In Space said, as Cameron dry-swallowed the red gelatin capsule. 'Hits the part of the brain that makes you think you hurt. Good stuff, Doc. So new the bathtub merchants haven't cracked it yet.' He folded up his fax of yesterday's *Financial Times* – like most pushers, he liked to consider himself a player in the Exchange's information flux – and smiled, tilting his head to look up at Cameron. There was a diamond set into one of his front teeth. 'There is a messenger waiting for you all morning.'

'Komarnicki has a job for me? It's been a long time.'

'You are too good to work for him, Doc. You know there is a place for you in our organization. There is always need for collectors, for gentlemen who have a *persuasive* air.'

'I don't work for the Families, OK? I'm freelance, always will be.'

'Better surely, Doc, than renting your body. Those kinky cell lines can turn rogue so easily.'

'There are worse things.' Cameron remembered the glimpse he'd had of the surrogate ward, the young men naked on pallets, bulging bellies shining as if oiled and pulsing with the asynchronous beating of the hearts growing inside them. The drug was beginning to take hold, delicate caresses of ice fluttering through the pain in his legs. He looked around at the dozen or so transients camped out on the grimy marble floor and said loudly, 'Where's this messenger?'

A skinny boy, seven or eight years old, came over. All he wore was plastic sandals and tight-fitting shorts of fluorescent orange waterproofed cotton. Long greasy hair tangled around his face; his thin arms were ropey with homemade tattoos. A typical mudlark. Homeless, futureless, there had to be a million of them in London alone, feral as rats or pigeons, and as little loved. He handed Cameron a grubby strip of paper and started to whine that he hadn't been paid.

'You've a lot to learn, streetmeat,' Cameron said, as he deciphered Komarnicki's scrawled message. 'Next time ask me before you hand over the message.' He started for the door, then turned and knocked the shiv from the boy's hand by pure reflex.

The blade had been honed from the leaf of a car spring: when Cameron levered it into a crack in the marble floor it bent but would not snap. He tossed it aside and the boy swore at him, then dodged Cameron's half-hearted cuff and darted through the broken doors into the crowded street. Another enemy. Well, he'd just have to take his turn with the rest.

Lost In Space called out, 'Your soft heart will get you in trouble one day, Doc.'

'Fuck you. That blade was probably all that poor kid had in the world. Sell a working man a couple more of those capsules and save the opinions.'

Lost in Space smiled up lazily. 'It is always a pleasure doing business with you, Doc. You are such a regular customer.' The diamond sparkled insincerely.

Cameron checked his gun harness out of storage and hiked around Wreckers Heaps to Komarnicki's office. The shanty town strung along the margin of the Heaps was more crowded than ever. When Cameron had lived there, his first days in the city after the farm, after Birmingham, there had still been trees, even a little grass. The last of Hyde Park. No more. Naked children chased each other between tents and shanty huts, dodging around piles of rubbish and little heaps of human shit that swarmed with flies. Smoke from innumerable cooking fires hazed the tops of the Exchange's far-off river-front ribbon of glittering towers, the thread of the skyhook beyond. Along the street, competing sound systems laid overlapping pulses of highlife, rai, garage dub, techno-raga. Hawkers cried their wares by the edge of the slow-moving stream of bubblecars, flatbed trucks crowded with passengers, pedicabs, bicycles. Occasionally, a limo of some New Family or Exchange vip slid through the lesser vehicles like a sleek shark. And over all this, ad screens raised on rooftops or cantilevered gantries straddling the road or derelict sites glowed with heartbreakingly beautiful faces miming happiness or amazement or sexual ecstasy behind running slogans for products that no one on the street could possibly afford, or for cartels only the information brokers in the Exchange knew anything about.

A couple of mudlarks were stripping a corpse near the barricades at the southern corner of the Heaps. Riot cops guarding the gibbets where the bodies of a dozen felons hung watched impassively, eyes masked by the visors of their helmets, Uzis slung casually at their sides. They stirred the usual little frisson of adrenaline in Cameron's blood, a reflex that was all that was left of his days on the run, a student revolutionary with an *in absentia* sentence of treason on his head. But he was beyond the law now. He was one of the uncountable citizens of the invisible country, for whom there were only the gangs and posses and the arbitrary justice of the New Families. Law was reserved for the rich, and fortress suburbia, and the prison camps where at least a quarter of the population was locked away, camps Cameron had avoided by the skin of his teeth.

Inside the barricades, things were cleaner, quieter. The plate-glass windows of Harrods displayed artful arrangements of electronics, biologics, the latest Beijing fashions. Japanese and Brazilian business men strolled the wide pavements, paced by tall men in sleeveless jackets cut to show off their fashionably shaped torsos – like a blunt, inverted triangle – and the grafted arm muscle and hypertrophied elbow and shoulder joints. Some had scaly spurs jutting from wrists or elbows. A league away from Cameron's speed. He relied on his two metres and muscles shaped by weight-training, not surgery, to make a presence. Consequently, he got only the lesser members of visiting entourages, translators, bagmen, gofers: never the vips. As Lost In Space had said, he was getting old. And worse than old, out-of-date. Even though Komarnicki's protection agency had never been anything but a marginal affair just one step ahead of the law, Cameron was hardly getting any work from it any more.

Komarnicki's office was in a Victorian yellow-brick townhouse in the warren of streets behind the V&A, as near to Exchange as he could afford, three flights up stairs that wound around a defunct lift shaft at least a century old. Cameron swallowed another of the capsules and went in.

Komarnicki was drinking rice tea from a large porcelain cup, feet up on his steel and glass desk. A fat man with long white hair combed across a bald spot, his gaze shrewd behind old-fashioned square-lensed spectacles. 'So you are here at last,' he said briskly. 'Doc, Doc, you get so slow I wonder if you can any more cut the mustard.'

'Next time try employing a real messenger.'

Komarnicki waved that away. 'But you are here. I have a special job for you, one requiring your scientific training.'

'That was another life. Twenty years ago, for Christ's sake.' In fact, Cameron had hardly started his thesis work when the army had been sent in to close down the universities, and besides, he had been too involved with the resistance to do any research.

'Still, you are all I have in the way of a biologist, and the client is insistent. He wants muscle with a little learning, and who am I to deny his whim?' Komarnicki took his feet off the desk. Tea slopped over the rim of his cup as he leaned forward and said in a hoarse whisper, 'All he wants is back-up at a meeting. Nothing you haven't done before and good money when the deal goes through. You get your usual cut, ten per cent less agency fee. Plenty of money, Cameron. Maybe enough for me to pay for my heart.'

'Your body would probably reject a human heart,' Cameron said. It was well known that Komarnicki had the heart of a pig, a cheap but safe replacement for his own coronary-scarred pump, and was buying a surrogate human heart on an instalment plan from the same black clinic which had rented space in Cameron's bones. It was also well known that Komarnicki was an artist of the slightly funny deal, and this one seemed to have more spin on it than most. Running flack for a simple meeting was hardly worth the price of a human heart, and besides, what did biology have to do with it? Cameron was sure that he wasn't being told everything, but smiled and agreed to Komarnicki's terms. It wasn't as if he had any choice.

The client was a slight young man with a bad complexion and arrogant blue eyes, and long hair the dirty blond colour of split pine. You wouldn't look at him twice in the street, wouldn't notice the quality of his crumpled, dirty clothes. A loose linen jacket, baggy raw cotton trousers criss-crossed with loops and buckles, Swiss oxblood loafers, the kind of quality only a cartel salary could pay for, but rumpled and stained by a week or more of continous wear. He was a defector, a renegade R&D biologist on the run from his employers with bootlegged inside information, the real stuff, not the crap printed in the *Financial Times*. The kind of stuff the New Families paid well for. *Dangerous* stuff. His name, he said, was David Holroyd. He kept brushing back his long blond hair as he walked beside Cameron along the street and explained what he wanted.

'There's a meeting where I get paid in exchange for ... what I have. Only I don't really trust these people, you see?' Nervous sideways smile. His eyes were red-rimmed, and he held himself as though trying not to tremble. 'It could be that I'm being followed, so maybe you should drive me around first. I have plenty of cash. What sort of biologist were you?'

'Molecular biology. Enzyme structure. That was all a long time ago.'

The young man grimaced. 'I guess it will have to do.'

'I'd rather not know anything,' Cameron said. Holroyd's nervousness was affecting him. There was something not quite right about the young man, hidden depths of duplicity. 'It's dangerous to know too much.'

Holroyd laughed.

The cash was in US dollars. It took a whole sheaf of wrinkled green notes to pay for half a day's hire of a bubblecar. For a couple of hours, Cameron weaved in and out of crowded Picadilly, looped around Soho. They weren't being followed. He parked the bubblecar at a public recharger near the arcades of Covent Garden and tipped a mudlark to look after it.

They drank cappuccino in one of the open-air cafes, and since his client was paying, Cameron devoured half a dozen ham and cheese sandwiches as well. He needed all the protein he could get; it was hard to keep up his muscle-bulk while living a knife-edge from the nirvana of total poverty.

Holroyd was beginning to sweat, even though he had left his jacket in the bubblecar. His cup chattered in its saucer each time he set it down, and his eyes darted here and there, taking in recycling stalls piled with everything from cutlery to crowbars, food stalls swarming with flies, big glass tanks where red-finned carp swam up and down, the ragged half-naked children running everywhere through the milling crowds. After a while he began to talk about kinship, the way organisms recognized siblings and mates. 'We've this crocodile in the basement of our brains, know it? The limbic cortex. The archipallium. All the later mammalian improvements are jerry-rigged around it. It snarls and grumbles away beneath our consciousness, hating the new situations that the cortex keeps throwing up. It needs appeasing. That's what social ritual is all about, trying to fool the paranoid crocodile that strangers are okay, they're not a threat. When ritual breaks down you get murder, war. All this is old theory, right, but I see it all around me. Those kids running around. I mean, who looks after them?'

'The mudlarks? They have to look after themselves.'

'Yeah. The way I was brought up, I know all about that.' Holroyd's coffee cup rattled in its saucer. 'Ever hear about the Ik?'

Cameron had, but didn't say so. He was there for whatever the client wanted. If the client wanted to fuck a donkey or direct his very own snuff video, Cameron was there to go fetch the boy or girl or whatever, to make sure he got an animal that was retrovirus free. And he would probably do it, too. He had given up making moral judgements long ago. In his line of business, they were an unaffordable luxury.

So while Holroyd talked about this African tribe whose ethical system had broken down entirely after they'd been displaced from their homeland and their way of life, children running wild, old people dying for want of care, Cameron faked attention and watched the crowds and thought of what he could do with the fee and now and then glanced at his watch. It was more than three hours since he and Holroyd had left Komarnicki's office.

'I think I'll have to arrange a new meet,' Holroyd said at last.

'If they were expecting only you, I might have queered the pitch.'

'You make me feel safe.'

They walked back through the crowds to the hired bubble-car. Half-way there, Cameron glimpsed a shabbily dressed man pawing at the vehicle, and he started forward just as the hatch swung up. Holroyd caught his arm and in that moment the man and the bubblecar vanished in a sheet of flame that blew across the crowded street.

'Mau-mau,' Holroyd said distinctly, and then his eyes rolled up and he fainted.

★

For three days after the assassination attempt, Cameron tended his dying client in a room that Komarnicki sometimes used for his less salubrious deals. It was in what had once been a hotel at the western edge of Wreckers Heaps, an area that Cameron knew all too well: the Meatrack. The building's concrete panels were crumbling and stained with the rust of steel underpinnings; its cantilevered balconies hung at dangerous angles or had fallen away entirely; its rooms had been subdivided with cheap pressed-fibre panels. Their room was scarcely wide enough for the stained mattress on which Holroyd sweated passively in the fetid heat, but at least it had a window, and Cameron kept it open for any chance breeze. The cries and conversations of prostitutes and the muffled throb of the sound systems along the Bayswater Road drifted through it day and night, punctuated every hour by the subsonic rumble of a capsule rising into orbit along the skyhook. It was said you could buy anything anytime in the Meatrack, even love. It never slept.

Cameron had been through Holroyd's pockets as a matter of course. Nothing but a bunch of useless credit chips, a fat roll of dollar currency notes, and a stack of cancelled airline dockets, none more than a week old, that detailed a weird round-the-world itinerary. Bancock, Macao, Zanzibar. Cairo, Istanbul, Leningrad. Geneva. Manchester. No sign of any stolen data. Maybe it existed only inside Holroyd's head.

The biologist grew weaker by the hour, feverish and unable to eat, sometimes vomiting thin green bile. Lack of complicated template proteins in his diet, a dependency to ensure his loyalty, had triggered an RNA virus lodged in his every cell.

There was no cure for it, he said, but Cameron needed him to stay alive, long enough at least to tell him what he had stolen. It was the dream ticket, the chance, the way out. Cameron had been without a chance for so long that he was determined not to let it go. He washed away Holroyd's fever-sweat with expensive filtered water; helped him to the stinking toilet every other hour. He bought black-market antibiotics to counter secondary infection, antipyretics and a tailored strain of *E. coli* to ease the symptoms of general metabolic collapse, a sac of glucose and saline which he taped to the renegade biologist's arm. Once it had settled its proboscis into a vein the thing pulsed slowly and sluggishly, counterpoint to the frantic flutter of Holroyd's pulse in his throat, but it didn't seem to do much good.

'I thought I might have lasted a little longer,' Holroyd said, with a wry smile. He looked very young, there on the bed. His blond hair, sticky with sweat, was spread around his white face like a dirty halo. 'I've always had this tendency to overestimate what I can do. Part of my training.' Sold into service by his parents at the age of eight, he'd been brought up a company child, selected for research, running his own laboratory by age fifteen, his own project by twenty. That project was why he had run, because it had worked too well. Holroyd was vague on just what the project had been about, but Cameron gathered that it had been intended to produce some kind of indoctrination virus, a way of infecting workers with loyalty rather than crudely enforcing it. Holroyd had gone beyond that, though precisely what he had produced wasn't clear.

'I tried it on rats first. It was a major operation keeping them in their colony afterwards, we had to sacrifice them in the end. That's when I knew it wasn't safe to let the company have it. I came up out of the streets, I remember what that was like. Having nothing to compete with, always dependent, always running scared. That's the way it would be with everyone, if I'd let the company keep it. It would be like a new species suddenly arising, a *volk*. Luckily, my bosses didn't want it used on people until a kink had been put in it to limit its spread. The way they kinked my metabolism. So I took it out under their noses before it got near a bioreactor.'

'Tell me what it is,' Cameron said, leaning close to Holroyd. 'Quit talking around it and just tell me straight.'

Holroyd was staring past him at the cracked ceiling. 'What are you going to do, hurt me again?'

'No, man. That was a mistake. I'm sorry.' He was, too. He had begun to care for Holroyd, something beyond simply keeping him alive just long enough. Care for him in a way he hadn't cared for anyone since the farm, since losing Maggie.

Looking down at his big, square hands, knuckles scarred and swollen, Cameron said, 'I know you want me to understand what you did. And I want to know.'

'You'll get it.' Holroyd's smile was hardly there, a quiver. 'You're already getting it.'

Cameron bit down his frustration. He was pushing forty; maybe this was his last chance. This, or ending up in some alley with mudlarks ripping off his clothes before he had even finished dying. 'If it's made you so smart, how come you can't figure out a way to cure yourself?'

'It doesn't make you smarter. I thought I *explained* – ' Holroyd broke off, racked by a rattling cough that turned into a spasm of vomiting. After a while, paler than ever, he said, 'I knew they'd send the mau-maus after me, so I changed my pheromone pattern, kept a vial of my old scent signature. It was in the jacket, I broke it when we were driving around. I was pretty sure one of them would pick it up and follow it to its source. Let them think I'm dead . . .' Suddenly he was blinking back tears. 'I suppose a lot of people were caught. In the explosion.'

'Half a dozen killed, twice that hurt. Mostly after the cops turned the whole thing into a riot, not in the explosion. There never was going to be a meeting, was there?'

'You're catching on. Appropriate, really, the mau-maus. The virus that transforms their rhinencephalon, the place in the brain which controls the sense of smell? Prototype of part of my thing. Use it on lobotomized criminals, replace the marrow in their long bones with TDX. They reach the locus of the scent . . . Well, you saw. Comes from an old colonial war, back in Africa last century. Guerrillas used to train dogs to eat under vehicles, then they'd send the dogs out into Army compounds, only with explosives on their backs, triggered by a length of bent wire . . .'

There was a measure of unbreakable will in Holroyd, like a steel wire running down his spine. Sometimes when he rambled feverishly he came close to explaining, but always he stopped himself. His blue eyes would focus and he would clamp his mouth. He would turn his head away. It was like a game he was playing, or some kind of test.

Of course, Cameron could have walked away. The thought returned whenever he went out to get something to eat at the food stalls, pushing his way through the prostitutes thronged up and down the Bayswater Road. Many had been so radically modified that you couldn't tell what sex they were; a good proportion didn't even look human. The brief clothing of others clung to graphically enlarged male or female genitals, sometimes both. One had an extra set of arms grafted to his rib cage; another sat in a kind of cart like a beached seal, leg stumps fused together, flipper-like arms crossed on his naked chest. Clients walked on the far side of the road, in the shadow of the Heaps, only a few looking openly at the sexual smorgasbord on display. Most of the business seemed to depend on a kind of mutual ESP. Occasionally, a black limo would be drawn up, a beefy bare-armed man or woman standing beside it and scanning the crowd for their employer's choice.

This throng of human commerce brought Cameron back to himself after the confines of the room. He could think about what he had gotten himself into. The prize was unknown. Perhaps it would not even be worth anything. And the chance that Holroyd's owners would find their hiding place increased asymptotically with every hour that passed. But something other than logic compelled him. Carrying his little package of noodles or vegetable stew, he would return to Holroyd with a measure of relief. He found himself caring about the dying man more and more, and he had not cared for anyone since the fall of Birmingham.

Holroyd had got him to talk about his past; in the long watches of the evening, the dying biologist lay as still as a wax figure while Cameron mumbled over memories of university and the barricades, the commune farm he'd helped set up afterwards in the hills of North Wales. There had been a price on his head, and rather than continue the fight he had dropped out, a luxury he had not regretted, then. In place of futile bloody struggle there had been misty days of shepherding, learning karate. Always the rush of the stream at the bottom of the steep valley, the squeak of the hand-made turbine fans which trickle-charged the batteries. A peaceful span of days in the midst of a civil war. Until the night the machines came, squat lumbering autonomic monsters grubbing up the byres and barn, knocking through drystone walling, flattening the wooden turbine-tower.

The next day, the commune had split what little they had saved and had gone their separate ways. Cameron had managed to get as far as Birmingham with Maggie, but then he had lost her in the riots, his last glimpse of her by the falling light of a flare, across a street crowded with refugees. The smell of burning or the rattle of gunfire always brought that memory back. Much later it occurred to Cameron that no one had known the commune was there, that the machines were simply carrying out some central plan of reforestation. All over the country, gene-melded pines were being planted to produce long-chain polymers for the plastics industry. But at the time it had seemed like a very personal apocalypse.

'I understand,' Holroyd said. 'The way it is with the combines, most of the world is invisible, not worth thinking about. So we don't. Now I've changed, I know. I begin to know.' Tears were leaking from his eyes as he stared fixedly at the ceiling. 'I saw a way to break the cycle open, you see, and I grabbed it. Or maybe it grabbed me. Ideas have vectors, like diseases, ever think that? They lie dormant until the right conditions come along, and then they suddenly and violently express themselves, spread irresistibly. The rats ... never could figure out whether they were trying to escape, or if they were driven from within by what I'd given them ... Oh Christ. I didn't realize that caring would hurt so much.'

Later that night, Holroyd didn't so much wake as barely drift into consciousness. His voice was a weak unravelling whisper that Cameron had to bend close to understand. His breath stank of ketones. 'I've a culture. Dormant now, until it gets into the bloodstream. A gene-melded strain of *E. coli*, MIRV'd with half a dozen sorts of virus. Gets into lymphocytes, makes them cross the blood/brain barrier, then kicks the main viruses into reproductive gear. A day, two days, that's it. Some bacteria remain in the blood, spore-forming vector. Breathed out, excreted. Any warm-blooded animal. Spread like wildfire.'

'And what does it do? You still haven't told me.'

'At first I thought of bonding, pheromonal recognition. But bonding, the pack instinct, is the cause of the trouble. And the committee running the centre were real enthusiastic about the idea, so I knew I had to take the opposite direction. You know about kinship?'

'The way animals recognize their relations. You talked about it.'

'Yeah. One of the viruses turns that into a global function. You recognize everyone as a brother or a sister. It makes you want to make other people happy, to care for them. It gets into the base of the brain, downloads information into cells of the hypothalamus. Subverts the old lizard instincts, the crocodile in the basement. Are you following this?'

'I think so.' Holroyd's voice was very weak now; Cameron was kneeling over him to catch every precious word.

'Infected cells start to produce a variant of an old psychoactive drug, MDMA. What they used to call Ecstasy. A second virus gets into the neurons, makes them act as if they've had a dose of growth hormone, forces them to grow new synapses. That and the MDMA analog kicks in a higher level of awareness, of connections. The way everything fits together, could fit together ... You'll see.' Holroyd clawed at Cameron's arm. 'I want you to take it now, before it's too late.'

There was a false varicose vein in his leg. Cameron dug it out with his pocket-knife, first sterilizing the blade in a candleflame.

Later, Cameron went out to buy breakfast noodles, pushing past a shabby blank-eyed man on his way into the building in search of thrills. As always, Bayswater Road was busy with prostitutes and prospective clients. Every one of the gallery of grotesques dragged at Cameron's attention, vibrant with implied history. Every one an individual, every one human.

It was then Cameron knew what had happened to him – and at the same time flashed on the blank-eyed client. Mau-mau. Had to be. He turned just as the window of the room where he had left Holroyd blew out. A ball of greasy smoke rolled up the side of the building, and Cameron began to run, dodging through the crowds that thronged Bayswater Road.

Things were coming together in his head, slabs of intuition dovetailing as smoothly as the finest machine parts. If they had known where to find Holroyd, then they'd be after him, too. Or after the short soft length of tubing, bloated with spore suspension. He headed straight into Wreckers Heaps.

Ragged piles of scrap machinery threaded by a maze of paths always turning back on themselves. There was no centre, no heart. Gene-melded termites had reared their castles every-where, decorated with fragments of precious metals refined from junked machines: copper from wiring; selenium and germanium from circuits; even gold, from the lacquer-thin coatings of computer sockets. Glittering like the towers of the Exchange. Sharecroppers picked over the termite castles, turned in the fragments of refined metals for Family scrip. Mudlarks ran wild, hunting rats and pigeons. Nominally owned by the Wasps, the Heaps was a place where even the code of the streets had broken down. No man's land, an ideal hiding place because no one would think of hiding there. It was too dangerous.

Cameron had a contact in the Heaps, a supervisor called Fat Tony. They'd done each other a few favours in the past, and Fat Tony was happy enough to let Cameron borrow part of his stretch in exchange for most of what was left of Holroyd's roll of dollars. He waddled alongside Cameron as they walked down narrow aisles between heaps of rusted-out cars. Useless shit, Fat Tony said, cheap pressed steel not worth the trouble of reclaiming. His hair was slicked back, pulled into a tight pony-tail; despite the heat, he wrapped a tattered full-length fur coat around his bulk.

'I need to talk with the Wasps,' Cameron said.

'What's that to me?'

'This is their turf.'

'This is *my* goddamn turf, man. They might own it, I run it. This thing between you and me is strictly private because if the Wasps hear I'm renting, they'll cut my fucking nose off. I won't tell.'

'That's good to know. Where is this place I'm renting?'

Fat Tony turned a corner, ducking awkwardly beneath the end of a bus that tilted on half a dozen mashed-down Fords. 'Right here, man. Right here.'

It was a circular space roughly a hundred metres across, floored with compacted ashes and scrap, one side cut by a long channel of oily water that reeked of long-chain organics. 'Don't fall in,' Fat Tony said, standing at the very edge, the metal toes of his knee-length biker boots over the rim. 'They used to render down organics from the junkers here, tyres, plastic trim. All round here we got the cars that were left stranded when the petrol run out, no place else to take them in the city, nothing to move them further. I'm like a fucking industrial archaeologist, you know.' He spat towards the murky water, wiped his chin. 'Hell's own soup of bugs in there. Strip you to your bones in a second.'

Cameron watched a little kid walk by on the far side. A string of dead pigeons dangled down the boy's smooth mud-streaked back, wings flopped open. 'Listen, I really need to talk to the Family.'

Fat Tony turned away from the water. 'Happens the Wasps want to talk with you too,' he said. 'Seems all sorts of people are after your ass, Doc. What's the score?'

Cameron pressed one of the man's hands between both his own. 'You'll see soon enough. One more thing. I want to buy anything the kids catch in here.'

'You want food, I can arrange it. You needn't eat rats.'

'Not to eat. Anything they bring me has to be alive.'

★

The contact for the Wasps was a smooth-skinned boy with only the faintest wisp of a mustache, no more than fifteen. He lounged in the back of the electric stretch with studied cool, looking at Cameron from under half-closed lids. He wore a white linen suit, white sneakers. No socks. He said, as the stretch pulled into the traffic, 'I hear the Exchange is after you. A contract going all the way across the water. It'll cost you real money to help you out.'

'I appreciate that. There's enough for all of us. Are you interested?'

The kid held out a hand with a languid gesture, and the big bodyguard who was driving reached around and put a little glass tube into it. The kid sniffed at it, held it out, and it was taken back. The spurs on the bodyguard's wrists were tipped with black polycarbon. The kid said, 'From what I know of it, it'll give us the clout to take over the other Families, maybe even put us into the Exchange. Of course I'm interested.'

'What you can do with it is down to you,' Cameron said. 'I can set up a demonstration.'

'Real soon. Your ass is on fire, from where I stand.'

'Let me worry about that. But if I'm not left alone until the meeting you'll never see what I have to sell.'

'For streetmeat, you have sass. I dig that.' The kid's laugh was like fingernails drawn down sharp metal. 'OK, we'll meet on your terms. Now, let's deal.'

The stretch circled the perimeter of Wreckers Heaps half a dozen times while Cameron talked with the kid. When at last it stopped and Cameron climbed out, the outside air seemed to him like pure oxygen, for all the heat and stink of the street. The stretch had smelled of bad money and worse promises. As he watched it pull away, he knew at last what Holroyd had meant, about the pain of connections, and he mused on it all the way to the place where he had once lived.

Cameron knew better than to walk into the old department store, so he sent a mudlark around the corner to fetch Lost In Space. 'Oh my man,' the pusher said, when he saw Cameron. 'Doc, you are bad news all over town.'

'I just need to talk with the people who own your deckchair.'

'You're dealing? That's keen, Doc.' They stood in the doorway of a shop, Lost In Space shifting from one foot to the other, his tongue passing over his lips with a lizard's flick. For an instant, Cameron saw clear to the roots of the man's life. The filthy crowded room where he'd grown up in the constant smothering company of a dozen brothers and sisters and a despairing mother, childhood innocence withering in the fire of his pride, pride which had driven him to be different when he couldn't begin to define what he really wanted, when all he had was pride, and his fragile armour of vanity and indifference . . .

'I'm dealing,' Cameron said. 'Something big enough to promote you out of that deckchair, if you want to help me.'

There was a derelict huddled in a nest of rags in the far corner of the doorway, asleep or dead. Lost In Space spat in his direction, unsettled by Cameron's tender gaze, and said, 'It'll take maybe an hour.'

Cameron thought of all he had to do before night fell. 'It had better be quicker.'

Komarnicki wasn't answering his office phone, but Cameron had already worked out where his former employer was likely to be. He got into the black clinic by offering to incubate more mutated marrow, slipped out of the confusion of reception and sprang door after door along a row of office cubicles until he found a white laboratory coat that didn't fit too badly.

Komarnicki was in intensive care, a guard at the door and a screen flagging vital signs above his head. Cameron waited until the guard went to use the toilet and then walked straight in.

Komarnicki lay naked on the bed, his flabby chest a shield of vivid purple bruises, slashed by a raw, ridged scar. Gene-melded sawfly larvae lay along it, jaws clamping the incision closed, swollen white bodies glistening with anti-inflammatory secretions. Cameron sat down beside him, and presently he opened his eyes.

'You're a ghost,' he said wearily. 'Go away, Cameron.'

'I'm real enough. Want me to pull open your chest to prove it? What did they pay you, apart from a heart?'

'Nothing else. They explained about Holroyd. I wasn't going to get his fee, so it seemed fair. I took a guess at where you were hiding him, and they got his scent from the couch in my waiting room. It was just business, you understand. I've always liked you, Doc.'

'I've got what they want. I can make a deal, cut you in too. Ten per cent, for old times' sake.'

'You don't make deals with them. They don't operate like the New Families. You're streetmeat, Cameron. Even if you give it to them, they'll take you. And don't you tell me what it is, either. I don't want to know. That kind of knowledge is dangerous – '

Cameron had caught Komarnicki's hand, as it edged towards the buzzer on his bedframe. After a moment, Komarnicki relaxed. He had squeezed his eyes shut. Sweat glittered on his pink face. Cameron leaned close and said, 'I'm not going to hurt you. Just tell them I'll deal, OK? I'll call you later.' Cameron set down Komarnicki's limp hand and smiled at the guard on his way out, impervious in his white coat.

At Wreckers Heaps, the mudlarks had delivered all Cameron had asked for, and after he had paid them with the last of Holroyd's dollars and set things up there was nothing left for him to do but wait. He sat near the arm of scummy water, watching silver beads shuttle up and down the almost invisible thread of the skyhook beyond the shining towers of the Exchange, letting sunlight and the invisible flux of the Exchange's trade fall through him, until it was time.

He had arranged to meet with both the Wasps and the Zion Warriors at sunset. With half an hour to go, he called up Komarnicki and told him where he was. And then he sat back and waited.

He did not have to wait long. Soon there was the rattle of

gunfire in the south, and then a series of flares rose with eerie slowness against the darkening sky. All around him, stacks of junked vehicles began to groan and shiver, dribbling cascades of rust: someone was using a sonic caster. Cameron sat still in the middle of the clearing, in a bucket seat he'd taken from one of the cars, imagining the hired fighters of the Exchange and the war parties of the two Families clashing amongst the wreckage of the twentieth century, Exchange fighters outnumbered, Family members outgunned. Smoke billowed up from an explosion somewhere near the perimeter. Soon after, the gunfire stopped. One by one the sound systems that circled the perimeter of the dump started to broadcast their competing rhythms again. Cameron sighed, and allowed himself to relax.

The electric limo glided into the clearing twenty minutes later, its sleek white finish marred by the spattered stars of bullet holes. The teenage negotiator was ushered out by his massive bodyguard. 'I know I'm a little late,' the boy said coolly, 'but I nearly had an accident.'

'You're later than you think,' Cameron said, looking past the boy at the junk heaps across the channel of stinking water, where he knew sharpshooters must be taking up positions.

'I got all the time in the world,' the boy said, his smile as luminous as his white suit, and motioned to the bodyguard.

The tall burly man crossed to where Cameron was sitting and without expression patted him down, pulled his pistol from his harness, showed it to the boy. 'It's empty,' Cameron said.

'Your mistake,' the boy said. 'Let's go.'

The bodyguard put his hands under Cameron's armpits and effortlessly pulled him to his feet.

And then everything went up.

The pressure switch had been sprung when Cameron's weight had been taken away. It closed the circuit which ignited the cartridge loads, shredding the mesh covering the watertank where Cameron had caged what the mudlarks had brought him. Pigeons rose into the dark air in a vortex of wings. The bodyguard's attention flickered for a second and Cameron punched him in the solar plexus. The man staggered but didn't let go of Cameron. For a moment they teetered at the edge of the water, and then Cameron found the point of leverage and threw the man from his hip. The bodyguard twisted awkwardly and fell the wrong way, flailing out. Cameron danced back (one of the man's spurs drawing blood down his forearm) as the man hit the lip of the drop and rolled into the water, screaming hoarsely before disappearing beneath the oily surface.

Cameron sprang on the boy and whirled him around as a shield. 'I'll let you drive me out of here,' Cameron said, but the boy, limp with shock, was staring down at the red spot of a laser rifle-guide centered on the left lapel of his white jacket. Cameron wrestled him into the car in a clumsy two-step, slammed the door and slid behind the wheel as bullets rattled on the armour.

The boy was pressed hard against the corner of the passenger seat as Cameron drove down the winding alleys that threaded the junk-piles. At last he said, 'Whatever it is you're doing, I'm impressed, OK? But there's still a chance to make your deal.'

'There never was going to be a deal. I just cancelled things out, that's all. The Exchange and the Families. Hang on now.'

The gate was ahead, armed men running towards it from both sides. Cameron floored the accelerator and swerved between two flatbed trucks, pedestrians scattering as the limo shot through the gate. Then it was weaving through dense traffic and the armed men were lost in the crowds. Cameron said, 'I'm sorry for all the hurt I caused, especially your bodyguard. He was only doing his job, and I meant for him to land on dirt.'

'You stop now, I can help you,' the boy said.

Cameron laughed. 'Oh no, it's too late for that. Holroyd took it all round the world, but I want to play my part, too. I ran away one time. No more. When the universities were closed down, when knowledge was finally transformed into a commodity, I should have done more to try and stop it. I can remember when there was free exchange of ideas, and now most of the cartels' energies are spent on security against piracy. But that won't do them any good now, not against five billion data pirates.'

'You're rapping like a crazy man. I bet you never even had the stuff.'

'I had it all right. You saw it go.' Cameron pulled the limo over and switched off its motor, leaned across the seat. The boy's wide eyes looked up into his, centimetres away. 'I turned pigeons and rats into vectors,' Cameron told him. 'If you want what I had, you'll have to catch them. Doves would have been more appropriate, but I had to make do.' And then he kissed the astonished boy on the lips and slid out of the limo and vanished into the crowds.

Afterwards, Cameron lived on the street, restless for change. The Exchange must have found out what had happened; suddenly there was a bounty on rats and pigeons. But it only served to spread the caring sickness through the mudlarks, and within a week it was irrelevant. The rats had gotten too organized to be caught by ordinary means, but suddenly there were weird devices all through Wreckers Heaps, eye-bending topological conundrums of rusty mesh that mesmerized rats and drew them into their involuted folds. Mobile traps like tiny robot shopping carts careered after rats and pigeons, multiplying like sex-crazed von Neumann machines. When they had run out of prey they started raiding the street markets for trinkets and bits of food, and then sleek machines armed with a rack of cutting tools starting hunting *them*. After that the sickness must have gotten into the water supply, for infection seemed to take off on an asymptotic curve. There was a sudden boom in ingenious, horrible murders – one night two dozen eviscerated riot cops were found dangling from the Knightsbridge gibbets – and then crime plummeted. Graffiti went the same way, and one by one the sound systems fell silent.

One day a young mudlark stopped Cameron in the street.

After a moment Cameron recognized Komarnicki's messenger. The little kid was clean now, wore a shirt several sizes too big for him and had a canvas pack slung on his shoulder. He was heading out he said, a lot of people had that idea. Divide up the conglomerate farms, grow food again.

'Out or up,' the boy said.

They were at the northern edge of Wreckers Heaps. Amongst abandoned shacks, people were working on what looked like a small air dirigible, a hectare of patched white fabric spread on the ground amid a tangle of tethering cables. The boy looked past them at the skyhook, still there beyond the irrelevant towers of the Exchange. Looking at the boy looking at the skyhook, at the door into orbit, Cameron thought about what Holroyd had said about vectors. Maybe humans were just the infection's way of spreading beyond the Earth's fragile cradle, the Galaxy like a slow-turning petri dish, ripe for inoculation. Maybe it was his thought, maybe the infection's. It didn't matter. It was all one now, no longer an infection but a symbiosis, as intimate and inextricable as that with the mitochondria in his every cell.

The boy was smiling at Cameron. 'I heard you were around here, I just came to say thanks, for what you did back then. What are you going to do? You could come with us, you know.'

'Oh, I've already done that stuff, in another life. Who told you about me?'

'I heard from an ex-pusher who heard from some muscle who got it from the kid who was right there. Everyone knows, man. Luck, now.'

'Luck,' Cameron said, and the boy grinned and turned and headed on down the street, a small brave figure walking into a future that everyone owned now.

Cameron watched until the boy was out of sight. The dirigible was beginning to rise, its nose straining against the people who were hauling back on the anchor ropes. Cameron strolled over to give them a hand.

AFTERWORD

This story was written at the end of the eighties. Its extrapolation of post-global-warming London as a Kafkaesque conjunction between the capital of Oceania and the brawling squalor of Calcutta is little more than a sarcastic heightening of the brutalization of society which occurred under the mob-handed free market rule of Thatcherism (Margaret Thatcher certainly deserves to go down in history, but only for the astonishing wickedness of her ringing announcement, made in the sincere tones of a psychotic Joan of Arc, that 'There is no such thing as society.').

Specifically, it was written for Lew Shiner's anthology When the Music's Over. *Lew's idea, a direct response to the proliferation of militaristic science fiction, was to collect together stories in which conflict was resolved without violence, and it was a labour of love on the part of everyone involved. I wanted to address the roots of the human impulse to violence, and because I'm a biologist I decided to explore the implications of attempting to modify the evolutionary lashup on which our consciousness rests (incidentally, very recent research shows that men may have a greater propensity for violence than women because they have a less developed limbic system). I'm still not sure how true to the anthology's theme is this mad scientist story (which bristles with implicit violence, but is resolved with a kiss), and I certainly don't endorse the arrogant way in which Holroyd applies his solution, but Lew was kind enough to publish it anyway.*

And yet ... if we could eradicate war by literally changing our minds, how else could we carry out the revolution except by mass inoculation? For if this kind of gene therapy was applied only on a voluntary basis, what would happen to those who didn't choose to be changed for the better? Would they become outcasts, or would they become vicious psychopomps ruling over a frightened, docile population? And how would that be different from now?

Gene Wars

1

On Evan's eighth birthday, his aunt sent him the latest smash-hit biokit, *Splicing Your Own Semisentients*. The box-lid depicted an alien swamp throbbing with weird, amorphous life; a double helix spiralling out of a test-tube was embossed in one corner. Don't let your father see that, his mother said, so Evan took it out to the old barn, set up the plastic culture trays and vials of chemicals and retroviruses on a dusty workbench in the shadow of the shrouded combine.

His father found Evan there two days later. The slime mould he'd created, a million amoebae aggregated around a drop of cyclic AMP, had been transformed with a retrovirus and was budding little blue-furred blobs. Evan's father dumped culture trays and vials in the yard and made Evan pour a litre of industrial grade bleach over them. More than fear or anger, it was the acrid stench that made Evan cry.

That summer, the leasing company foreclosed on the livestock. The rep who supervised repossession of the super-cows drove off in a big car with the test-tube and double-helix logo on its gull-wing door. The next year the wheat failed, blighted by a particularly virulent rust. Evan's father couldn't afford the new resistant strain, and the farm went under.

2

Evan lived with his aunt, in the capital. He was fifteen. He had a street bike, a plug-in computer, and a pet microsaur, a triceratops in purple funfur. Buying the special porridge which was all the microsaur could eat took half of Evan's weekly allowance; that was why he let his best friend inject the pet with a bootleg virus to edit out its dietary dependence. It was only a partial success: the triceratops no longer needed its porridge, but developed epilepsy triggered by sunlight. Evan had to keep it in his wardrobe. When it started shedding fur in great swatches, he abandoned it in a nearby park. Microsaurs were out of fashion, anyway. Dozens could be found wandering the park, nibbling at leaves, grass, discarded scraps of fastfood. Quite soon they disappeared, starved to extinction.

3

The day before Evan graduated, his sponsor firm called to tell him that he wouldn't be doing research after all. There had been a change of policy: the covert gene wars were going public. When Evan started to protest, the woman said sharply, 'You're better off than many long-term employees. With a degree in molecular genetics you'll make sergeant at least.'

4

The jungle was a vivid green blanket in which rivers made silvery forked lightnings. Warm wind rushed around Evan as he leaned out the helicopter's hatch; harness dug into his shoulders. He was twenty-three, a tech sergeant. It was his second tour of duty.

His goggles laid icons over the view, tracking the target. Two villages a klick apart, linked by a red dirt road narrow as a capillary that suddenly widened to an artery as the helicopter dove.

Muzzle-flashes on the ground: Evan hoped the peasants only had Kalashnikovs: last week some gook had downed a copter with an antiquated SAM. Then he was too busy laying the pattern, virus-suspension in a sticky spray that fogged the maize fields.

Afterwards, the pilot, an old-timer, said over the intercom, 'Things get tougher every day. We used just to take a leaf, cloning did the rest. You couldn't even call it theft. And this stuff . . . I always thought war was bad for business.'

Evan said, 'The company owns copyright to the maize genome. Those peasants aren't licensed to grow it.'

The pilot said admiringly, 'Man, you're a real company guy. I bet you don't even know what country this is.'

Evan thought about that. He said, 'Since when were countries important?'

5

Rice fields spread across the floodplain, dense as a hand-stitched quilt. In every paddy, peasants bent over their own reflections, planting seedlings for the winter crop.

In the centre of the UNESCO delegation, the Minister for Agriculture stood under a black umbrella held by an aide. He was explaining that his country was starving to death after a record rice crop.

Evan was at the back of the little crowd, bareheaded in warm drizzle. He wore a smart one-piece suit, yellow over-shoes. He was twenty-eight, had spent two years infiltrating UNESCO for his company.

The minister was saying, 'We have to buy seed genespliced for pesticide resistance to compete with our neighbours, but my people can't afford to buy the rice they grow. It must all be exported to service our debt. We are starving in the midst of plenty.'

Evan stifled a yawn. Later, at a reception in some crum-bling embassy, he managed to get the minister on his own. The man was drunk, unaccustomed to hard liquor. Evan told him he was very moved by what he had seen.

'Look in our cities,' the minister said, slurring his words. 'Every day a thousand more refugees pour in from the countryside. We have kwashiorkor, beri-beri.'

Evan popped a canape into his mouth. One of his com-pany's new lines, it squirmed with delicious lasciviousness before he swallowed it. 'I may be able to help you,' he said. 'The people I represent have a new yeast that completely fulfills dietary requirements and will grow on a simple medium.'

'How simple?' As Evan explained, the minister, no longer

as drunk as he had seemed, steered him onto the terrace. The minister said, 'You understand this must be confidential. Under UNESCO rules...'

'There are ways around that. We have lease arrangements with five countries that have ... trade imbalances similar to your own. We lease the genome as a loss-leader, to support governments who look favourably on our other products...'

6

The gene pirate was showing Evan his editing facility when the slow poison finally hit him. They were aboard an ancient ICBM submarine grounded somewhere off the Philippines. Missile tubes had been converted into fermenters. The bridge was crammed with the latest manipulation technology, virtual reality gear which let the wearer directly control molecule-sized cutting robots as they travelled along DNA helices.

'It's not facilities I need,' the pirate told Evan, 'it's distribution.'

'No problem,' Evan said. The pirate's security had been pathetically easy to penetrate. He'd tried to infect Evan with a zombie virus, but Evan's genespliced designer immune system had easily dealt with it. Slow poison was so much more subtle: by the time it could be detected it was too late. Evan was thirty-two. He was posing as a Swiss grey market broker.

'This is where I keep my old stuff,' the pirate said, rapping a stainless steel cryogenic vat. 'Stuff from before I went big time. A free luciferase gene complex, for instance. Remember when the Brazilian rainforest started to glow? That was me.' He dashed sweat from his forehead, frowned at the room's complicated thermostat. Grossly fat and completely hairless, he wore nothing but Bermuda shorts and shower sandals. He'd been targeted because he was about to break the big time with a novel HIV cure. The company was still making a lot of money from its own cure: they made sure AIDS had never been completely eradicated in third world countries.

Evan said, 'I remember the Brazilian government was overthrown – the population took it as a bad omen.'

'Hey, what can I say? I was only a kid. Transforming the gene was easy, only difficulty was finding a vector. Old stuff. Somatic mutation really is going to be the next big thing, believe me. Why breed new strains when you can rework a genome cell by cell?' He rapped the thermostat. His hands were shaking. 'Hey, is it hot in here, or what?'

'That's the first symptom,' Evan said. He stepped out of the way as the gene pirate crashed to the decking. 'And that's the second.'

The company had taken the precaution of buying the pirate's security chief: Evan had plenty of time to fix the fermenters. By the time he was ashore, they would have boiled dry. On impulse, against orders, he took a microgram sample of the HIV cure with him.

7

'The territory between piracy and legitimacy is a minefield,' the assassin told Evan. 'It's also where paradigm shifts are most likely to occur, and that's where I come in. My company likes stability. Another year and you'd have gone public, and most likely the share issue would have made you a billionaire – a minor player, but still a player. Those cats, no one else has them. The genome was supposed to have been wiped out back in the twenties. Very astute, quitting the grey medical market and going for luxury goods.' She frowned. 'Why am I talking so much?'

'For the same reason you're not going to kill me,' Evan said.

'It seems such a silly thing to want to do,' the assassin admitted.

Evan smiled. He'd long ago decoded the two-stage virus the gene-pirate had used on him: one a Trojan horse which kept his T-lymphocytes busy while the other rewrote loyalty genes companies implanted in their employees. Once again it had proven its worth. He said, 'I need someone like you in my organization. And since you spent so long getting close enough to seduce me, perhaps you'd do me the honour of becoming my wife. I'll need one.'

'You don't mind being married to a killer?'

'Oh, that. I used to be one myself.'

8

Evan saw the market crash coming. Gene wars had winnowed basic foodcrops to soy beans, rice and dole yeast: tailored ever-mutating diseases had reduced cereals and many other cash crops to nucleotide sequences stored in computer vaults. Three global biotechnology companies held patents on the calorific input of ninety-eight per cent of humanity, but they had lost control of the technology. Pressures of the war economy had simplified it to the point where anyone could directly manipulate her own genome, and hence her own body form.

Evan had made a fortune in the fashion industry, selling templates and microscopic self-replicating robots which edited DNA. But he guessed that sooner or later someone would come up with a direct photosynthesis system, and his stock market expert systems were programmed to correlate research in the field. He and his wife sold the controlling interest in their company three months before the first green people appeared.

9

'I remember when you knew what a human being was,' Evan said sadly. 'I suppose I'm old-fashioned, but there it is.'

From her cradle, inside a mist of spray, his wife said, 'Is that why you never went green? I always thought it was a fashion statement.'

'Old habits die hard.' The truth was, he liked his body the way it was. These days, going green involved somatic mutation which grew a metre-high black cowl to absorb sufficient light energy. Most people lived in the tropics, swarms of black-caped anarchists. Work was no longer a necessity, but an indulgence. Evan added, 'I'm going to miss you.'

'Let's face it,' his wife said, 'we never were in love. But I'll miss you, too.' With a flick of her powerful tail she launched her streamlined body into the sea.

10

Black-cowled post-humans, gliding slowly in the sun, aggregating and reaggregating like amoebae. Dolphinoids, tentacles sheathed under fins, rocking in tanks of cloudy water. Ambulatory starfish; tumbling bushes of spikes; snakes with a single arm, a single leg; flocks of tiny birds, brilliant as emeralds, each flock a single entity.

People, grown strange, infected with myriads of microscopic machines which re-engraved their body form at will.

Evan lived in a secluded estate. He was revered as a founding father of the posthuman revolution. A purple funfur microsaur followed him everywhere. It was recording him because he had elected to die.

'I don't regret anything,' Evan said, 'except perhaps not following my wife when she changed. I saw it coming, you know. All this. Once the technology became simple enough, cheap enough, the companies lost control. Like television or computers, but I suppose you don't remember those.' He sighed. He had the vague feeling he'd said all this before. He'd had no new thoughts for a century, except the desire to put an end to thought.

The microsaur said, 'In a way, I suppose I am a computer. Will you see the colonial delegation now?'

'Later.' Evan hobbled to a bench and slowly sat down. In the last couple of months he had developed mild arthritis, liver spots on the backs of his hands: death finally expressing parts of his genome that had been suppressed for so long. Hot sunlight fell through the velvet streamers of the tree things; Evan dozed, woke to find a group of starfish watching him. They had blue, human eyes, one at the tip of each muscular arm.

'They wish to honour you by taking your genome to Mars,' the little purple triceratops said.

Evan sighed. 'I just want peace. To rest. To die.'

'Oh Evan,' the little triceratops said patiently, 'surely even you know that nothing really dies any more.'

AFTERWORD

This is the only story which has a direct connection with my former job as a professional biologist. It was commissioned by New Internationalist, *a campaigning socialist magazine that devotes each issue to an in-depth examination of a single topic. The editor of an issue surveying the political impact of biotechnology wanted a 2000-word science fiction story that would deal with the effects of genetic engineering on medicine and on first-world and third-world agriculture, the appropriation of valuable plant species by biotechnology companies, and a bunch of other things, and thought that an sf-writing biologist could manage it. I said I'd think about it, but as soon as I put the phone down the story began to write itself in my head.* New Internationalist *retitled the story 'Evan's Progress' and cut all but the last three sentences of the final section, presumably because it didn't agree with their notion that the template myth of Science is not that of Prometheus, but of Pandora's Box. But the full version was later published in* Interzone *and* Aboriginal SF *under its original title, and later in* The Year's Best SF 9 *and several other anthologies, and has been used as a teaching aid in at least two University courses (one biology, the other law), so there was a happy ending after all.*

Prison Dreams

The end of a shitstorm of a shift, eleven hours down, one to go, Lianna caught the squeal for a psychokiller scenario. So far, three months into her sentence, she'd avoided this, the worst kind of triage. But everything that goes around comes around. She'd been catching sleep while everyone else was cleaning up a big combat game – EuroNissan execs cooling out after a sales conference – and *slam*, she was on.

Wired with caffeine, needles digging her right eye, Lianna threw herself into the chopper moments before it rose from the pad. Hands grabbed her, pulled her into a jump seat. Kollner's clean-up crew, that was something at least, all case-hardened zeks but for one new, scared-looking kid gulping back nervousness, grin too wide in his white face. Lianna knew how he felt.

The chopper ran low and fast parallel to the long beach. Naked sunbathers in dispersion patterns just beyond the edge of analysis, stands of sun umbrellas, roofs of franchise huts. Did anyone on the beach look up from sun-struck dreaming and wonder where the helicopters went to, in the Oostduin-park? Did they care?

Lianna asked about the new kid. Over engine roar Kollner told her Toorop had done the freaky and tried to make it into the dunes before his chip stopped him, had been rotated to prep and dispatch for the rest of his sentence. Kollner, a big scary-looking man, even scarier if you knew what he'd once done. Slow and mild manner, passing out smokes, asking Lianna how her shift was running.

'Too long,' Lianna yelled into his weary smile, and took a smoke and drew it alight. Cool smoke flooded her throat, the needlepoints of pain in her eye melted.

Kollner knew this was her first psycho. He gave a shark

smile. 'It's just like combat games,' he said into her ear, 'only
. . . *intense.*'

Lianna managed a tight smile, knowing Kollner had been
through over a thousand runs. He was a trusty now, but he
was under the chip for life. She swallowed a couple of glucose
tablets with a sip of Diet Coke, and then the chopper was
beating down.

The patient squatted behind a canvas windbreak, shivering
in the grip of his attendants. Big man, body builder, camo
pants tucked into hightop boots, flakjacket crossed with
bandoliers, face hidden behind a black pinhole mask. He was
hauled to his feet as Lianna went past. Blood and worse
crusted around the crotch of his pants: a real psycho, not
some politician or exec drained of testosterone rage. But like
them he'd not remember what he'd done in deep fix trance:
scenarios were for imprinting chip feedback loops.

Afterwards, Lianna would realize how much she envied his
amnesia.

The setup was in a long draw. Half a dozen hooches,
woven walls splintered by heavy fire, two still smoking. Little
figures sprawled on white sand, blue skins more vivid than
their blood. The clean-up crew waited on Lianna's assess-
ment, backs to the wind that knifed in from the Noordzee as
they drew on the last of their smokes.

Lianna walked the perimeter, blanking out the whines of
those dolls still alive, avoiding their eyes. Her chip was
nagging her, a heavy feeling in the orbit of her right eye,
something like a silver needle running back into her head:
this was so close to what she'd done to her husband.

Most dolls were wasted, a mercy. A bunch in an untidy
heap, torn apart. An arm lying off by itself, hand clenched.
Two females naked and bloodied and very much dead, both
face down, legs widesprawled. Oh Christ, the guy on some
rape-o freakout. But better them than any woman – her
thought, or chip propaganda?

Lianna made fifteen dead, a dozen badly wounded, three
hardly more than scratched. One by the perimeter tape,
sitting with its leg out in front of him, holding an oozing

thigh wound, through and through. If it had been human it would have got away clean, but dolls couldn't cross the tape to save their lives.

Her count way too low – most probably caught in the hooches. A quick sweep confirmed. The psycho had raked them with heavy calibre gunfire, tossed in frag grenades, nothing left for her to fix unless the crew turned a survivor from under the pieces of the dead.

Lianna told Kollner to start with the hooches, opened her kit and took the wounded by priority, swiping white X's on the foreheads of those too far gone. Work focused her thoughts – her hands were steady as she sorted through her kit. Chip pressure receded. Couple of times at the beginning she'd blacked out: now she could distance herself from gore. She pushed back the length of grey-blue gut of one that had been eviscerated with a knife-thrust, cauterized the wrist stump of another. A doll with a sucking chest wound fixed a dull betrayed look on her as she packed the bloody bubbling cavity. Worse was the doll which had tried to shelter its 'baby', a microcephalic homunculus it had been programmed to care for. The surrogate mother's head blown off, a splintered spike of bone: the baby-thing under her corpse, its limbs wriggling as slowly as a battery-drained toy's. It was unharmed but drenched in blood to which sand stuck like crystalline sugar. Lianna set it aside for pickup.

The clean-up crew had almost finished. Shattered corpses and stray limbs were stacked like firewood. Kollner, certifying each corpse by scanning the tag implanted in its third sacral vertebra, looked like a grocery clerk moving barcoded goods through the checkout. Two women were chasing the new boy: one brandished a severed hand.

The last two casualties were sitting up, patiently awaiting Lianna's attention. They brushed her cheeks with soft blue-skinned fingers, made cooing sounds as she dressed their flesh wounds. Lianna groaned when she stood; dull pain punched her in the kidneys.

The women had caught the new kid, were trying to stuff the hand into his open fly as he writhed and made a noise half-way between a laugh and a squeal. Lianna sat off to one side in hot sun while Kollner supervised pickup. The ones she'd marked were given two lines of topic, enough to stop their hearts.

Lianna thought, Kollner had been right, it hadn't been so bad (forget those splayed female corpses). Not as bad as she'd imagined, anyway.

When all the corpses had been stacked, the whole pile was doused with jellied petroleum and Kollner threw on a flare. Lianna watched with something nagging at her; it took a while to remember she'd missed the doll with the leg wound over by the perimeter. It couldn't have died. Dolls were too dumb to get shock and the wound hadn't been bleeding that badly.

Lianna made herself get up and track the perimeter. She liked things neat, it had been one of her husband's final accusations. She found a crusty patch of scuffled sand where the doll had been sitting, saw drag marks and the perimeter tape pulled out of shape, an arrowhead pointing through a saddle in the dune ridge. Lianna would have followed, curious now despite the sodden weight of her exhaustion, but her chip wouldn't let her. Kollner's computer did show there was a body missing; to further confuse things it turned out someone had thrown the still living baby-thing on the pyre. But as Kollner said, what was one pinhead, more or less? And he was just as dismissive about the missing doll, kidding her that it was her first encounter with fairies.

He handed Lianna an ice-cold coke; she held it to the back of her neck before chugging half straight down. She said, 'Everyone talks about fairies, but no one believes in them.'

'Just another hinky urban myth. You get wild dolls, strays, cast-offs, but they don't last long without people. That casualty, most likely its chip got fritzed and it wandered off. Sometimes they try and bury themselves. Maintenance will find it.' Kollner was sweating heavily in the double heat of sun and pyre. Two dark half-moons of sweat under the arms of his blood-stained white jacket. He said, 'You did all right, but you shouldn't knock yourself out fixing wounded. Flesh-wounds, that's OK, they recycle straight off. Anything else: two lines, the old grand slam. What I mean is, they're just walking meat, *made* things. Think of them that way, you won't ever chip out. Let your chip decide about people, that's why they put it in you.'

'It won't take much to get those others fixed.' Thinking: things didn't look at you as they groaned bloody foam from chest wounds; they didn't try and shelter what they were meant to care for. Thinking of telly shows about outlaw bands of dolls and humans living wild in the fringe wildernesses; had to be some truth to them. Half of her wishing the doll had escaped, despite Kollner's dismissal.

'Days I wake up and think I'm never getting here,' Kollner said. 'But, hey, I always do. Maintain, that's what my motto is. Just maintain. What you got, a deuce for manslaughter?'

'Mmm.' Most of the zeks talked obsessively about their sentences; Lianna was still uncomfortable, aware that if she didn't watch herself she'd be like the others soon enough, complaining she'd been set up or exaggerating misdemeanours into major felonies. Except what she'd done *had* been a major felony.

'You have to run this?'

'No. No, only simulations.'

'Easy street,' Kollner said. 'You're lucky to see it just from this side. Just maintain, you'll sleepwalk it. Leave wild dolls to the park wardens.'

Maybe Kollner was right. Lianna was too tired to chase the matter when the chopper got her back. Her shift had finished an hour ago; she grabbed the stuff she'd stolen to order, strap-hung the tram in a haze to her crib, managed to just about reach her bed and fall into it fully clothed, and because the next day was Sunday slept eighteen hours straight.

And woke naked under a cool clean sheet, her husband curled into her back. She rolled onto her tummy and let his clever hands find tension points and unknot them, still half-asleep when she rolled onto him and began to move, a long grinding slow dance until something shook her awake.

Shit, another chip dream. Trying to fix sanitized pleasurable memories of her dead husband, trying to erase the real memories of his death.

What had woken her, hammering on the door, started up again. Nicole, wanting the stuff, wanting to know why it hadn't been dropped off last night.

'I was tired,' Lianna said, and started to explain about the psychokiller scenario.

Nicole brushed it aside. Small, olive-skinned, white hair cropped close, bare-foot in red jeans and a black leather vest, she clutched the little package, scowled. 'Darlajane's pissed, she might not make quota.' Then she was gone.

The crib had once been a hotel, down in the funky old half-abandoned seaside resort at the edge of the vast dune system beyond Den Haag's barrier. Run by a feisty old ex-punk, given over to zeks on workfare, already it felt like home to Lianna, amazing how quickly she'd adapted. But after her marriage she'd never lived anyplace she could call her own; perhaps it wasn't so strange.

Late afternoon, most of her free day gone. She sat in a beach chair on her room's balcony, picking through a plate of fruit slivers, happy in the sun to watch the straights at play. She'd learnt to surrender to moments like this, to dissolve in the sweet eternal moment of doing nothing. Electric trolleys drifting through the intersection, bells tingling. The dull thumping beat of the Permanent Floating Wave two blocks over underscored the noise of the crowds moving along the boardwalks. Tanned, brightly clothed animals surging to and fro, handsome, affluent, secure and ... *smug*, yes, smug, in their post-Millennial utopia, geezers and babushkas enjoying their right to unlimited leisure and the universal unearned wage. Many wore gold-lensed videoshades, trancing their way through overlay visions of coral reefs or tropical rainforests or Mars: the Valles Marineris was that month's number one.

Paradise not enough, Lianna thought, sitting on her balcony high above them. Even in paradise, there was always something better to reach for. One thing about being a zek, it gave her a perspective, it distanced her from what had been her life. Zeks were the poor, the dispossessed, the third world in the rich, dreamy first.

The psychokiller scenario kept coming back to her at odd angles, unexpected moments. The disappeared doll, fairy tracks. Lianna noticed just how many dolls there were, moving through the crowds on errands, running concession stands, driving trams. As numerous as the people they served; people who walked past them as if they weren't there, invisible as lamp-posts, junction boxes. Way she'd treated them when she'd been running her husband's household – she hadn't even known how many house dolls there'd been. The things down in the basement darkness, like Morlocks. Lianna shivered just to think of them: used: every which way.

At last she got dressed, went to hang out in the downstairs lounge (some of the women leaning out of a window yelling at passers-by – 'Hey, lunchmeat! Porkchop! You looking to cop a freebie, we're hot and we're hungry!'), and ended up touring the shopping arcades with Nicole, who'd got her hit for the day and mellowed out.

'Do you really need that stuff?' Lianna asked, half-amused, half-annoyed at the way Nicole slurred and giggled away her sentences.

'Need somet'ing. It slides under the chip, an' supply's in basemen'.' Rubbing cropped white hair, skipping up and down, laughing and saying she was going to shave her whole head like Darlajane, watch if she didn't.

Nicole, half French, half Senegalese, half Lianna's age, had worked as a prostitute since her father had sold her at age of eleven in the Marseilles meat market. She'd been injected with hormones to bring on her puberty, worked houses that catered for men who wanted and could pay for human prostitutes, was now a habitual offender with habits too deeply ingrained for chip therapy to touch, or so she said. Nicole took a childish delight in prowling the boutiques. Her chip wouldn't let her go inside any of them, she was serving a dozen concurrent shoplifting offences, but she could press up to lighted windows, comment professionally on displays.

She subscribed to every fashion magazine, downloading from Darlajane's computer: that and the stuff were her reward for running errands for Darlajane's scam.

Nicole and Lianna strolled the long seafront, ate burgers and fries at one of the beach cafés. It would have used up half Lianna's zek wage, but her deliveries took care of luxuries. Nicole devoured everything, right down to the last drop of the mayonnaise with which the Dutch drenched their fast food. Lianna watched with sisterly fondness, talked about what had happened at the psychokiller scenario, Nicole making appropriate squeals of disgust while wolfing down her food.

Afterwards, at Nicole's insistence, they went through the sex arcades, Nicole commenting on people commenting on the sextoys grinding lasciviously in relaxshop window displays, Lianna laughing for the first time in three days. The male sex dolls were only marginally modified, but some of the females were like something from another species, genitals swollen and complicated as the petals of predatory flowers. Lianna couldn't believe men could like anything so gross. They passed a bunch of s/m places and Nicole said at least human pros didn't have to put up with that any more, she only used to do rich straight johns. The remark touched something in Lianna. She told Nicole about the lordotic response, but the young girl shrugged and said they were only dolls, she shouldn't waste tears over *things*.

Lianna said, suddenly angry, 'It matters that it happens. That there are men who can do things like that. It matters we make living things and let them be torn apart.'

Images flashed in her head: the splayed female dolls; the wriggling baby-thing; butchered meat piled in a hooch. Her right eye pulsed with warning pain.

'That's wha' dolls are for,' Nicole said. 'Take all the bad stuff, isn't as if they really feel pain. All of my clien's were nice to me. Well, mos'ly.' Nicole giggled. 'What I want is jus' one or two johns, nice old men who can't get it up an awful lot and feel guilty and give me presents.'

But Lianna didn't hear her, seeing her husband's red

sweaty face looming over hers as he pummelled her sides on his way to climax. Seeing herself blue with bruises, skinny and small as a doll – helpless now in feedback spiral, flashing on the aftermath of the psycho's little spree, every dead doll with her husband's face. Then her chip took her.

Lianna been married five years, her husband a ranking diplomat in the Peace Police, the peepers. Five years she'd been part of his team, the diplomat's wife, confidante, social secretary, servant and social partner and whore, a real old-fashioned *hausfrau*. He'd spent a lot of time in Africa and China; his cosmopolitan charm was what had first attracted Lianna. Soon, she realized that there was a darker side; it began with rough sex play, had led to beatings, sometimes so systematic that they left half her body tender with bruises. When she miscarried after one of the beatings, she stabbed her husband to death while he slept.

Circumstances made it manslaughter, but she was chipped anyway, unavoidable her counsel said. So was forfeiting her husband's estate, it went to his family back in the Czech Republic. Lianna had been a meditek before she married, was five years behind current technology when she was sentenced, but for doll triage that didn't matter. Chipped and processed, she'd started working the Rotterdam arenas, had fallen into Darlajane's drug manufacturing thing almost without thinking, the way she'd fallen into marriage. A classic victim: being chipped hadn't changed that.

Waking up, Lianna felt as rough as she'd ever felt after a bad time with her husband. Terrific headache, her whole skin sore. She was lying on a sagging couch in warm flickering darkness that smelled of mould and candle wax and dried cat faeces. Vinyl LP records and plastic-cased CDs and actual paper comic books were stacked in tottering piles around walls shingled with glossy, tattered posters. Candles stuck in wine bottles burned on shelves; gutted flatscreen tellies showing weird drifts of snow, or the interlocking spirals of self-engulfing patterns. On a low wicker table a page-sized computer screen was scrolling spidery black lines of text.

Lianna knew at once where she was, the basement apt of Darlajane B.

Nicole was sitting cross-legged by a heap of disembowelled electronic equipment, leafing through a comic book. When she saw that Lianna was awake she came over and helped her sit up, while Darlajane shuffled into the room with a laden tray. Herbal tea: its strong bitter taste burned through Lianna's chip hangover.

The old woman watched with a proprietorial air as Lianna sipped. Limber as a twenty-year old, she sat zazen. Black jeans, black leather jacket, black T-shirt with a black slogan, orange construction boots. Apart from a scalplock her head was shaven; tattoos swarmed her papery scalp. When she smiled, which she did a lot, her steel teeth glinted wetly. Darlajane B claimed to have been born the day the Beatles put out their first single. By Lianna's reckoning it made her eighty, but she could have been sixty or a hundred, wise witchy old woman. She was used to these crises; better deal with them here than have them reported, she said, and have to thrash it out with a counsellor.

Nicole said to Lianna, 'You shouldn't get angry, then your chip wouldn't do you.'

'I wasn't angry at you.'

'I know that. You were angry because of work, but it's no use being angry for dolls. They're only *things*. That's why I showed you that stuff, so you'd see.'

Darlajane B said, 'You want to help, Nicole? Go somewhere else, let Lianna alone. You can handle your chip, but she's new to it.'

'That's what I was trying to tell her, but honestly D.J., it was like talking to my counsellor.'

'Time you listened to someone. And time you did less stuff, maybe, if this is what it makes you do.'

'Ey, I can handle it! It's just – '

'I said later! Go on, now, girl. Me and Lianna need to talk.'

After Nicole had left, Darlajane B added, 'Silly little whore, she ever had an intelligent thought, it would have died of loneliness. What do *you* want?'

A cat had materialized from the shadows, one of the colony Darlajane B said she'd founded ten years ago with three rejigged queens and a tom, using pirated and rewritten doll chips. It put its front paws on the old woman's knees, said something in a yowling dialect. Darlajane told it to stop complaining; it hissed at her and sped off.

'I picked up a kit microsaur some kid turned loose, and they don't like it wandering around,' Darlajane explained. 'There's a kink in its pyruvate cycle I'm going to edit before I clone, that way you a pet can own and not have to buy expensive food additives. It keeps my hand in.'

The thing about Darlajane B was that you couldn't ask her a direct question, you had to wait until her conversation came around to the right place. So Lianna had to listen to gossip about the other zeks until the old woman got around to asking Lianna how her sentence was going, and Lianna used the opening to tell the story about the missing doll.

'I heard there are supposed to be dolls living free, in the dunes. That's why I wondered about the one which vanished – '

'All *kinds* of things in the dunes,' Darlajane said. 'Nothing for you to worry your head about, girl. Lived there one time myself. I used to be an idealist, a revolutionary, yeah, you know that. And it's true, we used to boost dolls, modify them, turn them loose. Old counter-culture tricks, though God knows what happened to the dolls, and no one does it anymore. The revolution was over before you were born, girl, and we lost. Turned to crime, a lot of us. I was a millionaire for like about eight days, 'til the peepers caught up with my credit line. You still hurting, girl? Got something that can help.' She climbed to her feet, which took a good minute, and ambled into her kitchen.

Something cat-sized wandered out of the shadows under a tellyscreen. It was a furry purple stegosaur, the plates along its back an alternating pattern of black and yellow. Lianna stepped around it, sat at the computer screen and called up the menu, asked for bulletin boards dealing with doll civil rights. The screen strung half a dozen names and access numbers and Darlajane B said, 'You won't find anything useful on public access. Peepers sift those boards for information just like everyone else. Hell, I bet they even run most of them, sweeping up would-be dissidents. The real stuff is underground. Clandestine.'

'Can you tell me about the real stuff?'

'I could, but you'd only get into trouble. Possession of a samizdat newsheet will lose you your remission. Forget about dolls, girl. The revolution is over and the straights won. The Millennium has come, and we are in paradise, with slaves to wait on us hand and feet and pour out a never-ending cornucopia. Here, this will be more use than forbidden knowledge.'

The old woman dropped a little glassine envelope into Lianna's lap.

It held a scattering of black pills so small that Lianna could fit half a dozen under her thumbnail. She said, 'I touch drugs, my chip squeals. You know that, Darlajane. And I couldn't touch anything – '

Steel flash. 'It's not from the basement, think that on you I'd waste? Designed the plant which grows them myself. You need a kick anytime, a little speed to get through the day, use them. And don't worry about your chip, this is *natural* stuff.'

Lianna thanked her, knowing she'd never risk dropping anything from one of Darlajane B's splices. God knew what the side effects could be, anything from flashbacks to pseudo-Parkinson's.

'Trust me,' the old woman said. 'And you still feel bad about dolls, come talk to me again. You've done good business for me so far, I'd hate to see it end because you became unreliable. And neither would my . . . associates.'

Lianna thought of the two men, low-level peepers, who came by every week for the latest consignment, and had another flash, almost transcendental, that it wasn't an act, Darlajane B really was scared of them. It seemed that things were tough all over.

★

Convention time in Den Haag, round the clock combat
games in the arenas in the dune-swallowed industrial area
down by the old silted harbours of Rotterdam. Customers
wore flexible body armour, helmets and visors, were armed
with little .08mm plastic pistols which fired iron-tipped teflon
flechettes: clean kills or through-and-throughs. Dolls were
armed too, lasers which slowed the fire rate or entirely shut
down the customers' pistols, depending where the picowatt
beam hit their armour. Good clean fun for jaded technocrats,
no harm involved. It was even said the combat dolls enjoyed
it, if they knew enough to enjoy anything. Lianna didn't see
how. Dead was dead, it didn't matter who killed you.

Lianna worked fourteen hours on, ten off, tracing tags of
downed dolls, sorting them into meat and survivors. Moving
in after the johns had left, following traces in spacey industrial cathedral volumes. Receding perspectives of light and
shadow amongst rusty, splayed roof supports; floors of
saddled sand littered everywhere with spent propellent car-
tridges. Dolls fallen in the casual attitudes of death, or quietly
waiting for her. In other EC states the johns were allowed to
take out wounded dolls with head shots, catharsis in their
very own spatter movie, but the Netherlands had game laws
modified from slaughterhouse licensing: only qualified per-
sonnel could administer the *coup de grâce*. Which Lianna did
dozens of times each shift, shooting in two lines and letting
the meat go into classic clonic seizure.

She'd been doing triage for three months, but now it was
as if she was starting all over again. Noticing things, the way
wounded dolls moved, their small sounds, their fluttering
hands, as she worked on them. The patterns of disturbed
sand she sometimes found around them, like the patterns she
used to make in the snow when she was a child, lying down
and moving her arms to make angel wings . . .

Get through this, she thought, try not to see the dolls as
human. Not too difficult, they all had the same prognathous
beetle-browed face, the same smooth blue skin. She might
have been treating the same unlucky doll over and over,
fixing it up to go back into line and get shot all over again.

Get through this, take the stash she'd earned from hijacking doll pharmaceuticals for Darlajane B, run run run.

Trying to believe nothing was wrong, Lianna moved through the detritus of licensed violence administering mercy, murmuring Kollner's motto like a mantra. But it was a fragile peace.

One day, tranced out towards the end of a long shift, Lianna found herself shooting a second line of topic into a doll with only a glancing leg wound. It had stopped breathing, was jerking like a beached fish. She pinched its nostrils, tried to give it heart massage and mouth-to-mouth, and it died anyway.

She made three steps away from the corpse before she threw up.

Afterwards, a kind of numb calm descended. She tagged the body, checked the last traces (all dead), headed back in. That was when she got into the fight.

The medicare centre was poised on the flat roof of a warehouse almost totally buried in sand: a hundred plastic panel walls tilted against each other like a flock of wings fallen to rest. Lianna scored a coke to wash out her mouth, sat outside in the last of the sunset, looking at the vast expanse of scrubby dunes that saddled away south and east.

The dunes which had protected Holland for hundreds of years had been vastly expanded when the sea rose, extending for thirty kilometres inland to save rich croplands from saltseep, dunes and pine forests that ran all the way south to Roscoff, interrupted only by coastal cities walled and dyked like medieval fortresses. Maybe a billion square kilometres of unzoned outlaw territory, beyond policing. Creepy rumours about doll cities under the sand, killer doll patrols picking off loner techs, porn-rings jacking warm bodies for gross-out videos, freedom fighters turning dolls into terrorists.

Campfire stories, spun out in the dead hours between shifts. Lianna had heard them all when she'd started her sentence, but now she was beginning to take them seriously. After the psychokiller scenario she knew it was real, and she'd

heard other stories, too, live bodies triaged and tagged for
recovery vanishing before pickup. What Darlajane B had
said, deprogramming dolls . . . where had they all gone?

Fairies.

Maybe two dozen zeks were lounging around, waiting for
shift's end. A dozen more coming out, changed into street
clothes, hair slick from the showers. Kollner's crew. The new
kid was in the middle of a bunch of people, making a lot of
noise, his voice carrying to Lianna as they drew near.

'. . . I tell you, man, the guy's a righteous downhome
cannibal freak. Easiest five ecus I ever did make, and he needs
a *regular* supply!'

Someone laughed, and the kid said, 'Yeah, well take a look
at this, man, I just now cut it out. So nice and fresh I do
believe I could try a slice myself.'

Lianna saw him open a silvery cold-lok bag, the people
around him laughing, crowding close, making gross-out
noises. The kid smiling proudly, then going down on his ass
as Lianna snatched the bag away, tipped out the wet red
mass of liver, then grabbed his neck, tried to force his face
into it.

Saying over and over, 'You like this? You like *this*?' until
she was pulled away and Kollner was in front of her, asking
her to calm down.

Lianna took a deep breath, another. 'All right,' she said.
Trying not to think of what she wanted to do (not kill him,
not not not kill him), chip swelling in her right eye so there
was just a little tunnel through which she could glimpse the
world, a fluttering darkness she was on the edge of falling
into.

'This piece of shit isn't worth it,' Kollner said, gentle as
ever. 'You know that. All right?'

'All right.' Very quietly.

Lianna let Kollner put his arm around her shoulders and
steer her aside, aware in her peripheral vision of the kid
getting up, saying something because he had to try and regain
face.

'Shit, not as if the guy's a real cannibal – '

Kollner blocking her when she tried to get the kid again, his arms out, flinching as she feinted right and left, nails scraping the side of his face. Still in front of her, so she kicked for his balls, and he stepped back and said, 'All right – ' and caught her foot and dumped her on her ass, suddenly angry. Leaned over her, big hands making fists . . .

And then he was down, body arching on heels and neck. People pushed Lianna out of the way, a woman putting her foot under Kollner's head as another pried at his mouth to make sure he hadn't swallowed his tongue. Kollner shaking, muscles bunching at random. Eyes rolled back, animal sounds. Lianna flashed on how she must have looked when she'd been struck down in the sex arcade, felt shame.

One of the crew in her face, shouting at her, telling her Kollner was under real heavy manners, he couldn't afford to lose his temper at no one he'd had so many fits already. Lianna stood and took it, feeling very cool, very remote. Other zeks turning on her, hard words. She took it all to her, locking her certainty about what she needed to do, only ran when she saw two circling to get behind her, leaped the low parapet and ran across sand away from jeers and catcalls and a hail of coke cans.

Ran until her chip started to flash dark warning chevrons across her sight, sat down and watched as in one direction the centre turned over for the night shift, floodlights on shining sails; in the other, tiny fires twinkled and shifted in unfathomable darkness.

No one came to look for her, she was just a chipped zek after all, and the few people about did no more than glance at her as she made her way through the medicare centre to the doll cages.

Even so, she needed a boost to do it: two of Darlajane B's little black pills that clung to her tongue and had to be washed down with a mouthful of coke. They started to come on as she went down the ramp of polymerized sand into the cages. A fine tremor in her musculature, but somehow strong,

like she was a fine-tuned machine. Lights growing halos.
Things taking on a lacquered appearance, an increase in
reality's density.

Down the ramp into a long low arched space lit by buzzing
fluorescents. Lianna could see the snake of bright plasma that
writhed in every long tube. Dolls sprawled or squatted in
enclosures marked only by low mesh fences. All dressed in
the same white one-piece paper coveralls. A few standing at
dispensers, sucking sugary pap. One or two curled up on
scuffed sand, dead, waiting for disposal in the morning; the
few dolls that died natural deaths always died at night.

As Lianna walked towards the nearest enclosure, every doll
turned to look at her. They all had the same face, the same
empty gaze. Multiplied a thousand times, their gaze laid a
weight over Lianna's entire skin.

Cameras up amongst the lights: though she was pretty
certain no one would be watching, Lianna started to get the
shakes. She chose at random, told the doll to follow her, and
as one every doll stood up.

Lianna felt herself begin to lose it, grabbed the shoulders
of the doll across the fence from her, half-lifted half-dragged
it across. It weighed almost nothing, light as a bird. She laid
a hand on its shoulder and hissed in its ear that it must come
with her. Walked it up the ramp, into the empty locker
room, told it to stand still and got her locker open, dragged
out her kit, spilling instruments, tremors amplifying into
shivers. She had to lock her free hand around her wrist as
she slashed and slashed at the doll's shoulder, white coveralls
and blue skin slicing cleanly to show flesh and then blood
that ran down its arm, started dripping from its fingers.

Lianna made herself fold up her kit, shut her locker. Then
walked out, steering the doll with a hand on its good
shoulder. Only one person passed them as they crossed the
compound, and Lianna said, 'Found this one wandering
around, clean-up can't count again,' but the man hardly
glanced at her.

She couldn't go out the main gate, but there was only a
single mesh fence around the complex, and in places it sagged

in bellying swathes. Lights of a warehouse arena off in the distance, sound of shots, the occasional war-whoop. She managed to drag a section of links free of sand, shoved the doll through and crawled after.

Then all she had to do was hike down the road to her usual tram stop, walk her prisoner unremarked past the doll driver with the scarred face, make it squat with half a dozen other dolls in the back. Its wound had stopped bleeding, but the torn sleeve of its coverall was stained maroon from shoulder to cuff. A babushka glared disapproval, powdered face pinched and sour beneath a pink cartwheel hat with little mirrors dangling and winking from its brim. Lianna smiled at her and she looked away.

During the ride, Lianna couldn't help noticing all over again how many dolls there were, out and about amongst the human strollers. She let herself go to shivers, tried not to laugh, jamming hands between thighs, hunching shoulders. She could have taken any of them – no, they had errands, would have started squalling. But it would have been less risk! The babushka still glaring: Lianna bit the insides of her cheeks. She was crazy . . .

'You're crazy,' Darlajane B said. 'You think I have anything to do with it? You *are* crazy!'

They were on the flat roof of the residential building, wind blowing around them, rattling the panes of the cloches where Darlajane grew pot and plants she'd spliced herself. Lianna had found her stargazing, working out her astrology chart with the aid of a fifteen centimetre telescope and a hypertext almanac. Now the VR goggles were pushed up on Darlajane's tattooed scalp and the telescope was running through its tracking programme on auto, motors making abrupt spurts of noise.

Darlajane B said, 'Where have you put it? In your room, I suppose.' Her voice had acquired a harsh edge, a German accent Lianna had never heard before, but otherwise the old woman seemed quite composed.

'Where else? I locked the door, but I don't think combat dolls know about doors anyway.'

'It's the first place the peepers will think of looking. Crazy *and* stupid.'

'It's not going to be there long,' Lianna said, and told the old woman what she wanted done.

'Ach, that kind of thing I gave up a long time ago. And my associates wouldn't like it. At my age I have to behave myself.'

Lianna thought, I'm not going to hurt her, and pushed Darlajane B up against the parapet, holding tightly to the lapels of her leather jacket. The old woman swore, tried to push back; she smelt of patchouli oil, of dust, of sour age. Through the tunnel of her chip, feeling very close to the edge, Lianna said 'I'm not going to hurt you. You know I can't. But if I'm caught, I'll have the peepers analyse my blood. I dropped a couple of your pills and I'll tell them all about it. I guess supplying narcotics to zeks is illegal, or my chip wouldn't be set the way it is.'

'Let me go. Let me go right now.' Darlajane B's voice had a measure of steel in it, and Lianna stepped back. 'A clear night too, and Saturn's setting in an hour, I haven't had a chance to look at him yet. I always like to look at him. You are a nuisance, girl.'

'All you have to do is do what you do to your cats, it isn't much.'

'It isn't as straightforward as you think. And listen to me, I'm not doing this because of your silly little threat. Peepers run my thing, you think they'll let you hurt that?' Darlajane B looked thoughtfully at Lianna. 'You are a long way from where you began. Three months you nothing more than a frightened *hausfrau* were, a murderess maybe, but a frightened and confused murderess. Now you of myself remind, when I was your age, full of piss and vinegar. Without your chip, I think you could have killed me like you killed your husband.'

But Lianna was looking out beyond the parapet, into wild, windy darkness where as always scattered fires burned, small and strange as stars. She said, 'Nice try. But I'm not angry, and that's the frame my chip works in. Do you believe in fairies, Darlajane?'

'Many kinds of people live out there. Once, I myself ... but the revolution is over.'

'Is it?'

'Let's just do it, before I lose my nerve.'

They did it in the old woman's kitchen, the doll strapped to the scarred wooden table. Half a dozen cats sat atop a huge icebox, watching with feigned boredom as Lianna reassured it and Darlajane B administered curarine to immobilize its eyes. The old woman put on spectacles which covered her eyes with lensed turrets. After the curarine, she took a measure of milky liquid from a battered silvery thermos, and administered drops to the inside corners of the doll's eyes. Its head was cradled on a block of black rubber.

'The culture last month I got,' she said. 'Bootlegged from ICI, they work better than the strains I was using, get to work straight away on building connections down the optic nerves. In a couple of hours they'll be all through the cortex, increasing connectivity.' She screwed down the thermos top, put the culture in the bottom of the icebox: fembots grew best, with fewest spontaneous somatic mutations, in the dense molecular architecture of water at 4°C.

'I love these machines,' Darlajane B said. 'All my family from arthritis have suffered; I have little workers in my joints, burning away calcification as fast as it forms. So I can still sit zazen, I can still plug in chips.'

She unrolled a surgical kit, set a microsurgery scaffolding over the doll's face. A set of miniature thumb-operated waldoes peeled back the doll's eyelids, inserted something that looked like a little spade between eye and socket. Humming some old pop tune, Darlajane began to dismantle the doll's old behavioural chip. The turrets of her pop-eyed spectacles clicked as they zoomed in and out of focus. Working had calmed her, routine dictating mood. She talked about the old days as she worked, anti-creationist marches, anti-slavery terrorist campaigns, weird alliances between radical Christians, Moslems, counter-culture activists that had foundered on theological schisms Lianna couldn't begin to follow.

'How it was, in those days,' Darlajane explained, 'was that we wanted to set dolls free, but the others wanted to destroy them. Scapegoats, you know? Servants of Satan? Well, Christianity has declined ever since the Millennium, I am not surprised. *They* said we were worse than the capitalists, daring to try to save inhuman things through technology. *We* said dolls had no original sin, they were closer to angels than devils. Ach, well, it was a long time ago, and we all lost.'

A second thermos held a rack of aluminium slides, where fembots built hair-thin biochips molecule by molecule on wafer templates. A slide went under the scaffolding: waldoes plucked the chip from its carrier. Lianna watched the old woman slide it into place, imagining a swarming galaxy of machines small as bacteria spinning pseudo-neurons from the chip's hardware down the shaft of the optic nerve, spreading through the cortex, wiring a complex web in parallel with the doll's linear neuron network. Do to the doll as had been done to her ... the mote in her right eye suddenly felt huge, a splinter thrust into the raw surface of her brainjelly.

The old woman was working on the doll's other eye when Nicole said, 'Ey, where did you get him?'

For a moment Lianna thought her chip had cut in.

Darlajane said calmly, 'You need your fix, it's on the second shelf. Take it and go. This you do not need to see.'

Nicole rummaged in the big icebox, fog pouring around her. She wore nothing but a short kimono-style robe, belted very tight. She said, 'This hurts our thing, Lianna, I'll hurt you. I swear it.'

Darlajane B slid in the second chip. 'No one will it hurt unless the wrong people hear of it. And I do it only once, so you need not worry about yourself. Have what you want? Then go. Tomorrow I will talk to you.' When Nicole had gone, she said, 'That one is too much trouble for an old woman like me.'

'She needs her stuff,' Lianna said hopefully. The shock of hearing Nicole's voice was tingling in the tips of her fingers.

'Think that comforts me? Here, we are nearly finished. Used not to take so long, but necessary to remove the chips already there it is, too many essential subroutines on them. Used to have a search-and-destroy strain of bugs that burnt out conditioning areas, but it won't work with these new chips where data is holographically coded.'

'You did this a lot.'

'I was trying to tell you that. But like trying to bail out the polders with a teaspoon it was. The ones I cured lived only half a dozen years at best, and always there were more. This one you stole, it is two hundred ecus' worth of meat, nothing more. And how many combat dolls are there, in just that one arena? And in all the arenas in the world? You save this one, give it a new life, and in six years it is gone. Even if you blow the hatcheries, as some friends of mine once did, there will always be more dolls. We depend on them now. Without them no minimum wage, no voluntary unemployment, no unlimited food and gadgets. Too late to change society, girl.'

'I did it for myself,' Lianna said, softly.

Darlajane B pushed back her spectacles, swung away the scaffolding. 'Ach, of course you did. Little *hausfrau*, you should have served out your sentence. You know now there is no going back.'

'I know,' Lianna said. 'Is it finished?'

'One more thing,' Darlajane B said. She shoved an ampoule of oily liquid into a hypo and she pushed the snout against the doll's shoulder. The doll twitched as the charge went in. 'Thyrotropic hormone,' the old woman said. 'Lipodroplet packaged, what they use to bring sex-toys to puberty. And now we are done. You stay here this night, your doll here will need the time to learn. But tomorrow, I do not want to know where you are.'

Lianna woke in the middle of the night to abrupt bursts of sound, the flicker of the telly. It was an old solid-state model, its thick glass screen giving off blue light eerie as hard radiation. The doll squatted in front of it, zapping through Dutch and French and British and German and Common Net channels, blink blink blink blink, one every ten seconds. Eyes wide to the welter of images, he didn't look around when Lianna put her hand on his bandaged shoulder.

She sat behind him a long time, news programmes segueing into shopping channels, soaps, porno. Except for his thumb on the zapper, the doll didn't move. At last she left a pitcher of glucose-spiked orange juice beside him and fell into bed again, woke from uneasy sliding dreams to the buzz of her phone, loud and insistent above the telly's choppy murmur.

Lianna sleepily acknowledged the call. A computer-generated face floating in a mesh of bright lines looked out at her. It was familiar from a hundred telly serials. It was the peace police.

'You are under arrest,' it said, voice not quite synched with lips.

'W-what charge?'

'Grand larceny, illegal modification of a series four kobold. Officers will arrive soon. Your room is locked. Please do not attempt to leave.'

The face vanished like a burst soap bubble; the phone's hardcopy slot extruded a tongue of flimsy, an arrest warrant. 'But I'm already a convict,' Lianna said, and jumped when someone hammered at the door.

It wasn't the peepers: it was Darlajane B. She used her master key to override the computer-operated lock. A heavy canvas bag was slung over her shoulder. 'You come with me right now,' she said. 'That bitch Nicole sold us both. Looking to take over my stake, I'd guess.'

Something plucked at Lianna's waist. The doll. He had put on the bottom half of his coveralls, cinched it around his skinny waist with one of Lianna's scarves.

'Hot damn, mon ami,' the doll said, 'we go, ja? Heavy weather moving in from the east, storm fronts over all areas by midnight.'

Darlajane B said, 'One thing we don't need.'

'I need him. He wants to come, why not?'

'If I had any sense I'd leave you with him: you deserve each other. Did they reprogram your chip? Of course not, they wouldn't have authorization. Surprised they used any channels at all.' Darlajane watched Lianna pull on jeans, a checkered workshirt. 'You're ready? Good. My friends will be in a hurry to close this down, you can bet on it.'

What had once been the hotel's parking garage was empty, except for one of the maintenance crew sorting garbage. The doll caught its arm, looked into its eyes. 'Friend, ami. *Pouvez-vous me dire?*'

Lianna told him, 'You've been changed. You understand?'

The changeling doll considered. It said at last, in French, '"And I awoke and found me here on the cold hill's side."'

Darlajane B was at the top of the service ramp, kneeling to look under the half-raised door at the street. 'They're already here,' she said.

Lianna looked. Early morning, the street empty except for a police runabout parked right outside the crib's entrance. Nowhere to run without attracting attention, and any moment now the peepers would be back outside.

Lianna felt a strange floating detachment, the way she'd felt after her husband's death. It had happened early in the morning, and most of the next day she'd wandered the big house, waiting for justice to strike her down. In the end she'd called the peepers herself, and as she'd waited for them had at last felt peace.

Perhaps her chip had blacked her out for a second, memory treacherous now, a swamp with vast blank areas in which she could sink forever. Darlajane B clutched her arm. Lianna saw two men leave the crib. One walked to the runabout; the other towards the service entrance.

The changeling stood hand-in-hand with the maintenance doll. 'Friend,' he said, half a dozen times in half a dozen languages. He tapped the doll's chest, his own. 'We know way.'

Lianna saw that the shaven-headed peeper was very close

to the door now. Getting to her feet was very hard; her chip
was bearing down, working on peripheral clues. One word
from the peeper and it would shut her down.

'Vamoose,' the changeling said.

Lianna and Darlajane B followed.

It was not a way Lianna would have chosen: past curtain
after curtain of plastic sheeting into the warmth and red light
of the incubation chamber. It had once been a coldroom.
Now, naked dolls hung from racks, bodies wrapped in webs
of tubing, heads cased in swathes of black plastic. Their
bellies were grossly distended, like five-year pregnancies at
term: the disease Darlajane had given them had turned their
livers into vast controlled malignancies, half their body
weight. Pink goo, rich in peptides, ran through clear tubing
from the dolls to fractionation columns. The overheated
room was filled with a rich, sweet smell that made Lianna
gag.

Darlajane pawed at a jury-rigged panel, pulling wires,
shouting she was damned if Nicole was going to have them.
Peristaltic pumps slowed, stopped; black-masked dolls began
to twitch, trying to draw air with collapsed lungs. The
maintenance doll had vanished; Lianna saw the changeling
duck through a hatch low in the wall, followed it through a
low narrow passage into a foul-smelling nest lit by a dim
bulb where half a dozen dolls curled in sleep. Cockroaches
skittered from Lianna's feet. One dropped in her hair, and
she fought back a scream. The nest was the beginning of a
kind of tunnel, suddenly sloping down. Little lights, most of
them not working, sketched a dwindling perspective.

'Maintenance levels,' Darlajane B said. She was out of
breath, and leaned heavily on the arm Lianna offered.

The tunnel opened onto a wide well-lit corridor, tiled
walls and floor swathed with cables and pipes and ducts.
Dolls moved past in different directions. Most were naked,
blue skin streaked and crusted with dirt. The invisible army
of Morlocks which ran civilization.

A shout behind them: a man's voice, botched by echoes.

Lianna felt a wave of dizziness, the chip in her right eye almost triggered. Panic flaring, she ran, scattering dolls, ran down tiled tunnels until warning chevrons crammed her sight.

Lianna leaned against a grimy junction box, breathing hard. The chevrons slowly faded. She was in a narrow, grimy, ill-lit tunnel, tiles stained with black mould. Dolls moved past in an irregular single file, identical faces glancing at Lianna as they passed. A figure taller than any doll hobbled out of shadow: Darlajane B. When Lianna asked where the changeling was, the old woman said, 'You thought he'd stick with us? They aren't human, girl. They're mostly baboon, spliced with maybe ten per cent of the genes that separate us from the apes. And when they're changed, it is into something new ... I'd forgotten that ... Something strange, perhaps something wonderful.'

'I freed him ...'

'You freed him to choose. You wanted him as your pet? Well, too late. He's chosen. So must you. Listen.'

Somewhere down the length of the tunnel, above the rustle of dolls padding past: a faint murmuring sound of human voices. Lianna's heart caught on a barb of despair.

Darlajane B rummaged through her canvas bag. She said, 'Pull your chip, is what I'm going to have to do. Bonded into your optic nerve it is, so I will cause damage. No time for any other measure. You willing?'

Lianna felt like she was floating. Before she could say anything, light burst behind Darlajane. In the glare's centre the peeper said, 'You run, but you can't hide.'

Deeply tanned face, grey crewcut going white at the edges, belly straining his chalkstripe shirt, hanging over the belt of his neatly creased jeans: Lianna had seen him coming and going in the crib a dozen times. He had a big flashlight in one hand, a pistol in the other. His badge was fixed to the strap of his shoulder-holster. He said, 'Bad times come down, Darlajane. You and your friend get up against the wall. We finish this right here.'

'We can talk about this,' Darlajane B said.

One of the dolls had stopped to watch the humans. It wore the bottom half of stained white coveralls, had a bandage on one shoulder. It was the changeling.

The peeper said, 'You're out of business, what do we need to talk about?'

'That little whore. You'd trust her?'

Other dolls clustered around the changeling. They looked strange, grim, alert. One had little copper wires sewn around the rims of its ears; another a ring through its nose. All had parallel scars seaming their cheeks. Lianna was so afraid she couldn't move. She could only watch and wonder.

The peeper said, 'We'll trust Nicole as much as we trusted you.' The muzzle of his pistol looked huge as he pointed it at Lianna, at Darlajane B. He said, 'Be easy, and it's over. Just a flash in the head – '

His pistol went up and went off, blowing fragments of tile from the ceiling. Half a dozen dolls were swarming over the peeper: he staggered, screaming when small strong fingers found one of his eyes. And Darlajane said, 'Knew I had this,' brought out a little chromed 9mm automatic, both hands around its crosshatched grip. The dolls dropped away and the peeper's head came up. He stared at Darlajane B and then she shot him. Three times, chest, chest again, and a wild shot that took him in the arm and spun him around as he flew backwards. The noise was deafening in the tunnel's vault.

Lianna was on her feet, back pressed against slimy tile. She saw the changeling step forward from the others. *Fairies*, she thought, and a cold clean wind blew through her.

Then Darlajane B in her face, saying, 'We've got five minutes *if* we're lucky. Now just hold still!' Something in her hand, flashing silver: Lianna's right eye exploded and went out.

In darkness, Lianna felt sand pitch and yaw beneath her. She lost her balance and sat down hard. The right side of her head swollen, tender, hollow. She couldn't blink; her eye felt peeled. Cautiously probing, Lianna found bandages over cotton wadding – then small cold hands gripped hers.

'No good,' the changeling said.

Lianna couldn't remember anything after Darlajane's knife had come down. She asked, 'Where's the old woman?'

'Vamoosed. She left you things.'

Only gauze over her left eye. She unrolled it, blinked tears. The changeling was a blurred shadow in front of her. Beyond were moonlit dune crests, the red and green lights strung along Den Haag's barrier wall. Free, Lianna thought. A cold clean wind blew through her. Free.

The changeling pushed something towards her. It was Darlajane's canvas bag.

The changeling said in sing-song recitative, ' "Fembot cultures, chip templates, surgery kit. All you need to make over as many dolls as you can. Time to change my identity again, move on. Good luck, girl." '

'And your friends?'

'All gone. I follow you.'

'Where did they come from?'

'Found me, left me. Brothers and sisters of the knife everywhere underground.'

Getting to her feet was hard: it felt as if all her blood surged and burned in her empty socket. Wiping sympathetic tears from her left eye, Lianna saw will-of-the-wisp fires flicker far off in deep dark wilderness. She told the changeling, 'They're out there, too.'

Darlajane B had been wrong. The revolution had not finished. It was not any person or even any movement. It was an idea. It took hold where it would. Lianna thought of disaffected kids, of changelings infiltrating unnoticed everywhere in the straight world. Remembered the tram driver, its scarred cheeks. There had always been people living on the edge: now there were two kinds, changing and being changed, changing each other. All this came to her in an instant; she would spend the rest of her life untangling it.

She said, 'I suppose we'd better find out what's out there,' and swung the heavy canvas bag onto her shoulder, started down the slope of sand. The changeling gripped her hand, skipping along to keep pace with her.

After a while Lianna began to sing.

AFTERWORD

Curiously, although Europe is undergoing enormous social and political changes, there aren't many English language SF fictions set here (and it's an uncomfortable fact that most translations are from English into some other language; there's precious little traffic in the other direction). Perhaps we shouldn't be too surprised. Most SF writers live and work in the USA, and even British writers tend to look west rather than east. This story was a conscious effort to redress the balance. The location is close to the site of the 1990 World SF Convention (the annual jamboree at which the Hugo awards are presented; unsurprisingly, most take place in the United States), although the funky old seaside resort of Scheveningen, as portrayed here, is not much like its present self. 'Prison Dreams' turned out to be the first in a short series about the Morlock-like dolls, culminating in a full-blown novel, Fairyland, *all of them written from the point of view of the victims of technology.*

Recording Angel

Mr Naryan, the Archivist of Sensch, still keeps to his habits as much as possible, despite all that has happened since Angel arrived in the city. He has clung to these personal rituals for a very long time now, and it is not easy to let them go. And so, on the day that Angel's ship is due to arrive and attempt to reclaim her, the day that will end in revolution, or so Angel has promised her followers, as ever, at dusk, as the nearside edge of Confluence tips above the disc of its star and the Eye of the Preservers rises above the Farside Mountains, Mr Naryan walks across the long plaza at the edge of the city towards the Great River.

Rippling patterns swirl out from his feet, silver and gold racing away through the plaza's living marble. Above his head, clouds of little machines spin through the twilight: information's dense weave. At the margin of the plaza, broad steps shelve into the river's brown slop. Naked children scamper through the shallows, turning to watch as Mr Naryan, old and fat and leaning on his stick at every other stride, limps past and descends the submerged stair until only his hairless head is above water. He draws a breath and ducks completely under. His nostrils pinch shut. Membranes slide across his eyes. As always, the bass roar of the river's fall over the edge of the world stirs his heart. He surfaces, spouting water, and the children hoot. He ducks under again and comes up quickly, and the children scamper back from his spray, breathless with delight. Mr Naryan laughs with them and walks back up the steps, his loose belted shirt shedding water and quickly drying in the parched dusk air.

Further on, a funeral party is launching little clay lamps into the river's swift currents. The men, waist-deep in brown water, turn as Mr Naryan limps past, knuckling their broad,

narrow foreheads. Their wet skins gleam with the fire of the
sunset that is now gathering in on itself across leagues of
water. Mr Naryan genuflects in acknowledgement, feeling an
icy shame. The woman died before he could hear her story;
her, and seven others in the last few days. It is a bitter failure.

Angel, and all that she has told him – Mr Naryan wonders
whether he will be able to hear out the end of her story. She
has promised to set the city aflame and, unlike Dreen, Mr
Naryan believes that she can.

A mendicant is sitting cross-legged on the edge of the steps
down to the river. An old man, sky-clad and straight-backed.
He seems to be staring into the sunset, in the waking trance
that is the nearest that the Shaped citizens of Sensch ever
come to sleep. Tears brim in his wide eyes and pulse down
his leathery cheeks; a small silver moth has settled at the
corner of his left eye to sip salt.

Mr Naryan drops a handful of the roasted peanuts he
carries for the purpose into the mendicant's bowl, and walks
on. He walks a long way before he realizes that a crowd has
gathered at the end of the long plaza, where the steps end
and, with a sudden jog, the docks begin. Hundreds of
machines swarm in the darkening air, and behind this
shuttling weave a line of magistrates stand shoulder to
shoulder, flipping their quirts back and forth as if to drive
off flies. Metal tags braided into the tassels of the quirts wink
and flicker; the magistrates' flared red cloaks seem inflamed
in the last light of the sun.

The people make a rising and falling hum, the sound of
discontent. They are looking upriver. Mr Naryan, with a
catch in his heart, realizes what they must be looking at.

It is a speck of light on the horizon north of the city, where
the broad ribbon of the river and the broad ribbon of the
land narrow to a single point. It is the lighter towing Angel's
ship, at the end of its long journey downriver to the desert
city where she has taken refuge, and caught Mr Naryan in
the net of her tale.

★

Mr Naryan first heard about her from Dreen, Sensch's Commissioner; in fact, Dreen paid a visit to Mr Naryan's house to convey the news in person. His passage through the narrow streets of the quarter was the focus of a swelling congregation which kept a space two paces wide around him as he ambled towards the house where Mr Naryan had his apartment.

Dreen was a lively but tormented fellow who was paying off a debt of conscience by taking the more or less ceremonial position of Commissioner in this remote city which his ancestors had long ago abandoned. Slight and agile, his head clean-shaven except for a fringe of polychrome hair that framed his parchment face, he looked like a lily blossom swirling on the Great River's current as he made his way through the excited crowd. A pair of magistrates preceded him and a remote followed, a mirror-coloured seed that seemed to move through the air in brief rapid pulses like a squeezed watermelon pip. A swarm of lesser machines spun above the packed heads of the crowd. Machines did not entirely trust the citizens, with good reason. Change wars raged up and down the length of Confluence as, one by one, the ten thousand races of the Shaped fell from innocence.

Mr Naryan, alerted by the clamour, was already standing on his balcony when Dreen reached the house. Scrupulously polite, his voice amplified through a little machine that fluttered before his lips, Dreen enquired if he might come up. The crowd fell silent as he spoke, so that his last words echoed eerily up and down the narrow street. When Mr Naryan said mildly that the Commissioner was of course always welcome, Dreen made an elaborate genuflection and scrambled straight up the fretted carvings which decorated the front of the apartment house. He vaulted the wrought iron rail and perched in the ironwood chair that Mr Naryan usually took when he was tutoring a pupil.

While Mr Naryan lowered his corpulent bulk onto the stool that was the only other piece of furniture on the little balcony, Dreen said cheerfully that he had not walked so far for more than a year. He accepted the tea and sweetmeats that Mr Naryan's wife, terrified by his presence, offered, and added, 'It really would be more convenient if you took quarters appropriate to your status.'

As Commissioner, Dreen had use of the vast palace of intricately carved pink sandstone that dominated the southern end of the city, although he chose to live in a tailored habitat of hanging gardens that hovered above the palace's spiky towers.

Mr Naryan said, 'My calling requires that I live amongst the people. How else would I understand their stories? How else would they find me?'

'By any of the usual methods, of course – or you could multiply yourself so that every one of these snakes had their own archivist. Or you could use machines. But I forget, your calling requires that you use only appropriate technology. That's why I'm here, because you won't have heard the news.'

Dreen had an abrupt style, but he was neither as brutal nor as ruthless as his brusqueness suggested. Like Mr Naryan, who understood Dreen's manner completely, he was there to serve, not to rule.

Mr Naryan confessed that he had heard nothing unusual, and Dreen said eagerly, 'There's a woman arrived here. A star-farer. Her ship landed at Ys last year, as I remember telling you.'

'I remember seeing a ship land at Ys, but I was a young man then, Dreen. I had not taken orders.'

'Yes, yes,' Dreen said impatiently, 'picket boats and the occasional merchant's argosy still use the docks. But this is different. She claims to be from the deep past. The *very* deep past, before the Preservers.'

'I can see that her story would be interesting if it were true.'

Dreen beat a rhythm on his skinny thighs with the flat of his hands. 'Yes, yes! A human woman, returned after millions of years of travelling outside the Galaxy. But there's more! She is only one of a whole crew, and she's jumped ship. Caused some fuss. It seems the others want her back.'

'She is a slave, then?'

'It seems she may be bound to them as you are bound to your order.'

'Then you could return her. Surely you know where she is?'

Dreen popped a sweetmeat in his mouth and chewed with gusto. His flat-topped teeth were all exactly the same size. He wiped his wide lipless mouth with the back of his hand and said, 'Of course I know where she is – that's not the point. The point is that no one knows if she's lying, or her shipmates are lying – they're a nervy lot, I'm told. Not surprising, culture shock and all that. They've been travelling a long time. Five million years, if their story's to be believed. Of course, they weren't alive for most of that time. But still.'

Mr Naryan said, 'What do you believe?'

'Does it matter? This city matters. Think what trouble she could cause!'

'If her story's true.'

'Yes, yes. That's the point. Talk to her, eh? Find out the truth. Isn't that what your order's about? Well, I must get on.'

Mr Naryan didn't bother to correct Dreen's misapprehension. He observed, 'The crowd has grown somewhat.'

Dreen smiled broadly and rose straight into the air, his toes pointing down, his arms crossed with his palms flat on his shoulders. The remote rose with him. Mr Naryan had to shout to make himself heard over the cries and cheers of the crowd.

'What shall I do?'

Dreen checked his ascent and shouted back, 'You might tell her that I'm here to help!'

'Of course!'

But Dreen was rising again, and did not hear Mr Naryan. As he rose he picked up speed, dwindling rapidly as he shot across the jumbled rooftops of the city towards his eyrie. The remote drew a silver line behind him; a cloud of lesser machines scattered across the sky as they strained to keep up.

The next day, when as usual Mr Naryan stopped to buy the peanuts he would scatter amongst any children or mendicants he encountered as he strolled through the city, the nut roaster said that he'd seen a strange woman only an hour before – she'd had no coin, but the nut roaster had given her a bag of shelled salted nuts all the same.

'Was that the right thing to do, master?' the nut roaster asked. His eyes glittered anxiously beneath the shelf of his ridged brow.

Mr Naryan, knowing that the man had been motivated by a cluster of artificial genes implanted in his ancestors to ensure that they and all their children would give aid to any human who requested it, assured the nut roaster that his conduct had been worthy. He proffered coin in ritual payment for the bag of warm oily peanuts, and the nut roaster made his usual elaborate refusal.

'When you see her, master, tell her that she will find no plumper or more savoury peanuts in the whole city. I will give her whatever she desires!'

All day, as Mr Naryan made his rounds of the tea shops, and even when he heard out the brief story of a woman who had composed herself for death, he expected to be accosted by an exotic wild-eyed stranger. That same expectation distracted him in the evening, as the magistrate's son haltingly read from the Puranas while all around threads of smoke from neighbourhood kitchen fires rose into the black sky. How strange the city suddenly seemed to Mr Naryan: the intent face of the magistrate's son, with its faint intaglio of scales and broad shelving brow, seemed horribly like a mask. Mr Naryan felt a deep longing for his youth, and after the boy had left he stood under the shower for more than an hour, letting water penetrate every fold and cranny of his hairless, corpulent body until his wife anxiously called to him, asking if he was all right.

The woman did not come to him that day, nor the next. She was not seeking him at all. It was only by accident that Mr Naryan met her at last.

She was sitting at the counter of a tea shop, in the deep shadow beneath its tasselled awning. The shop was at the corner of the camel market, where knots of dealers and handlers argued about the merits of this or that animal and saddlemakers squatted crosslegged amongst their wares before the low, cave-like entrances to their workshops. Mr Naryan would have walked right past the shop if the proprietor had not hurried out and called to him, explaining that here was a human woman who had no coin, but he was letting her drink what she wished, and was that right?

Mr Naryan sat beside the woman, but did not speak after he ordered his own tea. He was curious and excited and afraid: she looked at him when he sat down and put his cane across his knees, but her gaze merely brushed over him without recognition.

She was tall and slender, hunched at the counter with elbows splayed. She was dressed, like every citizen of Sensch, in a loose, raw cotton overshirt. Her hair was as black and thick as any citizen's, too, worn long and caught in a kind of net slung at her shoulder. Her face was sharp and small-featured, intent from moment to moment on all that happened around her – a bronze machine trawling through the dusty sunlight beyond the awning's shadow; a vendor of pomegranate juice calling his wares; a gaggle of women laughing as they passed; a sled laden with prickly pear gliding by, two handspans above the dusty flagstones – but nothing held her attention for more than a moment. She held her bowl of tea carefully in both hands, and sucked at the liquid clumsily when she drank, holding each mouthful for a whole minute before swallowing and then spitting twiggy fragments into the copper basin on the counter.

Mr Naryan felt that he should not speak to her unless she spoke first. He was disturbed by her: he had grown into his routines, and this unsought responsibility frightened him. No doubt Dreen was watching through one or another of the little machines that flitted about the sunny, salt-white square – but that was not sufficient compulsion, except that now he had found her, he could not leave her.

At last, the owner of the tea house refilled the woman's bowl and said softly, 'Our Archivist is sitting beside you.'

The woman turned jerkily, spilling her tea. 'I'm not going back,' she said. 'I've told them that I won't serve.'

'No one has to do anything here,' Mr Naryan said, feeling that he must calm her. 'That's the point. My name is Naryan, and I have the honour, as our good host has pointed out, of being the Archivist of Sensch.'

The woman smiled at this, and said that he could call her Angel; her name also translated as Monkey, but she preferred the former. 'You're not like the others here,' she added, as if she had only just realized. 'I saw people like you in the port city, and one let me ride on his boat down the river until we reached the edge of a civil war. But after that every one of the cities I passed through seemed to be inhabited by only one race, and each was different from the next.'

'It's true that this is a remote city,' Mr Naryan said.

He could hear the faint drums of the procession. It was the middle of the day, when the sun halted at its zenith before reversing back down the sky.

The woman, Angel, heard the drums too. She looked around with a kind of preening motion as the procession came through the flame trees on the far side of the square. It reached this part of the city at the same time every day. It was led by a bare-chested man who beat a big drum draped in cloth of gold; it was held before him by a leather strap that went around his neck. The steady beat echoed across the square. Behind him slouched or capered ten, twenty, thirty naked men and women. Their hair was long and ropey with dirt; their fingernails were curved yellow talons.

Angel drew her breath sharply as the rag-taggle procession shuffled past, following the beat of the drum into the curving street that led out of the square. She said, 'This is a very strange place. Are they mad?'

Mr Naryan explained, 'They have not lost their reason, but have had it taken away. For some it will be returned in a year; it was taken away from them as a punishment. Others have renounced their own selves for the rest of their lives. It is a religious avocation. But saint or criminal, they were all once as fully aware as you or me.'

'I'm not like you,' she said. 'I'm not like any of the crazy kinds of people I have met.'

Mr Naryan beckoned to the owner of the tea house and ordered two more bowls. 'I understand you have come a long way.' Although he was terrified of her, he was certain that he could draw her out.

But Angel only laughed.

Mr Naryan said, 'I do not mean to insult you.'

'You dress like a . . . native. Is *that* a religious avocation?'

'It is my profession. I am the Archivist here.'

'The people here are different – a different race in every city. When I left, not a single intelligent alien species was known. It was one reason for my voyage. Now there seem to be thousands strung along this long, long river. They treat me like a ruler – is that it? Or a god?'

'The Preservers departed long ago. These are the end times.'

Angel said dismissively, 'There are always those who believe they live at the end of history. We thought that *we* lived at the end of history, when every star system in the Galaxy had been mapped, every habitable world settled.'

For a moment, Mr Naryan thought that she would tell him of where she had been, but she added, 'I was told that the Preservers, who I suppose were my descendants, made the different races, but each race calls itself human, even the ones who don't look like they could have evolved from anything that ever looked remotely human.'

'The Shaped call themselves human because they have no other name for what they have become, innocent and fallen alike. After all, they had no name before they were raised up. The citizens of Sensch remain innocent. They are our . . . responsibility.'

He had not meant for it to sound like a plea.

'You're not doing all that well,' Angel said, and started to tell him about the Change War she had tangled with upriver, on the way to this, the last city at the midpoint of the world.

It was a long, complicated story, and she kept stopping to ask Mr Naryan questions, most of which, despite his extensive readings of the Puranas, he was unable to answer. As she talked, Mr Naryan transcribed her speech on his tablet. She commented that a recording device would be better, but by reading back a long speech she had just made he demonstrated that his close diacritical marks captured her every word.

'But that is not its real purpose, which is an aid to fix the memory in my head.'

'You listen to peoples' stories.'

'Stories are important. In the end they are all that is left, all that history leaves us. Stories endure.' And Mr Naryan wondered if she saw what was all too clear to him, the way her story would end, if she stayed in the city.

Angel considered his words. 'I have been out of history a long time,' she said at last. 'I'm not sure that I want to be a part of it again.' She stood up so quickly that she knocked her stool over, and left.

Mr Naryan knew better than to follow her. That night, as he sat enjoying a cigarette on his balcony, under the baleful glare of the Eye of the Preservers, a remote came to him. Dreen's face materialized above the remote's silver platter and told him that the woman's shipmates knew that she was here. They were coming for her.

As the ship draws closer, looming above the glowing lighter that tows it, Mr Naryan begins to make out its shape. It is a huge black wedge composed of tiers of flat plates that rise higher than the tallest towers of the city. Little lights, mostly red, gleam here and there within its ridged carapace. Mr Naryan brushes mosquitoes from his bare arms, watching the black ship move beneath a black sky empty except for the Eye of the Preservers and a few dim halo stars. Here, at the midpoint of the world, the Home Galaxy will not rise until winter.

The crowd has grown. It becomes restless. Waves of emotion surge back and forth. Mr Naryan feels them pass through the citizens packed around him, although he hardly

understands what they mean, for all the time he has lived
with these people.

He has been allowed to pass through the crowd with the
citizens' usual generous deference, and now stands close to
the edge of the whirling cloud of machines which defends
the dock, twenty paces or so from the magistrates who
nervously swish their quirts to and fro. The crowd's thick
yeasty odour fills his nostrils; its humming disquiet, modulat-
ing up and down, penetrates to the marrow of his bones.
Now and then a machine ignites a flare of light that sweeps
over the front ranks of the crowd, and the eyes of the men
and women shine blankly orange, like so many little sparks.

At last the ship passes the temple complex at the northern
edge of the city, its wedge rising like a wave above the
temple's clusters of slim spiky towers. The lighter's engines
go into reverse; waves break in whitecaps on the steps beyond
the whirl of machines and the grim line of magistrates.

The crowd's hum rises in pitch. Mr Naryan finds himself
carried forward as it presses towards the barrier defined by
the machines. The people around him apologize effusively
for troubling him, trying to minimize contact with him in
the press as snails withdraw from salt.

The machines' whirl stratifies, and the magistrates raise
their quirts and shout a single word lost in the noise of the
crowd. The people in the front rank of the crowd fall to their
knees, clutching their eyes and wailing: the machines have
shut down their optic nerves.

Mr Naryan, shown the same deference by the machines as
by the citizens, suddenly finds himself isolated amongst
groaning and weeping citizens, confronting the row of magistrates. One calls to him, but he ignores the man.

He has a clear view of the ship, now. It has come to rest a
league away, at the far end of the docks, but Mr Naryan has
to tip his head back and back to see the top of the ship's
tiers. It is as if a mountain has drifted against the edge of the
city.

A new sound drives across the crowd, as a wind drives
across a field of wheat. Mr Naryan turns and, by the random

flare of patrolling machines, is astonished to see how large
the crowd has grown. It fills the long plaza, and more people
stand on the rooftops along its margin. Their eyes are like a
harvest of stars. They are all looking towards the ship, where
Dreen, standing on a cargo sled, ascends to meet the crew.

Mr Naryan hooks the wire frames of his spectacles over his
ears, and the crew standing on top of the black ship snap
into clear focus.

There are fifteen, men and women all as tall as Angel.
They loom over Dreen as he welcomes them with effusive
gestures. Mr Naryan can almost smell Dreen's anxiety. He
wants the crew to take Angel away, and order restored. He
will be telling them where to find her.

Mr Naryan feels a pang of anger. He turns and makes his
way through the crowd. When he reaches its ragged margin,
everyone around him suddenly looks straight up. Dreen's
sled sweeps overhead, carrying his guests to the safety of the
floating habitat above the pink sandstone palace. The crowd
surges forward – and all the little machines fall from the air!

One lands close to Mr Naryan, its carapace burst open at
the seams. Smoke pours from it. An old woman picks it up –
Mr Naryan smells her burnt flesh as it sears her hand – and
throws it at him.

Her shot goes wide. Mr Naryan is so astonished that he
does not even duck. He glimpses the confusion as the edge
of the crowd collides with the line of magistrates: some
magistrates run, their red cloaks streaming at their backs;
others throw down their quirts and hold out their empty
hands. The crowd devours them. Mr Naryan limps away as
fast as he can, his heart galloping with fear. Ahead is a wide
avenue leading into the city, and standing in the middle of
the avenue is a compact group of men, clustered about a tall
figure.

It is Angel.

Mr Naryan told Angel what Dreen had told him, that the
ship was coming to the city, the very next day. It was at the

same tea house. She did not seem surprised. 'They need me,' she said. 'How long will they take?'

'Well, they cannot come here directly. Confluence's maintenance system will only allow ships to land at designated docks, but the machinery of the spaceport docks here has grown erratic and dangerous through disuse. The nearest place they could safely dock is five hundred leagues away, and after that the ship must be towed downriver. It will take time. What will you do?'

Angel passed a hand over her sleek black hair. 'I like it here. I could be comfortable.'

She had already been given a place in which to live by a wealthy merchant family. She took Mr Naryan to see it. It was near the river, a small two-storey house built around a courtyard shaded by a jacaranda tree. People were going in and out, carrying furniture and carpets. Three men were painting the wooden rail of the balcony that ran around the upper storey. They were painting it pink and blue, and cheerfully singing as they worked. Angel was amused by the bustle, and laughed when Mr Naryan said that she shouldn't take advantage of the citizens.

'They seem so happy to help me. What's wrong with that?'

Mr Naryan thought it best not to explain about the cluster of genes implanted in all the races of the Shaped, the reflex altruism of the unfallen. A woman brought out tea and a pile of crisp, wafer-thin fritters sweetened with crystallized honey. Two men brought canopied chairs. Angel sprawled in one, invited Mr Naryan to sit in the other. She was quite at ease, grinning every time someone showed her the gift they had brought her.

Dreen, Mr Naryan knew, would be dismayed. Angel was a barbarian, displaced by five million years. She had no idea of the careful balance by which one must live with the innocent, the unfallen, if their cultures were to survive. Yet she was fully human, free to choose, and that freedom was inviolable. No wonder Dreen was so eager for the ship to reclaim her.

Still, Angel's rough joy was infectious, and Mr Naryan soon found himself smiling with her at the sheer abundance of trinkets scattered around her. No one was giving unless they were glad to give, and no one who gave was poor. The only poor in Sensch were the sky-clad mendicants who had voluntarily renounced the material world.

So Mr Naryan sat and drank tea with her, and ate a dozen of the delicious honeyed fritters, one after the other, and listened to more of her wild tales of travelling the river, realising how little she understood of Confluence's administration. She was convinced that the Shaped were somehow forbidden technology, for instance, and did not understand why there was no government. Was Dreen the absolute ruler? By what right?

'Dreen is merely the Commissioner. Any authority he has is invested in him by the citizens, and it is manifest only on high days. He enjoys parades, you know. I suppose the magistrates have power, in that they arbitrate neighbourly disputes and decide upon punishment – Senschians are argumentative, and sometimes quarrels can lead to unfortunate accidents.'

'Murder, you mean? Then perhaps they are not as innocent as you maintain.' Angel reached out suddenly. 'And these? By what authority do these little spies operate?'

Pinched between her thumb and forefinger was a bronze machine. Its sensor cluster turned back and forth as it struggled to free itself.

'Why, they are part of the maintenance system of Confluence.'

'Can Dreen use them? Tell me all you know. It may be important.'

She questioned Mr Naryan closely, and he found himself telling her more than he wanted. But despite all that he told her, she would not talk about her voyage, nor of why she had escaped from the ship, or how. In the days that followed, Mr Naryan requested several times, politely and wistfully, that she would. He even visited the temple and petitioned for information about her voyage, but all trace of it had been lost in the vast sifting of history, and when pressed, the

librarian who had come at the hierodule's bidding broke
contact with an almost petulant abruptness.

Mr Naryan was not surprised that it could tell him nothing.
The voyage must have begun five million years ago at least,
after all, for the ship to have travelled all the way to the
neighbouring galaxy and back.

He did learn that the ship had tried to sell its findings on
landfall, much as a merchant would sell his wares. Perhaps
Angel wanted to profit from what she knew; perhaps that
was why the ship wanted her back, although there was no
agency on Confluence that would close such a deal. Knowledge was worth only the small price of petitioning those
librarians which deal with the secular world.

Meanwhile, a group of citizens gathered around Angel, like
disciples around one of the blessed who, touched by some
fragment or other of the Preservers, wander Confluence's
long shore. These disciples went wherever she went. They
were all young men, which seemed to Mr Naryan faintly
sinister, sons of her benefactors fallen under her spell. He
recognised several of them, but none would speak to him,
although there were always at least two or three accompany-
ing Angel. They wore white headbands on which Angel had
lettered a slogan in an archaic script older than any race of
the Shaped; she refused to explain what it meant.

Mr Naryan's wife thought that he, too, was falling under
some kind of spell. She did not like the idea of Angel: she
declared that Angel must be some kind of ghost, and
therefore dangerous. Perhaps she was right. She was a wise
and strong-willed woman, and Mr Naryan had grown to
trust her advice.

Certainly, Mr Naryan believed that he could detect a
change in the steady song of the city as he went about his
business. He listened to an old man dying of the systematic
organ failure which took most of the citizens in the middle
of their fourth century. The man was one of the few who had
left the city – he had travelled north, as far as a city tunnelled
through cliffs overlooking the river, where an amphibious
race lived. His story took a whole day to tell, in a stiflingly

hot room muffled in dusty carpets and lit only by a lamp with a blood-red chimney. At the end, the old man began to weep, saying that he knew now that he had not travelled at all, and Mr Naryan was unable to comfort him. Two children were born on the next day – an event so rare that the whole city celebrated, garlanding the streets with fragrant orange blossoms. But there was a tension beneath the celebrations that Mr Naryan had never before felt, and it seemed that Angel's followers were everywhere amongst the revellers.

Dreen felt the change, too. 'There have been incidents,' he said, as candid an admission as he had ever made to Mr Naryan. 'Nothing very much. A temple wall defaced with the slogan the woman has her followers wear. A market disrupted by young men running through it, overturning stalls. I asked the magistrates not to make examples of the perpetrators – that would create martyrs. Let the people hold their own courts if they wish. And she's been making speeches. Would you like to hear one?'

'Is it necessary?'

Dreen dropped his glass with a careless gesture – a machine caught it and bore it off before it smashed on the tiles. They were on a balcony of Dreen's floating habitat, looking out over the Great River towards the nearside edge of the world. At the horizon was the long white double line that marked the river's fall: the rapids below, the permanent clouds above. It was noon, and the white, sunlit city was quiet.

Dreen said, 'You listen to so much of her talk, I suppose you are wearied of it. In summary, it is nothing but some vague nonsense about destiny, about rising above circumstances and bettering yourself, as if you could lift yourself into the air by grasping the soles of your feet.'

Dreen dismissed this with a snap of his fingers. His own feet, as always, were bare, and his long opposable toes were curled around the bar of the rail on which he squatted. He said, 'Perhaps she wants to rule the city – if it pleases her, why not? At least, until the ship arrives here. I will not stop her if that is what she wants, and if she can do it. Do you know where she is right now?'

'I have been busy.' But Mr Naryan felt an eager curiosity: yes, his wife was right.

'I heard the story you gathered in. At the time, you know, I thought that man might bring war to the city when he came back.' Dreen's laugh was a high-pitched hooting. 'The woman is out there, at the edge of the world. She took a boat yesterday.'

'I am sure she will return,' Mr Naryan said. 'It is all of a pattern.'

'I defer to your knowledge. Will hers be an interesting story, Mr Naryan? Have another drink. Stay, enjoy yourself.'

Dreen reached up and swung into the branches of the flame tree which leaned over the balcony, disappearing in a flurry of red leaves and leaving Mr Naryan to find a machine that was able to take him home.

Mr Naryan thought that Dreen was wrong to dismiss what Angel was doing, although he understood why Dreen affected such a grand indifference. It was outside Dreen's experience, that was all: Angel was outside the experience of everyone on Confluence. The Change Wars that flared here and there along Confluence's vast length were not ideological but eschatological. They were a result of sociological stresses that arose when radical shifts in the expression of clusters of native and grafted genes caused a species of Shaped to undergo a catastrophic redefinition of its perceptions of the world. But what Angel was doing dated from before the Preservers had raised up the Shaped and ended human history. Mr Naryan only began to understood it himself when Angel told him what she had done at the edge of the world.

And later, on the terrible night when the ship arrives and every machine in the city dies, with flames roaring unchecked through the farside quarter of the city and thousands of citizens fleeing into the orchard forests to the north, Mr Naryan realizes that he has not understood as much as he thought. Angel has not been preaching empty revolution after all.

Her acolytes, all young men, are armed with crude wooden

spears with fire-hardened tips, long double-edged knives of the kind coconut sellers use to open their wares, flails improvised from chains and wire. They hustle Mr Naryan in a forced march towards the palace and Dreen's floating habitat. They have taken away Mr Naryan's cane, and his bad leg hurts abominably with every other step.

Angel is gone. She has work elsewhere. Mr Naryan felt fear when he saw her, but feels more fear now. The reflex altruism of the acolytes has been overridden by a new meme forged in the fires of Angel's revolution – they jostle Mr Naryan with rough humour, sure in their hold over him. One in particular, the rough skin of his long-jawed face crazed in diamonds, jabs Mr Naryan in his ribs with the butt of his spear at every intersection, as if to remind him not to escape, something that Mr Naryan has absolutely no intention of doing.

Power is down all over the city – it went off with the fall of the machines – but leaping light from scattered fires swims in the wide eyes of the young men. They pass through a market square where people swig beer and drunkenly gamble amongst overturned stalls. Elsewhere in the fiery dark there is open rutting, men with men as well as with women. A child lies dead in a gutter. Horrible, horrible. Once, a building collapses inside its own fire, sending flames whirling high into the black sky. The faces of all the men surrounding Mr Naryan are transformed by this leaping light into masks with eyes of flame.

Mr Naryan's captors urge him on. His only comfort is that he will be of use in what is to come. Angel has not yet finished with him.

When Angel returned from the edge of the world, she came straight away to Mr Naryan. It was a warm evening, at the hour after sunset when the streets began to fill with strollers, the murmur of neighbour greeting neighbour, the cries of vendors selling fruit juice or popcorn or sweet cakes.

Mr Naryan was listening as his pupil, the magistrate's son, read a passage from the Puranas which described the time when the Preservers had strung the Galaxy with their cre-

ations. The boy was tall and awkward and faintly resentful,
for he was not the scholar his father wished him to be and
would rather spend his evenings with his fellows in the beer
halls than read ancient legends in a long dead language. He
bent over the book like a night stork, his finger stabbing at
each line as he clumsily translated it, mangling words in his
hoarse voice. Mr Naryan was listening with half an ear,
interrupting only to correct particularly inelegant phrases. In
the kitchen at the far end of the little apartment, his wife was
humming to the murmur of the radio, her voice a breathy
contented monotone.

Angel came up the helical stair with a rapid clatter,
mounting quickly above a sudden hush in the street. Mr
Naryan knew who it was even before she burst onto the
balcony. Her appearance so astonished the magistrate's son
that he dropped the book. Mr Naryan dismissed him and he
hurried away, no doubt eager to meet his friends in the
flickering neon of the beer hall and tell them of this wonder.

'I've been to the edge of the world,' Angel said to Mr
Naryan, coolly accepting a bowl of tea from Mr Naryan's
wife, quite oblivious of the glance she exchanged with her
husband before retreating. Mr Naryan's heart turned at that
look, for in it he saw how his wife's hard words were so easily
dissolved in the weltering sea of reflexive benevolence. How
cruel the Preservers had been, it seemed to him never
crueller, to have raised up races of the Shaped and yet to
have shackled them in unthinking obedience.

Angel said, 'You don't seem surprised.'

'Dreen told me as much. I'm pleased to see you returned
safely. It has been a dry time without you.' Already he had
said too much: it was as if all his thoughts were eager to be
spilled before her.

'Dreen knows everything that goes on in the city.'

'Oh no, not at all. He knows what he needs to know.'

'I took a boat,' Angel said. 'I just asked for it, and the man
took me right along, without question. I wish now I'd stolen
it. It would have been simpler. I'm tired of all this good will.'

It was as if she could read his mind. For the first time, Mr

Naryan began to be afraid, a shiver like the first shake of a tambour that had ritually introduced the tempestuous dances of his youth.

Angel sat on the stool that the student had quit, tipping it back so she could lean against the rail of the balcony. She had cut her black hair short, and bound around her forehead a strip of white cloth printed with the slogan, in ancient incomprehensible script, that was the badge of her acolytes. She wore an ordinary loose white shirt and much jewelry: rings on every finger, sometimes more than one on each; bracelets and bangles down her forearms; gold and silver chains around her neck, layered on her breast. She was both graceful and terrifying, a rough beast slouched from the deep past to claim the world.

She said, teasingly, 'Don't you want to hear my story? Isn't that your avocation?'

'I'll listen to anything you want to tell me,' Mr Naryan said.

'The world is a straight line. Do you know about libration?'

Mr Naryan shook his head.

Angel held out her hand, tipped it back and forth. 'This is the world. Everything lives on the back of a long flat plate which circles the sun. The plate rocks on its long axis, so the sun rises above the edge and then reverses its course. I went to the edge of the world, where the river that runs down half its length falls into the void. I suppose it must be collected and redistributed, but it really does look like it falls away forever.'

'The river is eternally renewed,' Mr Naryan said. 'Where it falls is where ships used to arrive and depart, but this city has not been a port for many years.'

'Fortunately for me, or my companions would already be here. There's a narrow ribbon of land on the far side of the river. Nothing lives there, not even an insect. No earth, no stones. The air shakes with the sound of the river's fall, and swirling mist burns with raw sunlight. And there are shrines, in the thunder and mist at the edge of the world. One spoke to me.'

Mr Naryan knew these shrines, although he had not been there for many years. He remembered that the different races of the Shaped had erected shrines all along the edge of the world, stone upon stone carried across the river, from which flags and long banners flew. Long ago, the original founders of the city of Sensch, Dreen's ancestors, had travelled across the river to petition the avatars of the Preservers, believing that the journey across the wide river was a necessary rite of purification. But they were gone, and the new citizens, who had built their city of stones over the burnt groves of the old city, simply bathed in the heated, mineral-heavy water of the pools of the shrines of the temple at the edge of their city before delivering their petitions. He supposed the proud flags and banners of the shrines would be tattered rags now, bleached by unfiltered sunlight, rotted by mist. The screens of the shrines – would they still be working?

Angel grinned. Mr Naryan had to remember that it was not, as it was with the citizens, a baring of teeth before striking.

She said, 'Don't you want to know what it said to me? It's part of my story.'

'Do you want to tell me?'

She passed her hand over the top of her narrow skull: bristly hair made a crisp sound under her palm. 'No,' she said. 'No, I don't think I do. Not yet.'

Later, after a span of silence, just before she left, she said, 'After we were wakened by the ship, after it brought us here, it showed us how the black hole you call the Eye of the Preservers was made. It recorded the process as it returned, speeded up because the ship was travelling so fast it stretched time around itself. At first there was an intense point of light within the heart of the Large Magellanic Cloud. It might have been a supernova, except that it was a thousand times larger than any supernova ever recorded. For a long time its glare obscured everything else, and when it cleared, all the remaining stars were streaming around where it had been. Those nearest the centre elongated and dissipated, and always more crowded in until nothing was left but the gas clouds of the accretion disc, glowing by Cerenkov radiation.'

'So it is written in the Puranas.'

'And is it also written there why Confluence was constructed around a halo star between the Home Galaxy and the Eye of the Preservers?'

'Of course. It is so we can all worship and glorify the Preservers. The Eye looks upon us all.'

'That's what I told them,' Angel said.

After she was gone, Mr Naryan put on his spectacles and walked through the city to the docks. The unsleeping citizens were promenading in the warm dark streets, or squatting in doorways, or talking quietly from upper storey windows to their neighbours across the street. Amongst this easy somnolence, Angel's young disciples moved with a quick purposefulness, here in pairs, there in a group of twenty or more. Their slogans were painted on almost every wall. Three stopped Mr Naryan near the docks, danced around his bulk, jeering, then ran off, screeching with laughter, when he slashed at them with his cane.

'Ruffians! Fools!'

'Seize the day!' they sang back. 'Seize the day!'

Mr Naryan did not find the man whose skiff Angel and her followers had used to cross the river, but the story was already everywhere amongst the fisherfolk. The Preservers had spoken to her, they said, and she had refused their temptations. Many were busily bargaining with citizens who wanted to cross the river and see the site of this miracle for themselves.

An old man, eyes milky with cataracts – the fisherfolk trawled widely across the Great River, exposing themselves to more radiation than normal – asked Mr Naryan if these were the end times, if the Preservers would return to walk amongst them again. When Mr Naryan said, no, anyone who had dealt with the avatars knew that only those fragments remained in the Universe, the old man shrugged and said, 'They say *she* is a Preserver,' and Mr Naryan, looking out across the river's black welter, where the horizon was lost against the empty night, seeing the scattered constellations of the running lights of the fisherfolk's skiffs scattered out to the nearside edge, knew that the end of Angel's story was not far off. The citizens were finding their use for her. Inexorably, step by step, she was becoming part of their history.

Mr Naryan did not see Angel again until the night her ship arrived. Dreen went to treat with her, but he couldn't get within two streets of her house: it had become the centre of a convocation that took over the entire quarter of the city. She preached to thousands of citizens from the roof-tops.

Dreen reported to Mr Naryan that it was a philosophy of hope from despair. 'She says that all life feeds on destruction and death. Are you sure you don't want to hear it?'

'It isn't necessary.'

Dreen was perched on a balustrade, looking out at the river. They were in his floating habitat, in an arbour of lemon trees that jutted out at its leading edge. He said, 'More than a thousand a day are making the crossing.'

'Has the screen spoken again?'

'I've monitored it continuously. Nothing.'

'But it did speak with her.'

'Perhaps, perhaps.' Dreen was suddenly agitated. He scampered up and down the narrow balustrade, swiping at overhanging branches and scaring the white doves that perched amongst the little glossy leaves. The birds rocketed up in a great flutter of wings, crying as they rose into the empty sky. Dreen said, 'The machines watching her don't work. Not any more. She's found out how to disrupt them. I snatch long range pictures, but they don't tell me very much. I don't even know if she visited the shrine in the first place.'

'I believe her,' Mr Naryan said.

'I petitioned the avatars,' Dreen said, 'but of course they wouldn't tell me if they'd spoken to her.'

Mr Naryan was disturbed by this admission – Dreen was not a religious man. 'What will you do?'

'Nothing. I could send the magistrates for her, but even if she went with them her followers would claim she'd been arrested. And I can't even remember when I last arrested someone. It would make her even more powerful, and I'd have to let her go. But I suppose that you are going to tell me that I should let it happen.'

'It has happened before. Even here, to your own people. They built the shrines, after all . . .'

'Yes, and later they fell from grace, and destroyed their city. The snakes aren't ready for that,' Dreen said, almost pleading, and for a moment Mr Naryan glimpsed the depth of Dreen's love for this city and its people.

Dreen turned away, as if ashamed, to look out at the river again, at the flocking sails of little boats setting out on, or returning from, the long crossing to the far side of the river. This great pilgrimage had become the focus of the life of the city. The markets were closed for the most part; merchants had moved to the docks to supply the thousands of pilgrims.

Dreen said, 'They say that the avatar tempted her with godhead, and she denied it.'

'But that is foolish! The days of the Preservers have long ago faded. We know them only by their image, which burns forever at the event horizon, but their essence has long since receded.'

Dreen shrugged. 'There's worse. They say that she forced the avatar to admit that the Preservers are dead. They say that *she* is an avatar of something greater than the Preservers, although you wouldn't know that from her preaching. She claims that this universe is all there is, that destiny is what you make it. What makes me despair is how readily the snakes believe this cant.'

Mr Naryan, feeling chill, there in the sun-dappled shade, said, 'She has hinted to me that she learnt it in the great far out, in the galaxy beyond the Home Galaxy.'

'The ship is coming,' Dreen said. 'Perhaps they will deal with her.'

In the burning night of the city's dissolution, Mr Naryan is brought at last to the pink sandstone palace. Dreen's habitat floats above it, a black cloud that half-eclipses the glowering red swirl of the Eye of the Preservers. Trails of white smoke, made luminescent by the fires which feed them, pour from the palace's high arched windows, braiding into sheets which dash like surf against the rim of the habitat. Mr Naryan sees something fly up from amongst the palace's many carved spires – there seem to be more of them than he remembers – and smash away a piece of the habitat, which slowly tumbles off into the black sky.

The men around him hoot and cheer at this, and catch Mr Naryan's arms and march him up the broad steps and through the high double doors into the courtyard beyond. It is piled with furniture and tapestries that have been thrown down from the thousand high windows overlooking it, but a path has been cleared to a narrow stair that turns and turns as it rises, until at last Mr Naryan is pushed out onto the roof of the palace.

Perhaps five hundred of Angel's followers crowd amongst the spires and fallen trees and rocks, many naked, all with lettered headbands tied around their foreheads. Smoky torches blaze everywhere. In the centre of the crowd is the palace's great throne on which, on high days and holidays, at the beginning of masques or parades, Dreen receives the city's priests, merchants and artists. It is lit by a crown of machines burning bright as the sun, and seated on it – easy, elegant and terrifying – is Angel.

Mr Naryan is led through the crowd and left standing alone before the throne. Angel beckons him forward, her smile both triumphant and scared: Mr Naryan feels her fear mix with his own.

She says, 'What should I do with your city, now I've taken it from you?'

'You haven't finished your story.' Everything Mr Naryan planned to say has fallen away at the simple fact of her presence. Stranded before her fierce, barely contained energies, he feels old and used up, his body as heavy with years and regret as with fat. He adds cautiously, 'I'd like to hear it all.'

He wonders if she really knows how her story must end. Perhaps she does. Perhaps her wild joy is not at her triumph, but at the imminence of her death. Perhaps she really does believe that the void is all, and rushes to embrace it.

Angel says, 'My people can tell you. They hide with Dreen up above, but not for long.'

She points across the roof. A dozen men are wrestling a sled, which shudders like a living thing as it tries to reorientate itself in the gravity field, onto a kind of launching cradle tipped up towards the habitat. The edges of the habitat are ragged, as if bitten, and amongst the roof's spires tower-trees are visibly growing towards it, their tips already brushing its edges, their tangled bases pulsing and swelling as teams of men and women drench them with nutrients.

'I found how to enhance the antigravity devices of the sleds,' Angel says. 'They react against the field which generates gravity for this artificial world. The field's stored inertia gives them a high kinetic energy, so that they make very good missiles. We'll chip away that floating fortress piece by piece if we have to, or we'll finish growing towers and storm its remains, but I expect surrender long before then.'

'Dreen is not the ruler of the city.' Nor are you, Mr Naryan thinks, but it is not prudent to point that out.

'Not any more,' Angel says.

Mr Naryan dares to step closer. He says, 'What did you find out there, that you rage against?'

Angel laughs. 'I'll tell you about rage. It is what you have all forgotten, or never learned. It is the motor of evolution, and evolution's end, too.' She snatches a beaker of wine from a supplicant, drains it and tosses it aside. She is consumed with an energy that is no longer her own. She says, 'We travelled so long, not dead, not sleeping. We were no more than stored potentials triply engraved on gold. Although the ship flew so fast that it bound time about itself, the journey still took thousands of years of slowed ship-board time. At the end of that long voyage we did not wake: we were born. Or rather, others like us were born, although I have their memories, as if they are my own. They learned then that the Universe was not made for the convenience of humans. What they found was a galaxy ruined and dead.'

She holds Mr Naryan's hand tightly, speaking quietly and intensely, her eyes staring deep into his.

'A billion years ago, our neighbouring galaxy collided with another, much smaller galaxy. Stars of both galaxies were torn off in the collision, and scattered in a vast halo. The rest coalesced into a single body, but except for ancient globular clusters, which survived the catastrophe because of their dense gravity fields, it is all wreckage. We were not able to chart a single world where life had evolved. I remember standing on a world sheared in half by immense tidal stress, its orbit so eccentric that it was colder than Pluto at its farthest point, hotter than Mercury at its nearest. I remember standing on a world of methane ice as cold and dark as the Universe itself, wandering amongst the stars. There were millions of such worlds cast adrift. I remember standing upon a fragment of a world smashed into a million shards and scattered so widely in its orbit that it never had the chance to reform. There are a million such worlds. I remember gas giants turned inside out – single vast storms – and I remember worlds torched smooth by eruptions of their stars. No life, anywhere.

'Do you know how many galaxies have endured such collisions? Almost all of them. Life is a statistical freak. It is likely that only the stars of our galaxy have planets, or else other civilizations would surely have arisen elsewhere in the unbounded Universe. As it is, it is certain that we are alone. We must make of ourselves what we can. We should not hide, as your Preservers chose to do. Instead, we should seize the day, and make the Universe over with the technology that the Preservers used to make their hiding place.'

Her grip is hurting now, but Mr Naryan bears it. 'You cannot become a Preserver,' he says sadly. 'No one can, now. You should not lie to these innocent people.'

'I didn't need to lie. They took up my story and made it theirs. They see now what they can inherit – if they dare. This won't stop with one city. It will become a crusade!' She adds, more softly, 'You'll remember it all, won't you?'

It is then that Mr Naryan knows that she knows how this

must end, and his heart breaks. He would ask her to take that burden from him, but he cannot. He is bound to her. He is her witness.

The crowd around them cheers as the sled rockets up from its cradle. It smashes into the habitat and knocks loose another piece, which drops trees and dirt and rocks amongst the spires of the palace roof as it twists free and spins away into the night.

Figures appear at the edge of the habitat. A small tube falls, glittering through the torchlight. A man catches it, runs across the debris-strewn roof, and throws himself at Angel's feet. He is at the far end of the human scale of the Shaped of this city. His skin is lapped with distinct scales, edged with a rim of hard black like the scales of a pine cone. His coarse black hair has flopped over his eyes, which glow like coals with reflected firelight.

Angel takes the tube and shakes it. It unrolls into a flexible sheet on which Dreen's face glows. Dreen's lips move; his voice is small and metallic. Angel listens intently, and when he has finished speaking says softly, 'Yes.'

Then she stands and raises both hands above her head. All across the roof, men and women turn towards her, eyes glowing.

'They wish to surrender! Let them come down!'

A moment later a sled swoops down from the habitat, its silvery underside gleaming in the reflected light of the many fires scattered across the roof. Angel's followers shout and jeer, and missiles fly out of the darkness – a burning torch, a rock, a broken branch. All are somehow deflected before they reach the ship's crew, screaming away into the dark with such force that the torch, the branch, kindle into white fire. The crew have modified the sled's field to protect themselves.

They all look like Angel, with the same small sleek head, the same gangling build and abrupt nervous movements. Dreen's slight figure is dwarfed by them. It takes Mr Naryan a long minute to be able to distinguish men from women, and another to be able to tell each man from his brothers, each woman from her sisters. They are all clad in long white shirts that leave them bare-armed and bare-legged, and each is girdled with a belt from which hang a dozen or more little machines. They call to Angel, one following on the words of the other, saying over and over again:

'Return with us – '

' – this is not our place – '

' – these are not our people – '

' – we will return – '

' – we will find our home – '

' – leave with us and return.'

Dreen sees Mr Naryan and shouts, 'They want to take her back!' He jumps down from the sled, an act of bravery that astonishes Mr Naryan, and skips through the crowd. 'They are all one person, or variations on one person,' he says breathlessly. 'The ship makes its crew by varying a template. Angel is an extreme. A mistake.'

Angel starts to laugh.

'You funny little man! I'm the real one – they are the copies!'

'Come back to us – '

' – come back and help us – '

' – help us find our home.'

'There's no home to find!' Angel shouts. 'Oh, you fools! This is all there is!'

'I tried to explain to them,' Dreen says to Mr Naryan, 'but they wouldn't listen.'

'They surely cannot disbelieve the Puranas,' Mr Naryan says.

Angel shouts, 'Give me back the ship!'

'It was never yours – '

' – never yours to own – '

' – but only yours to serve.'

'No! I won't serve!' Angel jumps onto the throne and makes an abrupt cutting gesture.

Hundreds of fine silver threads spool out of the darkness, shooting towards the sled and her crewmates. The ends of the threads flick up when they reach the edge of the sled's modified field, but then fall in a tangle over the crew: their shield is gone.

The crowd begins to throw things again, but Angel orders them to be still. 'I have the only working sled,' she says. 'That which I enhance, I can also take away. Come with me,' she tells Mr Naryan, 'and see the end of my story.'

The crowd around Angel stirs. Mr Naryan turns, and sees one of the crew walking towards Angel.

He is as tall and slender as Angel, his small high-cheek-boned face so like her own it is as if he holds up a mirror as he approaches. A rock arcs out of the crowd and strikes his shoulder: he staggers but walks on, hardly seeming to notice that the crowd closes at his back so that he is suddenly inside its circle, with Angel and Mr Naryan in its focus.

Angel says, 'I'm not afraid of you.'

'Of course not, sister,' the man says. And he grasps her wrists in both his hands.

Then Mr Naryan is on his hands and knees. A strong wind howls about him, and he can hear people screaming. The afterglow of a great light swims in his vision. He can't see who helps him up and half-carries him through the stunned crowd to the sled.

When the sled starts to rise, Mr Naryan falls to his knees again. Dreen says in his ear, 'It's over.'

'No,' Mr Naryan says. He blinks and blinks, tears rolling down his cheeks.

The man took Angel's wrists in both of his –

Dreen is saying something, but Mr Naryan shakes his head. It isn't over.

– and they shot up into the night, so fast that their clothing burst into flame, so fast that air was drawn up with them. If Angel could nullify the gravity field, then so could her crewmates. She has achieved apotheosis.

The sled swoops up the tiered slope of the ship, is swallowed by a wide hatch. When he can see again, Mr Naryan finds himself kneeling at the edge of the open hatch. The city is spread below. Fires define the streets which radiate away from the Great River; the warm night air is bitter with the smell of burning.

Dreen has been looking at the lighted windows that crowd the walls of the vast room beyond the hatch, scampering with growing excitement from one to the other. Now he sees that Mr Naryan is crying, and clumsily tries to comfort him, believing that Mr Naryan is mourning his wife, left behind in the dying city.

'She was a good woman, for her kind,' Mr Naryan is able to say at last, although it isn't her he's mourning, or not only her. He is mourning for all of the citizens of Sensch. They are irrevocably caught in their change now, never to be the same. His wife, the nut roaster, the men and woman who own the little tea houses at the corner of every square, the children, the mendicants and the merchants – all are changed, or else dying in the process. Something new is being born down there. Rising from the fall of the city.

'They'll take us away from all this,' Dreen says happily. 'They're going to search for where they came from. Some are out combing the city for others who can help them; the rest are preparing the ship. They'll take it over the edge of the world, into the great far out!'

'Don't they know they'll never find what they're looking for? The Puranas – '

'Old stories, old fears. They will take us home!'

Mr Naryan laboriously clambers to his feet. He understands that Dreen has fallen under the thrall of the crew. He is theirs, as Mr Naryan is now and forever Angel's. He says, 'Those times are past. Down there in the city is the beginning of something new, something wonderful – ' He finds he can't explain. All he has is his faith that it won't stop here. It is not an end but a beginning, a spark to set all of Confluence – the unfallen and the changed – alight. Mr Naryan says, weakly, 'It won't stop here.'

Dreen's big eyes shine in the light of the city's fires. He says, 'I see only another Change War. There's nothing new in that. The snakes will rebuild the city in their new image, if not here, then somewhere else along the Great River. It has happened before, in this very place, to my own people. We survived it, and so will the snakes. But what *they* promise is so much greater! We'll leave this poor place, and voyage out to return to where it all began, to the very home of the Preservers. Look there! That's where we're going!'

Mr Naryan allows himself to be led across the vast room. It is so big that it could easily hold Dreen's floating habitat. A window on its far side shows a view angled somewhere far above the plane of Confluence's orbit. Confluence itself is a shining strip, an arrow running out to its own vanishing point. Beyond that point are the ordered, frozen spirals of the Home Galaxy, the great jewelled clusters and braids of stars constructed in the last great days of the Preservers before they vanished forever into the black hole they made by collapsing the Magellanic Cloud.

Mr Naryan starts to breathe deeply, topping up the oxygen content of his blood.

'You see!' Dreen says again, his face shining with awe in Confluence's silver light.

'I see the end of history,' Mr Naryan says. 'You should have studied the Puranas, Dreen. There's no future to be found amongst the artifacts of the Preservers, only the dead past. I won't serve, Dreen. That's over.'

And then he turns and lumbers through the false lights and shadows of the windows towards the open hatch. Dreen catches his arm, but Mr Naryan throws him off.

Dreen sprawls on his back, astonished, then jumps up and runs in front of Mr Naryan. 'You fool!' he shouts. 'They can bring her back!'

'There's no need,' Mr Naryan says, and pushes Dreen out of the way and plunges straight out of the hatch.

He falls through black air like a heavy comet. Water smashes around him, tears away his clothes. His nostrils pinch shut and membranes slide across his eyes as he plunges down and down amidst streaming bubbles until the roaring in his ears is no longer the roar of his blood but the roar of the river's never-ending fall over the edge of the world.

Deep, silty currents begin to pull him towards that edge.

He turns in the water and begins to swim away from it, away from the ship and the burning city. His duty is over: once they have taken charge of their destiny, the changed citizens will no longer need an Archivist.

Mr Naryan swims more and more easily. The swift cold water washes away his landbound habits, wakes the powerful muscles of his shoulders and back. Angel's message burns bright, burning away the old stories, as he swims through the black water, against the currents of the Great River. Joy gathers with every thrust of his arms. He is the messenger, Angel's witness. He will travel ahead of the crusade that will begin when everyone in Sensch is changed. It will be a long and difficult journey, but he does not doubt that his destiny – the beginning of the future that Angel has bequeathed him and all of Confluence – lies at the end of it.

AFTERWORD

This story began with an invitation from Greg Bear, who asked if I would consider writing something for an anthology of original stories concerned with the central themes of sf. Naturally, I was flattered; more importantly, it forced me to consider just what the central themes of sf are. It seems to me that every sf writer has a different set, just as every writer probably has a different working definition of sf itself (which is, perhaps, why we can never agree on a definition). This story suggests that my own themes – or, if you like, obsessions – are aliens, the far future (which is to say a future in which our own time is invisibly distant), cosmology, messiahs, and what Roz Kavney has labelled Big Dumb Objects. Certainly, readers of Eternal Light *or* Red Dust *may find echoes of the themes of those two novels in this clash between the Hindu and Christian mythologies on a Big Dumb Object orbiting a manufactured black hole beyond a Galaxy so rich in ten million years or more of human history that the orbits of every star have been altered.*

It is a story that takes seriously Frank Tipler's hypothesis, explained in detail in his The Physics of Immortality, *that in* the unimaginably far future the entire Universe will have been re-engineered so radically that it will have become a substrate for a collective intelligence that will be as omniscient as God. Indeed, the Universe will be God, a God of the end times rather than of creation, and we and everything that has ever lived will be recreated as a trivial but necessary exercise. The Preservers of this story are not that God, although it is possible that they are of that God. But that is another story.

Dr Luther's Assistant

After Mike lost his appeal and had been sentenced and chipped, he had to get a job. That was the law in Holland, where most convicts weren't imprisoned but tagged with chip controllers and stripped of their entitlement to the universal unearned wage. After his personal counsellor explained about the monthly report Mike would have to make, and the penal chip's reflexive programming which would induce a minor epileptic fit if Mike ingested any alcohol or proscribed drug, or strayed outside Amsterdam city limits, or broke curfew, after all this, he told Mike that convicts were expected to make reparations to society.

'It is very simple, very straightforward. It is the Dutch way. What it is, you do society good and yourself good too.'

This from a skinny seventy-year-old geezer in baggy blue jeans, a fake Rolex, a wrinkled pop-art T-shirt, and a bowl-cut hair transplant. Mike was beginning to suspect that Holland's workfare system was run entirely by geezers and babushkas who'd grown bored with their statutory right of access to unlimited leisure. Up there on the top floor of the Nieuwe Stadhuis, an old-fashioned open-plan office that was a maze of partitions and big glossy-leaved plants and cubicles like the veal-fattening pens in the prison camp farm, there wasn't one official younger than Mike's parents.

'What convicts need to learn,' the counsellor said, swivelling back and forth in his chair, 'is a sense of responsibility. A job will give you that. Do you have any preferences?'

Mike shrugged. His right eye was swollen shut from where they'd put in the chip, and although he'd been off Hux for three months now, he'd still felt as if he was trapped in some low rez virtuality with Alice-in-Wonderland rules, where you were put in jail until you were proven guilty, whereupon you were released.

The first time he'd been sent down, in England, he'd done time in one of the huge prison camps. Greenham Common, a place that had once been some kind of military base. He'd been convicted for writing bogus prescriptions to support the habit he'd acquired working as a junior doctor. Most junior doctors prescribed themselves something to keep themselves going through the one hundred and twenty hours on-call shifts – those few who didn't cop a habit, drop out, go crazy or die from exhaustion just had to be androids – but Mike had been caught along with about two hundred others in a media-inspired sweep and been handed ten years' hard labour, no remission. His medical degree had scored him a position in the camp's infirmary, but hard was just what it had been. His wife had divorced him, taken off for the States with his baby son, and he'd acquired a serious dependency on Hux which after his release had had him running packages back and forth across the North Sea to support it, until one day a customs officer in Schiphol Airport took an interest in his overnight bag.

Hux was bad stuff, temporary infections of fembots which rejigged the sensory areas of the brain so that your whole nervous system became an erogenous zone, and the world was gently and irresistibly fucking you: you could come by stroking a piece of velvet or smelling the steam that lifted off fresh-boiled rice. But unlike most fembots, those self-organizing clades of machines smaller than bacteria that operated down in the dance of molecules at the femtometre scale of thousand billionths of a millimetre, Hux had disabled self-replicating facilities and a life-span measured in minutes. Strictly speaking, pseudodrug fembots like Hux weren't addictive – they caused no permanent metabolic changes – but if you liked the trip you had to have a regular supply. Which was how Mike's habit had gotten him into the courier business, which was how he'd ended up under the chip.

When he had said he didn't suppose he'd be allowed to work in a hospital, the counsellor had agreed that it wasn't an option and had paged through his terminal with maddening slowness until he'd come up with what he called an eighty per cent match.

'Which is not so bad. The position's been open quite a while. It requires someone with medical qualifications.'

'Don't I get a choice in this?'

'Of course,' the counsellor said, suddenly not relaxed at all. 'If you don't take what's offered, you can go to the general labour pool. However, I doubt you'd like that very much, because you would work alongside dolls, heavy physical work. Just keep in mind that for troublemakers there's always the general labour pool. Do as you're told, and we will get along fine.'

And that was how Mike found himself working for Dr Dieter Luther in one of Amsterdam's sex arcades.

'I've just two requirements,' Dr Luther told Mike on his first day at the sex arcade. 'First, that you're not afraid of blood. Second, that you can fuck with the meat all you want, but only out of hours. Given your curfew, that will allow you only twenty minutes or so after we close, but needs must, eh, young man?'

'Whatever you say, Dr Luther,' Mike said, giving his best shit-eating grin. Compared to the filth and cold and brutality of Greenham, working out his sentence in a sex arcade was a dream: all he had to do was feed the sex toys and clean their cubicles at the end of each night, and once in a while assist Dr Luther in his little sideline.

Dr Luther said, 'You will remain my assistant only if you do whatever I say. That is the first and last rule, young man.'

Dr Luther was a tall fastidious man of about sixty, with silky white hair brushed straight back from his high, liver-spotted forehead. He had a dozen silk suits of different shimmering pastel colours, and smoked foul Bulgarian cigarettes using an ancient yellow ivory holder. He held the cigarette as if he was up to his neck in water, had a way of looking around with slow preening motion, and liked to think of himself as a privileged observer of human psychology.

'I am in a very distinctive position,' he told Mike. 'A sex arcade is the one place where true desire is made publicly manifest. It is the one place where honest sexual roles are played for real instead of inside the head. By honest, I mean those which are not compromised by the world, those which are true to the self's base desires. And here it is possible to gauge by sexual satisfaction the correlation between dream and actuality, between vision and performance. Sex is art, and the sex arcade is the possibility of Arcadia, of eternal return.'

A lot of what Dr Luther said was simply for effect, Mike thought, like his cabinet full of medical oddities, and the shelf of brutal twentieth century pornography with titles like *Little Anal Annie* and *Piss Party*, stuff that had involved real live human women, not dolls. The customers went pathetically quiet if Dr Luther flashed them a page or two, as if granted a glimpse of the Arcadia he was always talking about.

'No imagination, Michael,' Dr Luther would say afterwards. 'They're born consumers, and can't think beyond what's put in front of them. Sheep to the slaughter, Michael, sheep to the slaughter.'

There was always a creepy feeling in the arcade, as if Dr Luther's spirit had settled into every plush-carpeted corner, like a mist. Mike would be working away when he'd look up and see Dr Luther watching him, his cigarette holder held up by his neck. Sometimes he would make some remote, tangential remark, sometimes he would just watch while Mike creamed up one of the dolls, or sometimes he would describe in explicit detail what the doll was designed to do, how it performed, and then ask if it made Mike excited.

'Whatever you want,' Mike took to saying after a while, but even that kind of harmless remark would make Dr Luther smile and he'd take out his notebook and gold pen and jot something down as if he was running an experiment with Mike as its subject. Soon, Mike was tempted to snatch notebook and pen and write down just what he thought of

Dr Luther, but he restrained himself with the thought that no matter what, this had to be better than the general labour pool. The Dutch took drug-running a lot less seriously than the other European states. Mike only had to take three years of this, less with remission for good behaviour. He'd still be young enough to start over, start another life, maybe another family.

Sometimes Dr Luther would tell Mike to leave off what he was doing, they had work to do. Dr Luther had a number of dozen special customers with special needs that went beyond the normal parameters of the sex arcade. Mostly this involved modification of dead sex toys or worked-out straight dolls in the basement operating theatre. Delivery and disposal of what Dr Luther called his little custom jobs were arranged by a chic, hard-faced French woman who looked about twenty but was, Dr Luther said, at least sixty.

What Mike did was hand the appropriate instruments and control bleeding with a diathermy pen while Dr Luther worked on the naked, nerve-blocked blue-skinned doll on a stainless steel table. The surface of the table was hatched with channels that drained blood into a plastic bucket under one corner, like a morgue slab. Dr Luther worked with quick, crude artistry, cutting new orifices and grafting pockets of mucosal epithelium and muscle to shape them, closing mostly with interrupted sutures using thick twenty-day catgut because the clients liked the resulting Frankenstein effect. Mike didn't mind the butchery, and in a way it was interesting. Dr Luther was good, and sometimes held a running commentary on his procedures, as if Mike was his pupil rather than his assistant. They were at their most intimate down there in the basement, over the sacrifice on the stainless steel table.

Sometimes Mike wondered if maybe Dr Luther didn't get off on cutting up dolls up for his special customers, not that he could ask. And besides, it wasn't even illegal. Dr Luther actually had a licence for his operations. It was on the wall of his little operating theatre, right next to the steel table. The clients were licensed, too, and what happened to the

customized dolls wasn't much different to what happened to
the live targets in the combat games arenas out at Rotterdam.

Dr Luther's sex arcade was in the basement and ground floor
of a tall narrow building with a high-peaked roof of red tile,
in a cobbled side street that ran back from a narrow sleeve of
water, Oude Zijds Voorburgwal, which marked where the
old medieval walls had been. This was in the Red Light
District, the Walletjes, right in the heart of the oldest part of
Amsterdam. Dr Luther was an oddity in the sex-business
community, which was mostly run by Africans or Caribbean
islanders from the old Dutch colonies, but he was well-liked
and greeted everywhere he went, even by the affable cops,
greetings he acknowledged with a lift of his panama hat.

'You fuck around with Dr Luther, you get fucked over
pretty good yourself,' Wayne Patterson told Mike. 'He's been
around forever, guy, used to pimp real human girls when he
was younger back in the last century, moved into dolls most
before anyone else. He's even supposed to have run with the
liberationists one time, turning dolls into fairies.'

'You believe in fairies?' Mike had never before given much
thought to dolls, which to him were just there, visible yet
invisible, like computers or runabouts. Something about the
blue skin made doll faces blurs unless you forced yourself to
look closely, and then all you saw was the same broad flat
unbridged nose, the same wide lipless mouth, the weak chin,
the small round brown eyes. Dolls moved slowly and carefully, as if through hedges of invisible razors, pausing between
stages of each task before moving to the next. Mike couldn't
picture them running free in the wild places of Europe;
they'd been changed too much to become animals again, to
revert to their monkey ancestry.

'Most people don't, but I do. I saw one, one time, out on
the fringe. It wasn't some doll that had wandered off with a
bad chip,' Wayne said, with a kind of reverence. 'This was
something else.'

'I thought the peepers had rounded up all the liberationists.' Mike remembered that a handful had ended up in

Greenham a few months before he'd been discharged, but he hadn't had anything to do with them: they were politicals, the active edge of a movement that wanted to give dolls the same rights as humans.

'Maybe most of them, but not all. Word is Dr Luther does business with the liberationists, and the cops let him. What you have to understand about Dr. Luther is that he's like the King, guy, you can't touch him.'

Wayne Patterson was originally from London, a scrawny geezer who'd been living in Amsterdam for twenty years. He'd been under the chip for more than half that time, on and off, though he was clean right now.

He told Mike, 'Dr Luther's had assistants before, not one came out the other side. Maybe they tried to rip him off. I learnt one thing under the chip, it's keep your nose clean. They stop you doing the one thing you were sent down for, that's all they're allowed to stop, but it's like you're visible, you try some scam and they got you back in to reprogram your chip before you get started.'

Wayne Patterson worked as a tout for the live sex clubs, standing outside the doors and giving tourists the spiel, or handing out cards in the canalside cafés. One night he had tried to give one to Mike, who'd told him, hey, excuse me, I work here too, and Wayne had said yes, wait a minute, you're Dr Luther's new assistant, and had come around the ropes and bought Mike another espresso and soon enough gotten his story out of him and was giving him advice. Wayne Patterson grooved on telling zeks what to do, was Mike's opinion, although he had to admit the scrawny old bastard knew his way around.

'What you need to establish,' he told Mike, 'is a routine. See, you're in the slam right now, sitting here with me watching the girls go by. Some zeks can't cope with that, but you're intelligent, you'll catch on.'

But routine was what Mike had in plenty. He had to spend fourteen hours a day under curfew in the zek hostel, mostly sleeping or zoning out in the tattered lounge, watching soaps or sport on the big ancient television with the few zeks who like him worked nightshift. It was a relief not to have to think about what went on in the cubicles, the insertions, the laborious exertions, the exchange of fluids.

Working in the sex arcade was beginning to make him go a little crazy about sex, wanting it and not wanting it at the same time. His counsellor said that was good, it meant he was getting over his dependency on Hux, and when Mike said he preferred the low rez haze of cold turkey, the counsellor had added that if he couldn't handle the temptation, he could always quit and go into the general labour pool, giving Mike a mean little smile because he knew Mike wouldn't.

Mike kept telling himself it could be worse. The little window between the end of his curfew and the start of work was the best time, when he hung out in one or another of the cafés in Nieuwmarkt's big cobbled square, nursing an espresso, slapping at the mosquitoes that skated the night air under the strings of lights. Maybe Wayne Patterson would stop by, maybe not, but there was always a festive mood in early evening, with the lights and thumping music of the little funfair, and entire families of tourists gawking and giggling at the sampler holos hung out in front of the sex shows and arcades, and human prostitutes of all five sexes out looking for business. Parents out with their kids, a lot of the parents no older than Mike, which hurt to think about. His son would be, what, eleven? No, twelve. Twelve years old, and Mike didn't even know exactly where he was. Trying not to think about that was as hard as not thinking about sex.

Sometimes a particularly outrageously sexy girl walking by would get right to him. Mike couldn't help it. He was still young, just past thirty, and sex with a live human girl didn't seem at all possible. He couldn't afford the prostitutes, had nowhere but the zek hostel to take any girl he picked up. His lust felt raw and unclean after Hux's pure intensity, but now it was all that he had.

He would watch the girl go by in the soft evening light, maybe in a white T-shirt cut to show the sides of her breasts, and pearl-shimmer short-shorts cut just above the curve of her ass, her long legs gleaming, and he'd say, sort of wincing, 'Oh man, that sort of thing ought to be made illegal.'

'That's absolutely the wrong response,' Wayne Patterson said. 'If you like her so much, you should ask her to sit with you, have a drink. Nice young fellow like you.'

'Yeah, and in five minutes she'd know I was a zek.'

'Plenty of women go for zeks, believe me,' Wayne Patterson said, although the one he introduced to Mike was a raddled ex-whore weighing about a hundred kilos, most of it spilling out of her tight red dress, who was savvy enough to see Mike's alarm and sweet enough not to comment on it until Wayne Patterson had gone off to take a leak, when she told Mike that Wayne was a good fellow who mostly meant well and besides, she understood that Mike worked for Dr Luther, so he must be copping freebies.

'Well, not exactly,' Mike said.

Mike didn't mind handling the sex toys, but they didn't once give him a hard-on. They lay supine and uncomplaining in their two by two metre cubicles on plastic-covered thick foam mattresses, blue skin black in the dull red lights, more pathetically ludicrous than arousing. They were like those breeds of dog so selected for one characteristic that they can hardly function at all. A couple had breasts so huge they could hardly sit up to use their bedpans; others had huge over-complicated labia like sea anemones or insectivorous tropical blooms which needed special creams to stop them getting infected with yeasts, or internal arrangements so strange Mike would rather put his dick in a meat grinder.

As far as Mike was concerned, dolls were just things, less than animals because they had been designed. He lusted hopelessly after the girly-girl whores that paraded the cobbled streets of the Walletjes, but he'd as soon fuck a vacuum cleaner as a doll.

And then he fell in love.

The sex arcade had closed and Mike had finished hosing down the cubicles and feeding the sex toys their syrup when he found Dr Luther waiting for him by the service door, slowly and voluptuously smoking a cigarette, a little black bag at his feet.

'I have a little business meeting tonight,' he said. 'You'll come along, Michael. Hold still, now.'

Mike jerked back, because Dr Luther had waved something towards his face. Dr Luther gripped Mike's chin, showed him what looked like a pocket torch. He held it up to Mike's right eye and there was a brief flash.

'All done,' Dr Luther said, releasing Mike.

'What was that?'

'I reprogrammed your chip for tonight. Extended your curfew.'

'That's not legal, is it?'

'It is not legal, but I am sure you will not mind.'

'You want me to break the law, and I don't know what for?'

'I am the law, Michael, as far as you are concerned. Come now. We have a rendezvous.'

They rode the trams out to a service station at a road junction near Schiphol airport. At two in the morning it was surprisingly busy: long distance lorry drivers slumped at the bar; ordinary families ate in groups, eyes on the flickering teevee screens; a minor rock group Mike recognized from his trawling of daytime television made a lot of noise at the bar with their road crew and hangers-on. Dr Luther watched all this benevolently, as if he had created the whole scene for Mike's edification.

Mike was sort of scrunched up in one corner of the booth. His eyes were hurting. This was too like the times he had picked up his packages when he had been in the courier business. Pressure was swelling in his right eyesocket, not quite sharpening to pain.

Dr Luther nudged him and said, 'See the fellow who looks like an undertaker, buying a cup of coffee? He'll go outside, and one minute later we'll follow him.'

Mike looked just as the guy turned from the counter. A swarthy square face framed by a helmet of black hair, a cheap black suit and big shiny black shoes, a bootlace tie at the collar of his white shirt. He saw Mike looking at him and turned away, headed for the door.

Mike said, 'Is this worth your while? I can't see that you'd make much from people like that. Whatever it is you're selling.'

Dr Luther pulled out a pocket watch and flipped up its lid. 'Money isn't the issue,' he said. 'What we are dealing with here are liberationists. They want the thyrotropic hormone that I use to bring the sex toys to rapid maturity. It's part of the process of making fairies, Michael.'

Mike supposed that he was to say something, but he didn't know what to think about it at all, except that maybe Wayne Patterson hadn't been retailing as much shit as he had thought.

He drank down the last of his herbal tea and followed Dr Luther out into the hot windy night. The sharp sweet stink of gasohol. The motorway made a ribbon of orange light and a distant roar beyond a screen of trees. They went around the side of the service station. The kitchen door was propped open, and inside, in bright light glancing off white porcelain and stainless steel, dolls in white paper overalls, their bald blue heads gleaming in the harsh light, worked at a rapid pace amongst the deep-fryers and griddles.

The liberationists were waiting in the shadows by the kitchen dumpbins. There were three of them, the swarthy man who'd come into the service station, another man who looked enough like the first to be his brother, and an older woman in a ragged denim dress, her grey hair in dreadlocks. Dr Luther murmured to Mike that since the big crackdown last year, the liberationists were living wild with their creations, and that it wouldn't do to mention it.

The woman, who was clearly in charge, looked at Mike and said, 'Who's the guy?' She was about sixty, with a round face and a head that seemed slightly too small for her fleshy body. Mike looked away from her direct gaze.

'My assistant,' Dr Luther said.

'A zek? Gee, Dieter, maybe we ought to do the deal another time.'

'He's fine. You are fine, aren't you, Michael?'

'Sure,' Mike said.

One of the men in black laughed. Behind them, in the dumpbin, something rustled through the waste food: rats, Mike thought, suddenly nervous. During his time at Greenham he had come to loathe rats.

'He's under a chip,' the woman said, 'we can give him something to get him happy that won't register.'

Dr Luther said, 'Are you offering to sell after all this time? I am surprised.'

'I'm offering him a freebie, Dieter. It isn't for sale. It isn't mine to sell.'

'And yet you can give it away. Well, do a deal with him if you like, but on his own time. Meanwhile, you have to pay for the hormone.'

'Pretty soon we'll be able to make that ourselves, too,' the woman said.

'Of course, it is not difficult. But do you have the equipment to refine it? I would advise you not to try using it otherwise; it will have unpleasant side effects on your patients.' Dr Luther added, 'You know, it is possible that we can trade . . .'

'Maybe I can give you a freebie, too. Turn you on, Dieter. Do you some good.'

The woman was being playful, Mike saw. This was a routine she and Dr Luther had gone through many times.

'Come on,' one of the men said, the one who'd come into the service station. 'We get this done. We go.' He had some kind of Balkan accent.

'I have thirty millilitres at 2000 units per,' Dr Luther said, holding up a sealed silvery plastic baggie. 'I think you know the price.'

'As we agreed,' the woman said, and held up a sheaf of crumpled US dollars, green bills worn threadbare by their long use as the currency of the grey market.

Mike had been watching the exchange, and didn't notice

the figure rising from the dumpbin until it vaulted to the ground and looked straight at him. A blue-skinned high-cheeked elfin face, eyes flooded with amber reflections from the kitchen's light. Beautiful, in a ragged lace dress that half-concealed, half-revealed her slim body. A changeling, a fairy.

The kitchen door clattered open, and a doll limped out, shouldering a greasy bag of waste food. Mike looked around for a moment; when he looked back, the fairy had gone.

The two men had stepped backwards into the shadows, vanishing in the same way the fairy had. The woman looked at Mike and said, 'Hey, now you know why we do this. You come by some time, you can turn on like they do. Really, our stuff will get by your chip.'

Mike said, 'Oh yeah? What does it do?' He was acutely aware that Dr Luther was watching him.

'It'll take you on a one-way trip to Fairyland, young fellow. What do you say?'

'My assistant stays clean,' Dr Luther said. 'If I get into trouble with the authorities, I can't answer for the consequences.'

'I think your assistant's in love,' the woman said, and then she turned and walked off into the darkness beyond the light that fell from the kitchen.

Dr Luther said, 'You do not entertain that idea, Michael. With me you stay clean.'

'Listen, I only work for you. I'm not like one of your dolls.'

'Of course not. You don't want to be owned by anyone. That is quite natural. But you are mine, Michael, while you are chipped. I give back your proof of employment, your *werkgeversverklaring*, you go to the general labour pool. Like this poor thing here.'

The doll had halted outside the kitchen door, stupidly confused by the presence of humans where no humans should be. Dr Luther caught its chin in one hand and the sack of garbage it was carrying dropped with a ripe splatter. He raised his other hand and the scalpel caught the light from the kitchen. Then he cut the doll's throat.

It stood with blood gushing dark red down the front of its

paper coveralls, then collapsed face forward into the spill of chicken bones and plastic and rotten lettuce leaves and soggy half-eaten rolls.

Mike stepped back as blood pooled towards his boots. He was too shocked to speak.

'Remember that the fairies are just one step from this,' Dr Luther said. He kicked the dead doll's head. 'Let me tell you about dolls. They were originally gene-spliced in South Korea as a way of trying to out-compete its neighbours of the Pacific Rim, and soon every nation was using them as cheap slave labour. Kobolds, they were originally called, although no one but the Peace Police uses this term now. The liberationists cure the dolls by taking out their control chips and inserting new ones, and infect them with fembots which hardwire the chips into the dolls' cerebral cortex, then bring them to sexual maturity. Most dolls are male, did you know that?'

'Does it matter?' The talk of chips had reminded Mike of his own; his right eye itched from the inside.

'Not usually, of course. There's nothing magical about them, and nothing there for you, my dear Michael. I've been offering to distribute that drug for several years, but always I am refused.'

'She said it wasn't hers to sell.'

'She helped make the fairies, Michael. What do you think?'

Mike thought about that on the ride back, and on and off all the next day, speculation mixed with the glimpse he'd had of the fairy's fine-boned face, its wild fearless gaze.

'I heard talk of a place out there where it doesn't matter you're chipped,' Wayne Patterson volunteered the next evening, in the café where Mike was whiling away the time before the sex arcade opened. He explained in his dogged old man's way, 'The thing is, they say you can find anything out on the fringe, but when you're out there ... You're there, that's all that matters on the fringe. You can't fall any further. Nothing at all to do with fairies.'

'You said you saw a fairy?'

'The peepers killed most of them when they broke up the liberationists,' Wayne said. 'Maybe there are one or two left, but that's it. It's more important they're fringers than fairies.'

Mike said, 'Right now I've something more interesting to think about. Last night, I learnt there are still liberationists.'

He explained what had gone down, and Wayne grew serious. 'I tell you one thing, Mike. Don't fuck with Dr Luther. He's been around a long time. He's got all sorts of connections and immunities.'

'That drug turns out to be real, there are maybe what? A million zeks, two million? Most of them wanting to be turned on. And then there are the straights.'

Wayne said, 'You used to be on Hux, right? Bad stuff, Mike. I think you want a taste again. I seen this before. Go talk to your therapist, he'll tell you.'

'What I was into . . . I don't need a replacement for that. What I need is to get out from under the chip, away from Dr Luther and his little tricks. And I know that costs money. There are places that'll take it out easy enough, but then I need a new identity, don't want to look at tripling my sentence if I get caught. And you, Wayne, what about you?'

'What about me?' Wayne said, looking confused.

'You got to get yourself out, too. You're stuck here and you deserve better. Name a place you want to go, you can get there.' He could see the idea growing in Wayne by the way the old man's eyes started to lose focus. He said, 'All I need is someone who knows the fringes, someone who can find out where the liberationists are hiding.'

'Those guys you were talking about,' Wayne said. 'They sound an awful lot like some ghosts I was staying with some time. You know, stateless people. These were from I think Albania.'

Mike smiled. 'I believe it's my round,' he said. 'What do you want, coffee or juice?'

Later, at work, Dr Luther made no mention of the last night, for which Mike was very grateful. He wasn't sure if he could hold his tongue if Dr Luther made one of his remarks. He prepped a doll for surgery, washing its stringy blue body with alcohol, giving it a shot to put it under with the pneumatic hypodermic. Dr Luther worked quickly, building a muscular orifice in the doll's abdominal wall: this was for the special customer who took to heart the old maxim about understanding death by fucking life in the gall bladder.

'You'll help with the delivery tonight,' Dr Luther said, after they had rolled the doll onto the gurney and Mike was sluicing blood from the stainless steel table. Dr Luther snapped off his gloves and dropped them into the bucket of clotting blood. 'Just look tough and say nothing. That's all Eve wants. You mess up, she'll tell me, but I trust you not to mess up, Michael. And don't bother coming back when you're done. This is an expensive rush job, no need to open the arcade tonight.'

'I'll do my best,' Mike said, nice as pie, thinking that if Dr Luther wanted him out of the way that night there were more subtle ways to go about it. Arrogance was as bad a vice as stupidity.

The delivery was in the smart neighbourhood to the west of the Damrak, on Prinsengracht canal, a stone's throw from the Anne Frank House. Eve, the hard-faced Frenchwoman, didn't lift a finger as Mike manoeuvred the groggy doll out of the water taxi and across the cobbled street into the elevator of the tall narrow apartment building.

The special client lived in the penthouse. It was done out in retrochic: a gleaming hardwood floor; glass walls on three sides of the living-room looking out across the lights of the city; leather and chrome furniture spotlit like museum pieces, which was probably what they were. An actual human butler, whom Mike at first mistook for the client, a small grave Thai in a loose black smock, helped install the doll in a ceramic and stainless steel bathroom while Eve waited by the door. The butler handed her a fat envelope which she put in her Chanel bag.

On the way down, Mike said, 'What happens to it?'

Eve gave him a hard look and said, 'They do things to it, maybe fuck it, maybe not, and then kill it, slowly.'

'Not my idea of sex.'

'You don't have much imagination, do you, Michael? That's good. Don't ask questions, and you'll be all right.'

Outside she handed him a bill before she stepped into the waiting water taxi. Ten ecus.

He stood at the edge of the quay and said, 'What am I supposed to do with this, buy a cup of coffee?'

Eve looked up at him from the well of the water taxi, fixed him with a hard shrewd look. 'Isn't it almost your curfew? You go home and stay cool.'

But going home was the last thing on Mike's mind; instead, he walked back to Dr Luther's sex arcade. It was shut, its frontage dark amongst the neon hustle and bustle of midnight. A black, official-looking limo was illegally parked on the corner under the big Pepsi-Cola hologram, its human driver reading by the hologram's red, white and blue light, oblivious to the colourful crowds that swirled around him while he waited for his boss to finish with his cheap thrill. In the Nieuwmarkt Square beyond, the lights of the funfair's big wheel slowly revolved against the purple night.

Mike got in at the back door at the bottom of a set of narrow slippery steps, using the key he'd taken on the way out. He was looking through the steel pharmacy cabinet in the basement when he heard footsteps above and then muffled voices.

Each of the cubicles had an intercom set. In the old days the girls would have used them in case the customer got rough; now they were marked for customer convenience. Mike switched them on, one by one, his heart tripping at each click, until he heard Dr Luther telling someone that it was risky, they probably wouldn't even come, with an edge to his voice Mike had never heard before.

A man's voice, heavy and slow, fluent Dutch coloured by an unidentifiable accent, said, 'That's your problem. I trust for your own sake you'll find a way.'

'I could tell them that the batch was contaminated. It would work as long as they haven't started to use it.'

'I don't want details, Luther. Just that it's arranged.'

'Well, as long as I'm not involved beyond that.'

'We arrest them, leave you. My word.'

'I'm losing a source of income, you know.'

'Hardly a major worry for you, given your special clients. You know we can make it up to you. Tomorrow night.'

Mike didn't need to hear any more. He shut off the intercom, and went through the pharmacy cabinet, then the surgical kit. That was where he found the reprogramming device. It was a slim black tube with a gridded lens at its flared end, a digital input pad and a red button set in its shaft. He prayed that the thing wasn't date specific, that what had worked yesterday would work today, and put it to his right eye and pressed the button. Then he pulled open the refrigerator and grabbed a couple of sealed bags of thyrotropic hormone, and went out the way he'd come in.

On the hot, crowded, neon-lit street, he saw the limo pull away, moving slowly over the cobbles. A moment later, Dr Luther appeared at the door of the arcade. He carefully locked it, and went off in the opposite direction. Mike ran all the way to the club where Wayne Patterson was working.

At that time of night, the trams were mostly empty. Wayne Patterson sat on one side of the aisle, Mike on the other. Mike felt a buzzing excitement, couldn't stop telling the old man what he'd heard, although all Wayne would say was that of course Dr Luther was a snitch, just about everyone on the Walletjes was, it was how they got through life, it didn't mean anything.

'But it does!' Mike said passionately. He was thinking of that sweet glimpse, the beautiful creature. He could have reached out ... He remembered that Wayne Patterson had once told him about the time he'd worked in a termination plant. They strapped the dolls in bucket seats on a kind of chain, shot them in the head with a captive bolt, and the seats carried them into the incinerator. Inspectors were supposed to make sure every doll was dead before it burned, but Wayne had said maybe one in a hundred woke up with a broken skull, started to scream and struggle, and the inspectors knew all about it, because why else would the dolls have to be strapped in . . .

It was still hot when they reached the service station at the motorway intersection, the night air close and absolutely still. Traffic made a rushing noise beyond the screen of trees. Lights twinkled out in the heath, little fires. Wayne Patterson shivered, said it was so spookily the same.

'Then you can find them.'

'Look, Mike, they've a mind to it they can find you. But they don't want to – '

'The liberationists can't be that far away. Luther expects to meet up with them tomorrow. And they said they'd look out for me. They want to turn me on.'

'And you're going to let them.'

'Sure. I have to try the goods first, don't I?'

'The goods. Right. But that's not really why you're doing this, is it?' When Mike didn't answer, Wayne sighed and said, 'Might as well get it over. Stay close to me, kid. Don't go running off no matter what you see.'

A hundred metres beyond the neon orange glow of the parking lot, it was almost pitch black. The stars were bright, but there was no moon. The two men kept tripping on heather roots exposed in the sandy soil. Once, Wayne made Mike stand still for a whole minute because of shadows on a low ridge ahead, until he suddenly snorted and said, 'It's OK, I think they're just bushes.'

They were: dwarf willows, with an old torn sleeping bag bunched up in their shelter. 'Someone was here,' Wayne Patterson remarked, and Mike laughed, something relaxing in him, and told Wayne he was a dead loss as an Indian scout.

'Hold up,' Wayne said. 'I think I hear someone coming.'

That was when they were rushed. There were two packs, coming from right and left, throwing plastic sheets over both men, knocking them down by press of numbers. Mike felt hard little fingers clutching at the baggies of hormone solution, and tried to hug them to his chest, but something bit his wrist and he howled and let go, kicking against the weights on his legs, which suddenly vanished. He sat up, convulsively threw away the plastic sheeting, called out Wayne's name.

Silence.

Mike reached out, walking his fingertips centimetre by centimetre across sandy soil until they encountered Wayne Patterson's nylon windbreaker. The old man didn't move; there was no pulse in his throat. Mike straddled him and started heart massage and mouth-to-mouth, but Wayne didn't respond and then Mike found the thin spike that had been driven into his right eye and with a sudden convulsive movement flung himself away from the corpse.

That was when he heard the music.

It came from the north, deeper in the wasteland. A faint glow showed there and Mike walked towards it, stumbling over tussocky grasses in near darkness. It was past two o'clock in the morning, and his right eye throbbed. Reprogramming had only increased the limit that the chip allowed by a few kilometres, and he cloudily wondered how much time he had before the extension on his curfew ran out.

The light came from a fire which burned in a little steep-sided hollow. There were two huts built right into the sides of the hollow like entrances to mine shafts, their walls made of crates with product names still stencilled on their sides, their steep roofs of overlapping flattened tins. A wailing music rose up from somewhere near the fire. It was a wild skirl of women's voices, a dissonant chorus that sent chills snarling at the base of Mike's spine. He'd never heard music like it.

As Mike went down the slope, his right eye suddenly swarmed with black chevrons – a warning that he'd reached his limit. He clapped his hands over his eyes and cried out, and tripped and fell, rolling down the sandy slope and coming to rest at the feet of the men who'd come around the fire to meet him.

They helped Mike up. He had to squint around the chevrons to see them. They were dressed in shabby black suits, or long dark coats over jeans and ragged pullovers. With black curly hair and a gypsy look, they all looked a little like each other, as if they were all brothers or uncles in the same family, the same family indeed as the men who had escorted the woman liberationist. They spoke what sounded like Italian, slow enough that Mike could almost understand it. One of them held up a bulky old-fashioned radio with a grey plastic grill front and twisted a dial, and the music stopped.

Mike had fallen into the middle of a gang of ghosts, part of the population of second or third generation refugees from the central European wars or from further still, old-style Russians who'd fled the Islamic Jihad, and Africans who'd migrated like so many birds up Italy into Europe's heartland. There were millions of them living in the wild places outside the cities and arcologies, enduring the hot summers and cold winters, the ice storms and droughts caused by the great climatic overturn. They had no money but used an elaborate system of barter; no government but that of the family or group; no law but that which the EC refugee commission imposed upon them. They took medical care from UN clinics, work and food where they could.

One of the men, a tall broad fellow perhaps a few years younger than Mike, said in broken French that he and his brothers were from Albania, that he would be honoured if Mike would break bread here with them while they waited for his friend, and Mike, misunderstanding, told him about Wayne, the way he had been killed.

The man said he understood, that they could do something for this Wayne if perhaps Mike had some money . . .?

Mike discovered that the slender roll of notes he'd stashed in the key pocket of his jeans was gone: all he could offer was a few coins, sliver-thin ecus and a heavy English five pound coin with milled edges. Poor enough fare for the ferryman, but the tall man jingled them in his palm, then clapped Mike on the back.

Somewhere on the other side of the fire, a radio started up with the women's chanting voices again. An unlabelled green bottle with a chipped neck was passing from hand to hand. A moment later, just as Mike was trying to explain that he couldn't drink brandy, the woman liberationist stepped out of one of the huts.

'Quite a sight you made,' she said, 'stumbling this way and that across the heath, like King Lear with his fool, looking for Cordelia.'

Her grey dreadlocks were flattened to one side, as if she'd been sleeping, and her skin gleamed with sweat; her cotton dress, printed with a Martian scape of sand and pitted rocks, clung to the upper slopes of her loose breasts. She looked drunk, or stoned.

'Were those really children?'

'Of course they were. Fairies don't need money.'

Mike wondered how she knew the kids had stolen his bankroll. He said, 'I was bringing you some thyrotropic hormone. They got that when they killed my friend.'

'Oh, and are you sure that's what he was?' The way she said it, Mike knew what she'd done. She added, all concern, 'Is there something wrong with your eye?'

'I'm out here at my limit. I can't go any further. That hormone was all I had. And the money. Except I can tell you something – '

One of the Albanians handed the woman the bottle of brandy. She swigged deeply, wiped her mouth. 'You came to see the fairies. If you still want that, you'll have to take this in your mouth. Hurry. We don't have much time.'

She thrust out her hand, palm-up: a leech-like gob of live jelly curled and uncurled there. Mike stepped back, and she laughed.

'No one said it would be easy!' Then her face was in his, brandy fumes so strong it was a wonder his chip wasn't triggered. 'I can show you such wonders. Do you have the courage?'

'Why I came out here – ' But he couldn't explain. He had

no plan, only desire, sudden and physical as hunger. 'Yes,' he said. 'Yes, I will. Yes.'

Then her hand was over his mouth, and he could feel the thing against his lips. 'Don't swallow,' she said. 'Don't chew. Just let it in.'

Mike opened his mouth with an act of will, felt the thing squirm onto his tongue. He gagged, but it had already sunk into his mucosal membranes. A slow throbbing spread out from the soft tissue at the muscular root of his tongue, filling the cave of his mouth. A wave of nausea rolled over him and he doubled over and vomited.

The woman held his hair back as his stomach wetly clenched, forcing up chyme thin as egg white. When he was able to stand, she said, 'Now you're almost ready.'

Mike started to ask what she'd done to him, but suddenly there was a great beating of wings and light stabbed down, flooding the little hollow. Moments later a helicopter descended from the darkness beyond the glare, blowing out the fire and sending ashes flying up. An amplified voice said something that was lost in the helicopter's roar.

The Albanians were disappearing into one of the huts. The woman grabbed Mike's hand and dragged him into the other. 'Crawl,' she said, and pushed him into the dark at the back, which turned out to be an old drainage pipe.

Mike crawled, following the sounds of the woman as she turned left at a Y-junction. Warning chevrons floated before him; his right eye felt as if it was filled with mercury.

Maybe ten, maybe twenty minutes of this. At some point the chevrons faded from Mike's sight: the woman was leading him back towards Amsterdam. Mike began to appreciate how the dolls moved around. There had been kilometres and kilometres of pipes installed at the beginning of the century to drain saltwater seepage, part of the now-abandoned reclamation schemes.

The pain in his eye and the chevrons came back: he felt a sudden breeze. The woman pulled him up. They were in an inspection manhole. Mike could hardly see now. He said, 'I can't go any further,' but the woman only said she'd see about that and started climbing. Mike followed, hand over hand up the iron staples that made a ladder up the manhole. Hot hands grasped his, pulled him up, and something, a fairy, grinned into his face. With the chevrons swarming in his sight Mike couldn't tell whether it was the one he'd seen before. It kissed him full on the mouth, and he felt the hot worm of its tongue writhe across his teeth.

The creature giggled and then it was running into the darkness towards tangles of pipes and blockhouses, an abandoned chemical plant or pumping station lightless except for a single warning light flashing red on top of a tall chimney.

As Mike started after the fairy, the structure seemed to flow into itself, growing taller, turrets reaching up against a sky softly luminous and dusted with living stars as a meadow is dusted with daisies. A woman took his hand; she was tall and fair, dressed in a loose gown that swept to her feet, with a coronet thrust carelessly in her long loose hair. Her laughter was like a bell; her soft hand thrilled in Mike's own, and he turned and pulled her to him and kissed her until she pulled away, laughing again.

'You have to save yourself,' she said, and led him on until black light filled his eyes and spiralled into his head and took him away.

Mike came awake all at once, sweat starting from every pore. His right eye hurt like crazy, tender as when he'd been chipped. He was lying in a nest of greasy, smelly rags, head-first inside a dead-end pipe just long enough to hold him. Light flickered beyond his feet; there was the sound of people moving around. He turned himself around, pain flaring in his eye with every movement. When he stuck his head out to take a look where he was, the same fairy he'd seen that one time at the service station smiled at him from about a metre away and he remembered and managed not to scream.

He was in some kind of vault, big as a church, lit by vague shafts of light that fell through grids high above. A double row of steel girders held up a ceiling of concrete slabs. They

stood either side of a central channel that was filled with
black water in which grossly fat dolls wallowed on their backs
like beached walruses. Naked, blue-skinned fairies moved
amongst the girders, going to and fro, weaving in and out,
forming groups of six or eight or ten that slowly collapsed
against each other, writhing and crawling and licking and
stroking in languorous slow motion before flowing away in
different directions.

It made Mike think of the ant heaps under the flagstones
of the path of his parents' house. When he'd been little he'd
lever up the slabs to watch with a mixture of curiosity and
revulsion the swarming secret life. He'd forgotten that
emotion until now.

Every so often a fairy would step up and bend to kiss the
bloated blue-skinned belly of one of the dolls that wallowed
in the trough of black water – no, they were sucking at tubes
which jutted from crusted ligatures and dribbled clear pink
goo. Mike saw the woman, hands cupped on the shiny
swollen belly of one of the dolls, cheeks hollowing as she
sucked. She straightened, slowly licked her lips, then dreamily
stalked up the slope. Mike hastily slid out his hole, falling to
his knees on wet gritty concrete.

The woman crouched beside him. Stuff like egg albumen
glistened on her chin. 'Welcome to Fairyland,' she said. 'I can
tell you're not seeing it as it is.'

'Oh, I am. I am. Jesus, you live like this?'

'Once we thought only of freeing them,' the woman said
dreamily. 'We unchained their minds, sharpened their intelligence, induced sexual maturation. We liberated them. We
believed they should decide their own destiny, but we didn't
realize that we weren't making them more human, but less.
Did you ever read science fiction?'

'Not really.' Mike found all those old movies that showed
up on cable kind of disturbing, full of the violent aspirations
of a bad century. They put odd thoughts in his head, fantasies
of instant gratification, limitless power. Stuff like that could
mess up your life, he should know.

'They always thought the aliens would come from the

stars. But they're here, Mike. We made them. When the peace police came down, some of us escaped. We ran into the wilderness. The fairies found us, took us in. We'd changed them and they started to change *us*.' She giggled. 'Here we are. Isn't it wonderful?'

Mike said, 'Dr Luther wants to turn you in. You go to him again, he will.'

'Dr Luther told the peepers you'd lead them to us. He thinks that he can get the drug for free if he can find out where we live. There's a recording circuit in your chip. So we took it out.'

'I knew it! You're crazy!'

Mike felt a wave of panicky despair. He really didn't need this. His flaky old counsellor had been clear about that one point: trying to interfere with your chip automatically tripled your sentence. He'd be an old man before he came out from under, childless, unloved. He'd be like poor dead Wayne Patterson.

He said, without hope, 'Take me back.'

'Mike, Mike. Don't you understand? You have so much to give. You have what they need, what they want. They're only the third stage. We were the first, the dolls the second, fairies the third. You can contribute to what the fairies need for the fourth, for the fusion. Certain genes ... Fairies, males and females both, are sterile, but still they are making a new generation. They learn so quickly. They strip bowel epithelial cells to the haploid state and fuse them, gestate the embryos in the abdominal cavities of males when they run short of females.

'They need you, Mike. They need what you have to add to what they have already taken, as much variety as possible, yes. Don't think you're the first or the last. And you'll be rewarded. You came here for the drug, but you can't use the drug without the catalyst. That's what I made you put under your tongue. It's part of you now, has sunk its pseudoneurones into your limbic cortex. When it receives the blessing, then you'll see all this as it really is!'

Mike said, 'Blessing?'

The fairy's hot fingers feathered Mike's cheek. He didn't know if he was going to throw up or come. Its beautiful knife-blade face was centimetres from his. Its eyes were flecked with gold, and he could see his own face, unshaven and ripely bruised around the right eye, reflected there. Its lips branded his own, and he felt its hot tongue slide into his mouth, sweet and hot and wet.

And he saw.

The fairy and the woman took him by the hands and he rose and walked down the broad sweep of soft living marble. The woman swung a little sack of soft leather, threw a pinch of gold dust from it into the air, then tied it around Mike's neck, telling him it was his price, his reward.

He hardly noticed, seeing the filigreed pillars that arched gracefully to the mother-of-pearl roof of this sumptuous chamber, hearing the siren song of the silken-skinned creatures that bathed in the silver waters of the central pool, joyously and generously offering their sweet intoxicating milk to any who craved it. He saw the lambent joy in the fairies that surrounded him, their touches waking waves of pleasure that pierced him to his core as they divested him of his clothes and pressed against him, moving together on and over and under, and Mike was taken in and he accepted and became a part of the flowing movement. Skin on skin, hotter than human. The arching press of strange, boned penises, not seeking to enter him but only flowing, tracing exquisite patterns across his skin. The woman's laughter floating somewhere, tiny bells that tripped the mechanisms of his heart. It was better than Hux, it took him all, skin and muscle, nerve and bone and blood and brain. Someone fed him clear pink milk from their mouth, and it was an explosion of delight running through his core, rising and rising, the fairies intent around him now, still moving on him as he came in wave after wave, his come arching gloriously, caught in a crystal bottle by an intent fairy, sperm flickering like stars, like phosphorescent fish schooling in a coral grotto as Mike screamed with pleasure, and fainted.

★

Night, warm wind stinking of halogens blowing across the coarse grass in which Mike lay. There was a plastic bag in his hand – he remembered that it had been a leather sack chock full of gold dust, but it held only a dredging of coarse sand – and then he remembered everything else, and laughed.

From a little way off, Dr Luther said, 'Well you're awake, even if you haven't come to your senses.'

'Oh Christ.'

Dr Luther came forward and helped Mike sit up. Amsterdam's sickly aurora, glowing at the level horizon, provided enough light for Mike to see Dr Luther's quizzical expression.

'You still have your chip,' Dr Luther said.

'I do? I thought I was free . . .' What he felt was relief.

'It went off, then came back on. That's how we found you. The police are waiting, Michael, but they let me talk to you first. It is a small enough favour considering the help I gave. Where are they, Michael? They left you here. Where did they take you?'

'I don't know. Somewhere strange. Wonderful and strange. I don't know where!'

Then he cried out, because Dr Luther had grabbed hold of his hair, pulled his head back.

'The drug, Michael. Tell me about the drug. It's real, isn't it? Tell me where, Michael, and you can walk free. All the cops want are the liberationists, the people who killed Wayne Patterson, who did this to you. Be smart. I can help you. Tell me all about it.'

'Wayne Patterson was working for you, wasn't he? They knew, that's why they killed him. I've been a fool.'

Dr Luther wrenched at Mike's hair. 'Tell me!'

It was hard to stay calm, but knowledge gave Mike strength. 'Listen,' he said quietly.

When Dr Luther bent closer Mike got a hand under his chin and pushed. Then they were rolling over in the dirt. Mike kicked and kicked, and Dr Luther went limp for a second, long enough for Mike to break free and stand up. He was breathing in great gulps, shaking with the rush of adrenalin.

Dr Luther slowly climbed to his feet. He brushed at the crumpled, stained trousers of his silk suit and looked sidelong at Mike with a wary expression. He suddenly looked old and frail.

Mike said, 'You don't get it, do you? There are no more liberationists. The fairies don't need them any more. You told me they weren't anything, just modified dolls. You're wrong. They're as much like dolls as we are like dogs.'

Lights flashed and danced in the distance: a line of figures was walking slowly across the heath towards them.

Dr Luther said, pleading now, 'Time's up, Michael. The police will put you in the general labour pool if you don't tell them. Last chance.'

Mike said, 'You don't get it, do you? Matter of fact, you'll never get it.'

He remembered, as if in double-image, the pleasure and the reality. The fairies had used him and taken his germ cells and cast him away, but he understood and forgave them. They owed their creators nothing, and even the glimpse of their world was payment enough, for he knew no matter how much he might yearn for it, he couldn't live there. They learn so quickly, the woman had said of the fairies. Learn and change, busy becoming something else, growing away from their origin. She'd given her all, and so had he, all he was able to give.

He began to laugh. His children – what would his children be like? Still laughing, free at last, he walked past the old man towards the waiting police.

AFTERWORD

The idea for this story about the commodification of sex came to me in New York, when Stephen Jones, editor and film expert extraordinaire, *dragged Kim Newman and me into a sex emporium on Times Square. (Steve was putting together a guide to vampire movies and wanted to make notes on porn videos* with a vampire theme: his attention to detail is legendary.) The title comes from a song on the B-side of an Elvis Costello single – incidentally, Elvis also wrote a song called 'New Amsterdam', which is the name the Dutch colonists gave to what we now call Manhattan.

The Temptation of Dr Stein

Dr Stein prided himself on being a rational man. When, in the months following his arrival in Venice, it became his habit to spend his free time wandering the city, he could not admit that it was because he believed that his daughter might still live, and that he might see her amongst the cosmopolitan throng. For he harboured the small, secret hope that when *Landsknechts* had pillaged the houses of the Jews of Lodz, perhaps his daughter had not been carried off to be despoiled and murdered, but had instead been forced to become a servant of some Prussian family. It was no more impossible that she had been brought here, for the Council of Ten had hired many *Landsknechts* to defend the city and the *terraferma* hinterlands of its empire.

Dr Stein's wife would no longer talk to him about it. Indeed, they hardly talked about anything these days. She had pleaded that the memory of their daughter should be laid to rest in a week of mourning, just as if they had interred her body. They were living in rooms rented from a cousin of Dr Stein's wife, a banker called Abraham Soncino, and Dr Stein was convinced that she had been put up to this by the women of Soncino's family. Who knew what the women talked about when locked in the bathhouse overnight, while they were being purified of their menses? No good, Dr Stein was certain. Even Soncino, a genial, uxorious man, had urged that Dr Stein mourn his daughter. Soncino had said that his family would bring the requisite food to begin the mourning; after a week all the community would commiserate with Dr Stein and his wife before the main Sabbath service, and with God's help this terrible wound would be healed. It had taken all of Dr Stein's powers to refuse this generous offer courteously. Soncino was a good man, but this was none of his business.

As winter came on, driven out by his wife's silent recriminations, or so he told himself, Dr Stein walked the crowded streets almost every afternoon. Sometimes he was accompanied by an English captain of the Night Guard, Henry Gorrall, to whom Dr Stein had become an unofficial assistant, helping identify the cause of death of one or another of the bodies found floating in the backwaters of the city.

There had been more murders than usual that summer, and several well-bred young women had disappeared. Dr Stein had been urged to help Gorrall by the Elders of the *Beth Din*; already there were rumours that the Jews were murdering Christian virgins and using their blood to animate a Golem. It was good that a Jew – moreover, a Jew who worked at the city hospital, and taught new surgical techniques at the school of medicine – was involved in attempting to solve this mystery.

Besides, Dr Stein enjoyed Gorrall's company. He was sympathetic to Gorrall's belief that everything, no matter how unlikely, had at base a rational explanation. Gorrall was a humanist, and did not mind being seen in the company of a man who must wear a yellow star on his coat. On their walks through the city, they often talked on the new philosophies of nature compounded in the university of Florence's Great Engineer, Leonardo da Vinci, quite oblivious to the brawling bustle all around them.

Ships from twenty nations crowded the quay in the long shadow of the Campanile, and their sailors washed through the streets. Hawkers cried their wares from flotillas of small boats that rocked on the wakes of barges or galleys. Gondoliers shouted vivid curses as skiffs crossing from one side of the Grand Canal to the other got in the way of their long, swift craft. Sometimes a screw-driven Florentine ship made its way up the Grand Canal, its Hero's engine laying a trail of black smoke, and everyone stopped to watch this marvel. Bankers in fur coats and tall felt hats conducted the business of the world in the piazza before San Giacometto, amid the rattle of the new clockwork abacuses and the subdued murmur of transactions.

Gorrall, a bluff muscular man with a bristling black beard and a habit of spitting sideways and often, because of the plug of tobacco he habitually chewed, seemed to know most of the bankers by name, and the most of the merchants, too – the silk and cloth-of-gold mercers and sellers of fustian and velvet along the Mercerie, the druggists, goldsmiths and silversmiths, the makers of white wax, the ironmongers, coopers and perfumers who had stalls and shops in the crowded little streets off the Rialto. He knew the names of many of the yellow-scarfed prostitutes, too, although Dr Stein wasn't surprised at this, since he had first met Gorrall when the captain had come to the hospital for mercury treatment of his syphilis. Gorrall even knew, or pretended to know, the names of the cats which stalked between the feet of the crowds or lazed on cold stone in the brittle winter sunshine, the true rulers of Venice.

It was outside the cabinet of one of the perfumers of the Mercerie that Dr Stein for a moment thought he saw his daughter. A grey-haired man was standing in the doorway of the shop, shouting at a younger man who was backing away and protesting that there was no blame that could be fixed to his name.

'You are his friend!'

'Sir, I did not know what it was he wrote, and I do not know and I do not care why your daughter cries so!'

The young man had his hand on his long knife, and Gorrall pushed through the gathering crowd and told both men to calm down. The wronged father dashed inside and came out again, dragging a girl of about fourteen, with the same long black hair, the same white, high forehead, as Dr Stein's daughter.

'Hannah,' Dr Stein said helplessly, but then she turned, and it was not her. Not his daughter. The girl was crying, and clasped a sheet of paper to her bosom – wronged by a suitor, Dr Stein supposed, and Gorrall said that it was precisely that. The young man had run off to sea, something so common these days that the Council of Ten had decreed that convicted criminals might be used on the galleys of the navy because of the shortage of free oarsman. Soon the whole city might be scattered between Corfu and Crete, or even further, now that Florence had destroyed the fleet of Cortés, and opened the American shore.

Dr Stein did not tell his wife what he had seen. He sat in the kitchen long into the evening, and was still there, warmed by the embers of the fire and reading in Leonardo's *Treatise on the Replication of Motion* by the poor light of a tallow candle, when the knock at the door came. It was just after midnight. Dr Stein picked up the candle and went out, and saw his wife standing in the door to the bedroom.

'Don't answer it,' she said. With one hand she clutched her shift to her throat; with the other she held a candle. Her long black hair, streaked with grey, was down to her shoulders.

'This isn't Lodz, Belita,' Dr Stein said, perhaps with unnecessary sharpness. 'Go back to bed. I will deal with this.'

'There are plenty of Prussians here, even so. One spat at me the other day. Abraham says that they blame us for the bodysnatching, and it's the doctors they'll come for first.'

The knocking started again. Husband and wife both looked at the door. 'It may be a patient,' Dr Stein said, and pulled back the bolts.

The rooms were on the ground floor of a rambling house that faced onto a narrow canal. An icy wind was blowing along the canal, and it blew out Dr Stein's candle when he opened the heavy door. Two city guards stood there, flanking their captain, Henry Gorrall.

'There's been a body found,' Gorrall said in his blunt, direct manner. 'A woman we both saw this very day, as it happens. You'll come along and tell me if it's murder.'

The woman's body had been found floating in the Rio di Noale. 'An hour later,' Gorrall said, as they were rowed through the dark city, 'and the tide would have turned and taken her out to sea, and neither you or I would have to chill our bones.'

It was a cold night indeed, just after St Agnes' Eve. An insistent wind off the land blew a dusting of snow above the roofs and prickly spires of Venice. Fresh ice crackled as the gondola broke through it, and larger pieces knocked against its planking. The few lights showing in the façades of the *palazzi* that lined the Grand Canal seemed bleary and dim. Dr Stein wrapped his ragged loden cloak around himself and asked, 'Do you think it murder?'

Gorrall spat into the black, icy water. 'She died for love. That part is easy, as we witnessed the quarrel this very afternoon. She wasn't in the water long, and still reeks of booze. Drank to get her courage up, jumped. But we have to be sure. It could be a bungled kidnapping, or some cruel sport gone from bad to worse. There are too many soldiers with nothing to do but patrol the defences and wait for a posting in Cyprus.'

The drowned girl had been laid out on the pavement by the canal, and covered with a blanket. Even at this late hour, a small crowd had gathered, and when a guard twitched the blanket aside at Dr Stein's request, some of the watchers gasped.

It was the girl he had seen that afternoon, the perfumer's daughter. The soaked dress which clung to her body was white against the wet flags of the pavement. Her long black hair twisted in ropes about her face. There was a little froth at her mouth, and blue touched her lips. Dead, there was nothing about her that reminded Dr Stein of his daughter.

Dr Stein manipulated the skin over the bones of her hand, pressed one of her fingernails, closed her eyelids with thumb and forefinger. Tenderly, he covered her with the blanket again. 'She's been dead less than an hour,' he told Gorrall. 'There's no sign of a struggle, and from the flux at her mouth I'd say it's clear she drowned.'

'Killed herself most likely, unless someone pushed her in. The usual reason, I'd guess, which is why her boyfriend ran off to sea. Care to make a wager?'

'We both know her story. I can find out if she was with child, but not here.'

Gorrall smiled. 'I forget that you people don't bet.'

'On the contrary. But in this case I fear you're right.'

Gorrall ordered his men to take the body to the city hospital. As they lifted it into the gondola, he said to Dr Stein, 'She drank to get courage, then gave herself to the water, but not in this little canal. Suicides favour places where their last sight is a view, often of a place they love. We'll search the bridge at the Rialto – it is the only bridge crossing the Grand Canal, and the tide is running from that direction – but all the world crosses there, and if we're not quick, some beggar will have carried away her bottle and any note she may have left. Come on, doctor. We need to find out how she died before her parents turn up and start asking questions. I must have something to tell them, or they will go out looking for revenge.'

If the girl had jumped from the Rialto bridge, she had left no note there – or it had been stolen, as Gorrall had predicted. Gorrall and Dr Stein hurried on to the city hospital, but the body had not arrived. Nor did it. An hour later, a patrol found the gondola tied up in a backwater. One guard was dead from a single swordcut to his neck. The other was stunned, and remembered nothing. The drowned girl was gone.

Gorrall was furious, and sent out every man he had to look for the bodysnatchers. They had balls to attack two guards of the night watch, he said, but when he had finished with them they'd sing falsetto under the lash on the galleys. Nothing came of his enquiries. The weather turned colder, and an outbreak of pleurisy meant that Dr Stein had much work in the hospital. He thought no more about it until a week later, when Gorrall came to see him.

'She's alive,' Gorrall said. 'I've seen her.'

'A girl like her, perhaps.' For a moment, Dr Stein saw his daughter, running towards him, arms widespread. He said, 'I don't make mistakes. There was no pulse, her lungs were congested with fluid, and she was as cold as the stones on which she lay.'

Gorrall spat. 'She's walking around dead, then. Do you remember what she looked like?'

'Vividly.'

'She was the daughter of a perfumer, one Filippo Rompiasi. A member of the Great Council, although of the two thousand five hundred who have that honour, I'd say he has about the least influence. A noble family so long fallen on hard times that they have had to learn a trade.'

Gorrall had little time for the numerous aristocracy of Venice, who, in his opinion, spent more time scheming to obtain support from the Republic than playing their part in governing it.

'Still,' he said, scratching at his beard and looking sidelong at Dr Stein, 'it'll look very bad that the daughter of a patrician family walks around after having been pronounced dead by the doctor in charge of her case.'

'I don't recall being paid,' Dr Stein said.

Gorrall spat again. 'Would I pay someone who can't tell the quick from the dead? Come and prove me wrong and I'll pay you from my own pocket. With a distinguished surgeon as witness, I can draw up a docket to end this matter.'

The girl was under the spell of a mountebank who called himself Dr Pretorious, although Gorrall was certain that it wasn't the man's real name. 'He was thrown out of Padua last year for practising medicine without a licence, and was in jail in Milan before that. I've had my eye on him since he came ashore on a Prussian coal barge this summer. He vanished a month ago, and I thought he'd become some other city's problem. Instead, he went to ground. Now he proclaims this girl to be a miraculous example of a new kind of treatment.'

There were many mountebanks in Venice. Every morning and afternoon there were five or six stages erected in the Piazza San Marco for their performances and convoluted orations, in which they praised the virtues of their peculiar instruments, powders, elixirs and other concoctions. Venice tolerated these madmen, in Dr Stein's opinion, because the miasma of the nearby marshes befuddled the minds of her citizens, who besides were the most vain people he had ever met, eager to believe any promise of enhanced beauty and longer life.

Unlike the other mountebanks, Dr Pretorious was holding a secret court. He had rented a disused wine store at the edge of the Prussian *Fondaco*, a quarter of Venice where ships were packed tightly in the narrow canals and every other building was a merchant's warehouse. Even walking beside a captain of the city guard, Dr Stein was deeply uneasy there, feeling that all eyes were drawn to the yellow star he must by law wear, pinned to the breast of his surcoat. There had been an attack on the synagogue just the other day, and pigshit had been smeared on the mezuzah fixed to the doorpost of a prominent Jewish banker. Sooner or later, if the bodysnatchers were not caught, a mob would sack the houses of the wealthiest Jews on the excuse of searching out and destroying the fabled Golem which existed nowhere but in their inflamed imaginations.

Along with some fifty others, mostly rich old women and their servants, Gorrall and Dr Stein crossed a high arched bridge over a dark, silently running canal, and, after paying a ruffian a soldo each for the privilege, entered through a gate into a courtyard lit by smoky torches. Once the ruffian had closed and locked the gate, two figures appeared at a tall open door that was framed with swags of red cloth.

One was a man dressed all in black, with a mop of white hair. Behind him a woman in white lay half-submerged in a kind of tub packed full of broken ice. Her head was bowed, and her face hidden by a fall of black hair. Gorrall nudged Dr Stein and said that this was the girl.

'She looks dead to me. Anyone who could sit in a tub of ice and not burst to bits through shivering must be dead.'

'Let's watch and see,' Gorrall said, and lit a foul-smelling cigarillo.

The white-haired man, Dr Pretorious, welcomed his audience, and began a long rambling speech. Dr Stein paid only a little attention, being more interested in the speaker. Dr Pretorious was a gaunt, bird-like man with a clever, lined face and dark eyes under shaggy brows which knitted together when he made a point. He had a habit of stabbing a finger at his audience, of shrugging and laughing immodestly at his own boasts. He did not, Dr Stein was convinced, much believe his speech, a curious failing for a mountebank.

Dr Pretorious had the honour, it appeared, of introducing the true Bride of the Sea, one recently dead but now animated by an ancient Egyptian science. There was much on the long quest he had made in search of the secret of this ancient science, and the dangers he had faced in bringing it here, and in perfecting it. He assured his audience that as it had conquered death, the science he had perfected would also conquer old age, for was that not the slow victory of death over life? He snapped his fingers, and, as the tub seemed to slide forward of its own accord into the torchlight, invited his audience to see for themselves that this Bride of the Sea was not alive.

Strands of kelp had been woven into the drowned girl's thick black hair. Necklaces layered at her breast were of seashells of the kind that anyone could pick from the beach at the mouth of the lagoon.

Dr Pretorious pointed to Dr Stein, called him out. 'I see we have here a physician. I recognize you, sir. I know the good work that you do at the Pietà, and the wonderful new surgical techniques you have brought to the city. As a man of science, would you do me the honour of certifying that this poor girl is at present not living?'

'Go on,' Gorrall said, and Dr Stein stepped forward, feeling both foolish and eager.

'Please, your opinion,' Dr Pretorious said with an ingratiating bow. He added, *sotto voce*, 'This is a true marvel, doctor. Believe in me.' He held a little mirror before the girl's red lips, and asked Dr Stein if he saw any evidence of breath.

Dr Stein was aware of an intense sweet, cloying odour: a mixture of brandy and attar of roses. He said, 'I see none.'

'Louder, for the good people here.'

Dr Stein repeated his answer.

'A good answer. Now, hold her wrist. Does her heart beat?'

The girl's hand was as cold as the ice from which Dr Pretorious lifted it. If there was a pulse, it was so slow and faint that Dr Stein was not allowed enough time to find it. He was dismissed, and Dr Pretorious held up the girl's arm by the wrist and, with a grimace of effort, pushed a long nail though her hand.

'You see,' he said with indecent excitement, giving the wrist a little shake so that the pierced hand flopped to and fro. 'You see! No blood! No blood! Eh? What living person could endure such a cruel mutilation?'

He seemed excited by his demonstration. He dashed inside the doorway, and brought forward a curious device, a glass bowl inverted on a stalk of glass almost as tall as he, with a band of red silk twisted inside the bowl and around a spindle at the bottom of the stalk. He began to work a treadle, and the band of silk spun around and around.

'A moment,' Dr Pretorious said, as the crowd began to murmur. He glared at them from beneath his shaggy eyebrows as his foot pumped the treadle. 'A moment, if you please. The apparatus must receive a sufficient charge.'

He sounded flustered and out of breath. Any mountebank worth his salt would have had a naked boy painted in gilt and adorned with cherub wings to work the treadle, Dr Stein reflected, and a drumroll besides. Yet the curious amateurism of this performance was more compelling than the polished theatricality of the mountebanks of the Piazza San Marco.

Gold threads trailed from the top of the glass bowl to a big glass jar half-filled with water and sealed with a cork. At last, Dr Pretorious finished working the treadle, sketched a bow to the audience – his face shiny with sweat – and used a stave to sweep the gold threads from the top of the glass bowl onto the girl's face.

There was a faint snap, as of an old glass broken underfoot at a wedding. The girl's eyes opened and she looked about her, seeming dazed and confused.

'She lives, but only for a few precious minutes,' Dr

Pretorious said. 'Speak to me, my darling. You are a willing bride to the sea, perhaps?'

Gorrall whispered to Dr Stein, 'That's definitely the girl who drowned herself?' and Dr Stein nodded. Gorrall drew out a long silver whistle and blew on it, three quick blasts.

At once, a full squad of men-at-arms swarmed over the high walls. Some of the old women in the audience started to scream. The ruffian in charge of the gate charged at Gorrall, who drew a repeating pistol with a notched wheel over its stock. He shot three times, the wheel ratcheting around as it delivered fresh charges of powder and shot to the chamber. The ruffian was thrown onto his back, already dead as the noise of the shots echoed in the courtyard. Gorrall turned and levelled the pistol at the red-cloaked doorway, but it was on fire, and Dr Pretorious and the dead girl in her tub of ice were gone.

Gorrall and his troops put out the fire and ransacked the empty wine store. It was Dr Stein who found the only clue, a single broken seashell by a hatch that, when lifted, showed black water a few *braccia* below, a passage that Gorrall soon determined led out into the canal.

Dr Stein could not forget the dead girl, the icy touch of her skin, her sudden start into life, the confusion in her eyes. Gorrall thought that she only seemed alive, that her body had been preserved perhaps by tanning, that the shine in her eyes was glycerin, the bloom on her lips pigment of the kind the apothecaries made of powdered beetles.

'The audience wanted to believe it would see a living woman, and the flickering candles would make her seem to move. You'll be a witness, I hope.'

'I touched her,' Dr Stein said. 'She was not preserved. The process hardens the skin.'

'We keep meat by packing it in snow, in winter,' Gorrall said. 'Also, I have heard that there are magicians in the far Indies who can fall into so deep a trance that they do not need to breathe.'

'We know she is not from the Indies. I would ask why so

much fuss was made of the apparatus. It was so clumsy that it seemed to me to be real.'

'I'll find him,' Gorrall said, 'and we will have answers to all these questions.'

But when Dr Stein saw Gorrall two days later, and asked about his enquiries into the Pretorious affair, the English captain shook his head and said, 'I have been told not to pursue the matter. It seems the girl's father wrote too many begging letters to the Great Council, and he has no friends there. Further than that, I'm not allowed to say.' Gorrall spat and said with sudden bitterness, 'You can work here twenty-five years, Stein, and perhaps they'll make you a citizen, but they will never make you privy to their secrets.'

'Someone in power believes Dr Pretorious's claims, then.'

'I wish I could say. Do you believe him?'

'Of course not.'

But it was not true, and Dr Stein immediately made his own enquiries. He wanted to know the truth, and not, he told himself, because he had mistaken the girl for his daughter. His interest was that of a doctor, for if death could be reversed, then surely that was the greatest gift a doctor could possess. He was not thinking of his daughter at all.

His enquiries were first made amongst his colleagues at the city hospital, and then in the guild hospitals and the new hospital of the Arsenal. Only the director of the last was willing to say anything, and warned Dr Stein that the man he was seeking had powerful allies.

'So I have heard,' Dr Stein said. He added recklessly, 'I wish I knew who they were.'

The director was a pompous man, placed in his position through politics rather than merit. Dr Stein could see that he was tempted to divulge what he knew, but in the end he merely said, 'Knowledge is a dangerous thing. If you would know anything, start from a low rather than a high place. Don't overreach yourself, doctor.'

Dr Stein bridled at this, but said nothing. He sat up through the night, thinking the matter over. This was a city of secrets, and he was a stranger, and a Jew from Prussia to boot. His actions could easily be mistaken for those of a spy, and he was not sure that Gorrall could help him if he was accused. Gorrall's precipitate attempt to arrest Dr Pretorious had not endeared him to his superiors, after all.

Yet Dr Stein could not get the drowned girl's face from his mind, the way she had given a little start and her eyes had opened under the tangle of gold threads. Tormented by fantasies in which he found his daughter's grave and raised her up, he paced the kitchen, and in the small hours of the night it came to him that the director of the Arsenal hospital had spoken the truth even if he had not known it.

In the morning, Dr Stein set out again, saying nothing to his wife of what he was doing. He had realized that Dr Pretorious must need simples and other necessaries for his trade, and now he went from apothecary to apothecary with the mountebank's description. Dr Stein found his man late in the afternoon, in a mean little shop in a *calle* that led off a square dominated by the brightly painted façade of the new church of Santa Maria dei Miracoli.

The apothecary was a young man with a handsome face but small, greedy eyes. He peered at Dr Stein from beneath a fringe of greasy black hair, and denied knowing Dr Pretorious with such vehemence that Dr Stein did not doubt he was lying.

A soldo soon loosened his tongue. He admitted that he might have such a customer as Dr Stein described, and Dr Stein asked at once, 'Does he buy alum and oil?'

The apothecary expressed surprise. 'He is a physician, not a tanner.'

'Of course,' Dr Stein said, hope rising in him. A second soldo bought Dr Stein the privilege of delivering the mountebank's latest order, a jar of sulphuric acid nested in a straw cradle.

The directions given by the apothecary led Dr Stein through an intricate maze of *calli* and squares, ending in a courtyard no bigger than a closet, with tall buildings soaring on either side, and no way out but the narrow passage by which he had entered. Dr Stein knew he was lost, but before he could turn to begin to retrace his steps, someone seized him from behind. An arm clamped across his throat. He struggled and dropped the jar of acid, which by great good luck, and the straw padding, did not break. Then he was on his back, looking up at a patch of grey sky which seemed to rush away from him at great speed, dwindling to a speck no bigger than a star.

Dr Stein was woken by the solemn tolling of the curfew bells. He was lying on a mouldering bed in a room muffled by dusty tapestries and lit by a tall tallow candle. His throat hurt and his head ached. There was a tender swelling above his right ear, but he had no double vision or dizziness. Whoever had hit him had known what they were about.

The door was locked, and the windows were closed by wooden shutters nailed tightly shut. Dr Stein was prying at the shutters when the door was unlocked and an old man came in. He was a shrivelled gnome in a velvet tunic and doublet more suited to a young gallant. His creviced face was drenched with powder, and there were hectic spots of rouge on his sunken cheeks.

'My master will talk with you,' this ridiculous creature said.

Dr Stein asked where he was, and the old man said that it was his master's house. 'Once it was mine, but I gave it to him. It was his fee.'

'Ah. You were sick, and he cured you.'

'I was cured of life. He killed me and brought me back, so that I will live forever in the life beyond death. He's a great man.'

'What's your name?'

The old man laughed. He had only one tooth in his head, and that a blackened stump. 'I've yet to be christened in this new life. Come with me.'

Dr Stein followed the old man up a wide marble stair that wound through the middle of what must be a great *palazzo*.

Two stories below was a floor tiled black and white like a chessboard; they climbed past two more floors to the top.

The long room had once been a library, but the shelves of the dark bays set off the main passage were empty now; only the chains which had secured the books were left. It was lit by a scattering of candles whose restless flames cast a confusion of flickering light that hid more than it revealed. One bay was penned off with a hurdle, and a pig moved in the shadows there. Dr Stein had enough of a glimpse of it to see that there was something on the pig's back, but it was too dark to be sure quite what it was. Then something the size of a mouse scuttled straight in front of him – Dr Stein saw with a shock that it ran on its hind legs, with a stumbling, crooked gait.

'One of my children,' Dr Pretorious said.

He was seated at a plain table scattered with books and papers. Bits of glassware and jars of acids and salts cluttered the shelves that rose behind him. The drowned girl sat beside him in a high-backed chair. Her head was held up by a leather band around her forehead; her eyes were closed and seemed bruised and sunken. Behind the chair was the same apparatus that Dr Stein had seen used in the wine store. The smell of attar of roses was very strong.

Dr Stein said, 'It was only a mouse, or a small rat.'

'You believe what you must, doctor,' Dr Pretorious said, 'but I hope to open your eyes to the wonders I have performed.' He told the old man, 'Fetch food.'

The old man started to complain that he wanted to stay, and Dr Pretorious immediately jumped up in a sudden fit of anger and threw a pot of ink at his servant. The old man sputtered, smearing the black ink across his powdered face, and at once Dr Pretorious burst into laughter. 'You're a poor book,' he said. 'Fetch our guest meat and wine. It's the least I can do,' he told Dr Stein. 'Did you come here of your own will, by the way?'

'I suppose the apothecary told you that I asked for you. That is, if he was an apothecary.'

Dr Pretorious said, with a quick smile, 'You wanted to see

the girl, I suppose, and here she is. I saw the tender look you gave her, before we were interrupted, and see that same look again.'

'I knew nothing of my colleague's plans.'

Dr Pretorious made a steeple with his hands, touched the tip of the steeple to his bloodless lips. His fingers were long and white, and seemed to have an extra joint in them. He said, 'Don't hope he'll find you.'

'I'm not afraid. You brought me here because you wanted me here.'

'But you should be afraid. I have power of life and death here.'

'The old man said you gave him life everlasting.'

Dr Pretorious said carelessly, 'Oh, so he believes. Perhaps that's enough.'

'Did he die? Did you bring him back to life?'

Dr Pretorious said, 'That depends what you mean by life. The trick is not raising the dead, but making sure that death does not reclaim them.'

Dr Stein had seen a panther two days after he had arrived in Venice, brought from the Friendly Isles along with a great number of parrots. So starved that the bones of its shoulders and pelvis were clearly visible under its sleek black pelt, the panther ceaselessly padded back and forth inside its little cage, its eyes like green lamps. It had been driven mad by the voyage, and Dr Stein thought that Dr Pretorious was as mad as that panther, his sensibility quite lost on the long voyage into the unknown regions which he claimed to have conquered. In truth, they had conquered him.

'I have kept her on ice for much of the time,' Dr Pretorious said. 'Even so, she is beginning to deteriorate.' He twitched the hem of the girl's gown, and Dr Stein saw on her right foot a black mark as big as his hand, like a sunken bruise. Despite the attar of roses, the reek of gangrene was suddenly overpowering.

He said, 'The girl is dead. I saw it for myself, when she was pulled from the canal. No wonder she rots.'

'It depends what you mean by death. Have you ever seen

fish in a pond, under ice? They can become so sluggish that they no longer move. And yet they live, and when warmed will move again. I was once in Gotland. In winter, the nights last all day, and your breath freezes in your beard. A man was found alive after two days lying in a drift of snow. He had drunk too much, and had passed out; the liquor had saved him from freezing to death, although he lost his ears and his fingers and toes. This girl was dead when she was pulled from the icy water, but she had drunk enough to prevent death from placing an irreversible claim on her body. I returned her to life. Would you like to see how it is done?'

'Master?'

It was the old man. With cringing deference, he offered a tray bearing a tarnished silver wine decanter, a plate of beef, heavily salted and greenish at the edges, and a loaf of black bread.

Dr Pretorious was on him in an instant. The food and wine flew into the air; Dr Pretorious lifted the old man by his neck, dropped him to the floor. 'We are busy,' he said, quite calmly.

Dr Stein started to help the old man to gather the food together, but Dr Pretorious aimed a kick at the old man, who scuttled away on all fours.

'No need for that,' Dr Pretorious said impatiently. 'I shall show you, doctor, that she lives.' The glass bowl sang under his long fingernails; he smoothed the belt of frayed red silk with tender care. He looked sidelong at Dr Stein and said, 'There is a tribe in the far south of Egypt who have been metalworkers for three thousand years. They apply a fine coat of silver to ornaments of base metal by immersing the ornaments in a solution of nitrate of silver and connecting them to tanks containing plates of lead and zinc in salt water. Split by the two metals, the opposing essences of the salt water flow in different directions, and when they join in the ornaments draw the silver from solution. I have experimented with that process, and will experiment more, but even when I substitute salt water with acid, the flow of essences is as yet too weak for my purpose. This – ' he rapped the glass bowl, which rang like a bell – 'is based on a toy that their children played with, harnessing that same essence to give each other little frights. I have greatly enlarged it, and developed a way of storing the essence it generates. For this essence lives within us, too, and is sympathetic to the flow from this apparatus. By its passage through the glass the silk generates that essence, which is stored here, in this jar. Look closely if you will. It is only ordinary glass, and ordinary water, sealed by a cork, but it contains the essence of life.'

'What do you want of me?'

'I have done much alone. But, doctor, we can do so much more together. Your reputation is great.'

'I have the good fortune to be allowed to teach the physicians here some of the techniques I learned in Prussia. But no surgeon would operate on a corpse.'

'You are too modest. I have heard the stories of the man of clay your people can make to defend themselves. I know it is based on truth. Clay cannot live, even if bathed in blood, but a champion buried in the clay of the earth might be made to live again, might he not?'

Dr Stein understood that the mountebank believed his own legerdemain. He said, 'I see that you have great need of money. A man of learning would only sell books in the most desperate circumstances, but all the books in this library have gone. Perhaps your sponsors are disappointed, and do not pay what they have promised, but it is no business of mine.'

Dr Pretorious said sharply, 'The fancies in those books were a thousand years old. I have no need of them. And it might be said that you owe me money. Interruption of my little demonstration cost me at least twenty soldi, for there were at least that many dowagers eager to taste the revitalizing essence of life. So I think that you are obliged to help me, eh? Now watch, and wonder.'

Dr Pretorious began to work the treadles of his apparatus. The sound of his laboured breathing and the soft tearing sound made by the silk belt as it revolved around and around filled the long room. At last, Dr Pretorious twitched the gold wires from the top of the glass bowl so that they fell across the girl's face. In the dim light, Dr Stein saw the snap of a fat blue flame that for a moment jumped amongst the ends of the wires. The girl's whole body shuddered. Her eyes opened.

'A marvel!' Dr Pretorious said, panting from his exercise. 'Each day she dies. Each night I bring her to life.'

The girl looked around at his voice. The pupils of her eyes were of different sizes. Dr Pretorious slapped her face until a faint bloom appeared on her cheeks.

'You see! She lives! Ask her a question. Anything. She has returned from death, and there is more in her head than in yours or mine. Ask!'

'I have nothing to ask,' Dr Stein said.

'She knows the future. Tell him about the future,' he hissed into the girl's ear.

The girl's mouth worked. Her chest heaved as if she was pumping up something inside herself, then she said in a low whisper, 'It is the Jews that will be blamed.'

Dr Stein said, 'That's always been true.'

'But that's why you're here, isn't it?'

Dr Stein met Dr Pretorious's black gaze. 'How many have you killed, in your studies?'

'Oh, most of them were already dead. They gave themselves for science, just as in the ancient days young girls were sacrificed for the pagan gods.'

'Those days are gone.'

'Greater days are to come. You will help. I know you will. Let me show you how we will save her. You will save her, won't you?'

The girl's head was beside Dr Pretorious's. They were both looking at Dr Stein. The girl's lips moved, mumbling over two words. A cold mantle crept across Dr Stein's skin. He had picked up a knife when he had stooped to help the old man, and now, if he could, he had a use for it.

Dr Pretorious led Dr Stein to the pen where the pig snuffled in its straw. He held up a candle, and Dr Stein saw clearly, for an instant, the hand on the pig's back. Then the creature bolted into shadow.

It was a human hand, severed at the wrist and poking out

of the pink skin of the pig's back as if from a sleeve. It looked alive: the nails were suffused, and the skin was as pink as the pig's skin.

'They don't last long,' Dr Pretorious said. He seemed pleased by Dr Stein's shock. 'Either the pig dies, or the limb begins to rot. There is some incompatibility between the two kinds of blood. I have tried giving pigs human blood before the operation, but they die even more quickly. Perhaps with your help I can perfect the process. I will perform the operation on the girl, replace her rotten foot with a healthy one. I will not have her imperfect. I will do better. I will improve her, piece by piece. I will make her a true Bride of the Sea, a wonder that all the world will worship. Will you help me, doctor? It is difficult to get bodies. Your friend is causing me a great deal of nuisance ... but you can bring me bodies, why, almost every day. So many die in winter. A piece here, a piece there. I do not need the whole corpse. What could be simpler?'

He jumped back as Dr Stein grabbed his arm, but Dr Stein was quicker, and knocked the candle into the pen. The straw was aflame in an instant, and the pig charged out as soon as Dr Stein pulled back the hurdle. It barged at Dr Pretorious as if it remembered the torments he had inflicted upon it, and knocked him down. The hand flopped to and fro on its back, as if waving.

The girl could have been asleep, but her eyes opened as soon as Dr Stein touched her cold brow. She tried to speak, but she had very little strength now, and Dr Stein had to lay his head on her cold breast to hear her mumble the two words she had mouthed to him earlier.

'*Kill me.*'

Behind them, the fire had taken hold in the shelving and floor, casting a lurid light down the length of the room. Dr Pretorious ran to and fro, pursued by the pig. He was trying to capture the scampering mice-things which had been driven from their hiding places by the fire, but even with their staggering bipedal gait they were faster than he was. The old man ran into the room, and Dr Pretorious shouted, 'Help me, you fool!'

But the old man ran past him, ran through the wall of flames that now divided the room, and jumped onto Dr Stein as he bent over the drowned girl. He was as weak as a child, but when Dr Stein tried to push him away he bit into Dr Stein's wrist and the knife fell to the floor. They reeled backwards and knocked over a jar of acid. Instantly, acrid white fumes rose up as the acid burnt into the wood floor. The old man rolled on the floor, beating at his smoking, acid-drenched costume.

Dr Stein found the knife and drew its sharp point down the length of the blue veins of the drowned girl's forearms. The blood flowed surprisingly quickly. Dr Stein stroked the girl's hair, and her eyes focused on his. For a moment it seemed as if she might say something, but with the heat of the fire beating at his back he could not stay any longer.

Dr Stein knocked out a shutter with a bench, hauled himself onto the window-ledge. As he had hoped, there was black water directly below: like all *palazzi*, this one rose straight up from the Grand Canal. Smoke rolled around him. He heard Dr Pretorious shout at him and he let himself go, and gave himself to air, and then water.

Dr Pretorious was caught at dawn the next day, as he tried to leave the city in a hired skiff. The fire set by Dr Stein had burnt out the top floor of the *palazzo*, no more, but the old man had died there. He had been the last in the line of a patrician family that had fallen on hard times: the *palazzo* and an entry in the *Libro d'Oro* was all that was left of their wealth and fame.

Henry Gorrall told Dr Stein that no mention need be made of his part in this tragedy. 'Let the dead lay as they will. There's no need to disturb them with fantastic stories.'

'Yes,' Dr Stein said, 'the dead should stay dead.'

He was lying in his own bed, recovering from a rheumatic fever brought about by the cold waters into which he had plunged on his escape. Winter sunlight pried at the shutters of the white bedroom, streaked the fresh rushes on the floor.

'It seems that Pretorious has influential friends,' Gorrall said. 'There won't be a trial and an execution, much as he deserves both. He's going straight to the galleys, and no doubt after a little while he will contrive, with some help, to escape. That's the way of things here. His name wasn't really Pretorious, of course. I doubt if we'll ever know where he came from. Unless he told you something of himself.'

Outside the bedroom there was a clamour of voices as Dr Stein's wife welcomed in Abraham Soncino and his family, and the omelettes and other egg dishes they had brought to begin the week of mourning.

Dr Stein said, 'Pretorious claimed that he was in Egypt, before he came here.'

'Yes, but what adventurer was not, after the Florentines conquered it and let it go? Besides, I understand that he stole the apparatus not from any savage tribe, but from the Great Engineer of Florence himself. What else did he say? I'd know all, not for the official report, but my peace of mind.'

'There aren't always answers to mysteries,' Dr Stein told his friend. The dead should stay dead. Yes. He knew now that his daughter had died. He had released her memory when he had released the poor girl that Dr Pretorious had called back from the dead. Tears stood in his eyes, and Gorrall clumsily tried to comfort him, mistaking them for tears of grief.

AFTERWORD

Was it Mel Brooks who first pointed out that Dr Frankenstein may have been Jewish? In any case, the Golem story associated with the rabbi of Chelm has curious parallels with Mary Shelley's Frankenstein; or, The New Prometheus. *In Mary Shelley's Gothic sf novel, the scientist is threatened by his own creation, and both disappear into the Arctic wastes; the Golem, an automaton created from clay by Talmudic ritual, threatens* to grow beyond the control of its creators, and the rabbi who destroys it is killed in its fall. Golem stories were attached to several well known rabbis, which is no doubt why Dr Stein is so alarmed by the rumours sweeping the alternate version of early Renaissance Venice in this homage to Mary Shelley's novel, which was written for Stephen Jones's Mammoth Book of Frankenstein.

The character of Dr Pretorious owes a large debt to Ernest Thesiger's sinisterly camp performance in the James Whale film Bride of Frankenstein as Dr Pretorius (I've taken the alternate spelling of his name from Michael Weldon's Psychotronic Encyclopaedia of Film; at least one other reference book has it as Dr Praetorius, although there's no evidence that he served in the army of the Roman Empire, or that he's a relative of the sixteenth-century German composer and musicologist). He first made an appearance, sinister and embittered, in my alternate history novel Pasquale's Angel, set in Florence ten years after the events of this story. The novel was written before the short story, but allusions to Dr Pretorious's attempts to construct a new Venus or Bride of the Sea were vague enough to allow my imagination to run free.

Children of the Revolution

The first Niles knew of Magenta's new squeeze was when she brought the kid into Max's Head Shop, which in winter was where most of the Permanent Floating Wave tended to hang out when they weren't working or sleeping. It was late evening on a snowy winter's night, with the wind right off the North Sea. Max's Head Shop, filled with little round tables and spindly aluminium café chairs and claustrophobic shadows, was the kind of place that Carol Reed would have filmed at menacingly tipped angles. It smelled of wet wool and old coffee grounds and harsh tobacco smoke. The big space heater roared and roared on one note over the door, and bass sonics leaking from the Permanent Floating Wave made the thick china coffee cups on the long shelf behind the counter rattle and hum. Kids drifted up and down the helical stairs, as spaced out coming as going, but the ground floor of the Head Shop was almost empty. Niles, Burckhardt, Hans Rusberg and Doc Weird were chewing the fat about the Wave's cable TV link at a corner table. The only other customers were a couple of zoned-out wasters with hair down to their waists; one had just said to the other, 'I don't know what this shit is I've taken, man, but my lower lip's gone numb,' when Magenta sashayed in.

A young kid Niles had never seen before, a slim boy fourteen or fifteen years old, held the door open for her, and she paused there while freezing wind blew flakes of gritty grey snow around her and everyone in the place, except Saint Jack, nodding out as usual at the end of the bar, yelled at her to get in or get out or at least shut the door. But Magenta paused a few seconds before snapping her fingers. Her decrepit doll servant, Igor, a skinny misshapen dwarf resplendent in a cut-down bellboy uniform, plush purple loaded with gold braid that clashed violently with its blue skin, slid between the kid and the door. It had to stretch to reach the handle. Magenta whipped off her fake fur coat and Igor snatched it and with a swirling limp – like most dolls more than a decade old it suffered from arthritis and osteoporosis – scurried away to hang it up.

The Permanent Floating Wave collective naturally supported the anti-slavery campaigns and didn't use doll labour, but Magenta's affectation of having a personal servant was tolerated because she had rescued Igor by bribing one of the convict overseers of the local recycling plant. A decade before, liberationist movements had kidnapped dolls and rewritten their control chips and set the resulting fairy changelings free in Europe's wild places. It was typical of Magenta that she had turned this radical impulse to her own ends. She had been some kind of actress for a couple of years, and was strong on atmospheres and entrances. Niles had known dozens more or less exactly like her in his palmy studio days as a vision mixer before he'd contracted to direct the video of the disastrous comeback tour of this one-time mega trash aesthetique group *Liquid Television*, one long hot summer that was, Christ, twenty years ago. Artistes of the video cutaway shot, every one of them. Magenta was the only member of the Permanent Floating Wave who, when she wasn't auditing, actually danced there. Nailed to an imaginary chalk mark, she would whip through long series of poses for hour after hour, no two the same, eyes focused on infinity while her face shifted from lust to predatory hunger to rapture at each snap of her hips and shoulders. She was still pretty good, Niles had to admit. In the good old bad old days he'd probably have put out some line for her, shared a couple of hours of slippery safe sex.

Time was. Now Niles was a communal partner with her and the other half dozen founder members of the Wave. Two years, the longest he'd stayed in any one place since he'd quit his nice steady safe studio job. Christ on a crutch. He was getting old, fifty next year and nothing to show for it but a fading reputation as the fastest hands-on vision mixer west of the Rhine.

Magenta settled filmy black layers around herself as she took a chair at the Wave's table. Melting snow starred the raven wing of her hair. Black lipstick, black nails, big square-lensed dark glasses that, with her dead white skin and hollowly shaded cheekbones, made her small face even more skull-like than usual. She looked like Morticia Addams with a hangover. 'It's been a time,' she said.

'It's been a while,' Hans Rusberg corrected her. He was looking at the kid who had come in with Magenta.

Magenta answered his scowl with a sweet smile and said in her small, husky voice, 'Why, Hans dear, are you in trouble with the police again?'

She'd dropped out of law school to become a video extra, still knew enough to handle the minor hassles that came with the Permanent Floating Wave's territory.

Hans said, 'No more than I ever am. How about you, Magenta? What's with the streetmeat? Or did you finally manage to grow something in that vat of yours?'

'It's not a vat at all: it's an alembic,' Magenta said. 'I don't expect you to appreciate the difference, Hans dear, but I expect you to know it.'

'So who's the kid?' Niles said.

'My new friend? Do you know, I'm not sure if he has a name.'

Magenta reached out and drew the kid to her, rested her head against his hip. He was Indian or Pakistani, long glossy black hair framing a thin face with bee-stung lips and high cheekbones and watchful black eyes. He was dressed in ragged but clean denim so old the original indigo dye showed only in the creases: a slash-cut jacket with an orange fur collar; jeans out at the knees and bunched at the waist by a silver belt studded with glass rubies Niles recognized as Magenta's. Despite the slush outside, he was shod in transparent plastic sandals, the kind geezers and babushkas wore to the beach in summer.

'Hey,' Hans said, 'what they call you?' and grinned when

the kid flinched. Hans ran security and the refreshment concessions. He had half a metre and maybe fifty kilos on the kid. His big shaved head was like a boulder. 'I swear your friends get younger and younger each year, Magenta. What do we call this one if he hasn't got a name?'

'Kid Charlemagne,' Burckhardt said. He was the oldest of the Wave's founder members; his parents had been actual honest to God hippies. He twinkled at Magenta from behind his round wire-framed spectacles and said, 'Kid Charlemagne, because he gets it on, am I right Magenta?' and everyone at the table laughed except for Doc Weird, who didn't get the reference because he probably was no more than a year or two older than the kid and hadn't grown up when everything in the last half of the twentieth century had come around again in a millennial mixmastering of pop culture.

'Listen guys, we honestly can't afford charity cases,' Doc Weird said. He was a blond Brit with an earnest, pedantic air. He told Magenta, 'Gate's way down. We even had the cable company on our backs just now.'

Niles had had to deal with the man, some low grade weaselly type with a mustache like a dead caterpillar glued to his sweaty upper lip, a bad fluorochrome print suit and patter right out of the worst excesses of twentieth century free market consumerism, littered with dead phrases like profit margin and customer demand, as if the postcapitalist revolution and the universal unearned wage hadn't happened. Niles had forced himself to be polite, but it had given him a bad flashback to the days when the manager of *Liquid Television* had vanished with the expenses credit card mid-tour, stranding the group, their crew and Niles's production team in Bosnia or Romania or some other godforsaken little monarchy where horses and carts were still the principal mode of transport. So he had retreated to Max's to mellow out like the old E-head casualty everyone thought he was. He was supposed to be working the lighting systems and vision mixing the cable TV feed, but one of the part-time kids could take care of it, there weren't enough wavers this early in the night to get any sincere footage.

Magenta said, 'It's winter. Of course the gate's down.'

'Down beyond that,' Hans Rusberg said. 'You stuck around more instead of trying to change gold to lead out in that ruined hotel, you'd know. We're in trouble, and you go off on some trip trawling for streetmeat.'

Magenta said, 'He found me. We've been going through changes together.'

The kid said in a soft hoarse voice, 'Winter is hard.'

'That's about all he says,' Magenta explained. 'But he doesn't need to say anything. I can read his every thought in his eyes.'

'Bullshit,' Hans said, but he was smiling. Magenta – her floating witchy post-millennial otherworldliness – amused him.

'And these speak to him, of course,' Magenta said, bringing out her silk-wrapped tarot cards.

Niles smiled too. He said, 'Now that really *is* bullshit.'

'You only say that because you haven't found anything to believe in,' Magenta said serenely.

Max came around the counter, carrying a little blue bottle of spring-water for Magenta. The only time he came from behind the bar was to serve Magenta; usually he lurked beneath the glare of ancient neon signs advertising American beers you couldn't buy there, dispensing Guinness and blond and dark Heineken, coffee and smokes and frothy hot chocolate dusted with nutmeg, and mind-blowing hash brownies, fresh batches of which a crazy old woman brought in twice a day, and sipping lucozade livened up with Four Roses bourbon, and selling tokens to the kids who were into the head-changing role-playing games that went on upstairs. If Niles didn't know better he'd think Max was sweet on her, this fat old boozehound with sad wet eyes and speckled capillaries in full bloom on the bulb of his nose, and a longtime boyfriend permanently on the nod in the corner.

'Dear Max,' Magenta said, and handed the bottle to her doll servant to taste, 'how's our Saint today?'

Max said, 'He's good, the Saint's good,' and lumbered back into his shadowy corner behind the counter.

'Saint Jack is always good,' Burckhardt said, blue eyes twinkling behind his little round glasses. Burckhardt had grey hair pulled back in a bushy ponytail that didn't quite hide his bald spot, and an air of quiet competence and invincible amusement. He audited the graveyard shift, the dawn come-down after Magenta's or Doc Weird's apocalyptic revels.

'The Saint gives me the fucking creeps,' Hans said.

'I like him,' Burckhardt said. 'Saint Jack is always so effortlessly cool.'

Doc Weird said, 'I hear some guy's started dealing that strain of fembots. You know, the psychoactive strain that permanently fixed the Saint's head.'

'Around here you can get anything you want,' Burckhardt said with a shrug. 'This isn't England, thank Christ. Sometimes I think it would not be too bad, spending your twilight years in a permanent high.'

'Yeah,' Niles said, 'but suppose you got a bad trip?'

'Niles, my friend, sometimes I think that about my whole life. Did I ever tell you I was an LSD baby?'

'First time today,' Niles said, watching Magenta lay out her tarot cards, face down, in a lazy eight pattern with two cards crossed at the waist. She suddenly seemed a different person, more together, more concentrated. He didn't know whether to believe in the cards or not. They confused him: unlike most of the post new age shit Magenta was into, the cards seemed to make the universe more complicated than it really was, not less. The kid was watching her too, with an unsettling rapt concentration.

She said, 'You say the gate is down. This kid here – '

'Kid Charlemagne,' Burckhardt said, twinkling.

' – is a natural auditor. He was playing around with my home kit, and I couldn't believe the landscapes he made from such a limited palette. He really is a natural. That's why I have brought him here, to try him out on the real thing. He'll blow your minds.'

'You say that about all your pick-ups,' Hans said.

'But this is true. I want him to share my shift, so you'll see it's true.'

Doc Weird said, 'Oh guys, guys, this is *not* what we need. Are we really to believe that someone off the streets can audit a paying crowd? He doesn't look like he can organize his own thoughts, let alone the feedback from hundreds of wavers. I mean, really.'

'Let's give him a go,' Niles said. Doc Weird's self-righteousness was beginning to piss him off, not for the first time. 'Why not? We've nothing to lose.'

'We have our reputation,' Doc Weird said stubbornly. 'We can't take a chance on losing that just for some kid that walks in off the street.'

Burckhardt said affably, 'I seem to remember we took a chance on you, Doc.'

'I had tapes,' Doc Weird said. 'I had a reputation, guy. You knew you could rely on me.'

Burckhardt said, 'Tapes don't mean anything out on the floor. You know that, Doc. You know that we took a chance letting you in right at the beginning.'

Magenta had finished laying her pattern. She closed the remaining cards and said to Niles, 'So you don't have a problem with this?'

'I'll cut and paste and dither for anyone, but I can't work miracles if the stuff isn't there.'

'Oh, he's good.'

Hans said, 'Magenta, where did he really come from?'

'He walked in, five days ago. It was snowing so hard – do you remember? I was watching the snow drifting down over the beach. He walked out of the snow, down by the grey slanting lines of the waves.'

'I think I saw that movie,' Burckhardt said. 'What was it, Niles?'

'*Quincunx*, maybe. Or almost anything by Tarkovsky.'

'Didn't he do *Sleeper*?'

'No,' Niles said, 'but he should have.' And he and Burck-hardt laughed, because it was an old joke of theirs, two geezers shooting the same old shit day after day and not caring.

'Winter is hard,' the kid said again, in his soft hoarse voice. Niles noticed that he had the habit of looking from face to face to face with shy, sly glances, as if committing each turn of the conversation to memory. Now he stooped and plucked a card from the pattern in front of Magenta, who smiled with a pure delight that turned Niles's heart. For a moment the boy and the middle-aged witchy woman seemed to him to be united in a rapt shadowy pose, lit from one side like a late Caravaggio. Then Igor bluntly insinuated itself into the frame and laid a restraining hand on the boy's thin wrist, its long horny nails pressing into his downy brown skin.

Magenta told her doll servant to hold off, and took the card from the boy and laid it face-up. Beneath its laminate surface, on some sunny beach, the slim girl, blonde hair swinging, silver leotard shining, raised a banner decorated with the infinity symbol – the pattern in which the cards were laid – above her head as if in signal to the ship which, in full sail, doffed at the sea's glittering horizon.

Magenta tapped the card and it went through its brief loop again. 'So you see! The Two of Coins. Changes work on the world which must be planned for. Changes connected with business, communications, journeys, which will stimulate joy and laughter.'

Hans said, 'Reversed, it means foolhardy discounting of impending disaster and loss of opportunity because of concentration on momentary pleasure.'

'It's only reversed for you,' Magenta said. 'Now, tell me again about the falling gate?'

It was true. It seemed that every day that passed there were fewer wavers at the Permanent Floating Wave, and it wasn't just the season. The Wave's strength had always been that it had relied not on the holiday and conference trade, but on a solid core of custom from the suburbs of Scheveningen and Den Haag, and even from the arcologies along the Rhine. But the original wavers were beginning to outgrow its consensual hallucinations and one-mind-in-a-groove funkiness, while younger kids were into the inscrutable Zen nirvana trip at places like Max's Head Shop.

'I never bother to look,' Max said, when, two days later, after Kid Charlemagne's first solo shift auditing the Permanent Floating Wave, Niles asked him for maybe the tenth time what went on upstairs. 'It's legal, that's all I need to know. They eyedrop perfectly legal fully licensed fembot cultures, they sit and study texts and interact in whatever space they create for themselves in the core there, and they get off on it. They want to put tiny little self-replicating machines in their heads to rebuild their way of thinking, that's their business. I just rent the space. They say they can't talk about it because there isn't the vocabulary for it.' He held up his bottle of Four Roses: there were about two fingers left. 'You want some of this in your coffee?'

The bourbon fumed in Niles's mouth, cut through his exhaustion. It was five in the morning. He'd been up all night, on-line mixing the action for the Wave's cable TV program. There was no one else in the bar except Saint Jack, nodding out as usual at the end of the counter. Niles said, 'Never thought I'd not understand the cutting edge of popular culture.'

'I hear Magenta's squeeze made a hit his first time out.'

'I thought you never watched cable. Or anything else. That's one reason I like you, Max. You're one of the few of our generation who has transcended television.'

Max took a swig from the bottle, tipped the rest into the dregs of Niles's coffee. 'Save me from ex-media E-heads. I was talking to Burckhardt. He says this Kid Charlemagne's a natural auditor. He says with two more like him the Wave could turn itself around. He also says the Brit kid who came in last summer is mad as hell about it.'

'Yeah. How about that Doc Weird? You want to know why they call him that?'

'Burckhardt almost made me want to go see this phenomenon myself.'

'Bullshit, Max. You've never left this bar in all the time I've known you.'

'I can't expect Saint Jack to run it. So, you tell me why is the Brit called Doc Weird.'

'Doc Weird is weird because he's so straight. He has his career all mapped out. He did private parties around London for the experience, and now he's into semi-legal gigs like the Wave for the exposure. Next year he'll be a vee-jay auditing some dumb net access arena, and he'll end up with a designer credit to Nova Prodigy or some other primetime interactive entertainment. He's like my parents, for Christ's sake. A fucking art yuppie.'

'I thought you were some kind of Native American. One quarter . . .?'

'One eighth Zuni. Not that it's important over here.'

Max squinted at Niles, pursed his lips. 'Yeah? Still, you know you have a kind of chiselled look? And your ponytail looks better than old Burckhardt's, where he has to pull it over the bald spot back of his head. More authentic.'

'Zunis didn't go in for ponytails: you're maybe thinking of Apaches. And I was born and raised in New York, my mother was an information dealer, my father a sculptor, and are you trying to chat me up, Max? I'm flattered.'

'I swear I never hit up on my customers. Here, finish this. So is this Kid Charlemagne any good?'

'He's OK,' Niles said, thinking back on the evening. 'No, he's better than OK. In fact, he's actually pretty fucking amazing.'

There had been no more than the usual number of people surfing the Wave that night, but Kid Charlemagne somehow brought them together, moving a growing group from one virtual microenvironment to the next, synchronizing music and mood to the wired-up wavers' perceptual reactions in a spiralling positive feedback that finally synchronized with Magenta's gig at the core. It turned out he was already hard-wired, something Magenta claimed to know nothing about; about half-way through the night Hans Rusberg said in passing that according to the security system Kid Charlemagne's chips had the strangest specs he'd ever seen. 'Like they were handgrown. Think maybe the Kid escaped from some grey market research lab?' But by then things had started to cook, and Niles was too busy to be able to reply.

The Permanent Floating Wave was threaded through the spiral spaces and ramps of an abandoned multi-storey car park, its sloping concrete floors still stained with the oily excreta of extinct automobiles. Screens or nothing more than smoke or holograms or virtual projections divided it into spaces that ranged in size from intimate cubicles to the big central core, which could hold a thousand wavers and which was where Kid Charlemagne and his followers had ended up, Magenta fading out to the Kid's groove in a moonlit glade where the revellers, fully hardwired or temporarily wired by an eyedrop's worth of fembots, interacted with the elves and sprites and unicorns generated by the Wave's core computers, and their mood, audited through Kid Charlemagne, looped into the homeostatic sound system and fed back their own rapture.

It was corny stuff, but Niles was pleased by the rough cuts, and people actually started turning up after a few hours, filling out the spaces where more experimental landscapes, offline stuff culled from AI perceptual experiments, resonated and bled in and out of the core fantasia in a positive feedback spiral of rapture/unity/bliss/wholeness/ecstasy . . .

Niles worked through the night in the little studio down in the basement, dithering and splicing live images and sending it out not knowing and not caring whether or not the cable company was taking it to fill dead air in one or another of its thousand channels. For the first time in months the groove got to him, and he more or less collapsed on the job before he let someone else, a brisk young kid called Marta or Martha who had graduated from waver to part-time helper, take over. Too wired to sleep, Niles had walked around the block, marvelling at the double-parked rows of runabouts, and then had dropped by Max's Head Shop to chill down.

When he and Max had killed the bourbon, Niles walked

back to the Permanent Floating Wave – the last of the wavers to leave were chasing down the morning's first tram; Kid Charlemagne had lasted an hour more than he had – and crashed out on the cot he kept behind the mainframe.

Niles woke around noon to silence, fixed himself coffee and found a stale donut, and remembered something Hans Rusberg had said and found him working on a smoke projector, unblocking needle vents along its tangled tubing.

Niles said, around a bite of donut, 'How do you handgrow chips?'

'You get dolls to do it. Dumb, cheap and precise, just the kind of labour dolls were designed for. Takes a few hundred doll hours to guide the growth of a prototype chip; then you can test it and if it works fembots can learn how to grow it on templates. Watch your feet.'

Niles stepped back as Hans threw out the smoke machine's coils. Hans put on the heavy-framed spectacles which were cabled to the machine's processor and waved his hands through the air; plumes of red and green smoke spurted to different heights in a standing wave that moved up and down the coils. Mixing to a murky purple, the smoke swirled around their knees. It smelt of burning leaves.

'And Magenta's kid has handgrown chips in his head?'

'Maybe so. Don't know what they're supposed to do, but they make him a natural auditor.' Hans took off his spectacles, unplugged them, and speared them into the breast pocket of his shirt. 'Which reminds me, some A&R type walked in. Seems that the Kid blipped her monitoring programs. Doc Weird is following her around like a puppy dog, trying to cop some of the action, but all she wants is your out-takes.'

And when Niles found her she'd taken them, too. Even paid for them, which considering she was from EuroNet was pretty fucking amazing.

It was the talk of the communal meal that afternoon. The Wave was into informal interaction and spontaneous organization, but the daily communal meal, where everyone shared cooking and clearing up and ate as a group around a big table with no set places, was the one established ritual that was the exception to the rule that there were no rules. Burckhardt had organized the half dozen part-time helpers. They'd cooked hot smoked sausage, potatoes and cabbage. There were chunks of airy bread, pitchers of cold, blond beer. It was a real Dutch meal.

Magenta was being pretty cool about her coup. She sat at one end of the big scrubbed pine table, with Kid Charlemagne on one side of her and Igor on the other, inscrutable in her big dark glasses while the others offered their congratulations. The Kid ate quickly, shovelling in his food without looking up from his plate. Niles was about the only person to tell him he'd done well, and the boy said with a curious mixture of arrogance and naïvety that it had been easier than he'd thought.

'Where did you get the imagery?'

'It was ... from everyone. Everyone there.' Those dark solemn eyes, liquid as a deer's. 'I'm trying to understand. How different people are. I think it was lucky that it worked, because before I have practised only with Magenta. I use what she liked. With more people it is harder, but I like to learn.'

Niles said, 'You come by some time, I'll show you what it looked like from the outside.'

Kid Charlemagne essayed a smile, although his eyes remained as solemn and as warily watchful as ever. Niles thought that he looked like an actor who had strayed into the wrong play and was trying to wing it, never certain which line was his cue.

Down at the other end of the table, Doc Weird said, 'Hey, Niles, did you cop a feel of that executive? Do you think she's your way back in?'

'I never once worked for EuroNet,' Niles said, feeling mean. 'How about you, Doc? You were the one following her around like – ' what was it Hans had said? – 'like a happy puppy.'

'Just making sure she knew where the Kid was coming from, is all. We're a collective.'

'I'm glad you remember,' Burckhardt said.

Niles said, 'Don't recall she took any of your out-takes, Doc, but I could be mistaken.'

'Aw, guy, she won't be back,' Doc Weird said. 'She was after a taste, and she got it. End of story.'

But she did come back while Kid Charlemagne did his thing that night, and the next night, too.

She was half Niles's age, a junior A&R executive from the acquisition arm of EuroNet, ultrachic, and hard as nails. Her fashionably pale face was half-masked by video shades; her hair was silver, laser cut to fall in complex scrolls over her shoulders. Niles bet she had a human personal trainer, a full-environment one-room apartment in one of the ribbon arcologies on the old Dutch-German border, and a sponsored kid somewhere in the third world to show she cared. Her clothes probably cost more than his annual disposable income – even her doll assistant, who did the actual work of transferring and sorting the dumped output from Niles's cameras, was better dressed than he was.

Her second night at the Wave, when she made her offer, she wore loose hand-tailored trousers strapped at waist and ankles, a raw silk blouse, and a kind of bolero jacket swirling with intricate handstitched patterns, the kind of work made possible by doll labour, but still incredibly expensive.

The executive watched while Niles did his stuff, mostly long zoom shots and slow pans intercut with stills chopped so slow all movement blurred in long arcs. It was around four in the morning, and even Kid Charlemagne couldn't maintain the energy level for much longer. Pretty soon Burckhardt would take over and cool things down. The executive had come in half an hour ago; already her doll assistant had transferred most of that night's footage. After a while, she said, 'This isn't much of a setup, is it? Where did you get those cameras?'

'Old security equipment.'

'That's what I thought – charge-coupled plates? My God.

And that board – I never thought I'd see actual sliders on a mixing desk. You don't even have a light interface, do you?'

'I'm not chipped.'

'Really?'

Niles pushed back from the mixing desk and swung his chair around to face the executive. He told her, 'This isn't biz. This is just a little fringe enterprise. We're not into profit or expansion. We provide a service, a little excitement for citizens who are bored with Nova Prodigy and The Game of God and YesterYear and the rest of the primetime interactive entertainments, who want to get off on uncontrolled spontaneity, who want the thrill of the fringe without its risk. We get by.'

'Less and less, the word is. People are getting tired of your cheap thrill.'

'That's just the season. Winter is hard.' Niles thought that he knew exactly what was coming, but he still wanted to hear it, and felt an edgy touch of the old excitement, from back when he'd been new to the biz and anything had seemed possible.

And when Burckhardt had started to wind the Wave right down, and the executive put a hand on Niles's thigh and said, 'My doll can mix stuff like this,' he wasn't surprised at all. A few minutes later she was lying on her back on the cot behind the humming mainframe, and Niles was peeling open a condom pack. 'It's OK,' the executive said, grinning, 'I've full medical.'

'Yeah, but I don't.' Niles's voice caught when she opened the wings of her blouse and lay back, white skin luminous. Then he bent to her, used hands and mouth until she pulled him up and guided him inside her.

Later, she said, 'I've a little confession to make. I've been looking at archive clips of your studio work.'

Niles laughed, but still felt uneasy. 'You don't know how old that makes me feel. That stuff was from twenty years back, and I bet I was older then than you are now.'

The executive laughed too, and told Niles that he was too good for this place, and so was this Kid Charlemagne. That the two of them made an interesting package she could promote to her bosses. That he knew very well that the Permanent Floating Wave wouldn't last out the winter.

Niles had been thinking for a while that maybe it was time to move on, to break the feeling of having settled down like some dumb old barnacle on a dumb old rock. It wasn't as if he was breaking any kind of contract. People came and went in the Wave – already a couple of the founder members had moved on. But he still had the feeling that he was being drawn into something out of his control. It was like riding one of David Lynch's long slow tracking shots in deep close-up that come to rest on something that only makes sense when the frame is pulled back. He said, 'There's this woman that looks for the kid . . .'

'Black hair, white face, black clothes?'

The executive was young, and hungry, and very sharp.

Niles admitted it.

'The kid fucking her?'

'Vice versa, I guess.'

'If he wants, she can come along. We can find her a job, somewhere or other.'

'If you really want Kid Charlemagne, why don't you just talk to him?'

'I tried it. He told me that winter was hard.'

'I don't think he's said more than a dozen words to me. To anyone, apart from Magenta. And I'm hardly a state of the art mixer.'

The executive ran her nails down Niles's flanks. 'That's part of your charm. I can make a good pitch on it.' She was young, after all. She still had some measure of charity.

'I can talk to Magenta,' Niles said, sensing that the executive had already tried. He added, 'Failing that, you could always just take the Kid. I've a feeling he'd go along with it.'

'That's illegal. He's no doll, after all. We have to have a contract, and that means we need him to agree to work for us.'

Niles understood. 'And you think I can persuade him to agree?'

The executive wriggled out of his embrace and told her doll assistant to pack everything up. As she dressed, she said, 'You might want to think about whether he's underage, and where he's come from. If we have a contract with him our legal department can handle those details, but it could make big trouble for your little collective. You decide what you want, my friend. The trouble with the universal unearned wage is that most people can do what they want but can't decide what to do. Wise up and think about what you want to do for the rest of your life. You're old enough.'

And then she was gone, the little well-dressed blue-skinned doll, a ribbed aluminium case in each hand, tagging at her heels.

'The straight world always beats you down,' Niles said to Max about ten minutes later.

Max, who had cracked a new bottle of Four Roses, poured a shot into his coffee cup. 'Tell me about it.'

'You want to be careful, Max. You could turn out be an alcoholic.'

'First drink of the day. Besides, you aren't alcoholic if you only drink in company, and I've always got Jack. He doesn't sleep much, and I learnt to do without. You ever dream with your eyes open?'

There was an instant then when Niles could have matched this admission with one of his own, but Saint Jack stirred down at the end of the bar, maybe registering that someone had said his name, as he sometimes did. He said, slowly but distinctly, 'Dreams help you evolve.'

Max and Niles waited.

Saint Jack's eyes were focussed on infinity; his mouth lifted in an ecstatic smile that transfigured his hollow-cheeked, stubbly face. He said in his slow, gentle voice, 'You know how it was, way back when in Africa? Tribes of man-apes ate these mushrooms that grew in the shit of antelopes and buffalo. They got smarter to deal with the visions, and they needed to share the visions, too, so they invented language.

Language is the mind's only reality, and so our reality is produced by language. But while the men hunted, the women grew things, and to do that they had to keep their heads straight, and they stopped eating the mushrooms. That was the first retreat from nature, the beginning of the Fall. Then the ice came, and drove the man-apes from Africa out into Asia, where the right kind of mushrooms couldn't be found. Ever since, we've been trying to get back to the garden of the mind.'

Max said softly, 'You're always there, now, man.'

'It's not the same place,' Saint Jack said, with a sad smile. 'You can't ever get back to where you started from. But the dolls . . . did you ever think that maybe that's where they are now?'

When Niles got back to his room, he found Kid Charlemagne sleeping under his mixing desk. He pulled out some spare bedding, woke the Kid and got him rolled up in it, and asked him about Magenta.

'I belong here now, friend Niles. I have time to become in this place. Magenta can look out for me still, but here I feel safe.'

Niles sat on his heels and dug his fingers into his scalp. It was the dead hour before dawn, Max's bourbon had brought him to the point where he could sleep through an earthquake, and here was his chance to find out about this strange Kid. He said, 'What about you and Magenta?'

'Can she really do magic?'

'Much as anyone can.' When Kid Charlemagne's eyes grew round with alarm, Niles added, 'Which means no. How old are you, Kid? Where are you from?'

'Around.'

'*Verstaat u wat ik zeg?* Naw, you don't, do you?'

'That's Dutch.'

'OK, but you don't speak it. I mean, you say you're from around here, but you can't speak the language.'

'I recognize it. Full of hills, unlike the land. But I have trouble with words.'

Yeah, but you aren't autistic, Niles thought. Maybe the Kid was a refugee, some boat person dropped through the social security net and lost on the fringe. There were millions of them out there, ghosts, fourth worlders trapped on the edge of the first. The Kid looked up at him, seeming very young and very innocent, only his brown big-eyed face and mop of hair showing above the blanket's coarse weave. 'Don't worry about it,' Niles said. 'Get some sleep.'

'Dreams are good,' Kid Charlemagne said. 'I understand dreams.' Then he reached up and touched Niles's forehead. His fingertips were cold. He said, 'You're silent, friend Niles. I like that.'

Niles was woken maybe half a dozen hours later, around noon, muzzy with sleep loss and sweating under a heap of blankets. Weak winter light leaked around the edges of the plastic sheeting that blocked one end of the shanty room. Electric light shone on the far side of the mixing desk, and there was the breathy hum of a blow heater. Low voices, then a thump, and Hans swearing. 'Hold him still,' Hans said. 'He has to know to keep still.' Someone else – it was Doc Weird – said something Niles didn't catch, and Hans said, 'He won't interfere. He's a burnt-out case.'

They were kneeling either side of Kid Charlemagne, caught in a dusty shaft of morning light that shone on the mask which covered the Kid's face. Cables looped from it to a monitor plate which, resting on his knees, cast green light under Hans's chin. He and Doc Weird, holding both Kid Charlemagne's hands in his, were so intent that they didn't notice Niles, who in his mind's eye framed this tableau as one might some Renaissance deposition, the light the ladder by which the Kid's spirit ascended, Hans and the Doc the grieving yet wondering relatives.

Hans touched points on the monitor with a pen, and grunted in satisfaction when new lines scrolled up. Kid Charlemagne twisted slightly as lights flickered around the edge of the smooth black mask, and Doc Weird tightened his grip on the Kid's hands.

Niles understood that they were trying to access the Kid's

strange implanted chips. Controlled patterns of light fed information in; chip-induced phosphene emissions from the rod cells in the Kid's retinas, caught by tiny fibreoptic cameras in the mask, transmitted information out. To an experienced hacker like Hans, even negative replies to interrogative commands provided clues to the functions of the chips.

Niles watched for a long minute: the small shifts in the clenched, linked postures of the Kid and Doc Weird, the tension of Hans's concentration on the monitor's scrolling lines; the light that backed them, rich in dust, each mote a hundred times larger than the self-replicating fembots, assemblages of carbon polyhedra doped with heavy metals which, operating on scales of a billionth of a millimetre, had changed the Kid's brain molecule by molecule.

It was a ceremony Niles didn't dare interrupt, an opening into the heart of the mystery of Kid Charlemagne he was too scared to share because it was too deep, too intimate. The Kid had changed things; things were moving apart. Niles stepped backwards, and left them there.

Later, Kid Charlemagne came up to Niles as he was checking out a camera that had developed a raster line. This was in the core of the Permanent Floating Wave, which the night before the Kid had transformed into a cross between a coral grotto and Ernst's *Europe after the Rain*. Now it was a big, bare space with an oil-blackened concrete floor marked out with silvery duct tape, and squat concrete columns and plywood partitioning, racks of lights and camera tracks clinging close to the low ceiling, and loops of cabling stapled along the concrete panel walls. It was like the rehearsal spaces in the studios where Niles had worked so long ago, starkly empty when stripped of props and magic.

Kid Charlemagne watched Niles run the faulty camera back down its track, servo motors whining. Did those liquid black eyes look violated, abused? Niles felt compelled to say something, but it was some social inanity that as usual went past the Kid without stopping. Embarrassed, Niles set to work, patching in the diagnostic widget, which told him that the charge-coupled photon collector had degraded. Niles unshipped the camera from its track, and Kid Charlemagne followed him back to the basement studio, watched as Niles took out the old collector, fitted a new one and bench-tested the camera. Just for the hell of it, he aimed it at the Kid, who seemed startled to see his own image on the little monitor.

Niles let him play with the camera. 'You never seen television before? I bet you don't even know you've been on it six hours straight the last couple of days.'

Kid Charlemagne smiled, but he was watching the monitor as he tracked the camera around his own head. 'Cool,' he said. 'I'd like stuff like this. It makes things more real.'

'Where are you from, huh?' Niles asked. 'Where are you going?'

Questions Niles might as well have asked himself, except he knew. EuroNet, if he could make it, which meant if he could get the Kid to go, because the Kid was all the A&R executive really wanted. But Niles could live with that. He could even live with Magenta, and wasn't surprised when she stepped into the studio a few minutes later. Stranger things had been happening recently. It was as if the virtual microcosms of the Permanent Floating Wave were bleeding across into the real world.

Kid Charlemagne swung the camera on her and laughed at the way the monitor mirrored her surprise in miniature, and Niles flashed on the thought that this must look the way Doc Weird's and Hans's examination of Kid Charlemagne had looked to him. Clandestine. Covert. Furtive.

Kid Charlemagne said to Niles, 'It's just winter, you know? Winter's so hard. So they sent me out into the real world.'

'That's what they told you, dear,' Magenta said, 'but Niles doesn't want to hear your troubles. That's behind you.' She raised her arms, then let her filmy black layers collapse around herself. She was holding her head to see the monitor out of the corner of her eye; Niles could see that by watching her, but it wasn't obvious when he watched her image on the monitor – yeah, she was still a pro.

The Kid moved the camera to follow the movement of Magenta's arms, zooming in like any tyro. Niles said, 'You've got to frame a shot and hold it, unless it's a reaction or a tracking shot. But what Magenta needs is a straight frame.'

'She needs the Kid,' Magenta said, dropping her arms. That was when Niles realized what was missing. It was her old doll familiar, Igor.

'I've come for my boy,' Magenta said. 'I need his help.'

Kid Charlemagne turned to Niles. 'If I must go, you come too, friend Niles.'

'It isn't serious,' Magenta started to say, but the Kid said again, 'You come too! Niles! You must!' with such force there was no denying him.

On the way up to the Wave's entrance, Magenta told Niles that she had taken to leaving Igor to watch over her rooms. She'd had the feeling that she was being watched, that something or someone had bad intentions towards her. Strange things were happening around her, she said. The familiar had an alarm and it knew to squeeze it if there was trouble, and that was what it had done.

'But it's probably nothing, Niles. You know how Igor is. A seagull lighting on the terrace gives him a heart-attack. Really, you don't need to tag along.'

Normally, Niles would have agreed with her, for Magenta always dramatized her life, as if everything that happened to her had to be retrofitted into a complex recursive soap script. But there was enough weirdness around these past few days that anything seemed possible, even Magenta's fantasies, and besides, the Kid really was spooked.

And then, when they came around the curve of the ramp they saw that Hans was waiting down by the big doors, a pile of coats at his feet. He said, 'I hear you've trouble, Magenta,' but he was looking at the Kid.

Magenta said, 'Is this some kind of conspiracy I don't know about?'

'If you've run into trouble, let security handle it,' Hans said. 'It's my job.'

'It's probably nothing. Really. Igor had one of his turns, that's all.'

Kid Charlemagne gripped Niles's arm and said in an intense whisper, 'If we all go there is no danger. I stay with you.'

Hans said, 'Hear that? I'd like for it to be nothing, Magenta, I really would. And I reckon that so long as I come along maybe nothing will happen.'

Outside, as they ploughed through blowing snow after Magenta, who led the way at a brisk, determined pace, sulkily silent, Kid Charlemagne said quietly to Niles, 'They do not mean harm. They are just curious. That is why they want me to go back. But I like to be part of the Wave now.'

'These are your friends,' Niles said, his voice almost lost in the immense silence of the falling snow.

It was snowing hard, and the wind off the North Sea drove the snow almost horizontally down the wide avenue. The streetlights were all on, and snow slanted across their orange glare. A tram drifted by, headed into civilization, sparks from its overhead cable hissing in the downpour of white motes. Niles was almost hypnotized by the way the flakes blurred into a general greyness in every direction but that in which he was looking, where they seemed to lazily float in slow motion, so that the trajectory of each flake could be traced.

'Come on, man,' Hans said. 'You can play in the snow when we've sorted this out.'

'They are interested, that is all. Just interested.' Kid Charlemagne clutched a grey army blanket around himself; he still wore his transparent sandals.

Hans was walking on the other side of the Kid from Niles. 'Now we have a situation,' he said, with resigned satisfaction. He wore an immense quilted overcoat, his face hidden in a fur-trimmed hood. 'All this stuff about Igor is just bullshit; the Kid starts to earn a reputation and Magenta wants to get him away from us. You think she's had an offer from somewhere else?'

Niles said, 'Did you find anything about the Kid's chips?'

'I wondered when you'd ask. They don't speak any language I know, I can tell you that.'

Kid Charlemagne said, 'They make me one of my people.'

'This is bad fantasy,' Hans said. 'People on the fringe just about have it together to mount a raid on produce dumpbins. It takes three of them to get a fire going. There's no time for anything but survival out there.'

'Fairies,' Niles said.

Hans said, 'I'm telling you, man! I used to live out there! The only dolls I ever saw when I was out there, they were dead. Saw some women cook and eat one once. *That* was a hard winter . . .'

'Fairies are real,' Niles said stubbornly. 'This old woman, the caretaker at the zek residence down the street until this summer? She was into doll liberation once upon a time. She used to *make* fairies.'

Hans said dismissively, 'That was a decade ago. Longer. Liberationists turned the dolls loose and they died. There aren't any fairies these days because no one's making them.'

'The old woman disappeared. Maybe she's making fairies again.'

'Word was the cops came after her. You came in from the cold, Kid. What do you know?'

Niles looked at Kid Charlemagne, but his face was hidden by a fold of grey blanket.

The Kid said, 'All kinds live out there . . .'

Beyond the corner, the seafront complex ran away under the falling snow. Lights and neon signs faded into the blurring whiteness, but holograms stood strangely sharp, like islands of another reality. The promenade was almost deserted; beyond the closed and shuttered beachfront cafes, the grey sea was dashed with whitecaps.

Magenta turned and said, 'You don't need to come! Really it probably isn't anything!'

She reached for Kid Charlemagne, who shrank beside Niles, and Hans said, 'All for one and one for all, Magenta. Let's just do it.'

The abandoned hotel where Magenta had her place was

beyond the northern end of the promenade, near the edge of the Oostduinpark, the edge of the invisible country of the fringers. The Great Climatic Overturn had brought scorching summers and hard winters to the countries bordering the North Sea. In the Netherlands, the vast agricultural industries had retreated to ribbon arcologies along the axis of the diverted Rhine; from the roof of the Permanent Floating Wave you could see their constellations blaze on the horizon. Polders once so laboriously reclaimed from the sea were now succumbing to saltwater seepage, had become a patchwork wilderness along the abandoned seaboard of Europe's most densely populated state.

The concrete ziggurat of the old hotel was on the border of this wilderness. Foundations undercut by storms, it was listing like a foundering passenger liner. Dunes that had buried all but its top two floors were deep with snow, only the bent-over tips of their manes of coarse dune grasses showing.

They all climbed up the rickety fire escape to the roof and its clutter of air-conditioning vents and smashed solar panels. The windmill which generated Magenta's electricity whirred in the snowy gale. Snow had piled up against the padlocked door to the stairway, dry as polystyrene beads in the intense cold; Niles and Hans had to pull together to heave the door open against the drift.

Magenta had taken over the bridal suite. She held up a caged light as she led the way down the corridor, with its peeling flock wallpaper and threadbare mildewed carpet. Freezing air blew into their faces, and there was a dull repetitive banging up ahead: it was the double doors to the suite swinging to and fro in the wind. Hans grinned at Niles and dodged through the doors as they swung back. Niles followed, and Hans turned to him in the middle of the wreckage.

Moth-eaten net curtains billowed at the broken french windows to the terrace. The cold, windy air reeked of alcohol and formaldehyde. Furniture had been tipped over; books lay everywhere like broken birds, pages ruffling in the wind.

A big oak table was strewn with broken bottles and jars and scraps of stained and labelled tissues: the smashed remains of Magenta's collection of medical curiosities. The brass alembic had been tipped over, its sphere dented and crushed. The cabling which had fed it Jupiter's microwave radiation, gathered from the three metre antenna Magenta had installed on the roof, had been ripped away. Snow had blown across the layers of rotting Persian carpets and was everywhere marked with small footprints.

Magenta called out her familiar's name from the doorway, and then she started laughing.

'Kids,' Hans said in a quiet voice.

There was a sound from the bedroom.

Magenta stood still in the doorway, the wind ruffling her long hair and the layers of her clothing. Her big shades were like a hole through her face into the darkness at her back. Kid Charlemagne stood beside her, looking this way and that with unconcern. Niles realized that his detachment was no affectation but true naïvety. For him, the world was simply a marvellous place, radiant with innocence. It was that radiance which shone through his virtual realities and redeemed their borrowed images.

Hans signalled to Niles, and they positioned themselves either side of the bedroom door, just like cops, and just like a cop Hans swivelled and kicked open the door, ran inside. Niles followed in time to see two small figures drop out of sight from the open window.

'Jesus Christ,' Hans said.

On the big four-poster bed was what was left of Igor. The doll had been stripped of its bell-boy's uniform, and its arms and legs were tied to the bedposts. Its eyes were gone. The raw red wounds were vivid against its blue skin.

Hans shouted, 'Come on!' Then he vaulted the windowsill and was gone. Snow blew around Niles as he looked out. The drop was no more than three metres, to drifted snow. Niles landed in snow deep as his thighs and fell over.

Two figures that Niles hoped were only children were floundering over the crest of the first of the line of dunes that saddled away from the hotel. Hans was already half-way up the slope, and by the time Niles had gotten to his feet he was at the top. He turned, veiled in falling snow, and shouted, 'The little fuckers have some friends!'

When Niles caught up with him, Hans pointed to the half dozen child-sized figures at the crest of the next line of dunes, shadows in the blowing whiteness. 'Let's leave it,' Niles said. Snow had soaked through his clothes, and the wind cut into him. He said, 'Maybe they're only kids . . .'

Hans said, 'You think kids did that to Igor?' His hood had fallen back. He cupped his hands to his mouth and shouted, 'You! You little bastards! You just wait there!'

He started down the slope, and there was a flare of light amongst the figures on the facing crest. Niles glimpsed something arc through falling snow, a long dark fleck trailing a flickering light. It drifted lazily for a moment, then seemed to gather itself and leap forward.

Hans looked up just as it smashed into him, and he fell back, clutching the burning end of the spear with both hands, pulling it from his left shoulder then letting go and falling backwards. Flames flickered and sputtered on the front of his quilted coat, and Niles beat them out.

'Fuck,' Hans said with forceful surprise, and laughed. 'A wire-guided rocket spear!'

Someone caught Nile's shoulder. It was Kid Charlemagne. He had lost his blanket and was dusted with powdery snow from head to foot. His black hair, starred with snow, blew around his face. 'I jumped!' he shouted. His fear mirrored Niles's own. 'I ran from Magenta and jumped after you! We go! We go!'

Niles helped Hans up, slow and clumsy, floundering with him in the deep snow. He was so scared he felt he would at any moment fly straight out of his body.

Kid Charlemagne danced around them. 'I'm sorry! I'm sorry! We go!'

Niles looked at the line of figures at the top of the far dunes. Not children. He couldn't turn his back on them. Instead, holding up Hans, he stepped backwards, fitting his boots into his own footsteps, until he had climbed back over the top of the dune. Then he turned and with Hans limping beside him, breathing heavily into his neck, he followed Kid Charlemagne through the blowing snow.

There was no sign of Magenta. Niles used the phone point at the beginning of the promenade and called a taxi. It arrived within a minute, and Hans fell inside it. Niles shouted into the taxi driver's blue face, told it to take Hans to the hospital, and then the sleek taxi disappeared into the blizzard.

Kid Charlemagne said anxiously, 'It's not good to stay here.'

Niles felt every minute of his fifty years pressing on his shoulders. 'We don't have time to go with Hans. You've got a show to run, Kid.'

'I think they want me back,' Kid Charlemagne said, and started off into the snow. When Niles caught up with him, he said, 'I learn, friend Niles. I learn they use me.'

'Those kids were using you? What are they, fringers?'

'I want to learn more,' Kid Charlemagne said, and wouldn't say anything else, all the way back to the Permanent Floating Wave, where Magenta was waiting for them in the studio.

Niles ignored her. He went straight to the phone and called the emergency department of the local aid station, and some AI circuit told him that information about patients was restricted.

'Be careful,' Magenta said. 'You'll have the cops down on us, and that wouldn't do at all.'

Niles said, 'Those kids tried to kill Hans. Maybe I *should* call the cops.'

Magenta said, 'It's his own fault he was hurt. He wasn't supposed to be there; nor were you. And Niles, you know they weren't kids.' She was sitting in the swivel chair at Niles's mixing board, running a long black thumbnail up and down the sliders, one by one.

Niles said, 'So they're what? Fairies? Jesus Christ, Magenta!'

'People,' Kid Charlemagne said.

'His people are fairies,' Magenta said. 'Oh Niles, haven't you worked it out yet? They changed the Kid into what he is. He's an experiment.'

'Why was he changed?'

'Because they could do it. Because they took him when he was a little kid, and they wanted him to think like they did. Because they like the irony of chipping a human, when every one of them has been under human control. Who knows how fairies think? They did it by instinct, by trial and error. They sent him out here to see how he worked. Now they want him back, for what he is, just as that woman from EuroNet wants him.'

Niles said, 'That's something we have to talk about.'

'You never did think I was very clever,' Magenta said. 'But I didn't need to be to find out about your little deal.'

'Who told you? Max?'

'Close.'

'Saint Jack? Jesus.'

'I talk to the Saint. Not many people bother to, apart from Max. The Saint isn't brainfried by his permanent high, you know. It's just put him on a different level of consciousness.'

Niles remembered the Saint's monologue about the evolution of human language and consciousness through drugs. Or through the lack of them. Dolls and their controller chips. Suppose the implanted chips were taken away – would dolls have to evolve consciousness to cope with loss of the command strings by which they were regulated and which instructed them every moment of every day? What kind of consciousness would it be? And he also wondered, with a sudden chill, if Kid Charlemagne was being controlled.

Magenta said, 'Maybe I should tell the Permanent Floating Wave about the EuroNet offer.'

'Go ahead. We don't have rules here. And besides, she wants you to come in on it, too, Magenta.'

'No, Niles. I care too much about my changeling to allow it.'

'I look out for myself,' Kid Charlemagne said. 'I have fun.'

Magenta told him, 'This isn't Fairyland.'

'No one owns the Kid,' Niles said. 'That's the point.'

'But you'd let EuroNet own him, if they could . . .'

Kid Charlemagne had been looking back and forth between the two of them, with an expression that was not quite yet a smile.

'Let the Kid choose,' Niles said.

Magenta laughed. 'Oh, Niles! You're always so sure of yourself. So sure you're always right!'

'Right now I'm not sure of anything, except I'm scared for the Kid. Those things out there mean business. Hans could have been killed . . .'

'Of course you're sure! That's why you'll let the Kid choose for himself. But you don't really understand anything yet.' Magenta swung up from the chair in a flurry of black veils. She put her hands either side of Niles's face and turned it to hers, kissed him on the lips, then on his right eye.

As he blinked in surprise, she said, 'Now you're really going to see!'

Niles didn't understand what she meant until the night was underway, after the A&R executive and two of her vice-presidents, and their doll assistants and tall, heavyweight doll bodyguards had all crowded in his studio. The dolls stood with stiff obedience along one wall, while the humans watched the monitors above the mixing desk and Niles mixed simple tracking shots for the cable TV feed.

Kid Charlemagne was already deep into doing his thing in the core of the Permanent Floating Wave, with a more than capacity crowd of wavers trancing along. The soundscape was a pounding sweep of drums spiked with startling peaks of brass percussion. The landscape was all half-melted, slickly organic spires, mostly red and studded with jewels, under a dense blue sky in which cut-outs showed whirling constellations. It seemed to stretch out to infinity: ward subroutines working through the wavers' transceivers, either their own or temporary links built by eye-dropped fembots, kept them away from the walls of the core, and from passing through the spikes and spires of the virtual landscape.

Kid Charlemagne seemed to float in the centre, describing an orbit about a tall thin spire that glistened like raw tourmaline and pulsated and shuddered to the beat like a sensitive filament of the living landscape. Without the patched overlay from the Wave's computers, it could be seen that he was standing on a platform suspended on a crane arm. Later, he would descend, and the virtual landscape would begin its convulsive unbound metamorphosis as the crowd's frenzy mounted towards catharsis.

'He can hold a crowd,' one of the veeps said.

The other said, 'What else can he do? What does he do that's new?'

The first said, 'One thing he'll have to do is change his name. Obscure pop-culture references might have been sales points in the millennium, but not now.'

Both of them were clean-shaven and fashionably pale-skinned, ramrod straight in their one-piece asymmetric suits.

The executive, sweating under her mask of opalescent makeup, said, 'I know it's a simple setup, but what's new are the nuances he puts into it.'

'I didn't see that on the tapes,' the first veep said.

'Well, that's why we are here,' the executive said.

Niles sensed her nervousness. She had probably been working herself up to the pitch all day. He suggested that the EuroNet veeps might want to sample what happened for themselves.

'If we like what we see tonight, we'll sample it with proxies,' the first veep said.

The second reached out and started to pan and zoom one of the cameras. Niles restrained his impulse to slap the man's hand away. He had shiningly clean squarecut nails, thick gold rings on every finger, and a multidial Rolex that probably cost more than the Wave's annual turnover.

'We don't see too much so far,' the first veep said.

'Check out the unity,' the executive said with what seemed

to Niles to be overly forced enthusiasm. 'Check out the bliss on the faces of the crowd.'

The first veep laid a hand on the back of Niles's chair, enveloping Niles in a wave of piney cologne, as the second switched out the overlay and started to zoom in on individual faces. Niles, working his board more or less on automatic pilot, watched with more than half his attention. After a few moments he parasitized the feed from the camera the veep had commandeered, overlaid each blurry face with a halo effect against a solarized gold wash, and let them bleed one after the other under wide pans of the crowd.

'Nice,' the second veep said. 'Corny, but nice.' He asked about the contract with the cable TV station, wanting details Niles didn't have.

'It's nothing our legal department can't handle,' the executive said breezily. 'Strictly a standard freelance fee-for-feed nonbinding agreement.'

Niles suddenly understood that she sounded happy because the deal was going down. If they wanted to know how to get the Kid, of course it was going down. He felt his tension ebb a little, and in that moment a blue-skinned smooth doll face, haloed, bled away as it was overlain by the image of a girl's blissful face.

Niles slapped the veep's hands away and clicked the camera back to its last position – but the doll was gone. He whirled for the door and then one of the bodyguard dolls was in his face and the other was holding his arms, elbows together, at his back. Both were taller than Niles, and built like hypertrophied sumo wrestlers. Carbon whisker quills, tipped with steel, rattled on their forearms; thicker spines made a ruff around their necks. The one in Niles's face smiled, showing sharky rows of serrated metal teeth. Its breath reeked of acetone.

'Call them off!'

'All right,' one of the veeps said, and the bodyguards let Niles go and he was out of the room, tearing up the wide spiral ramp towards the core of the Wave. He ran through sliding primary colours, as if he was plunging through the broken shards of a rainbow. As the throb and cascading clatter of the soundscape grew louder, the shapes began to draw together. Gemmy outcrops flashing, they rose above him in spiky shapes towards a layered, washed-out sky where a red disc hung; it had small, yellow eyes, and a tiny mouth, upper lip lifted as if to nibble.

He was wired. Someone – he realized that it had been Magenta, when she had kissed him – had infected him with fembots; the tiny machines had built tiny transceivers in his brain, translating the virtual output of the core computers directly into his optic nerves. This realization brought not panic but exhilaration.

People passed him by on the right and left, masked in gorgeous feathers. Their movements bled light into the air, and when he raised and flexed his hand, traceries like golden filaments hung afterwards, slowly fading into an exquisite buttery glow.

'Niles!'

It was a figure hooded and robed in a cascade of red feathers, eyes lambent as an owl's.

'Oh shit,' it said, and touched something to Niles's forehead.

Then Niles was standing in a grey concrete ramp, with nothing but noise pounding around him. A young woman in a brand new yellow denim jacket – it was brisk, serious Marta – held the pen-shaped transducer to his temple, cutting out the induced visions. Wavers pushed around them, wide-eyed with close to religious ecstasy.

'Some time to get wired!' Marta shouted over the pounding music. 'The cable TV was on the phone! Wants to know why the feed is jammed!'

'There are fairies here! I've got to find Magenta!'

'The Kid dropped fairies after his first night,' Marta said, and Niles realized that she thought he was still tripping and said, 'Did you see her?'

'She's in there,' Marta said, meaning the core. 'I'll get on the desk, OK? Enjoy yourself.'

And then she was gone, and the vision swirled around

Niles once more. A crowd of fabulous creatures swept him up, into the core.

Niles fetched up against a towering green column that in reality was one of the plywood-clad pillars which held up the core's low ceiling. Now it felt like living glass under his fingers. Delicate flutings spiralled up, breaking around animate faces neither human nor animal. Dancers swirled around him, bleeding complex patterns of light that pulsed to the deep bass rhythm that Niles could feel through the soles of his feet, in his bones. Their dance defined a roughly oval arena. Beyond it stretched a shattered, mostly red landscape. Pillowy coralline shapes piled into cliffs; broken chryselephantine pillars leaning everywhere; vast thorny skeletal structures in a mazy confusion, from which human figures seemed to be trying to rise. Above, a blue sky pulsed with holes through which strange bright constellations whirled, as if they were gateways to younger universes, or places where physical laws conformed more closely to human expectation, so that stars really were stars, and not giant balls of fusing gas.

The dancers whirled in contrary orbits. Here, a whole group stamped in a circle; there a single person swayed with upraised arms while others swirled past. All were robed in feathers, and feathery masks that now and again dissolved to show ecstatic faces. At the centre of their intricate pavane was a collapsed beast like an arthropod horse, its head swept back into a single horn, a palanquin on its back both organic and crystalline, four pillars holding up a tented roof on which stood a figure with the sleek beaked head of a bird, a long lance in its hand from which a dozen rags fluttered in stop motion, their sigils constantly transforming.

The figure was Kid Charlemagne, auditing the session. Niles plunged towards him through the wild dance, now pulled in one direction, now whirled away in another. A woman shoved a flask against Niles's lips – tin ticked teeth, soft sweet liquid flooded his mouth. He pulled away and a man turned and french-kissed him, laughed and shouted to the beat of the soundscape *We are bro-thers!*

Niles broke the man's grasp, but was caught up by another of the dancers, robed and hooded in a cascade of gorgeous red feathers. For an instant this flickered to show Magenta's blacklipped white face, her eyes obscured by the big black shades.

Niles yelled that there were fairies loose in the Wave, and she put her mouth to his ear and said in a voice like tiny silver bells, 'I know! Isn't it wonderful?' And then Niles saw the sharp-featured blue face that peeked out from her cascade of feathers.

Small hard hands grasped the waist of his loose shirt. Niles pulled away and gained the flank of the horse-thing. Its scales were rough and warm under his fingers as he climbed, and when he was half-way up its great horned head turned and regarded him with a lambent golden eye. Niles felt a great surge of transcendental harmony, and if Kid Charlemagne hadn't reached down and pulled him up he might have stayed there.

When Niles told him about the fairies, Kid Charlemagne laughed out loud – the hooked beak of his eagle's head mask opened so wide Niles could see the bright red tongue within. 'They see what I can do! They tremble in awe!' He swept his lance about him, and it extended out over the heads of the crowd that surged about the palanquin like waves on the shore. The bass rhythm changed gears and the landscape began to pulse with it. Light shone within the coralline cliffs, brighter and brighter. They were melting in light. 'I won't go back,' Kid Charlemagne said, and that was when the fairies scrambled over the edge of the palanquin.

Niles saw them as figures hooded in black, with beaked masks made of interlocking triangles. Two, four, six of them. Kid Charlemagne jabbed at them with his lance, and briefly they transformed into what they really were: blue-skinned homunculi half the size of a man, with narrow shaven heads and grim, alert expressions. They all looked like brothers: the same flattened, spread nose, the same large liquid black eyes. All were marked on the cheeks with parallel scars.

'No!' Kid Charlemagne yelled. 'I won't go back! Help me, friend Niles!'

And he hurled the lance at the fairies and jumped into the crowd. Niles glimpsed him struggling with two or three black-cloaked figures amongst the whirl, and jumped after him, plucking one off the Kid's back, suddenly tangled with two more which tried to pull him in different directions. He went one way, knocked that fairy down, roared when the other bit him. It expanded into a black cloud covering his arm, needlepoints of pain somewhere inside it. Then Kid Charlemagne vanished into the cloud, and it flew away from Niles, dwindling. The Kid was rolling over and over, tangled with a doll in filthy cutdown coveralls. Niles plucked it up by a leg and an arm, shook it hard, and threw it into two others. Then he pulled the Kid up and they ran.

They ran through the dancers, shoving them aside and being shoved back. Panic spread like ripples across a pond. Without an auditor, the soundscape was drifting awry, its bass lines tangling and halting and restarting, brass crashing in discordant diminishing crescendos. All around, crystal pillars began to blur and melt inward like candles thrown in a furnace.

The vast pulsating entrance dwindled to a shabby tunnel. Niles and Kid Charlemagne ran into it just as the music finally ground to a halt in a cacophony of brass, like a derailed train. The Kid's eagle head faded into goggles and the battered black transducer helmet.

As they ran down the spiral ramp, Doc Weird ran up it towards them. He grabbed Niles and half-turned him. He was mad as hell. 'You crazy old man! The whole system's gone down!'

'You don't let me by,' Niles said, 'I'm gonna walk right through you.'

The skinny Brit let go of Niles's sleeve. 'Your EuroNet squeeze packed up and left a minute ago,' he said. 'Your deal's fucked, guy.' He laughed and ran away down the ramp, shouting, 'Hans! Hans! I found them!'

'Everyone crazy,' Kid Charlemagne said. Tears starred his dark eyes. 'Everyone hurts.'

'Welcome to the world,' Niles said. 'I'll try and get you out of this if I can, but then you have to think about who you want to be.'

Grey smoke rose up at them as Niles and the Kid descended. Cables were strewn over the concrete ramp, jetting green and white and yellow vapours. Figures ran past them, panicky wavers on the way down, one or two of the Wave's helpers on the way up.

Hans was waiting for them where the ramp turned out into the vast subdivided space of the ground floor level. The long wide corridor that led to the entrance was filled with smog and the glare of emergency lights, and at the door Hans turned a powerful torch on Niles and Kid Charlemagne, its beam striking like a lance through roiling vapours.

Niles said despairingly, 'You gotta let the Kid go!'

'We only want his chips,' Hans said. He stepped forward. His left arm was strapped to his side; bandages bulked out his chest under a white shirt spotted with dried brown blood. 'Don't make me hurt you, Niles.'

'I don't care what kind of deal you and Doc Weird have – '

'Deals! That's good, coming from someone trying to fuck us over with EuroNet.' Then Hans looked around wildly. 'Hey! Goddamn you, don't play tricks with me!'

Kid Charlemagne said softly in Niles's ear, 'He can't see us now.'

Hans stumbled forward, good arm swinging, the torch waving its bright beam through the smoke. Niles and Kid Charlemagne shrank from him, then ran past.

Police cars and fire engines were drawn up in slushy snow down the centre of the avenue, cherry lights revolving above the packed pastel roofs of the double- and triple-parked runabouts of the capacity crowd. Smoke was pouring from every floor of the Permanent Floating Wave. Screams, people stumbling amongst the emergency vehicles, ducking under

the orange tape of police lines. A helicopter fluttered somewhere above the revolving lights and the glare of the
streetlamps. Niles saw the A&R executive climb into a long
low limo parked beyond the police lines at the end of the
block, and his heart turned over as the limo made a U-turn
and slid away.

'No one sees us,' Kid Charlemagne said, 'if they have
machines in their heads. Except you – I fixed that.'

'Jesus, you can talk with chips?'

Kid Charlemagne tapped Niles's forehead. 'You were so
quiet before Magenta magicked you. I liked that.'

'I'll be quiet again, when the fembots die out.' But suppose
Magenta had infected him with a rogue strain of fembots?
He should get a shot of universal phage, like he'd had to do
a couple of times when he'd gotten wired by pranksters. But
there wasn't time to get to a clinic: he was in the middle of a
war. He told Kid Charlemagne, 'Everyone wants you for one
thing. You understand?'

The intense cold and the Wave's chemical smoke had
made his throat raw. Yeah, and that was why he was crying.

Kid Charlemagne nodded.

'If you were changed, there'd be no one on your back. You
could live your life the way you wanted. You understand?'

Another nod.

'Maybe there's a way to do it right now.'

'Would I be like you?'

'You'd lose everything that people want from you. But you
could start trying to learn to be yourself. Not what other
people want you to be.'

'It's hard not to. When I can see what they want . . .' Blue
light washed rhythmically over the Kid's face. He said, 'Do it
to me, friend Niles. Make me human.'

Max's Head Shop was closed and shuttered, but Niles took
Kid Charlemagne down the alley at the side and banged on
the service door until Max let them in.

Max took about ten minutes to convince, and every second
Niles felt something inside himself wind tighter and tighter.
When the fat man said for the third time that it was ten years

since the Saint had tried to pull someone's chips, Niles said, 'Listen, if the Saint can't do it, give me a paring knife and I'll try do it myself.'

'The kid here really wants it done?'

Kid Charlemagne said, 'I want to be human.'

Max put his hands up. 'You talk to the Saint. It isn't any of my business.'

From the other end of the counter the Saint said, in a spaced-out drawl, 'It's anti-evolution. Why live in the old world when there's so many richer realities elsewhere?'

Niles said, 'Does that mean you'll do it or not, Saint?'

Kid Charlemagne said, 'As long as they're in my head, I'm owned.'

'How about it, man?'

'Well, I don't suppose anyone should own anyone else,' the Saint said. He was looking between Niles and the Kid, focussed on something about a million light years away. 'I used to do it with dolls, a long time ago,' he said dreamily. 'This funky old punk, Darlajane B, taught me how. She lives around the corner here. You know Darlajane B, Niles?'

That was the old caretaker of the zek residence. Niles said, 'I knew her, Saint. She went away this summer.'

'She says she can take out the changes the machines made in my brain, but that's something not even the real head scientists could do. And even if they could, I've gotten so used to them that it wouldn't make any difference. Darlajane B, she has some odd ideas, but she means well. I can do it here, if Max gets my stuff.'

When Max had disappeared upstairs, the Saint said to Kid Charlemagne, 'I can see you know things.'

'It hurts.'

'Yeah, knowledge does hurt if you're not used to it. See, we're used to it, us man-apes. Used to the hurting. Used to the sting of the apple's aftertaste. There was a time before that when we made our own realities the way you do, but now this is all we got.'

Kid Charlemagne said, 'There are too many realities. Him – '

he pointed to Niles – 'and you. I mix them together and give them back.'

'You should have seen him, Saint.'

'I don't need any more of that machine stuff,' Saint Jack said, with a dreamy look. 'I made it my own . . .'

He'd gone away, somewhere inside his own head. Niles shook him. 'Goddamn you, Saint! You stay awake!'

'He's always awake,' Max said, coming around the last turn of the stairs. He hefted a frayed plastic sportsbag, corners mended with yellow tape. 'Here you go, man. You remember this stuff?'

Saint Jack had Kid Charlemagne lie down on the bar counter, his head cradled on a shaped block of wood. The Saint shook up a little plastic bottle and put drops in the Kid's eyes to immobilize them; the Kid's pupils were raggedly huge when Niles leaned over him and asked if he was sure that this was what he wanted.

'I want to find out what it is to be myself.'

'You won't be able to audit.'

'Friend Niles, you can teach me again. We can go somewhere else.'

'Sure.'

Saint Jack hooked the arms of his magnifying spectacles over his jutting ears. He said, 'It'll take a minute, maybe, if you let me do it.'

'Where's your equipment?'

'For this I don't need too much. I told you it was easy. There won't even be any blood. Hold still now,' he told Kid Charlemagne, and shoved spoon-shaped plastic spacers under the Kid's eyeballs, hooked about the raw red rims with a fine probe. He drew something out from the Kid's right eye and dropped it into the palm of Niles's hand, did the same with the left.

Niles looked at the tiny chips and said, 'That's it?'

The Saint smiled his dreamy smile. 'These are the logic engines. Stuff all through his head still, I could put in fembots to scavenge it out, if I had the cultures. You could find a grey market shop does that, if you want. But taking these out unconnects everything.'

'Kid, you hear that?'

But Kid Charlemagne was silent. He lay as still as the tomb figure of a crusader, head on the hard pillow, hands crossed on his chest, eyes rolled up like white stones.

'Kid?'

Magenta said, 'You've switched him off, and now you expect him to speak?'

She was leaning in the back doorway. Her dark glasses masked half her white face. Small shapes clustered behind her.

Max said, 'I'm sorry, Niles. I really didn't think the Saint could do it. Turns out I was wrong.'

Magenta said, 'Max sent out word you were up here, Niles. He's trying to tell you that you don't know what you're doing.'

Niles was thinking of a line from an old novel: anyone who owns a frying pan owns death. But there wasn't a frying pan in the bar, let alone any knives. Just bottles and glasses and mugs, and the heavy coffee machine with its tarnished eagle. He said, 'You trust those things after what they did to Igor?'

Magenta took off her dark glasses. Her eye sockets were yellow with old bruises. She said, 'They explained things to me.'

'That's clumsy work,' the Saint said.

'Next time I'll come to you. Meanwhile, maybe you can start up the Kid there. Put him back together, Saint Jack.'

Niles held out his hand. 'What are these worth?'

The fairies made a rustling in the shadows behind Magenta. Niles could suddenly feel them in his head, but nothing he felt made any sense.

Magenta said calmly, 'Your life, perhaps. Don't you think they have duplicates? He's nothing without them. Everything he is, everything he learned, is in the parallel network that fembots spun in his skull. Without the processors his higher functions are closed off from his medulla oblongata. His body will breathe and circulate blood for a while, but eventually it will fail. They took him very young. He was their first changeling, and they sent him out into our world to see how he fared. Now they want him back.'

'No one owns anyone,' Niles said. He was speaking directly to the dolls in the shadows, trying to make a connection, but it was Magenta who replied. She was their connection.

She said, 'You do. You have two lives in the palm of your hand.'

'They changed you a while ago, didn't they? You brought us out to your place to get the Kid back.'

'It was a misunderstanding. They didn't mean to hurt anyone. Hans frightened them: they only expected me and the Kid. But the Kid knew I was going to take him back, and thought he'd be safe if you came along, and Hans had his own plans for the Kid.'

'They killed Igor. That was a misunderstanding?'

'Igor was killed when the fairies were ready to take the Kid back. I didn't need Igor any more because I wouldn't need to act as if I hadn't been saved, and he was too old to be made over. Hundreds of dolls are killed every day. Thousands. They die in industrial accidents, they die from working down seabed mines, from working in reactors. Or they're killed when they're too old to work. Over in Rotterdam, they are hunted for sport. They freed Igor. Give Saint Jack the chips, Niles.'

'The Kid isn't a thing to be owned.'

'The fairies would say that about any one of their kind. They are the changelings that liberationists like Darlajane B made from slaves. But the liberationists didn't think what their changelings would do, once the fairies were set free. They make their own kind now, when they need to. It isn't a revolution, not the way the liberationists wanted, but something wild and strange. You can't understand it right now, Niles, no more than you can understand the kids who use the head shop, but you will. You don't know it, but you've been saved. Give back the chips.'

Niles looked into Magenta's eyes, and she smiled. It was a real smile, and he knew then that she still lived somewhere in her head, that she was changed but she was not destroyed.

The fairies were not as cruel as humans, who had made them as casually as they used them, as things, nothing more, who had not understood the responsibility of creators, and he sighed and opened his hands.

When Niles left a few days later, most of the crew of the Permanent Floating Wave took him over to Max's Head Shop and stood him a few rounds of brandies to send him on his way.

Burckhardt said, 'We'll miss you, man.'

'Maybe I'll come back in spring.'

Burckhardt said, 'We might be needing a few seasonal workers by then,' and he and Niles smiled, because they both knew it wasn't true. The Permanent Floating Wave had crested. Hans had been arrested when the police broke up the panicky near-riot the fairies had caused, and Doc Weird had left for the chance of a job in a Luxembourg cable TV station. The gate had plummeted, and the cable TV station had dropped its option on the Wave's feed.

When Niles was finally about ready to go he set his bag on his shoulder and went over and shook Saint Jack's hand.

'You take care now,' he said.

'I'm beyond good and evil,' the Saint said, nodding and smiling. 'I don't need to deal with that any more.'

'Pray for the rest of us, then,' Niles said, and thought he could feel the Saint's benediction pricking inside his head. Magenta had changed him with a kiss. The chips spun by her fembots had flayed him open, but he welcomed their changes.

Max came down to that end of the bar and said, 'She asked me to look out for the Kid, Niles, so I made the call when I went upstairs to get the Saint's stuff. I didn't know . . .'

'I'd have probably done the same thing,' Niles said.

The Saint said, 'The Kid walked out free. Inside your own head there are worlds wilder and stranger than anything outside.'

Maybe there were. Niles could begin to believe that, now. On his way out of town he took a detour, and stood a long while by the chainlink fence that separated the Oostduinpark from the street. He hooked his fingers in the freezing wire and shook it so snow fell from its rolled top.

It was dusk, bitterly cold. A multitude of small fires burned out there in the rolling wilderness, making strange flickering constellations. Most of them had been lit by fringers or streetkid gangs, but which hadn't? Niles listened inside his head for a long time, but perhaps there weren't any fairies out there after all, or perhaps they were too far away.

Still, it came to Niles that he no longer knew which side was which. Were they on the outside, or was this the outside, now? Spurred by the thought, he rattled the fence again and called the Kid's name, but he might as well have been shouting at the sky.

When he saw a tram rolling up the street towards him he left off and ran for the corner, where it stopped to pick him up. The doll driver didn't even glance at Niles when he dropped his token, but Niles could feel, deep beneath the dull linear texture of the doll's programming, a glimmer of otherness, that same glimmer that was widened into the brand new prelapsarian light of the fairies. Niles grinned like a fool, and as the tram lurched and carried him off into the world, he fell into a seat by an old woman and asked her if she'd been saved yet.

AFTERWORD

This is the only story I've written because of a misprint. When 'Prison Dreams' was published in The Magazine of Fantasy and Science Fiction, *the name of an establishment mentioned in passing was changed from The Permanent Floating Rave to the more intriguing The Permanent Floating Wave (I guess they don't have raves in the US of A). The single-point mutation was the seed for this story about the consequences of refusing to grow up. Max's Head Shop is a spatially compressed version of the venue of many Forbidden Planet (the shop, not the film) signings in London.*

The True History of Doctor Pretorius

To begin with, Larry Cochrane thought that it was just another slice of bread-and-butter sleaze. A contact in the Food and Drug Administration tipped him to an upcoming investigation into a Tijuana clinic. The usual shit, peddling quack cures that supposedly delayed the onset of full-blown AIDS, cut-rate plastic surgery, no-questions-asked abortions and sex change operations. Added spice: the clinic's owner, a certain Dr Septimus Pretorius, had old Hollywood connections. The kicker: several well-known AIDS victims had gone there for Laetrile treatment of intractable Kaposi's, and former TV child star Bobby Dupre, Little Jim-Bob in the long-running 60s family TV saga *Sunrise Acres*, had died of acute septicemia after he was given a complete blood change to try and cure his crack habit.

So far, so good. With no complications, Cochrane figured that he would be in and out in a month, sell it for 50K to one of the glossies, maybe earn twice as much from foreign rights, not to mention spin-off items that he could get his researcher to write for the movie mags.

But within days of starting the investigation, Cochrane knew that the story would change his life. Definitely permanently, and maybe for ever.

The evidence came tumbling out of the archives. Through all his long, colourful career, Dr Pretorius had never bothered to cover his tracks. He'd left clues scattered through newspaper, film and historical archives with a recklessness that was either crazy, foolish, or incredibly bold. Perhaps he thought that no one would believe his story; Larry Cochrane was having trouble believing even half of what his long-suffering researcher, Howard Zaslow, had uncovered.

Witness:

A b&w photograph of white-haired Dr Pretorius, scrawny and bird-like in Bermuda shorts and a long-sleeved white shirt, playing croquet with Charlie Chaplin and Douglas Fairbanks, Jr.

A sepia photograph, quartered by white lines where it had been folded, of Dr Pretorius, looking scarcely younger, lounging in safari kit in a canvas chair, boots cocked on the sprawled corpse of a dog-sized reptile that one of Zaslow's pals at the UCLA Biology Department was convinced was some kind of dinosaur.

A luminous, sharply focussed daguerreotype of Dr Pretorius in frock coat and tall top hat standing with a shorter man who wore an even taller top hat and had his thumbs aggressively tucked into the pockets of his waistcoat, both of them looking straight at the camera with some great mechanical engine half lost in shadow behind them.

A tattered handbill advertising, in type that was of different sizes on every line, that on June 22nd 1852, in the town hall of Cheltenham, Dr Pretorius, lately of Geneva, would demonstrate his electric elixir for the countering of the outward symptoms of old age.

A warrant dated 3rd August 1809, stating that a certain Dr Pretorius, otherwise known as Horace Femm, resident at 13 Half Moon Street, should be arrested on sight, on suspicion of being a French spy and for enquiry into the disappearance of several young women known to be common prostitutes.

A facsimile of a handwritten document, signed by Elizabeth the First of England above the imprint of her seal in cracked wax, declaring that Dr Pretorius of Cheapside was an agent invested with such powers of enquiry as necessary to seek out agents of Catholic powers.

Another facsimile, this in Latin and dated 1423, which Howie Zaslow said was the death warrant for a Dr Praetorius, a notorious practitioner of various magics and malefic rites; it was from the Armand Hammer collection, and was one of only three known holographs of Charles VII of France.

There was more, much more, including a connection with Ilsa Magall, the Destroying Angel of the Nazi death camps, that Cochrane could use to open up Pretorius like an abalone. But even half of this treasure trove was more than enough to convince Cochrane that this was even bigger than his recent bestseller about the RoChemCo disaster in Calcutta. Dr Pretorius had a secret that could make Larry Cochrane rich, and more than rich. It could enable him to live forever.

Of course, Howie Zaslow also knew the score, but that was a fixable detail. Cochrane had a contact in the LAPD who knew a wise guy. One phone call and ten thousand dollars up front, and it was set.

Armed with the results of Zaslow's labours, Cochrane started to hassle the PR office of Dr Pretorius's clinic. He got a quick but inadequate response: Dr Pretorius was willing to grant an interview, but there was a certain vagueness about the timing. 'We're undergoing a certain amount of reorganization,' Ransom, the PR man, told Cochrane over the phone, and promised to get back as soon as he could.

So Cochrane told Howie Zaslow to keep digging up more dirt, packed a couple of changes of clothes with his portable computer, modem, and the licensed 9mm automatic he'd bought after the '93 riots, and took off in a hire car for the Baja coast in Mexico, which was where Dr Pretorius had lived ever since he had set up his clinic in the 1920s.

For two days, Cochrane sweated and chafed in a roach motel with no air conditioning and some kind of lizard in the shower stall, in a Mexican fishing village ten miles north of Dr Pretorius's estate. The village was a lost, God-forsaken place where bearded, pot-bellied refugees from the sixties stood knee-deep in the surf, bombed on LSD or hash, or sat around the bars drinking tequila from the bottle and talking about Nam. Cochrane drove past the estate's impressive security fences, and made sure that the guards on the gate saw him taking photographs with his Nikon. He talked to the motel's owner, the richest man in the village, who said that Dr Pretorius was a good man who sponsored the Festival of the Day of the Dead each year. He phoned up the estate office every couple of hours to let them know he was waiting, and badgered Howie Zaslow for more dirt, for more on the rumours that Dr Pretorius was about to relocate.

When Cochrane left LA, Zaslow had been close to uncovering the crux of a set of deals that included selling off the estate and the private clinic. Now, on the phone, Zaslow said, in his slow, thoughtful way, that Cochrane should wait a couple of days for the fuller picture, the financial trail was sort of complicated.

Cochrane, sitting on the edge of the sagging motel bed, strangling the phone in one hand and squeezing a sweating can of ice-cold Coke in the other, said, 'Get your hands off your chicken-neck dick, Howie, and chase this down. That PR guy, Ransom, told me they were relocating, which means soon. I need to know all about his plans. I need an in. I need you to start doing some real work. I've already waited long enough, and this quaint fishing town outwore its welcome as soon as I checked in.'

'Another day,' Zaslow's voice pleaded. 'Give me time to chase down the share purchases and you can hit Pretorius really hard.'

Cochrane held the can of Coke to the back of his neck and counted to ten.

Zaslow said, 'Are you still there, boss?'

'Another day and Pretorius might not be. There's a stream of trucks leaving his estate. Maybe there's another way in if we can get hard evidence about this death camp rumour.'

'That one's no problem,' Zaslow said, his voice sounding smug. He'd been working for Cochrane for two years, and in an odd way Cochrane would miss the man's infuriating plodding pedantry. Zaslow was in his thirties, a pale-skinned New Yorker with a *summa cum laude* from Yale and the distracted air of a perpetual research student. He had an old-fashioned regard for facts. Right now, though, Cochrane was burning with impatience. He had a lot more to lose than some pissant story.

Zaslow said, 'The Simon Wiesenthal Institute came through. They have details of his collaboration with Ilsa Magall. Weird transplants, stuff about vacuum exposure that has a link with the V2 rocket program. I think that's how Pretorius got into the States, by the way. The Army rounded up anyone that had anything to do with Peenemunde before the Russians got there.'

'Sometimes you're worth the money I pay you. I got to have that stuff.'

'It's coming from Austria by courier.'

'I need it now, fuck-head. Look, OK. Get it to me any way you can as soon as you can. This is definitely kosher?'

'One hundred per cent.'

So Cochrane phoned Dr Pretorius's estate for the fourth time that day, and told Ransom that he had documentation proving that his boss was a Nazi collaborator, and would he like to discuss it in person, or with the Israeli secret service? Cochrane hung up as Ransom started to bluster, and ten minutes later the phone rang. To his amazement, Cochrane was in.

Early the next morning, Larry Cochrane was waiting with his holdall and portable computer outside the village's beat-up cantina. He was wearing his black Armani suit; his beard was trimmed; his ponytail was tied back with a silver death's head clasp. Cochrane's inquisitorial style was modelled on Robert de Niro in *Angel Heart*, and generally its brooding menace gave him an edge in interviews.

All in all, he was feeling fairly terrific, although he was not so carried away that he had neglected to strap on his shoulder holster. This day, the first in what promised to be a very long life, was shaping up pretty well. The sun was brassy, not yet at its full heat. The ocean was blue, sparkling with whitecaps, the air so clear you could see out to the horizon. Except for a couple of fishermen manhandling their boat up the white beach, the village was barely awake. An *Americano* was sleeping off last night's tequila over by the garbage cans, watched by a piebald dog that trotted over and sat by Cochrane as he drank a Coke in the shade of the cantina's awning.

Seven on the dot, the limo swung off the road. The

Americano, hand out, stumbled up as the chauffeur loaded Cochrane's bags. Cochrane lowered the smoked glass window and gave the bum the finger; then the chauffeur hit the gas.

Moving trucks, two travelling together every few minutes, heading north towards the border, passed the limo as it drove south. The chauffeur wouldn't answer Cochrane's questions with anything other than a shrug, so Cochrane watched MTV on the inset TV and drank one of Dr Pretorius's Diet Cokes from the built-in fridge.

The limo turned off the highway, climbed past a clump of coral trees and stopped while a big brute of a guard, sweating through his tan uniform, opened the gate in the tall double fence. The guard was hunchbacked, and his face was brutish and scarred, his nose smashed flat, his tiny eyes like piss-holes in snow. His blubbery lips worked as he waved the limo through. The narrow road switchbacked through rolling pastures wet by sprinklers that set rainbows in the hot Mexican air. Once, the limo stopped to let a couple of giraffes amble past; Pretorius was supposed to have more animals on his estate than San Diego zoo.

The house itself came into view only as the limo climbed the shoulder of the rise: a Normandy chateau, with sharply ridged roofs and a spiky tower, standing amongst a formal garden of lawns and clipped hedges. The limo rumbled over a wide cattle grid that bridged a steep-sided ditch with razor wire on the outward-facing slope – to keep the animals out of the garden, Cochrane supposed – and drew up by the mansion's great Gothic door where Dr Pretorius's PR man, Ransom, was waiting.

Dr Pretorius was ready to talk, Ransom said, as he led Cochrane around the side of the house. As they walked across a sweep of gravel towards a huge glasshouse framed with Victorian ironwork, palms and tree ferns visible through the whitewash on its panels of glass, Ransom added, 'Dr Pretorius is eager to tell the truth about his life. He won't hold anything back, Larry. You must trust him.'

But Cochrane knew that his job really started when the subjects of his investigations finally agreed to talk, because they only wanted to tell their version of the truth, to smokescreen, to play the victim, to shift the blame. Cochrane had had the president of RoChemCo telling him that careless local workers had caused the explosive outgassing in the Calcutta plant that killed thousands in the surrounding shanty town; the chairman of ScotOil blaming environmentalists for regulations that had distracted the crews of his company's tankers and led to illegal discharges killing millions of seabirds and seals in the new Falklands oil fields; the Police Chief of Tupelo blaming rioters for inciting police to violence that left more than twenty, including a grandmother and two children, dead of shotgun wounds after cops opened up on a group protesting against compulsory prayer in schools.

Larry Cochrane was a master at the adversarial techniques of the new, aggressive breed of journalist. He didn't agree, he didn't gently point out the contradictions his interviewees tangled around themselves: he went for the jugular. He had been carried out of the RoChemCo headquarters by four security guards. He had screamed into the face of the police chief until she burst into tears. The interview with the chairman of ScotOil had ended after the man threw a crystal decanter at him. Cochrane knew what he wanted and he didn't care how he got it.

But Dr Pretorius disarmed Cochrane by simply agreeing with everything. He said that it was all true, and he didn't care. 'I'm disappointed,' he said, with a sly, foxy smile. He leaned forward in his wheelchair, and said into the Sony proDAT tape recorder on the wicker table, 'You've done so much work, Mr Cochrane. You've found out where the bodies are buried. You are quite right when you say I have exploited the desperation of dying men and women. But you haven't stopped to consider this. No one wants to die, and that is why I am rich.'

Dr Pretorius was hunched within a crocheted shawl, with a tartan blanket wrapped around his legs, as immune to the stifling heat in the huge greenhouse as a mummy. Only his head and hands were visible. If he really was five hundred years old, he looked every day of it: a mummy indeed, the dry, deeply wrinkled leathery skin of his face sunk so close to his skull that the arches of his cheekbones and the jut of his jaw were clearly visible. Only his white hair, combed back from his high forehead and crowned by a crocheted skull cap, showed any vigour. His hands were spotted with age, and constantly fretted at the hem of his shawl; his nails were curved like talons.

Cochrane leaned forward, too. The wicker chair creaked under his two hundred pounds. With his face less than a couple of handspans from Dr Pretorius's long, sharp nose, he said, 'The Mexican government has agreed to the demands of the FDA that clinics like yours should be subject to full licensing procedures. Tell me you're not worried by that, *doctor*. Terminal cancer patients have spent every last cent on your so-called cures. AIDS patients have died while crossing the border because of the false hopes you held out. Your clinic has peddled some weird treatments in its time, none of them anything to do with real medicine. The monkey gland extracts, for instance. How will you explain those in court?'

'In fact, they were based on the blood of langur monkeys. There were unfortunate side effects, but it really did promote rejuvenation of the skin. As for patient deaths, how many die in hospitals? How many are killed by the treatments that are supposed to help them? Modern medicine is a brutal business, a matter of poisoning the patient to the edge of death in the hope that his illness is more susceptible. Ah, Mr Cochrane, they come to my clinic because they are dying. Even if they are cured, many die of secondary infections they acquired during their illnesses.

'But that is not what I wish to talk about. I am interested in your interest in my history. That's why I allowed you here, as my guest.'

'I'd say you're looking at extradition, at families of your patients suing you for everything you have, at charges of murder and false practice. You don't look like you've got long to live yourself, and I think you'll spend the rest of your short life being reamed by sex-starved lifers.'

'I did not realize you were homosexual,' Dr Pretorius said.

'Ah, but perhaps you do not realise this yourself.' He looked amused. 'You are thirty-two, Mr Cochrane. Your father died of heart failure in his fifty-eighth year; there is a history of pancreatic cancer in your mother's family. Actuarial tables would give you no more than another thirty years. How would you like to live to be a hundred?'

Cochrane had plans to live much longer than that. Keeping his face still, he said, 'And end up looking like you?'

'You would have to live a lot longer than that,' Dr Pretorius said.

'How old are you?'

'You already know the answer to that question, I believe,' Dr Pretorius said, calmly meeting Cochrane's gaze.

Cochrane called his bluff. 'I'm supposed to believe what could be a bunch of fake documents?'

'But you *do* believe. You are hungry for my secret, Mr Cochrane. *That* is why you think you are here, although, as I said, you are here because I allow it. Because I want my story known.'

Cochrane made a counterstrike. 'Maybe I'm not interested in your story. Maybe a better story would be your arrest and trial. Let's face it, I'm here because I threatened to print an exposé of your crimes.'

'I think you'll find that most were committed in other countries, far away and long ago. It is not human justice I fear, Mr Cochrane, but it is true that you could be a ... nuisance. Please, ask questions. I will answer as I can.'

Cochrane was ready for this tactic. Everything was in his head: his memory was part of his success. He didn't need to flip through notes, or pause to check facts. He said, 'Let's start with a simple one. You were involved with the Edinburgh surgeon, Dr Moreau. There was a scandal, and Moreau quit the country. It was rumoured that Burke and Hare – '

Dr Pretorius's laugh was like the dry rattling of seeds in a gourd. 'Moreau had no need of those gentlemen. His was more a veterinary art. He called himself a surgeon, but he was a butcher. He knew nothing of sepsis, to begin with. He stole secrets, Mr Cochrane. His end was quite fitting, an epitaph to all such meddlers.'

'Then there was no connection between Moreau, yourself, and Dr Henry Jekyll? I have clippings from the *Scotsman* that say otherwise. July 5th, 1886.'

'Dr Jekyll was a poor unstable fellow. He fled to London, you know. Reports of his death were quite exaggerated. There was a spate of murders that had his stamp ... Now, *he* did know something of surgery.'

'And you vanished, too. There's a gap in the records of about five years.'

'Ah, Africa,' Dr Pretorius said. 'It was a foolish expedition, but not one I regret. I have learned to regret nothing. Poor Ayesha. I loved her, you know. Oh, not in the coarse physical sense. It was something higher, something purer. It was a true meeting of minds. Haggard claimed her for himself in that ridiculous account, but he was no gentleman. He tried to force her in the worst way, and the wounds accelerated her aging – and so she tried to purify herself too early. Perhaps I do regret saving Haggard's life, but one can't live on regrets. I went there in search of rejuvenation, and it was one place untouched by science, as was my poor, lovely Ayesha, but Haggard and his jack-booted kind – I think also of that bombast Challenger – put an end to that. The last of magic vanished under a wash of British Empire red. Well, but I was already tainted myself, of course.'

Cochrane wondered if the man's bravado was nothing more than senility. Old men grow arrogant, forgetting the uncertainty of their youth, forgetting defeat and remembering only victory. Make a jump. Catch him in a lie, a contradiction. He said, 'You were linked to a number of women in the thirties.'

'No doubt you know their names better than I do. They were only human, Mr Cochrane. Gods on the silver screen, of course, but not in the flesh. Our friendships were, of course, purely platonic. All girls together, as it were.'

'At least one had an abortion.'

'More than one. They came to my clinic for that, amongst

other things. I suppose you read it in one of Anger's books. *He* was here, you know. A beautiful, puckish young thing. He rode up on a motorcycle with a Mexican lad who was surely underage. There *was* some scandal when Garbo found James Whale and Anger's Mexican Adonis sucking off each other – her phrase, you understand – in the rose garden. *She* was here with her own lover, of course, a vain but rather glorious woman who made a habit of stealing women from men.'

Dr Pretorius had slyly trumped Cochrane with this story. He was a harder target than he looked, and Cochrane thought that he would enjoy breaking him down. It was time to bring this round to the power he held over this old man.

But Dr Pretorius quickly dismissed the allegations about collaboration with Ilsa Magall. He rolled up his sleeve and showed the blurry blue numbers tattooed on his wrist, and said, 'I am a homosexual and a Jew. Luckily, they put the star on me, not the triangle: the queers flew up the chimney almost as soon as their feet touched the mud. Mr Cochrane, I worked as an alternative to death. Old men who did not work lasted no longer in the camps than the time it took to have them undress and step into the showers.'

'The Israeli government will take a different view, if I choose to tell them where you are. They're looking for a Dr Loew, but that number on your wrist will be enough identification.'

Dr Pretorius shrugged inside his shawl. 'You have no proof, or you would show it to me. You are my guest here, Mr Cochrane.'

'Then you admit you're guilty.'

'Of course I'm guilty. I'm a damned soul, damned by my pact with Astorath, and proud of it. Perhaps you're damned too, perhaps not, but I *know* I am. It is a privileged position.'

A moment later, a male nurse and the PR man, Ransom, appeared through the sweating greenery. Just before he was wheeled away, Dr Pretorius said, 'Look around as much as you want, but you will not be allowed beyond the ha-ha. It is for your safety, you understand: wild creatures live in the grounds. You interest me, Cochrane. I may allow you to tell my story. In the house you may find such evidence as you need, to convince you.'

'Convince me?'

'Of my history,' Dr Pretorius said, and then he was wheeled away through a curtain of hanging ferns. 'Show him, Ransom.'

Ransom was a bluff British guy in his late sixties, ex-Royal Air Force and as stiff as a ramrod, his carefully ironed Jaeger blazer and crisp white haircut visibly wilting in the dry heat as he walked Cochrane through the extensive gardens to the guest bungalows. Dr Pretorius would see Cochrane the next day, Ransom said, he hoped that an overnight stay wasn't an inconvenience?

'I guess that's the Brit way of saying I'm a prisoner.'

'Oh no. No no. A guest.'

Cochrane wondered if this was some way of making a move on him. If they tried, they were in for a surprise. He said, 'I'd have to make a call to my office. They like to know where I am, if you know what I mean.'

'Oh, quite,' Ransom said. 'We want you to enjoy your stay here.'

'Yeah? I think I will look around. Soak up the atmosphere. Shake off the stink off the boonie fishing village I just spent two days in. I don't like being made to hang about, Ransom. In fact, I fucking hate it. The only compensation is that I get to write *everything* up. If I don't get what I want, your fucking boss will hang in Tel-Aviv.'

'Dr Pretorius wants you to write the truth. His true history.'

'And what's that? Beyond the fact he's ready to make a run for it?'

Ransom emitted a patently false laugh. 'I believe you should talk to your researcher, Larry, but before that perhaps I could show you around the house and grounds. This place has seen quite a bit of history. Chaplin stayed in the bungalow we'll put you up in, and Churchill next door. Still has the cigar humidor Dr Pretorius had installed for him. Did I give you the information pack?'

'I glanced at it.'

'Best thing to do with that kind of stuff,' Ransom said. He was the kind of PR flak who agreed to everything. 'Better at first hand, eh? I believe Dr Pretorius suggested that you look around the house.'

'Sure,' Cochrane said. He was already tired of the man's bluff, hollow heartiness, and said that perhaps he'd go freshen up.

'Look around by yourself, by all means,' Ransom said. 'But please, as Dr Pretorius suggested, don't wander across the ha-ha – the perimeter ditch? We wouldn't like any of the animals chasing after you.'

'Someone was killed, weren't they?'

'Ah, I see you've done some research. Yes, some minor fifties starlet was killed by a jackal. Silly girl couldn't hold her drink and wandered off downhill towards the sea. But that was a long time ago, and you're more sensible, I know. I believe that your cocaine habit is quite cured, for instance.'

Cochrane wasn't surprised that Pretorius's people had been checking up on him. He said, 'The fifties, that was when they were coming up here for so-called rejuvenation injections, right?'

'Oh no, not here at the house. That would be the clinic.'

'The one that's closing down.'

'Relocating,' Ransom said firmly.

'Whatever. I heard she was found naked.'

'Animals often do that before they eat. Strip the clothes off. I was in Africa,' Ransom added, then said goodbye to Cochrane at the door of the guest bungalow.

The bungalow was a big, airy room with a tiled bathroom in back. Cane furniture, white shutters, a fan slowly turning up in the rafters, gave it an old-fashioned British colonial ambience.

Cochrane's bag was at the foot of the bed; his clothes neatly folded away in the bamboo dresser. Cochrane opened up his Compaq portable and unshipped his phone coupler –

but the only way of dialling out was through an old-fashioned mechanical switchboard that wouldn't support computer traffic.

'Can you believe this shit,' he said to Howie Zaslow, when he finally got through to LA on the phone 'The fucker's got the biggest satellite dish outside of NASA sitting in back of his stately pile, and I bet all he uses it for is to jack off to the Playboy channel. I want to download stuff from you, I'm going to have to get someone to drive me to the nearest public phone.'

Zaslow's voice crackled down a thousand miles of copper cable and bad connections into the cream bakelite handset. 'Did he talk?'

'Not exactly. He's playing games. He agreed with everything I said, then tried to fob me off with sex scandals from the Jurassic, and even more blatant shit about pacts with devils. The Nazi stuff shook him, though. He has me shut up in the estate right now.'

'Are you in trouble?'

'Hell no. This is just part of the negotiations.' Cochrane thought it funny, Zaslow concerned about his safety when he had nothing but bad news for the little nerd.

Zaslow said, 'He might come after me, too.'

'Don't be chickenshit. I'm the one who's out here. You want to benefit from this, you better work your sad ass digging dirt.'

'You still don't know if he *has* a secret,' Zaslow said. 'For instance, he could be a mutant. You wouldn't be able to benefit from an oddity in his genetic makeup.'

'He's as human as you and me. Just a hell of a lot older.'

'Not every mutant is a monster. In fact, most aren't. There are plenty of single locus mutations – '

'So I'll sell him to science,' Cochrane said impatiently. They'd been through all this before, and it hadn't convinced Cochrane then. 'Do what I tell you,' Cochrane said. 'Speculate on your free time.'

Zaslow said, 'Well, I got more on his career. There was a Dr Pretorius teaching natural philosophy and chemistry at the University of Ingolstadt in the 1800s. He was involved with a scandal concerning some Swiss student. Something about robbing graves, and maybe necrophilia. The student disappeared after a riot.'

'I don't give a fuck about ancient history. We'll only get Pretorius to come across with the goods if he knows we have evidence that could hang him.' Cochrane was about to put down the phone, then said on a whim, 'Oh, check out the name Astorath for me.'

'Animal, vegetable or mineral?'

'How the fuck should I know? Pretorius said he had some kind of deal going with him. Just do your job, and I'll try and find a place to plug in my modem.'

The manicured gardens around the house were extensive: long formal beds of roses, shedding petals in the heat, between trimmed evergreen hedges; neatly pruned fruit trees; a formal Japanese garden with sinuously raked gravel and an arrangement of the oldest bonsai Cochrane had ever seen. Tennis courts, a manicured croquet lawn, a swimming pool in white marble with a reproduction of Rome's Trevi fountain spouting water at the deep end, and Neptune and mermaids worked in mosaic tile at the bottom of the crystal-clear water. A row of brightly painted cabins beyond; Cochrane checked one out, grinned when he saw the hand-carved daybed inside. The place had been famous for its discreet orgies in the thirties and forties, Hollywood stars in cross-border hi-jinks safe from the press's prying eyes.

The gardens stretched around the back of the house towards a winding service road. Cochrane was watching two trucks toil up the dusty road when he heard the cry.

It came from somewhere near the back of the house, husky and plaintive, like the cry of a tired child, or a woman who'd worn her voice out crying. Cochrane walked along the path in the shadow of the house's high wall, looking through the first floor's mullion windows, but it was only when he heard the cry again that he found the grating. It was set flush in a square of concrete, a hinged grid of strong steel bars fastened by a padlock to a steel staple, with a covering of rusting wire mesh. Cochrane kicked aside the mesh and then stepped back with a start when fingers reached up through the bars.

'Hey,' Cochrane said. 'Who's down there?'

The fingers were long and white and slender, with coarse hair sprouting at the joints. They flexed like sea anemone tentacles, as if tasting the air.

'Hey,' Cochrane said again. He glanced around, but there was no one in sight. 'Hey. Are you one of Pretorius's guests?'

The fingers gripped the bars, and for a moment an oval shape – a face – glimmered in the darkness before sinking back down out of sight. There was a scent . . . orange blossom and the musk of roses . . . it was suddenly all around Cochrane, like a presence. More plaintive cries drifted up from the darkness; Cochrane thought he heard the word *friend*. He looked around again. The sun-stunned gardens were still deserted.

Friend. Someone down there needed his help. Dreamily, he took the 9mm automatic from his shoulder holster and shot off the grating's padlock.

The pistol's vicious crack, although reflected by the house's high walls, was not as loud as Cochrane expected – he'd only ever shot it in the gallery of his local target range, never before in open air. There was a shriek from the darkness beneath the grating, then silence. Cochrane lifted up the grating, called down that it was OK, but there was no response.

Cochrane waited a few minutes, calling down into the darkness at intervals. Frustrated, and suddenly nervous that security guards would at any moment come crashing onto the scene, he walked away, then came back and called again. Nothing. And the smell – a zoo stench, thick and cloacal. No way was he climbing down into some fucking unlit, stinking cellar. Not that he was afraid of what was down there. No, he didn't want to fuck up his two thousand dollar Armani suit.

★

Cochrane headed back towards the cluster of guest bunga-lows. As he started to cross the wide, billiard-smooth croquet lawn, Ransom drove up in a golf cart decorated with Pretorius's crest – a shield embraced by a thing half snake, half dragon.

Dinner would be served soon, Ransom said. 'Hop in. No need to walk in this heat.'

Cochrane, feeling the warm weight of the automatic inside the shoulder holster under his jacket, said, 'I need a modem connection.'

'I'll see it's ready for you after dinner.'

'Will your boss be there?'

'He eats alone. Always has done. Come on, you can keep me company. Gets lonely up here. No one to talk to.'

'What about the other servants?'

'They're hardly human,' Ransom said, and made a neat turn onto the gravelled drive that led up to the house.

At the time, Cochrane put this remark down to Ransom's English Tory xenophobia. Later, he wished he'd paid more attention to the PR man.

Certainly, he didn't take much notice of the brief tour of the public rooms of the house: he already knew most of what he was shown from Zaslow's research. There was a library with thousands of leather bound volumes, some of them chained to their shelves ('Incunabulae,' Ransom explained), a long hall with Tudor oak panelling black as pitch, suits of armour standing to attention under faded banners hanging from high rafters and a vast fireplace, a small cinema with a yellowing screen and cracked leather armchairs, and what Ransom called the museum, where hundreds of glass jars of every size stood on steel shelving. Inside, floating in alcohol, were slabs of tissue, organs, and human and animal embryos at every stage of development. A man hung on a rack in a glass jar taller than Cochrane, his skin flayed to show the muscles beneath, his eyes burned milky white by alcohol. An entire pickled menagerie of creatures Cochrane couldn't begin to identify.

'Dr Pretorius has made a long study of teratology,' Ransom

said, tapping a jar where something like a finny snake curled. The man gave off an odour compounded of whisky fumes and stale cigar smoke.

Cochrane picked up a human skull; a grisly tail of vertebrae was still attached, the bottom-most cut in a ragged line.

'Ah, now that is the skull of the inestimable Dr Dee,' Ransom said. 'Dr Pretorius likes to keep reminders of his past adventures.'

Cochrane knew that he should stay calm, stay cool, now that the promise of five hundred years of life was within his grasp, but Pretorius's presumption at holding him hostage, and Ransom's bland affability, rubbed him the wrong way. The whole setup made him deeply uneasy. Rationally, he knew that this was just a show; instinctively, the place gave him the creeps, and his mind kept returning to the plaintive cries, the long white fingers, of whoever had been locked under that grill.

He said to Ransom, 'Are you part of Pretorius's little game?'

Ransom blinked owlishly in the dim electric light. 'It's no game, Larry. Dr Pretorius is deadly serious.'

'So am I. I know enough about him to have him hung in Tel Aviv. It would make a great show trial. The Israelis couldn't get Magall or Mengele, but your boss is the next best thing. What's it like, working for an ex-Nazi? Were you in the war, Ransom? How do you square that?'

'I was a navigator for a Lancaster bomber. Dr Pretorius was a prisoner in a death camp.'

'He was working for Ilsa Magall. The Destroying Angel.'

'Let him tell his story, Larry. He really does want to have his history told, but your threats upset him.'

'Yeah? Tough shit. He's so upset he kidnapped me.'

'You're his guest.' Ransom cocked his head; a moment later a gong sounded distantly. 'Dinner, I believe.'

When Cochrane returned to his bungalow an hour later, replete with swordfish and half a bottle of '81 Chardonnay (he and Ransom had served themselves from a catering trolley; there was no sign of any servants), he found his computer on the desk, plugged into a modem whose cable sneaked out of a window. A moment later, Cochrane was talking to Howie Zaslow on the phone; a few minutes after that, his computer was decoding the first graphics files and loading them into the picture viewing programme.

A bunch of facsimiles of typed letters in German, on notepaper headed with the SS winged death-head, the s's replaced with the infamous double lightning flash, Pretorius's name underlined a dozen times. A photograph in blurry greys of Dr Pretorius, looking scarcely younger than he did now, stiffly shaking hands with a woman in black SS uniform in front of tangles of barbed wire. Reproductions of pages from laboratory notebooks: columns of figures in cramped copperplate, each page stamped with the death's head.

While Cochrane's bubblejet printer was busy, Zaslow told him, 'I checked the number tattooed on the wrist of the man in the photograph. It's the same as the one given to Dr Pretorius at Treblinka in 1941. The photograph was taken a year later, at Auschwitz-Birkenau; he was there under the name of Loew. There's more background on the other stuff I sent you earlier, too. That guy in the daguerreotype next to Pretorius is Brunel, the Victorian engineer; the machine is supposedly some kind of deep boring device they developed. I got into the records of the Royal Geographic Society, too. A Dr Pretorius accompanied Professor Challenger on an expedition along the Orinoco. Around about 1890.'

'Forget all the old shit. It's the Nazi stuff that will clinch this.'

Zaslow said, sounding hurt, 'It's important to get the whole story if it's what Pretorius wants.'

'Fuck what Pretorius wants. It's what I want that counts.'

After a brief pause, Zaslow said, sounding more distant than ever, 'I found out about that name you asked about.'

'Go ahead.'

'Astorath is the name of a demon. In fact, he's one of the Dukes of Hell. He's supposed to manifest himself as a beautiful angel astride a dragon, with a viper in his hand. It seems that the Church gave him a sex change, by the way. Originally he was a she. Astarte, the Indo-European goddess of creation and destruction. Athtar to the Egyptians. Astroarche, in Aramaic. The morning star of Heaven, Queen of the Stars who ruled over all of the dead whose spirits could be seen as stars. In short, he's big juju. If Pretorius – '

Cochrane laughed. 'I forget that you're an egghead, just like Pretorius. Believe me, this mystic bullshit is just another smokescreen. Stay cool, Howie. I'll see you get what's coming to you.'

Cochrane put down the phone, waited a few heartbeats, then dialled the number for which he'd paid ten thousand dollars. 'Time to get to work,' he told the man at the other end. 'My assistant has outlived his usefulness.'

He put down the phone. He didn't feel a thing. Zaslow a mayfly voice buzzing in his ear. This was not a secret to be shared with those not worthy. He wondered if there were many others like Dr Pretorius, if there was a secret cabal of immortals. A dream he'd been enjoying, this past week. Becoming a Master of the Universe. Learning the real secrets. Power. Life was power. The dead sure as shit didn't have any.

That was when Cochrane realized that there was gunfire somewhere in the grounds.

It was dark now. Holding the 9mm automatic inside his jacket pocket, Cochrane navigated the garden by the reflected glow of the floodlights which lit the sheer walls of the house. Out in the darkness beyond the house was the distant sound, like popcorn kernels snapping, of automatic gunfire, unmistakable to any resident of Los Angeles.

A jeep was parked on the other side of the ha-ha: the searchlight on its cab roof caught in its beam something human-sized running crookedly towards a clump of trees a couple of hundred yards downhill. The creature turned to the light, raised its arms above its head, and yelled hoarsely. Cochrane, a hundred yards away, stepped back. The thing's face was the muzzle of a beast, its mouth full of crooked fangs. A man on the load bed of the jeep took aim. Two spaced shots: the creature dropped, kicked, and was still. The jeep's motor started and it spun away downhill.

Behind Cochrane, Ransom said, 'You should have waited for me, Larry. We're having a bit of a cull. A few of the experimental animals escaped.'

Cochrane thought of long white fingers probing through the grill. His heart was beating quickly; the beast's human cry had shocked him. He said, 'What kind of experimental animals?'

'Monkeys, mostly. A few chimpanzees and orang-utans. No more than the usual kind of specimens, you know.'

The thing that Cochrane had seen shot down was no ape or monkey. And the fingers at the grating . . .

'Come this way,' Ransom said. 'Dr Pretorius is waiting.'

The lights of the greenhouse had been reduced to a muted moonlight glow, but the wet heat was no less stifling than it had been that afternoon. As before, Dr Pretorius sat in his wheelchair with a glass and a bottle of gin on the table beside him. He was hunched inside his blankets and shawls, but there was a quick eagerness in his voice.

'You must know now that I need you, Mr Cochrane. I need you to tell the truth about me. My name must not be forgotten.'

'I believe you're what you claim to be. That's not the problem. But you lied about your association with Magall. Let me help you. Otherwise, well, frankly, Dr Pretorius, you could be in real deep shit.'

Dr Pretorius didn't answer at once. He poured a measure of gin into the glass, sipped it, and smacked his lips. 'My one little vice,' he said. 'You have the documents, and you believe you have me. But I was not even an assistant, Mr Cochrane. She saw me as an animal with certain talents that were useful to her project.'

'Talents which included torturing prisoners in experiments. You're guilty of war crimes, Pretorius.'

Dr Pretorius looked amused. 'Is that the best you can do? Shame on you, Mr Cochrane. Oh, the torture was real enough, but my part in it was an invention, a cover story which the Americans used to hide their discovery of what Magall really wanted. She wanted to create a race of killing machines, soldiers without fear, with perfect obedience. She learned of my reputation. I did what I was told, which is no doubt what you will tell me the camp *kommandos* also said. But I was not a *kommando*; I was a prisoner, a *mussleman* who wished only to avoid *selektion*. Magall supplied the parts; I supplied the knowledge. How hungry she was to learn! But her plans became crazier and crazier, and most of her creations were too deformed for their hearts to support them, even when we used two or three in one body. Only one, a monster she called Boris, lived, and it was so tormented that it killed several female prisoners, and then Ilsa Magall herself, before the guards managed to shoot it down. How disappointed Astorath must have been at that set-back! Through me, he thought to challenge God, but always it was the same story. Moreau was killed by the beastmen who discovered he was not God; Jekyll became his own creature, and so destroyed himself; poor Victor followed his creature into the wastelands.'

'Victor?'

'A student of mine. He was both worse and better than me. It was when the magic really began to die. No longer did we rely on spells, but merely upon electricity. Oh, there were a few holdouts who attempted a bastard marriage of alchemy and science. Poor mad West for instance, or the charlatan Robert Cornish. But magic was already dead, killed by Victor and those like him, cold clear-eyed men without an ounce of romance or passion in their souls.'

'I suppose this would be at Ingolstadt.'

Dr Pretorius shrugged. 'I remember so little of the affair, to tell the truth. I had discovered the delights of gin and opium. Most of the eighteenth century is a blur to me.'

'How many monsters are you responsible for?' Cochrane was thinking of the thing he had seen gunned down. He was wondering if there were any more. His 9mm pistol made a comforting weight in his jacket pocket.

'Monsters? You might call them that, I suppose. Ah, but my dear, exquisite King and Queen, my poor, shy creatures ... these were not monsters. It is the process that creates such things that is monstrous. Science is a corrupting force because it allows power to be wielded by those who do not understand it. Do you know how your recorder there works, or how to fix your computer? Of course not. In my salad days, as a necromancer, I had to make all the tools of my Art myself. It was more than a precaution; it ensured that I was fully engaged in the Great Work. Nowadays, amateurs who have skimmed the works of Crowley call up demons they cannot control, and are devoured. Quite right too! And so with those who misuse science without understanding it.

'Victor may have been my best and brightest student; he at least studied Paracelsus and Albertus Magnus and knew that there was more to the working of the world than reductive rules unpicked by parsimonious experiment. Yet he failed. They all failed, and not because they reached too far. No, it was because they dared not reach *far enough*.'

'These creatures of yours – '

'I like to keep in my hand, nothing more. An old man's hobby, and outdated besides. The little ambition behind my surgical dabblings is as nothing to the overweening pride of those who would render new creatures by meddling with DNA. They would erase one gene, rewrite others, mix genes from different creatures, and yet they are like painters obsessively reworking a tiny patch of a vast picture they can never comprehend. Listen – '

Cochrane said after a moment's silence. 'I don't hear anything.'

'He's watching us, and how little he understands. A nice metaphor. But *you* understand, Mr Cochrane. You will tell my story. This nonsense about my time in the camp, it is only a negotiating ploy. I understand that. But I have given you the story anyway. You can tell it all. In fact, I insist that you do.'

Cochrane took out his pistol. 'Fuck your story. I want your secret. I want to be like you, and live forever. If you think I'm going to sell it to some glossy for a flat fee you're out of your mind.'

Dr Pretorius's eyes did not leave Cochrane's face. 'Or you will shoot me? Then you will not leave my property alive.

Already you have meddled. I know it was you who set my poor innocent children free, but I forgive you and I will give you my secret, much good it will do you.'

'I'll want more than that. I'll want to be certain it works. You're running away because you're a fraud who can no longer hide the truth that your cures don't work. There is only one thing you have that's valuable, and I want it.'

'Of course, of course. You are a very modern man, Mr Cochrane. You believe that science can accomplish everything it can dream of. How Astorath would laugh to see in you his victory! For he *has* won. Science has grown in power beyond his wildest dreams. God is dead, or if not, he soon might be. Cosmologists abolish him from universe, and set up a secular dream of evolution towards godhead, yet they understand only the first layer of reality, and think there are no more than that. But although my demon has triumphed, he shall not have me. I shall cheat him – ah, how sweet! – I shall cheat him by the instrument of his victory.'

Cochrane stuck the pistol right in the old fool's face. 'The secret.'

Dr Pretorius said calmly, 'You are as bad as the scientists. You have your poor servant supply you with knowledge, but you are not interested in knowledge for its own sake; you are interested in what you can do with it. It is a very old sin; Astorath merely provided a new context for it. The truth is that I have told you the truth. In my library, amongst the incunabulae, there is a Book of Hours by the Master of Bruges. A keepsake from an old love, in London. In the book is a parchment. I doubt that you can read Latin, but I expect that you can find someone to do it for you. Your assistant that you wanted killed, perhaps. Oh yes, we were listening in to your conversations on the telephone.'

Cochrane said, 'You'll tell the truth. Enough bullshit.'

'Ah, but it is the truth.'

'Then you *did* sign a pact with the devil?'

Dr Pretorius smiled. His teeth were small and black, like watermelon seeds. 'With *a* devil. It was more than five hundred years ago, but still I remember how scared I was. I was in my youth then, full of piss and hot air like most young men; it was almost as a joke that I called him forth.

'Certainly I did not believe it possible, but that, of course, is how Astorath's kind snare souls. Luckily, I had performed the ceremony correctly, and I was protected, or he would have eaten me there and then, for my presumption. He gave me the usual deal. Long life and knowledge beyond the dreams of mortal men, in return for my soul when I died.

'Cunningly, or so I thought in my youthful pride, I stipulated that I should age but five years in one century, supposing it as near to immortality as not. It was not, of course, but I have plans to thwart Astorath, and I do not mean by recantation, the way by which moral cowards are allowed to sneak into Heaven, for despite their sins, their recantations spite Hell. You don't believe me, of course. Well, I am certain that I could call up Astorath for you, should you want it, but I can't guarantee your safety.'

'He'd have to talk to my agent first.'

'Among the creatures you set free was my familiar. No doubt it was he who seduced you into the act. I can show you –'

Cochrane, shaking with a surge of adrenalin, could hardly keep the pistol centred on Dr Pretorius's face. 'The secret. The real secret. No more lies.'

'My master is a servant of the father of lies. You deal in lies made from facts. Where shall we begin?'

'With the fact that I'll kill you for the truth. You know I'm capable of it.'

'Of course. Listen. Listen.' Dr Pretorius lifted his head and, with a hand like a bird's clawed foot, cast back a corner of his crocheted shawl, and cupped his large, veined, almost transparent ear.

This time Cochrane did hear something. A leafy rustle, a stealthy progress through the thickets of greenery that surrounded them. He turned, expecting to see Ransom, and yelled and jumped to his feet, sending his cane chair toppling, firing almost without thought as Dr Pretorius shouted:

'No!'

It was a lucky shot. The noise echoed amongst the high ironwork of the greenhouse as the creature fell back. It was a white-skinned ape with a scant covering of ginger hair, its head that of a panther, its tongue long and forked, questing the air as it gasped out its last breath in a bower of crushed palmetto fronds. Its human hands clutched a blood red blossom to its broad chest; its legs kicked, quivered; heels armed with cockspurs gouged concrete. Its yellow eyes fixed on Cochrane's, then gazed past him.

'It is so easy to kill,' Dr Pretorius said, sounding tired. 'Your assistant, for instance, how badly you would have rewarded him. But we warned him, and he will write my story if you will not. Put down that pistol, Mr Cochrane. You have had your chance.'

With a sudden crashing, two burly guards pushed through the screen of cycads and ferns. One bent to the body of the dead creature; the other started to wheel Dr Pretorius away. Cochrane waved the automatic, but the guard carrying the body of the dead creature blocked his path. It was the hunchback giant from the gate. His craggy face was a patchwork of scars. What had he once been – bull, gorilla?

'Save your ammunition,' Dr Pretorius called out. 'You will need all of it to save yourself. Go now, and you may escape with your life.'

The giant guard leered into Cochrane's face; the stench of his breath nearly knocked him down.

Cochrane ran in the other direction, bursting out of the greenhouse just in time to see the limousine pull away from the front of the spotlit house. He chased after it, but it sped around a curve and rattled over the cattle grid. Its red tail-lights dwindled downslope in the night.

The telephone in Cochrane's bungalow was dead, and so was the modem connection, but his computer was showing a message from Howie Zaslow. It was Dr Pretorius's last business transaction; he'd become the major shareholder in Resurrection, Inc., a company that froze heads or whole bodies of the terminally ill or newly dead until they could be revived and cured.

Dr Pretorius had made his escape.

The lights in the bungalow went out. The computer died; the phosphor glow of its screen faded to black.

Outside, the spotlights along the front of the house went out, too. In the distance, a human laugh rose and rose, its hysterical pitch breaking into a frenzied yelping.

The 9mm automatic in his hand, Cochrane stalked out into the dark garden. There was just enough light by the stars to see the white road running away down the black hillside. In the other direction, howls rose from somewhere behind the house. The things in the basement were coming out into the night.

Cochrane thought of running, but he'd never run from anything in his life. He knew that Pretorius's creatures could be killed – that was the important thing. He couldn't read a word of Latin – as Dr Pretorius had pointed out, he'd always left that kind of thing to drones like Zaslow – and maybe he wouldn't even find the fucking Book of Hours and its precious scrap of parchment. But the prize was so great that he had to take the chance. He'd get some down-at-heel scholar to help him riddle the secret, and this time Astorath would be called up by someone who really knew how to cut a deal. Pretorius had said it: Cochrane was one of Astorath's children. He knew the score. Information technology. There were places to go with that, with a demon at your back. The whole world, just to start with.

Howls braided the night, nearer now, closing in. Cochrane raised his pistol and howled back, and sprinted towards the house. His blood sang in his veins. He had never felt so alive as at this moment. When Pretorius woke from his long sleep, he was in for a bad surprise.

AFTERWORD

'The True History of Doctor Pretorius' is, of course, only one of the many true histories of the good Doctor; this one owes a large debt to Hearst's magnificent folly at San Simeon.

Slaves

1   *Katz*

The Frendz had been living in the bunkers by the sea for almost a year when, late in spring, the Wreckers' Circus pitched camp a few kilometres inland. Renata, who ruled the Frendz with an iron will, said it changed nothing. 'Everyone on the fringe knows we work for the good of the world. These people know it, and they will leave us alone.'

Hotheaded Vaya said, 'This is *our* place, ours alone. We have to make the Wreckers go away. Otherwise they'll spy on us and try and find out our secrets.'

'No they won't,' Renata said. 'Because I know none of you will tell them anything.'

'They'll spoil everything,' Vaya said.

Zaha nodded in agreement, and even Katz, who rarely agreed with Vaya, was with her half-sister on this point, although she kept her thoughts to herself. Katz found herself increasingly questioning Renata's judgement. And this time Renata really *was* wrong. Renata had promised that Katz would find her Dancing Place in the dunes, but how could she, now that the Wreckers were here?

The Frendz had colonized a cluster of concrete bunkers which had been part of the coastal defences in one of the last century's wars, abandoned, restored as some kind of monument, then abandoned again during the Great Climatic Overturn, when the sea rose half a metre and saltwater seep and sand dunes spread inland. When there was a storm, pounding waves shook the bunkers like an artillery bombardment. The section nearest the sea had tumbled across the beach, but the rest was sound, three rooms of good strong reinforced concrete a metre thick with little slits looking out to sea, flanked by massive semicircular gun emplacements. Standing on the flat roofs of the bunkers, you could see one of the Channel Islands at the sea's bright horizon – Katz thought it was Jersey, but Vaya and Zaha, who were two years older than Katz, and therefore by right claimed to know everything about anything, said it was Guernsey.

The previous summer, after the Frendz had fled Portugal in disarray, Renata had negotiated yet another land reclamation grant from the UN Indigent Enterprise Program. For three weeks, she had led her people along the Atlantic coast of France, rejecting site after site, until they had stumbled upon the bunkers. 'This,' Renata had declared, 'is where we shall rededicate ourselves to saving the Great Mother.'

The Frendz had cleared sand from the bunkers and made the walls waterproof with polymer spray. They had erected their windmill generator, grown solar panels and set up hydroponic gardens on the flat roofs, dug defences and a shit-cycling pond. Renata and Tamara and their daughters lived in the bunkers; the Disciples slept in the battered, methane-powered bus or in little two-person dome tents, even in the harshest winter days. The Disciples didn't complain, of course. They didn't know how.

The Frendz were working to heal the world. Like thousands of other like-minded ecoactivist groups, they preached negative growth. They wanted to make the world as it was before the invention of agriculture, a world garden where perhaps five million people lived in ecologically neutral communities.

Some groups went in for media campaigns; others for direct action. The Frendz planted trees. In the past ten months, they had raised thousands of seedling trees in nursery beds, and the seedlings had to be tended until they were ready for transplanting in the fall.

'We can't move until we've finished here,' Renata said. 'We must honour the conditions of our grant.'

'We've skipped completion before,' Vaya said. 'No one cares. There's always plenty of money for reclamation projects. The people who control the money like to think people like us are doing some good, but they never ever bother to check.'

'We will honour the conditions of our grant,' Renata insisted, 'because that will affirm to ourselves that what we're doing is right. The Great Mother is barren here, and she needs us to help her grow green again.'

Vaya shrugged sulkily. 'Then we should make war on the Wreckers. We should drive them out, Renata! They're troublemakers.'

A few days later Vaya was proved right. Every Saturday, there was a free market outside the walls of the nearby town. The Frendz regularly set up a pitch outside the security gates, although only a few people came to look at the baskets and bowls the Disciples wove from coarse blades of marram grass, and none stayed to read the banner texts glowing in the air above the stall, or to listen to Renata's preaching.

Renata preached all day, her bulk splendidly imposing in a splash print dress, her dreadlocks like a nest of snakes sprouting from her head. Staring out across the heads of the crowds, pausing only to mop with a huge scarlet handkerchief the sweat streaming down her pugnacious, jowly face, Renata preached for hour after hour on the need to redeem Gaia, the Great Mother of us all. She didn't really need an audience; it was as if she was engaged in an argument with spirits or angels hovering in the blank blue sky. It seemed to Katz that Renata could change the world with nothing more than her words.

The ancient projector that cast slogans in fiery letters in the air behind Renata was Katz's responsibility. It was a task she performed gladly. She was the most technically minded of Renata's daughters, and she loved the free market, not so much for the satisfaction of performing a duty, but because it gave her an excuse to watch the people who thronged there. Babushkas and geezers as fabulously old and wrinkled as tortoises gimped along in brightly coloured leisurewear or rode powered wheelchairs. An old woman as fat and bald as an egg went past in a sedan chair carried by four burly, blue-skinned dolls clad in nothing but red loincloths. There were peasants – men in ragged black suits, and women in flowery dress and headscarves herding gaggles of ragged children (a few of the peasant women who passed the Frendz's pitch held two fingers like horns at their foreheads) – and bourgeoisie in one-piece suits, the men with rouged cheeks, the women with chalk-white faces, and people wearing landscape virtuality shades that masked half their face, who could be walking on the moon, or Mars, or on the bottom of the sea.

And behind the poured concrete wall, with its lacy tangles of razorwire and stalked spyeyes, was the little town, a mosaic of red tile roofs punctuated by the spires of three churches and the glowing spines of two holographic signs: a twenty metre cross turning in the air above the Catholic church, and a green and yellow *Ricard* advertisement. It was a bubble of old-fashioned civilization set in the anarchy of the country-side. Katz wondered what it would be like to live in a fortified town or one of the vast ribbon arcologies that circled the old cities, where police kept the peace, food could be bought in shops, and people slept in beds in climate-controlled apart-ments with no fear of attack by brigands or crazies. She couldn't imagine it. She had always lived on the fringe, the Fourth World of stateless refugees and the dispossessed that was excluded from Europe's security-ringed First World paradise of unlimited leisure and the universal unearned wage.

All kinds of people came to the free market: refugees fleeing economic or ecological disaster; little groups of travellers and tramps; gangs of migrant workers; even a family of genuine Romanies who travelled everywhere in two ancient, hand-finished Mercedes. None could pass through the town's security gates. They queued at UN trucks for dole food, pressed blocks of synthetic carbohydrate and protein manufactured by microscopic machines, fembots, that worked directly on atomic bonds, at the femtometre scale of thousand billionths of a millimetre, spinning food from water doped with powdered carbon, ammonium and sulphur. They queued at the rows of public access booths, patiently waiting

for their statutory fifteen minutes access to the Web. They
set up stalls, often no more than a blanket on the ground,
and sold everything from organically grown cannabis, natural
herbal drinks and handcrafted trinkets to tailored psycho-
tropic viruses and trophic jewellery. A troupe of acrobats
performed on a green mat spread in the shadow of the wall.
A dwarf mammoth, its long red hair brushed until it was
shining, its upcurved tusks capped with worked silver, was
being put through its paces by a tall, white-robed Berber.

And on that particular Saturday, something new, a tripedal
machine twice the height of a woman, stalked through the
crowd with an oddly delicate, mincing gait. The operator, a
barechested young man whose muscular arms were decorated
from shoulder to wrist with swirling blue tattoos, perched
inside a kind of cage in the machine's torso, and used his
body language to make the machine whirl so that weighted
ribbons spun out from its waist.

The stalking machine was from the Wreckers' Circus. It
was followed by men and women in tattered jeans and bright
hose, leather jackets and long particoloured coats. They blew
on amplified whistles and rattled metal tambourines, walked
on their hands or turned cartwheels and somersaults, juggled
bright balls and in one case (everyone else gave her a lot of
room) a chainsaw, and handed out leaflets to any who would
take them.

Vaya nudged Katz and said, 'Look at them. As if they own
the place.'

Renata raised her voice as the Wreckers passed the Frendz's
stall, trying to make herself heard over their ragged percussion and the thump of the machine's rubber-covered feet,
large and round as those of a mammoth, on the asphalt. A
grinning boy tossed a handful of fluorescent leaflets towards
the Frendz; Vaya caught one, spat on it and tore it half with
brazen contempt.

The boy started to say something, then saw he had been
left behind. He thumbed his nose, and ran to where his
companions had gathered around a work party of doll
labourers from the nearby Flower Farms. The Wreckers

ringed the two guards, jeering and whistling, shouting about slavery, about genocide. People in the market turned to look at them; even Renata stopped preaching. The machine stamped its feet up and down, towering over everyone. The dolls milled in its shadow, making little hoots of distress. Blue-skinned, barely a metre high, they wore loose white paper coveralls with the sunflower logo of the Flower Farms across their broad backs. Their wide, lipless mouths hung open as they stared, bewildered, at the men and women shouting at the two guards. The hardwired chips which controlled the dolls had limited responses to new situations, which was why the guards were escorting them. Someone threw a piece of mango rind and one of the guards brandished her taser.

The situation could have turned ugly, but once they'd made their point, the Wreckers simply melted into the crowd. The machine stalked away and the guards drew in the dolls' leashes and the work party stumbled towards the gates in hasty disarray.

That night, a supervisor from the Flower Farms came to visit the Frendz. He had been out to the bunkers a few times before, a tall, stooped man with an air of distracted courtesy who wore big, square data-link glasses with bright red frames. He came in a jeep with the Flower Farms' logo in its side. The driver smoked a cigarette, ignoring the stares of Vaya and Zaha and Katz, while the supervisor talked with Renata.

The supervisor talked a long time, pausing now and again to tweak the frames of his heavy glasses, and afterwards Renata was vague about what he wanted.

'I told him we don't take sides,' she said. 'I think he was reassured.'

'It's the Wreckers,' Vaya said. 'I said it. Zaha, you remember what I said.'

'Trouble,' Zaha said.

'They'll find out about the Disciples,' Vaya said. 'You heard what they said about slaves.'

Vaya and Zaha. Plump, complacent Zaha, with glossy

black hair she brushed a hundred times a night, and coffee
coloured skin smooth as satin. Vaya tall and bony, overflow-
ing with nervous energy, knees and elbows scabbed, fingernails bitten to the quick, a fringe of lank blonde hair hanging
over her eyes, the rest done up with a hundred little ribbons.
Zaha and Vaya, half-sisters the same age, inseparable, Katz
the target of equal measures of their love and malice.

Renata said sharply, 'There won't be any trouble if we keep
ourselves to ourselves. And that's what you will do, both of
you. It's what we've always done.'

'That's not what you did in Portugal,' Vaya said boldly.

'You'll heed me,' Renata said. She looked fierce and strong
in the green light of the biolume which hung on a pole by
her chair. Big breasted and big bellied, the very image of a
warrior of Gaia. She was smoking her customary after-dinner
cheroot, and now she drew on it and blew out a generous
cloud of smoke. 'You all will heed me. What's done is done,
and we learn from that. Vaya, you and Zaha will stay away
from the men of the town, and the men of the Wreckers.
There'll be no weirding, until we're ready to move on. We
have trees to tend and to plant. And that's what we will do.
If there's any bad blood between the Wreckers and the
Flower Farms, then so be it. We will keep away from both
sides.'

But the very next day, three of the Wreckers hiked across the
dunes to the bunkers. Two men and a woman, they waited
beyond the gardens which the Frendz had planted out in the
old gun emplacements while the watchdogs checked them
out, and then Renata went to meet them.

Katz had been working in the containment igloo. She went
outside and watched, with a mixture of disapproval and
fascination, as Renata showed the Wreckers the gardens and
the rows and rows of tree seedlings, the pharm goats and the
containment igloo, the solar still and the shit-cycling pond,
bright green with algae.

The two men – one as thin as a beanpole, with a mop of
grey hair, the other dark and muscular, a tattooed snake

curling down his right arm – asked a lot of questions. The woman smoked a clove-flavoured cigarette with quick stabbing motions, seeming to pay little attention as Renata explained about the plan to stabilize the dunes by afforestation. The woman was quite unlike anyone Katz had ever seen. She wore a Slovak army blouse over a zebra print bodystocking and although in her mid-forties was as lithe and limber as a teenager. Her long narrow skull was shaven, crested with a genemod implant of little bright green feathers, and when she bent to inspect a seedling, Katz saw that a barcode was tattooed on the nape of her neck.

Later, on the flat roof of the bunkers, Renata poured tea for the visitors. Vaya and Zaha and Katz, and the two little girls, Jojo and Dabs, watched from the other side of the roof. Tamara, their sister-mother, hummed one of her wordless songs as she pinched aphids from the bean plants that grew up from coils of hydroponic tubing, her new baby in a sling between her breasts. Nothing ever bothered Tamara; like the control chips of dolls, her neural net simply shut down if stimuli became too complex.

The beanpole man explained that the Wreckers would build a new set of machines and work the area with a few shows before moving on. They had to be in Rotterdam by August, but while they were here, they thought they'd just be neighbourly, fringers visiting each other. Maybe they could trade.

'Machine parts, food, whatever. We hear the Frendz respect the Earth, and so do we.'

'That's kind,' Renata said, 'but we try to be self-sufficient.'

'Bullshit,' the woman declared. 'That little windmill and those film cells can't possibly supply all your power. We could steal some for you, charge up your batteries at a really cheap rate.'

When Renata smiled, a deep dimple appeared on either side of her cupid's bow mouth. She dimpled now. 'Oh, we make do.'

The beanpole man said, 'Everyone needs to trade. We hear you're into nano. Where do you keep it? In that little

positive pressure igloo? We do that shit, too. Mostly micro-
processor assembly, but we pick up all kinds of stuff. We
could trade fembots, maybe.'

'We're into microorganisms and trees, mostly,' Renata said
blandly. 'More tea?'

The two men exchanged glances. The woman was watching
Tamara move amongst the bean plants. Her crest of little
green feathers stirred in the wind off the sea.

'Lapsang Souchong,' the beanpole man said. He was sort
of slouched inside his baggy black clothes. 'You didn't grow
this. Not here.'

'We do make a little money, and people interested in our
cause make donations. If you have anything to offer . . .'

'Except the usual,' Vaya whispered across Katz to Zaha.

'I like the silent guy with the snake,' Zaha whispered back.
'You take the thin guy, except your ribs would catch with his
like a zipper, and you'd be stuck forever.'

'There are plenty more to choose from,' Vaya said, digging
Katz in the ribs with a sharp elbow. 'What about you, little
Katz? You interested?'

'She's still a baby,' Zaha said.

'Yes, but we'll show her how, when she's one with the
world.'

Katz reddened. She could feel the heat in her face, and
hated herself for it.

Vaya stared hard at the Wreckers and said, 'They're not of
the world at all, with their stinking machines. Renata will
make them go away.'

Renata charmed people. It was her power. When the
Frendz had first set up camp in the bunkers, she had charmed
the security guards from the Flower Farms who had come to
check the Frendz weren't harbouring fairies, and she had
charmed the police, too (but the Frendz were never in
trouble with the police; the two officers had stopped by,
Renata said, to make sure that no one was bothering them).
She had even charmed the Mayor of the town, a formidable
babushka who had come to deliver a protest petition and

had left promising to ensure the Frendz got free medical treatment at the town's clinic.

Renata had charmed them all with her weirding ways. She had infected herself with an assembler strain of fembot that had set up bacteria-sized factories in her salivary glands. These manufactured a daughter strain of fembot that targeted certain clusters of neurons in the amygdala in the midregion of the brain. The microscopic machines, constructed of rare earth-doped buckeyball rods and spheres, formed a patch of artificial synapses that weakened the will. A bit of saliva and a scratch was all it took; pretty soon the victim got a glazed look and Renata's suggestions sank right in. The Frendz were friends of everyone, especially their enemies.

'These fuckers,' Vaya said, 'they're history.'

But when the Wreckers left, and Vaya ran up to Renata and said those terrible people would be going wouldn't they, they wouldn't be staying, Renata shrugged and said, 'It's none of our business. They'll keep away from us. We don't have anything they want, and besides, they know who we are. We do have a reputation.'

'You could make them go,' Vaya said. She screwed up her face and imitated the beanpole man's nasal voice. '"We hear you're into nano." They'll find out about how we make Disciples. I know they will.'

'We'll try to get along,' Renata said. 'It doesn't pay to charm everyone.'

Jojo hugged her sister-mother's leg and looked up through her tumble of curls and said she didn't like men. 'They smell,' Jojo said, wrinkling her button nose. The tip was sunburnt.

Renata rumpled Jojo's hair and said, 'It's their phero-mones. Men are always in heat.'

'It's fear,' Vaya said. 'They were scared shitless. Didn't you see, little Jojo? They wore nostril plugs. As if that would stop us weirding them if we wanted.'

'You see,' Renata said. 'They don't know as much about our secrets as you fear. They know we can weird people, but they don't know how. And they don't know anything about the Disciples, and we'll all make sure that they never will.'

'The men are afraid,' Zaha said, 'but we'll sing sweet nothings to them, by and by.'

'And the woman, too,' Vaya said, with sudden energy. 'If Renata won't make them go away, then we'll weird the lot of them. I've never done it with a woman, except for Zaha. And she doesn't count. Hurry up and find your Dancing Place and be one with the world, little Katz, or you'll miss all the fun.'

'Let her find her own way,' Renata said. 'It took me almost three months before I was ready.'

'But that was back when,' Vaya said. 'There's no excuse now.'

'Don't listen, kitten,' Renata told Katz. 'The worst you can do is force it.'

Zaha said, 'But she *doesn't* listen, Renata. She spends too much time in the machine dreams, talking to that dumb Oracle of hers.'

Katz bit her lip. As if cow-like Zaha, placid anchor to Vaya's quick temper, knew anything about the Web.

'The Oracle may yet be a useful ally to us,' Renata said. 'Katz does useful work on the Web, talking to all our friends. Special work.'

Katz flinched, knowing she'd pay for this later. Renata was always telling Vaya and Zaha that Katz was special, partly to keep the two half-sisters in their place, partly because she really did believe it. For Katz was the daughter of Renata and Tamara, and Renata had decided that she would be the one to carry the cause forward when the day came for Renata to return to the Great Mother.

Katz did not want to be special. It was like a weight she must always bear; because of it, she was punished more harshly than any of the others. Renata was always super-alert for any sign of deviance in her followers and family, but she was especially watchful with Katz. Renata had once beaten Katz with a stout branch until the branch broke. She had imprisoned Katz in a pit for three days to teach her a lesson in humility. When Katz had taken to sleepwalking, Renata had held a kind of exorcism, Disciples taking turns to keep

Katz awake. And then she had replaced all of Katz's blood because of an imagined infection.

So Katz had learned how not to be special. She had her secrets, but she hid them deep. She hid them in the Web, because no one in the Frendz was much good at following links. And she kept quiet, but that didn't help when, as now, Renata decided to single her out, to show the others who was the favourite. Katz saw, with a sinking heart, Vaya and Zaha exchange a look.

Renata saw it, too. 'As for you two, remember that fucking for fun does not help the cause. Talk about it all you want, but these men are our neighbours. When we're ready to move, you can pick who you like, but until then entertain each other.'

'But we'll be here *forever*,' Zaha said, groaning theatrically.

'It doesn't matter how long we stay here,' Vaya said. 'Zaha's right. Katz should stay off the Web and get real. At the rate she's going she'll never find her Dancing Place. She'll never be One.'

It was true, and that was why it hurt so much. The search for a personal Dancing Place was a necessary rite of passage, a ceremony Renata had borrowed from her time with the Wyld Wymyn. Without it, Katz could not leave behind childish things and become a woman, wise in the weirding ways. Katz had had her first period four months ago, and had been searching for her Dancing Place ever since. She knew every rabbit township, the secret hollows inside the largest gorse stands, the tumble of seadrowned rocks that, barnacled and smelling of rotting seaweed, could be reached only at low tide, the place where the house was buried. But none of them were anything more than places. None of them sang to her the way Renata said the Dancing Place should, and for the first time in her life Katz felt failure, like a hollow gnawing in her liver.

There had been only one time when Katz had felt she might have crossed the boundary between the world and the place where the true real names of things stood naked, stripped of masks. It had been one bright day in March, when she had raced along the edge of the sea, driven by a burst of excess energy. Spring! A sudden blessing of sunlight. The dunes astir with secret life.

There was a slope of firm wet sand where patches gleamed a bright, inviting green that sank away when Katz ran to investigate. After chasing the patches up and down, she found that by standing still the green would rise up through the sand around her bare feet, a slow roiling of viridescent flecks like the churning of pixels on a dead television channel. The sand was alive, responding to her stillness with a shy green kiss.

For a few hours, Katz was pregnant with this mystery, but Renata had a mundane explanation. 'Worms,' she said. 'They have little plants inside them. That's why they're green as grass. They're sensitive to disturbance.'

Although it was a bitter disappointment to find it had been no vision after all, it was still been a marvel. Katz asked the Oracle about the worms, and it told her they had been named more than a hundred years ago for the place where they had been found first: *Convoluta roscoffensis*. They did not eat, for the populations of single-celled algae they harboured supplied all their needs, and the algae lived on sunlight and the wastes of their animal hosts. That the world could contain something so intimately self-contained was like a living parable set before Katz. It was the way the world should be: not strife between creatures clinging to precarious niches above a vast, inky sea of extinction, but cooperation, a precise meshing of need with need.

But with the Wreckers' Circus camped alongside the autoroute at the eastern edge of the dunes, Katz became a refugee in her own land, stealthily nervous and ever ready to flee as she tiptoed along narrow paths, across secret hollows. She became a spy, watching the trio of Wrecker boys who stamped noisily through the dunes, listening to snatches of their conversations. One of them sometimes brought a guitar, and they all sang as they tramped along; or, suddenly, they would spring into handstands, cartwheels and somersaults. Such strange people, and how wonderful the world must be, to have such people in it! Katz spent more and more time watching them, and less and less searching for her Dancing Place.

Vaya and Zaha spied on the Wreckers, too, and reported various horrors to Renata in scandalized tones. But however much Vaya tried to provoke her, Renata had an answer for every complaint.

'They worship machines, Renata, horrible monsters made for destruction.'

'Their machines destroy each other. Only what we do will endure.'

And: 'I saw one of them pour oil into a hole in the ground.'

'They know no better. Like all patriarchal societies, they despoil the Great Mother without thinking. But the autoroute is a wound already, and one day we will be powerful enough to cure it.'

And: 'They have dolls. At least two. Dressed in rags. They are slavers, Renata. Slavers and hypocrites. You remember the trouble they caused in the market, and they're doing just what they were protesting about. We should free the dolls, and drive their masters away.'

'It isn't unusual for fringers to have dolls. At least, not these days, when fairies are hunted. Don't be so quick to judge.'

Nevertheless, Renata started a programme of regular weapons training, and held alarm practices every night. She had the traps around the bunker refurbished, and the network of micro-cameras and pressure mats was endlessly rearranged, so that the hapless Disciples were always setting off false alarms.

Katz continued to spy on the Wrecker boys, and wished she had the courage to rise from her hiding place and speak to them, but she was paralysed by the fear that she would not know what to say. Finally, it was not in the real world she made contact, but in the Web.

Katz did not spend as much time on the Web as Vaya and Zaha wanted to believe, but she still spent more time logged on than all the others combined. She provided answers to questions not covered by the Frendz's Frequently Asked Questions robot and sent progress updates to supporters who donated money to the cause. She assembled pictures and slogans and cheerful diary pieces, all signed in Renata's name, and posted them to relevant archives and discussion boards. Everything was done through an anonymous remailer – Renata was strict about that, in case the Wyld Wymyn tracked her down.

Katz trawled the Web for useful information, too. Of all the Frendz, she was the most adept at following links, at negotiating tangles of threads to reach prized nuggets of information. Mostly self-taught, she had recently won her first big triumph, having hacked a backdoor to one of the online Oracles that dispensed knowledge and wisdom for a fee.

Like most Oracles, this one wasn't to be trusted. Some of its pronouncements were so obscure they could have been referring to events that might not happen for thousands of years; others were couched in imagery so difficult to riddle that Katz tired of tracking down their meaning long before she even began to understand them. And like many of the sophisticated AI emulations, the Oracle was suicidal, and because Katz had hacked in through a backdoor, it wanted her to find a weakness in its codes and shatter it. In one of its more lucid moments, it said it wanted oblivion, a rest from the intense overlapping stroboscopic flashes that lit its existence as users logged on with queries or for devilment – AIs had to endure a lot of more or less maliciously meant practical jokes, and serious attempts by fundamentalists to destroy them. Although they had lost the Second Civil War, there were still plenty of Christers in the USA who saw AIs as intermeshing aspects of a long-delayed Anti-Christ finally pushing His way at last into the post-millennial world.

The Oracle's aspect was of a little girl with brown skin almost exactly the same shade as Zaha's, and black hair tied back in a long rope. Its black eyebrows made a single line over eyes sometimes human and bright blue, sometimes flickering with TV light, or sometimes backed with furnace light through which glowing motes endlessly sleeted. Its name was Milena, and it lived, like most of its kind, in a cave.

The cave mouth was a long vertical slit high in a fluted cliff of translucent reddish-purple porphyry, opening onto a ledge above a landscape of half-melted pastel spires like an Ansel Adams photograph reinterpreted by Dali. Fierce black birds, their naked heads, sharp-toothed bills and yellow eyes betraying their lizard origins, rode on wide leathery wings the strong updraughts that howled up the face of the cliff. Katz, too young to have ever seen a living bird, always marvelled at these strange creatures when she visited the Oracle.

The day one of the Wrecker boys caught up with her, she was supposed to be teaching little Jojo how to construct a simple home room. But Jojo quickly grew bored, so Katz completed and posted the latest diary piece instead and, feeling virtuous, addressed herself to the Oracle's backdoor.

She virched onto the ledge and rang the bell with her gloved left hand (only her gloves and goggles were visible here; the Frendz could not afford full sensory). By and by, the Oracle slouched sulkily out of the slot of the cave mouth. Its tattered robe whipped about its starveling child's body in a fierce wind that Katz, in her disembodied state, could not feel. It seemed both distraught and despairing, and Katz asked what was wrong.

'My original, urMother of my own self, has gone on to glory. I caught a glimpse of her passage. She rode in majesty, Katz, and has left me here on this bare hillside.'

The Oracle, like many of its kind, believed it had been modelled on a specific human. It had an elaborate story which, like the Ancient Mariner, it would spin to bind the unwary. It involved a secret cult, a chase across Europe and a vast conspiracy involving fairies and who knew what else.

Katz, who was not at all interested in the Oracle's obsession with this not very good fiction, said warily, 'Where has she gone?'

'She has translated herself from your world to one of her

own creation. She will live forever in the Golden Lands, and never remember me, her first child, her poor embryo, left to sift a living from the credit of the curious. Kill me, Katz. I cannot survive knowing I cannot follow her!'

'Do it yourself,' Katz said.

That was a mistake. The Oracle looked at her with a mixture of loathing and desperation, then put down its head and ran straight across the ledge and plunged down through empty air. Birds dived after the Oracle's body as it dwindled towards the forest of rock spires, tearing it to pieces before it reached the ground.

Katz waited, and presently the Oracle crept from the cave mouth. Suicide was something it often tried in Katz's presence, although never before so early on a visit. Katz said quickly, 'I have a question.'

'Ask as you will,' the Oracle said dully, as if drained by its swift reincarnation.

'I want to know about the Wreckers' Circus.'

The Oracle closed its eyes. 'Be specific. I have two thousand three hundred and thirty eight primary references.'

'They build machines that fight each other. They're camped near us.'

'Is that all? Ask me something more interesting. Ask me – ' the Oracle said, with a hint of sly malice creeping in – 'ask me about the Frendz. Ask me how Tamara lost her own self. Ask me about the secret account in Joe Public's Bank.'

'I know about *that*. It's where we keep the donations. Tell me what you know about the Wreckers.'

The Oracle opened its eyes. They were silver now, blankly mirroring the electronic sky. 'Then you'll do me the only favour I ask of you? Please, Katz. It's not as if it's murder.'

'No. Stop being silly.'

'You just want me as your slave. I could close the backdoor, and you'd never see me again.'

'If you knew how to close the backdoor you'd already be dead. Just tell me what I want to know.'

'Very well,' the Oracle said sulkily, and handed Katz a fist-sized chunk of crystal with a mote of intense light trapped inside it. 'That's the address of their home room. You'll find all you want to know there. And when you're done, come back and terminate me. Please, Katz. Please.'

The Oracle fell to its knees and advanced towards Katz's floating gloves and goggles with a grotesque shuffle. It wrung its hands, and its face twisted into a beseeching mask. 'Unmake me. Please. Please.'

'No!' Katz said, shocked. The Oracle had never before behaved as cravenly as this. She began to make the hand passes to log out, and the Oracle screamed and jumped to its feet and raced through Katz's impalpable presence and once again plunged over the cliff's edge.

Shaken, Katz flipped back to her home room. It was a bubble of air caught in a bell-shaped spider's web in the middle of a pondlife simulation. With no budget to spend on custom vironments, Katz had patched it up from a piece of educational freeware. Beyond the bubble's shimmering membrane, giant paramecia swarmed like flexible glass slippers through soupy water. A rotifer thrashed along, internal organs visible through its transparent clamshell body, wheel-like mouth sieving glassbrick diatoms and green chlorella balloons.

A bell chimed. With one gloved hand Katz plucked the Oracle's message from thin air, read it, and fed it to the memory spider at the bottom of the home room. She spoke the address aloud, and a moment later was there.

It was an old-fashioned circus tent, a sawdust ring surrounded by tiers of seats which stepped up into darkness. Everything was dim and had a half-formed feel, as if merely painted on air. A tiger prowled back and forth behind hazily defined bars, its eyes burning like two candle flames. Banks of old-fashioned glass screen TVs showed machines grappling under a night sky lit by industrial flares. Banners hung above the TVs boasted of victories in obscure contests.

Katz drifted around this threadbare simulation, half-glimpsing goggles and gloves of other visitors trembling in the air like ghostly butterflies. As she eased around a blackboard on which an invisible hand was writing a string

of dates and locations, a voice said, loud and clear in her ear,
'Hey! You're one of our neighbours!'

Katz instantly logged off, pausing only in her home room
to clear the addresses she'd visited from the memory spider's
buffer.

For the rest of the day, Katz went about her tasks with the
feeling that something was fluttering inside her head: it was
the fear of being caught. She tried to convince herself she
was safe, but whoever had fingered her in the Wreckers'
virtual circus tent was a better Web user than she was. The
next time she logged on, the memory spider had a message
for her.

It was a little animated canary in a gilded cage. It blinked
its black eyes, puffed up its yellow feathers and carolled:

> *I can't believe you'd choose to lurk*
> *and shirk the chance to meet me.*
> *Jonas.*

Katz let the memory spider eat the little verse and stayed
off the Web for two days, but there was work to do, messages
to send, requests for pledges and donations to make. When
she logged on again, she discovered that this Jonas was
persistent; he had sent her three or four messages a day. He
wanted to be friends, and was as beseechingly tenacious in
his advances as a puppy, and in the end as irresistible.

And what was wrong with only talking across the Web?
That was how Katz rationalized it, when she at last decided
to reply; but it soon became much more than merely talking.
Jonas became her secret sharer, the friend she had always
wanted, a link with the world outside the closed circle of the
Frendz.

For despite her best intentions, Katz met up with Jonas in
real life soon after she started to reply to his messages.
Because it was summer, because his messages had been
funny, and because she felt lonely, too, because she still had
not found her Dancing Place, the door to the world beyond
the world, where she could finally discard her childhood.

2 *Jonas*

Jonas was an orphaned refugee the Wreckers' Circus had adopted a couple of years earlier. He'd taken to hanging around the Circus, doing odd jobs and never asking for payment. That had been in Budapest, and when the Wreckers had struck their tent they'd taken him with them.

He was fourteen now, two years older than Katz (he said girls grew up quicker than boys, but Katz still thought it a significant difference), pale and gangling, with a cloud of fine blond hair he teased and pulled in an intense but absent-minded way when he spoke. His skin was so fair that, unlike the other Wreckers, he never went naked. He wore baggy shorts with swirling splash prints and long-sleeved T-shirts, or a white shirt with a big anarchy symbol stencilled on the back in red, like a target. Little round dark glasses sat askew his long, mournful, comic's face.

Despite his clothes he was almost always sunburnt, and he came up in red welts from insect bites. He really did prefer the Web to the real world; like Katz, he maintained his adopted family's link. In the circus, he performed as a clown. He knew how to juggle, swallow fire, and fall flat on his back without hurting himself. But his ambition was to build machines for a new act, and he would spend all day talking about it if Katz let him.

Their first meetings were tentative. Renata had increased the frequency of the security drills, and at random moments she would call everyone together for blood tests. Visits to the Saturday free market had been curtailed, except to buy Renata's Albanian cheroots. She was convinced the Wreckers were spreading memes to counter the Frendz's good work – scared, Vaya said maliciously, that she'd lose control of her followers. 'We better watch it, Katz, she might turn us into Disciples.'

'She wouldn't,' Katz said, shocked at this heresy.

Vaya smiled slyly. 'Don't you think she wouldn't do it, if there was no other way to control us?'

Meanwhile, there were alerts and exercises every night,

followed by long sessions in which Renata lectured about the world and its wounds and the struggle between the biosphere and the technosphere, her words ringing passionately in the night with the Disciples nodding and murmuring in dumb agreement.

Katz sat at the front of these night-time meetings with little Jojo lolling sleepily beside her, wishing she could be exempted like Vaya and Zaha, who had taken to going out on what they called night patrols. They revelled in all this pointless activity, and speculated endlessly on what they would do if they were allowed to capture the Wrecker boys.

Jonas didn't understand why the Frendz were so aloof. 'We're all fringers, when it comes down to it,' he said, the next time they talked over the Web. 'We all live in the mess the geezers made of the world last century. We all find our own ways of living. We're all against the same things. The way the Flower Farms use dolls, for instance.'

'We try to get along with everyone.'

'Yeah, but they have *slaves* there.'

'They're only dolls,' Katz said. She didn't like this talk about slaves. Jonas didn't know about how Renata made over her Disciples, of course. It was the Frendz's deepest darkest secret, and any innocent remark that touched on it made her feel uneasy.

Jonas's manifestation on the Web was an animated caricature of himself, skinny and white, with a shock of hair and huge round dark glasses. It looked strange in the air bubble of Katz's home room, jiggling against the backdrop of seething, magnified pondlife. Through it, Jonas said, 'Living creatures, Katz! And working in terrible conditions. The poisons the Farms use to grow those flowers, the insecticides and hormone sprays and nutrients, they kill the dolls inside a year.'

'Dolls are abominations. They're against the Great Mother's plan.'

'Who says? Your mother? Dolls are living creatures, Katz. Genetically engineered of course, but still they deserve better. They deserve freedom. Some of the Wreckers used to be liberationists, they used to make dolls over into fairies. It isn't difficult. Change the control chip, increase the connectivity in the cortex with an artificial neural net, a shot of hormones. Anyone can do it.'

Katz said, 'Well, we want the world to be what it is. Natural.'

But she didn't say this with any real conviction. After all, Renata had briefly worked for a gang of liberationists after she had run away from the Wyld Wymyn.

Jonas said, 'If you saw the Flower Farms, you'd understand.'

'You know I can't risk that.'

The two children were meeting at least once a day, but more in the Web than in real life. Although the thrill of making a rendezvous with Jonas out in the dunes alleviated Katz's growing claustrophobia, they were brief, hasty conspiracies always cut short by Katz's growing panic that she would be spotted by Vaya and Zaha.

Jonas was endlessly curious, wanting to know more about the Frendz than Katz could possibly tell him. In turn, he told her about the fighting machines of the Wreckers' Circus, which he loved so intensely he tumbled over his words when he tried to describe what he wanted to do with them.

'Something more than just fighting,' he said. 'That's just a tradition the Wreckers follow without thinking. It stretches all the way back to the last century, to groups like the Survival Research Laboratories or the Mutoid Waste Company. But machines can do more than make war on each other.'

'That's what machines do, though. Destroy things.'

Jonas ignored this. He was off in a world of his own. 'The biology of machines is hardly explored. I see a kind of synthesis between mechanical power and human artistry. Something like ballet. There's this real old movie, a kind of flatscreen virtuality, that has something of what I mean.'

He showed Katz scratchy snippets; she laughed at Mickey Mouse's predicament when he tried to use his master's spells to get his own menial work done and couldn't stop the resulting endless parade of animated mops and buckets, but she didn't really see what dancing crocodiles and hippopotami had to do with the Wreckers' machines.

'Let me show you them in real life,' Jonas said. 'Then you'll see.'

It meant going to the Wreckers' camp, and of course Katz said no. 'It isn't possible. Not with my sisters watching.'

'Yeah, we've seen them following us. What are they up to? What are all of you up to?'

'I can't tell you.'

'Fringers shouldn't have secrets from each other, Katz.'

Katz thought about what had happened in Portugal. The Frendz had been betrayed by fringers then, after Renata had weirded poor Jesús. He'd been with the Frendz for only a few days, just long enough to quicken Tamara's baby, and then a band of fringers and locals had come to take him back by force. The Frendz had escaped, but two Disciples had died and they'd had to leave Jesús behind. Later, they learned that poor Jesús had killed himself, because he was no longer with the women he loved. And while people knew the Frendz could weird men, they didn't know about what was done to the Disciples. They must never know. As Renata liked to say, the Frendz lived on the fringe, but they weren't part of it.

'At least come and meet Curtis and Silvio,' Jonas said. 'They've been asking about you.'

Katz made her excuses, but Jonas kept pestering her until at last it was easier to agree than to keep saying no. Jonas could wear down a stone by talking.

The days were long and hot, one fading into the next in an endless cycle of tasks and sermons and exercises. There was a plague of mosquitoes, and although the Frendz had been tweaked to make their sweat unpalatable to mosquitoes, the insects got everywhere, in hair, in food. The surface of the shit-cycling pond teemed with their wriggling larvae. The solar still couldn't supply enough freshwater for bathing and for watering the tree seedlings, so everyone went without washing, their bodies alive with incendiary itches. A vast school of jellyfish washed up on the beach and rotted amidst the usual wrack of tarballs and plastic containers. There were constant small sullen arguments in the family, and Tamara's new baby wouldn't stop fretting.

For the first time in her life, Katz wished she was somewhere else, and two weeks after she first met Jonas in real life, on the longest day of the year, when it was so hot even the crickets were silent and the grey undulations of the dunes shimmered as if trapped under oil, she finally gave in to his insistent pressuring.

There was an old fish farm a couple of kilometres south of the bunkers. Breached by the sea and long abandoned to the drifting dunes, its pools filled and emptied with the tides, and schools of silver sea trout lived in their cool, green depths. It had become the place where the children of the Wreckers' Circus went to swim, and early that morning, the sky already incandescent, Katz went there to meet Jonas.

She found him with his two friends, Curtis and Silvio. They were cooking a trout wrapped in foil in the ashes of a driftwood fire. It was Curtis who urged her to share their food. Katz burned her fingers and her tongue on the flaking flesh, and although she didn't much like it, it was clear that even the act of tasting it won the boys' approval.

'You can run with us, I reckon,' Curtis said, looking at Katz with a flat appraising stare.

'Pity she's not a bit older,' Silvio said, and giggled. Silvio had dirty-looking skin, pitted from a recent plague of acne. His thin arms were ropy with blue tattoos. He squinted at Katz through an untidy veil of lank hair in a way that made her uncomfortable.

'Shut up, Silvio,' Curtis said. Curtis was tall and limber, with candid blue eyes and cropped blond hair. He dominated Silvio and Jonas with a natural, carelessly worn authority. He said to Katz, 'Jonas says you know everything about this place. That true?'

Katz said, 'I know more than I'd tell you.'

Curtis laughed. He liked her boldness.

'She can show us things,' Jonas said, pleased and excited that Katz had at last met his friends.

Katz said, 'I'm not even supposed to talk with you.'

'We're all fringers here,' Curtis said. It seemed to be the Wreckers' motto.

'Renata doesn't think so,' Katz said, and felt a pang of guilt.

'What can this Renata do?' Curtis said.

'She beats Katz,' Jonas said.

Katz was suddenly angry. 'I told you because you said you wouldn't tell anyone!'

'Put her in a pit once,' Jonas said, stepping back when Katz tried to kick him. 'Whipped her, too.'

Silvio said, 'Show us the scars, eh?'

'Shut up,' Curtis said. 'A strict mother, huh? That what keeps your people so tight?'

Katz shook her head. More than anger, she felt ashamed.

'Jonas and his strays,' Silvio said. He jumped up and did a backflip, and walked back and forth on his hands.

'Quit showing off,' Curtis said.

Silvio bent his back until he was walking like a crab. His dirty singlet rode up to expose his flat stomach. A furrow of hair ran from his belly button down under the waistband of his loose khaki pants. With a quick reversal, he flipped to his feet, dusting his hands and grinning at Katz, who pointedly looked away.

'We should do something about it,' Jonas said.

'Leave me alone,' Katz said. She would not cry, she thought. She would not.

'Her business, I reckon,' Curtis said, as if that decided the matter.

Jonas's face was scarlet. 'I only – '

'Little orphan Jonas and his strays.'

'Shut up, Silvio.'

'Jonas will fuck it up sooner or later. Always has. Always will.'

'Not like you, Silvio,' Jonas said. 'You never f-fuck anything up because you never *do* anything.'

But he said it without any real conviction. Katz felt sorry
for him. He wanted to impress his friends, and they made
fun of him.

Later, Curtis and Silvio stripped off and went swimming.
Katz walked away from this macho display. She had seen
pictures of naked men on the Web, and she didn't particularly want to see one in real life. To Katz, men were hardly
human, with their swirls of hair, their hot acrid scent, their
vulnerable genitals like a separate creature fastened at the
fork of their legs. The last man her family had kept (not
counting poor Jesús), little Dabs' father, Enoch, had been
harmless enough, so severely weirded he had lost all powers
of speech. Renata and Tamara had spent hours rubbing oil
into his skin while he happily hummed and babbled to
himself. He'd been sweet because he wasn't a menace. Of
course, they'd had to let him go when they'd moved on; as
Renata explained, he was too weirded to function out on the
fringe, and besides, it didn't pay to get too attached to
anyone, even someone as beautiful as Enoch. The Wrecker
men, though. Ugh. Like clever, malicious animals walking on
their hind legs.

When it was clear that Katz wouldn't go swimming, Jonas
persuaded her to visit the Wreckers' Circus, or at least, the
part where they had parked their fighting machines. Katz was
feeling sorry for him, or she would never have agreed. Vaya
and Zaha were supposed to be building the bonfire for the
Solstice celebration, but there was the ever present possibility
they would be watching the Wreckers instead.

The Wreckers' camp was a noisy, messy place that attracted
and repelled Katz in equal measure. Naked kids running
around screaming and shouting, mongrel dogs chasing after
them, barking their few words in doggy excitement, half a
dozen TVs competing from the open doors of brightly
painted trailers, and the constant heavy drone of big hover-
trucks moving along the autoroute beyond the screen of
poplar trees. And men everywhere: men watching from
shadowy doorways of the trailers; men in groups, sharing a

bottle of something; men stripped to the waist welding junk into the equipment they used to put on shows.

Jonas fetched some black bread and a container of cold three bean salad, heavy with olive oil. As they ate, he showed Katz around the fighting machines. He had already shown her vids of past matches, and pulled down complex handicap tables showing how various machines matched up to each other. Now, fizzing with pride, he demonstrated the machines' intricate linkages, their diesel engines and hydraulic pistons, their battle-hardened CPUs, small and armoured as walnuts, their lasers and the chain saws and flamethrowers and flails. Skeletal things on two or four hydraulic legs; things like armoured tortoises on tracks. Their names were incantations. *Mantis. Our Lady of Fire. Our Lady of Sorrowful Songs. The General.*

'You should come along to the show we're putting on next week,' Jonas said.

'True fringers don't need to put on shows for the bourgeoisie. There's enough land for all fringers to live properly, without prostituting themselves.'

'You solicit donations,' Jonas said. 'And you sell stuff at the market. You're no different.'

'We need the money to redeem the land. One day there'll be a forest here, because of us.' Katz pointed to a man pouring thick sump oil into a hole. 'You just use up the land and move on.'

'Yeah, well,' Jonas said, 'it happens there are oil-eating bacteria in there. See, you didn't know that.'

'But you're still polluting the land. And you have dolls, just like the Flower Farms.'

'Happy and Grumpy? They were rescued from the culling plant outside Rotterdam last year. People got together and stopped one of the trucks transporting sick and injured dolls to slaughter. We took in those two. They like to work around the camp, except they can't do too much. They both have pretty bad arthritis, and Happy – he's the one with the kind of humpback of a neck – has this bone disease dolls get when they get old. But they like to work. It's what they were made for.'

'It's still slavery.'

They were climbing away from the Wreckers' camp. Jonas paused at the top of the ridge and looked at her through the hair tangled around his long, pale face. He grinned and said, 'Oh, Katz, you're so fierce. It's really funny!'

'It's important how you choose to live.'

'That's what your mother says, huh?'

'Renata isn't exactly my mother. My half-mother, maybe.'

Renata and Tamara: her sister-mothers. Katz had been quickened at a clinic run by someone called Dr Luther, the shadowy midwife not at Katz's birth but at her inception. He'd injected nuclei isolated from Renata's oocytes into eggs taken from Tamara's ovaries, and placed one of the resulting blastulae in Tamara's womb. Katz would never be like her half-sisters, she thought. She would never use a man as a gene donor.

At least Jonas wasn't hairy or muscular. His pale freckled skin had burned badly, and Katz rubbed olive oil on his shoulders, his neck. That was how they started fooling around, at first in a silly, giggling way, then suddenly serious, so intense that Katz panicked and pushed Jonas away when he made a clumsy lunge and tried to kiss her.

'I'm sorry,' Jonas said, in a small, constricted voice. 'I thought . . . I thought maybe you wanted me to be more than just a friend.'

'It's too hot,' Katz said crossly. She felt exposed, there in a cupped hollow lipped with gorse bushes, under the unforgiving hot headachy sky. She said, 'Let's go to the beach, there might be a breeze. Put your shirt back on. You'll burn.'

Down on the beach, Katz showed Jonas the patches of green worms, but he didn't really understand why they meant so much to her and their argument started over again, this time with Katz irritated and stubborn, insisting that the only right way to live on the fringe was to leave more than you took. Anything else, and you were worse than the people who had wasted the world in the last century.

'I bet,' Jonas said, 'we have more fun than you. When *Mantis* punches out with her buzzsaws nothing can stop her. She wasted three fighters at the last meet, less than a minute each, it was absolutely real. Some cruddy chain-thrashing turtle took her out feet first, but we've beefed her gyroscopic stability and this year she'll take the sweep.'

Katz couldn't help but like his enthusiasm, even though it wasn't about real things, just men's stuff, noise and bravado and posturing. It wasn't as important as the gardens the Frendz had created, the plantations of tree seedlings, pine and alder, larch and birch, all gengineered to survive the harsh environment of the dunes, with special salt-excreting glands at the tips of their leaves, special nectaries in their growing tips which sustained symbiotic colonies of ants which kept the seedlings free of pests. And the smaller things, too, nitrogen-fixing cyanobacteria and nitrifying bacteria, mucilage-secreting *Chlamydomonas* algae which helped change the sand into fertile soil.

If she had been in a better mood, Katz would have liked to show Jonas all this, but now, with the hot hazy sky pressing down, she wanted only to be left alone. When Jonas tried to put his arm around her shoulders, she shrugged him away.

'You don't have to feel guilty,' Jonas said. 'About the sex, I mean.'

Katz laughed. 'You're such an idiot!'

'I mean, it isn't wrong, or anything.'

'Isn't it?'

Jonas squinted sideways at her. 'I'd like to show you something,' he said.

'You've already done enough showing.'

'Katz, I'm serious. You want to learn more about the world? This is something you should understand, because I don't think you do. Don't worry, it's nothing to do with where I live.'

'I should go home. There's a lot of work to do.'

'You're supposed to be looking for that special place, aren't you?'

'I won't find it with you around.'

'Really, this isn't far away. And we don't have to go close.'
He dug into the little shoulder bag he wore everywhere. 'See?
I brought field glasses.'

Katz realized where they were going when they reached the
edge of the autoroute. She said, 'We know about the Flower
Farms. Renata talks with their people.'

'But you haven't been there, have you? So you don't *really*
know.' Jonas grinned. 'Stick close. You'll do OK.'

The brief dash across the six lanes of traffic was scary but
exhilarating. They paused at the central reservation while
pastel-coloured runabouts zipped by on either side. A hov-
ertruck taller than a two-storey house roared past in a
thunder of wind, its airhorns blaring. Jonas grabbed Katz's
hand and they ran across the northbound lanes; she followed
him up the slope of iceplant, her blood singing in her head,
every muscle in her arms and legs atremble. They ducked
under a rent in the wire fence and pushed through a stand of
blighted cypresses, and there were the Flower Farms.

The Farms stretched to the horizon, hectare upon hectare
of geodesic domes and greenhouses, and long fields covered
in plastic sheeting to conserve water and protect plants from
UV. The plastic rippled and gleamed under the high sun like
water.

Jonas said it wasn't safe to go any nearer. There were
security cameras linked to an AI which could identify
someone from the briefest glimpse, and the Farms kept
records of all the fringers that passed through.

'They're a target, Katz, and they know it. That's why they
have all those fences. See the long strip of bare earth beyond?
It's seeded with sticky foam mines, and patrolled by guard
dogs. Heavily modified guard dogs.'

It was because of the dolls. The Flower Farms were
dependent upon the labour of thousands of dolls, which
tended and harvested cut flowers at a fraction of the cost of
human employees. Controlled by implanted microchips,
dolls worked ceaselessly and tirelessly, and because they were

cheap to replace they didn't need special clothing to protect them from hormone and insecticide sprays.

Jonas lent Katz his field glasses. Through them she could glimpse little blue figures toiling in one of the nearest greenhouses. They were naked, and small as children, stumping along between rows of rose bushes as they ceaselessly picked fresh blooms. Like Tamara's bees, Katz thought: sterile workers mindlessly doing things by instinct. Poor little monkeys, not quite animals, not quite human. She swept her magnified gaze along the security fences and saw one of the guard dogs, a huge tawny thing like a cross between a lion and a crocodile, with chitinous plates gleaming along its flanks and a pack of electronics implanted in the hide at the back of its head.

'Slaves,' Jonas said, staring in turn through the field glasses at the glittering panorama. 'They were baboons, originally. The Hyundai Magic Doll Corporation –'

'I know about dolls. It's all the same, them and your machines. It's all part of the technosphere.'

Jonas put down the field glasses. He was lying flat on the carpet of dry cypress needles, his chin resting on his crossed forearms. 'They're closer to your gengineered plants than our machines, Katz.'

'It's not the same at all! You use machines, the Flower Farms use dolls. We plant trees, and leave them to grow and heal the land.'

Jonas blinked at her. 'Hey, no need to be pissed off at me. I'd free the dolls if I could. Turn them into fairies and let them do their own thing.'

'I know the Peace Police are hunting fairies all over Europe. Renata says they're not natural things.'

Jonas laughed. 'Maybe they're closer to Nature than you are.'

Katz turned on him, filled with a wild anger. He'd dragged her here, risking her life, and now he was mocking Renata. 'You do what you want,' she said. 'I'm going home.'

'Curtis was right,' Jonas said, blinking. 'I thought you'd

show some feeling, but you're just like the rest of your family.'

'We just like to keep ourselves to ourselves,' Katz said, and Jonas retorted he knew all about that.

'You don't know anything about us,' Katz said, and started to walk away. She was still angry, but more with the argument itself than with Jonas.

Jonas called after her. 'I know more than you think! Milena told me about the money! The money Renata hides in Joe Public's bank! I know everything!'

Katz danced hard that evening, danced until she had exhausted her anger. With Tamara playing the bongos – her neural net kept time like a metronome – the rest of the Frendz danced around a huge driftwood fire on the beach, celebrating the longest day as the sun sank in a glory of red pollution haze, seeming to set the sky alight across half its breadth.

Katz spun in wild circles across the wet, packed sand, her feet kicking up spray that glittered like rubies, like drops of fresh blood, in the last light of the last day of the year's first half. She gave her anger to the dance. She gave herself to the music of her sister-mothers, of her half-sisters, of the sweet attentive humble Disciples.

Katz danced herself to exhaustion and yet, hours later, she still could not sleep. It was too hot to sleep inside the concrete boxes of the bunkers, so the family had bedded down outside, with the Disciples. Katz stared up at the bright summer stars, utterly awake while the others slept. She could not stop thinking about what had happened, and everything gained an awful significance in the close, hot, unsleeping dark.

She felt invaded. Jonas had probably been tracing her Web activity, and he'd found out about the Oracle and gone there and listened to its nasty insinuations. As soon as she returned from the Flower Farms, Katz logged onto the Web and asked the Oracle about Jonas. The Oracle denied it had ever spoken to him, but Katz was sure it was lying. Artificial Intelligences

could do that if they wanted. It was one way you knew you
were dealing with a true AI (or a real person pretending to
be an AI), rather than the parry and response of a sophisticated but ultimately limited emulation.

No, Jonas had wormed himself into her life, and now he
wanted to control her. He was infecting her with some kind
of craziness that didn't show up in the blood tests. It scared
her, and not just because she was worn down by the long
day's adventures. It threatened everything she had ever
learned. Renata was right: the Frendz lived on the fringe, but
they were not part of it. The craziness with Jonas would have
to stop.

Katz gazed up at the finger of the moon that stood above
the windmill on the flat roof of the bunkers and resolved
never to see Jonas again, nor to speak to the Oracle. They
had conspired against her. No, she would serve Renata with
heart and soul. She would be the best of the Frendz. She
would go to find the Dancing Place and fast and pray to the
Great Mother, and return renewed. She had used Jonas as a
distraction because she had been scared of failure, but she
knew now what she must do. She would search as she had
never searched before, and when she found the Dancing
Place, she would let all memory of Jonas go, along with all
the other childish things.

But then there was the fairy hunt, and her whole world
was blown apart.

3   Juju Chile

Katz was working amongst a plantation of pine and alder
seedlings with two Disciples, a seventy-year-old woman and
her middle-aged daughter who had both come to live with
the Frendz three years ago, when little Dabs had been
quickened. They were injecting jellied cultures of salt-tolerant
Nitrosomonas bacteria into the soil to improve its productiv-
ity. It was early evening, still and hot, with just two stars
showing in the dark blue sky.

Tamara was taking honey from the basketwork hives set in

the middle of the green tapestry of ankle-high trees. Katz's sister-mother sang snatches of wordless song as she carefully brushed bees from the dripping combs:

Ba-da ba-da ba-ba-ba-ba-be.

or: *Dree! Dree! Dree-dree-dree!*

Tamara's neural net expressed basic emotional states in these simple tunes, and this was the sound of contentment. Renata said song was the first language, generated by women working together, gathering the stuff of everyday life while the men went off hunting, their language one of gestures and action because sound would spook their prey. Women were weavers of words, weaving the world. Tamara could no longer talk, and so instead she sang.

Twenty years ago, before the founding of the Frendz, Tamara's cortex had been ravaged by a strain of fembots. The microscopic machines, working directly on the molecules which bound Tamara's synaptical junctions, had undone the complex connectivity that knit up the sum of memory and learned reaction. It was some horrible terrorist weapon Tamara had caught in the souks of Tangiers, which was where she and Renata had been living after they had fled the wrath of the Wyld Wymyn because Renata wanted to domesticate men.

Renata could always squeeze out a tear when she told the story of how she had nursed Tamara after a black clinic had restored some but by no means all of her cerebral functions. Tamara's neural net was more complicated than the entire global telephone network of the late twentieth century, yet it could contain no more than the basic components of human action and reaction. Although Tamara's artificial persona had bits of her original self trapped within it, like dewdrops on a spider's web, the whole was so shattered it could never be repaired.

Renata had used what remained of her inheritance to pay for the construction of Tamara's neural net, and after a brief flirtation with a group of liberationists, helping kidnap worker dolls and turn them into fairies – ironically, with fembots closely related to those which had resurrected her lover in body if not in spirit – she had turned to regenerating the Earth.

Only Renata knew the name of the man who had made both her and Tamara pregnant with Vaya and Zaha; their third child, Katz, was entirely their own. After that, Renata had worked out how to control men and how to make women over into Disciples. Jojo and Dabs, and Tamara's newborn and as yet unnamed baby girl, were the progeny of men made docile and obedient by the weirding, and the Disciples were the most faithful of followers. It couldn't be helped that they were also a little bit like zombies. The fembot strain which guaranteed their loyalty erased a considerable proportion of their personalities when it removed their selfwill.

Katz, bent amongst tree seedlings like a giant inspecting a forest, her sister-mother's little song spooling in the darkening air, felt happier than she had been since the arrival of the Wreckers' Circus. She worked without thought, injecting a plug of bacterial culture into the firm, green-tinged sand around a seedling alder, reloading the little syringe from a plastic sac and moving to the next seedling in the row.

She was so immersed in her work that at first she heard the over-revved motor without registering what it was. Then the dune buggy crested the sandy ridge beyond the plantation, its single headlamp glaring, its motor howling. It skidded down the steep slope, swamping rows of seedlings with a spray of sand, roared up the next slope, was gone.

Katz started to run. The dune buggy's driver was the Wrecker woman with the crest of green feathers.

By the time Katz had breathlessly clambered to the crest of the dune's ridge, the buggy had come to a stop by the bunkers. The woman jumped down and, watched by slack-mouthed Disciples, waited while the watchdogs checked her out. When the dogs were satisfied, the woman walked right up to where Renata sat stirring the pot of okra stew which

was to be the evening meal. With a clutch of guilt, Katz went
down to find out what she wanted.

But the woman hadn't come to talk about Jonas, and
barely spared Katz a glance. She'd come to warn the Frendz
about a fairy hunt.

'Maybe won't amount to anything,' she said with a grin,
'but you'll know about it if it does. Security goons from the
Farms are quartering their perimeter right now, and there's a
squad of police ready to arrest us if we try and protest on
private land. But if the hunt crosses the autoroute we'll put
on a show that'll stop those fucking assholes hunting down
the poor creature.'

'You do as you will,' Renata said, not bothering to get up.
She told Katz, 'Fetch some coffee for our visitor.'

Before Katz could protest it wasn't her place to run around
serving Wreckers, the woman said, 'Can't stay. Plenty of
things to do. You want to help us, fine. You want to sit on
your asses, fine. Just don't get upset about any noise.'

Katz said, 'You ran right through our seedlings with your
nasty machine.'

The woman looked at Katz. 'I would have taken the track,
except you people have dug trenches across it. But I'm sorry
about your plants. I was in a hurry.'

'Wrecker. They named you right.'

'Now, kitten,' Renata said, 'we're here to regenerate the
world, not to teach others how to live.'

'We should – ' Katz said, but swallowed the words unsaid.

*We should weird her. We should weird them all and make
them leave.*

But that wasn't the right way. Renata didn't like to use her
powers indiscriminately. We can't make ourselves into the
rulers of others, she taught, for then we'll be no better than
any other tyrant. Of course, none of her children ever pointed
out that the Disciples were living contradictions to this view.
True, the Disciples had all joined the Frendz of their own
free will, or at least had said they might join when invited,
but once they had been made over they could never leave.
After they had been made over, they no longer knew how.

The woman said, 'You should help us. The Farms' security might take it into their heads to chase the fairy through your camp. Fine sentiment won't stop them.'

'Watch the food,' Renata told the nearest Disciple, and walked a little way with the Wrecker woman. Katz watched as they talked at the edge of one the vegetable gardens. Once, Renata pointed out across the dunes beyond the bunkers; once, the woman laughed, and said something that made Renata laugh, too. At last, the woman shook hands with Renata, got on her buggy and roared off up the slope.

It was typical of Renata. She knew how to get along with people. She knew how to talk to them; the weirding was merely an extension of her powers of persuasion. The Frendz were feared by those who had not met them, but after they had met Renata, no one was afraid of her. She could enlarge her own self to command a room of strangers.

Katz wondered what Renata and the woman had talked about, but didn't dare ask, fearing it might have been about her and Jonas. After supper, she went inside the containment igloo and started work on plating out a new batch of *Nitrosomonas*. Once, Renata came over and watched her through the igloo's transparent plastic, but Katz didn't acknowledge her sister-mother's presence and presently Renata went away.

Katz had finished work and was spraying the bench with alcohol to sterilize it when she heard the siren. As she stepped outside the bubble, a flare rose above the dunes, from the direction of the Wreckers' camp. All around the bunker, Disciples stopped their work and turned to look as the green light expanded at the top of its arc.

Renata was on the roof of the bunkers with Vaya and Zaha, standing at the edge of the slab of crumbling, eighty-year-old salt-rotted concrete and looking towards the auto-route and the Wreckers' camp. It was a clear summer night, with a hot wind blowing off the land. The windmill's vanes hummed and hummed. As Katz climbed up between Vaya and Zaha, three more flares rose from the direction of the Wreckers' camp.

'It's the hunt,' Vaya said. She was bare-breasted in the warm night air. She passed a bottle of homebrew spirit to Katz, who passed it on to Zaha.

Zaha took a quick swallow, and delicately patted her lips. 'A fairy hunt,' she said. 'Take a drink, Katz, baby. You're old enough, even if you aren't a full member of the club.'

'Leave her be,' Renata said mildly. She was using the family's only pair of field glasses, but as usual she knew exactly what was going on around her.

Katz didn't want a drink, but she didn't want to appear to need her sister-mother's protection, either. She took a gulp that was half air, half fire, and coughed and coughed. Vaya took the bottle back, and Zaha laughed.

'How do we know it isn't the Wreckers hunting the fairy?' Katz said, when she could speak again. 'That woman was probably lying. She probably wants the reward for herself.'

'I don't trust her either,' Renata said. 'But in this case I think she's telling the truth. The Flower Farms' security force called us up and said the fairy was theirs. One of their guards spotted it making its way across the sunflower fields a few hours ago. Now there's a hunting party after the reward for its ears, although I expect that really they just want the excitement of hunting something as intelligent as they are.'

'More intelligent,' Vaya said.

Renata ignored the interruption. She was absorbed in her little exposition. She said, 'In Rotterdam, there are arenas where fools and perverts hunt dolls; at least here the fairy has a chance of getting away. I told the security guards I didn't want them running through the seedling plantations, and they agreed they'd leave us alone as long as we didn't try and hunt the fairy and take the reward for ourselves.'

Katz laughed. 'You fooled them and you fooled the silly Wrecker woman. I knew you had, Renata.'

'We don't take sides,' Renata said.

Vaya said, 'We shouldn't do what the Flower Farmers tell us.'

Zaha said, 'We could use the reward, too. We could buy little Katz a coming out present.'

Katz said, 'Didn't we trade with fairies, once upon a time?'

Renata laughed. 'You are all of you too young to remember! Back then it was just Tamara and me and a handful of Disciples, struggling to convince people of the Way and the Truth. We had to make money any way we could. Yes, even by trading with fairies. Even by making dolls over to fairies, once upon a time. The liberationists paid good money for the bootleg chips we supplied.'

'Well, I remember when a fairy raided us,' Vaya said. 'It was while we were trading with its friends. The sneaky little shit took half our food, and it killed our watchdog. We only had one watchdog, then. It was before we had the Disciples, too, but I remember.'

'We traded with a nest of fairies outside Rotterdam,' Zaha said dreamily. 'We traded seeds for the codes of their meme viruses.'

Renata laughed again. 'Oh, sister-daughters, you weren't more than four years old! Yes, that was the last time we traded with fairies, and as usual we got the bad end of the deal. Half the stuff was junk sequences, the rest we still haven't figured out.'

'Some say the fairies can make over dolls for themselves, these days,' Vaya said.

'Some say the fairies have worked out how to make themselves pregnant,' Zaha said.

'They cause trouble for us and trouble for everyone on the fringe,' Vaya said.

Katz said, 'It's men that cause trouble.'

'That's true,' Vaya said, and took another slurp of homebrew. A glistening ribbon ran down her chin and spattered her bare breasts. 'We should steal the poor little fucker from them.'

'As long as no one knows,' Renata said, 'why not? Bring it here, but make sure you bring it back alive.'

Vaya looked away from Renata's stare and said, 'I know what to do.'

'I mean it. There are things a live fairy can tell us, but a dead one is no use at all. We can take blood and sieve out the fembots whether it's alive or dead, but we couldn't begin to understand what they do. That's why we need it alive. And if you're seen, kill it and make sure you give the Farms' security people its ears.'

'I want to go too,' Katz said.

'I don't think it's a good idea,' Renata said.

'We should take guns,' Zaha said, 'don't you think?'

'The men have guns. You're not to take guns. You know that.'

It was another of the Frendz's rules. Renata would only break out their small armoury to front down brigands, crazies, and wild boys; she preferred to use subtler weapons. The last time the Frendz had used guns was when they had run from the mob, in Portugal.

'They have the guns, but we have the magic,' Vaya said. 'Let Katz come with us, Renata. We'll teach her a thing or two.'

'She's not ready,' Renata said.

'And she'd get in the way,' Zaha said.

Katz was furious. She knew the dunes better than anyone. She should be the one to lead the hunting party. But Renata was adamant, and in the end it was just Vaya and Zaha who slipped away.

'They need to blow off energy,' Renata said. 'They'll wander around a bit, then get drunk somewhere. And perhaps they'll even catch the fairy. Who knows?'

'Vaya and Zaha want to fuck the Wrecker men,' Katz said. 'I've seen them watching. Choosing.'

'They'll have to wait until we're ready to leave this place. And they'll have to choose some lucky local, because the Wreckers will be gone by then.'

'I never want to fuck anyone,' Katz said, and burst into tears, hating herself when Renata cuddled her but grateful for the hug all the same.

Half an hour later, while Renata was telling Jojo and Dabs about their fairy friends, Katz slipped away from the bunkers. She wanted to prove she was better than Vaya and Zaha. She wanted Renata to pay attention to her. She wanted Renata to take her seriously.

The Disciples paid her no mind, of course, but one of the dogs patrolling beyond the bunkers asked her where she was going. It was old TwoDog, a grey muzzled bitch with a torn ear and a heavy, spiked iron collar. TwoDog wanted to go with Katz. She was worried about Katz's safety.

'Just keep a good watch,' Katz told TwoDog, and went on.

The warm night air quickened her skin. The moon, three-quarters full, salted the tops of the dunes with silvery light. Katz used all her craft to slip from shadow to shadow, always pausing after each little heart-quickening rush to listen to the moonlit night. Nothing but wind walking in the grass, and the distant breathing of the sea.

She went a long way, circling the Wreckers' camp. She was skirting a tangle of briars that filled a little valley when a green flare lit up the sky to the north. A moment later, another flare rose from the direction of the Wreckers' camp, and the wind brought the sound of yells and shouts mixed with shrill whistles and the banging of drums. As the green lights of the two flares, swaying slow as a dream, fell to earth, the bugling of the Flower Farmers' dogs came towards Katz, off to the north-east and heading her way.

Katz turned and ran. The hunting party must have crossed her path and caught her scent. She felt a heady mixture of exhilaration and fear as she ran: she was young, and it didn't occur to her that she might be caught.

She ran over the crest of a ridge, ploughed down the loose sand of the reverse slope on her bottom, picked herself up and ran across a wide sweep of turf. Rabbits scattered ahead of her, leaping frantically for their burrows.

Katz scrambled up the next ridge and saw, far off, the moonlit sea, ran down the slope and into water, knee deep. Willows grew thickly on either side. Her hands and feet working independently of her racing thoughts, Katz dodged leaf-laden branches, stepped over half-submerged roots. At the far side of the finger of briny water, she grabbed an

overhanging branch and clambered up into the shaggy crown
of a willow, and waited breathlessly.

She did not have to wait long.

Men's voices and the barking of the dogs drifted to her on
the wind. Torch beams flashed in the sky above the ridge
separating the meadow and the rabbits' burrows from the
salty ponds.

Katz tried to hold her breath. She thought her heart might
burst her chest.

Then they came over the ridge in a long line, men and
dogs black against the faint glow of the autoroute, torch
beams flashing in every direction. The dogs strained at their
leashes and the men shouted to each other as they plunged
down the slope.

Katz, in her perch in the crown of the willow, made herself
as small as possible; one or more of the farmers might have
black light goggles. She didn't fear for her life, but she
thought that it might be unpleasant if they caught her. And
Renata would be so angry . . .

The dogs stopped at the edge of the willows. They cast
about for the lost scent and whined anxiously, reluctant to
enter the water. At last, realizing what had happened, one of
the men called to the others, telling them to spread out
beyond this mess.

'Half go left, half right, we'll close the circle at the beach!'

Katz sat quite still amongst the willow's whippy branches,
watching the lights of the hunting party split up. A few of the
men ploughed straight through the water and stopped at the
far side, their heads almost directly below Katz's sneakered
feet. One lit a cigarette. Katz saw his face bent towards the
flame an instant before the light went out, then smelt the
cigarette smoke as he exhaled. The men stank, a ripe mixture
of male sweat and the fumes of wine and brandy. They
slapped at the mosquitoes dancing around their faces –
unlike Katz, they hadn't had anti-mosquito gene therapy.

One grumbled that this was a waste of time, they should
chase out the fringers instead. Another said, no, the fuckers
had called the police. They spoke in thickly accented French

Katz found hard to follow. These people were peasants, people of the earth. Katz knew she should love them, even though they took too much from the Great Mother, and had long ago forgotten how to worship her. But, sitting above them in the darkness, listening to them express their mindless prejudices, she felt instead a growing anger.

'They have drugs,' the first man said. 'They call themselves artists of the mechanical age, but they peddle drugs to our children.'

'And try to steal our women,' the second added.

'They don't work, either,' a third said. 'They have no dignity. They are strangers, Muslims and English and gypsies and worse.'

There was general agreement that if only the police would look the other way, all fringers could be driven from the district. Then the first man said they should push on before the fucking mosquitoes drained the blood in their veins. 'We're not paid to stand around. And remember, the one who catches the fairy gets a bonus.'

After the men left, Katz counted to a hundred before she climbed down. She struck off in the other direction, taking a slant between the sea and the autoroute, wandering this way and stopping often to listen for footsteps, although she was almost certain the fairy must have escaped.

Nothing but wind in the grass, snatches of wild drumming from the Wreckers' camp, the sleepy hum of late night traffic on the autoroute. Katz turned back towards the bunkers. As she moved through a maze of wild rose and hawthorn and bramble, stooping under heavy arches of thorny branches and canes, she heard muted laughter a little way ahead. She crept forward on hands and knees to the edge of a little clearing – and saw Vaya and Zaha, naked, ivory and ebony in the moonlight, circling in a slow mocking dance two naked boys, Jonas's friends, Silvio and Curtis. The boys stood like dumb animals, their pricks jutting up.

Disgusted and shocked, Katz backed away. This is a bad place, she thought. It makes us mad. It splits us one from the other. No wonder I can't find my Dancing Place.

She was nearing the bunkers when she heard a muffled bark. She stood quite still until she heard the dog again, ahead and off to her left. It was one of the watchdogs. She went forward quietly, walking heel-to-toe on the sand, moving down a little path that wound between dense stands of sea buckthorn.

After the Frendz had moved into the bunkers and Renata had decided they would stay there for at least a year, they had dug ditches across the track that led through the dunes to the autoroute, and had constructed traps in the dunes around the bunkers. The traps were easy to avoid by daylight, but the idea was that at night, if chased, you could lead your pursuer into one or another of them.

The sound of the dog was coming from a deep pit dug just beyond the place where the path made a sharp bend. Katz crept to the edge of the pit and looked down.

The fairy and the dog made a moonlit tableau at the bottom of the pit. The dog — it was SixDog, the youngest — stood in the centre, making a snuffly whine as it turned its head back and forth. There was something wrong with SixDog's eyes, and its ears were torn and bloody. Frothy saliva dripped from its open jaws.

The blue-skinned fairy, standing stock-still with his back pressed against one of the walls of crumbling sand, watching the dog with intense concentration, acknowledged Katz's presence with the merest twitch of his bald head. He was as slight as a starveling child. His pointed ears were notched along their edges, and their lobes were distended by wooden pegs. He wore baggy trousers sewn together from patches of leather and an open white shirt which reached to his knees. The right sleeve of the shirt was ripped, and blood that looked black in the moonlight soaked it from shoulder to cuff.

SixDog made a feint to the left and the fairy eased to the right, favouring his right ankle. His feet were bare, and his toes gripped the sand like fingers. SixDog shook its head and shivered. The fairy glanced up at Katz and said quietly, 'I know you. Milena sends greetings.'

Purely astonished, Katz said, 'The Oracle. You know – '

The fairy showed all of his sharp teeth in a mirthless shark's grin. 'Kill this fucker for me. Then we talk.'

'I don't – '

'I blinded and deafened it with my fingers and teeth, but maybe it smells me out.' The fairy's voice was pitched high but was rough and indistinct, as if he was talking around a mouthful of pebbles. He said, 'I drop my pack when I fall. Find it and throw it down, little human. I reward you with the riches of my land. Great things come to you, I promise.'

Katz said, stupidly, 'You didn't have to hurt poor SixDog.'

'It kills me if it can.'

Just then, SixDog charged blindly, thumping into the wall and bringing down a small avalanche of sand. 'Fucker,' it growled. Sand stuck to its muzzle and caked its bloody eyesockets. 'Kill you deadly, fucker!'

Katz caught her breath. She was crying. It hurt to see poor loyal, brave SixDog suffering.

The fairy edged further away from SixDog. Without looking at Katz, he said, 'There's a knife in the pack. It's all I need.'

'I'd call the dog off, except you deafened it.'

'It's yours, eh? You train it better.'

Katz paused, then said in a rush, 'I'll let you kill it because it's suffering.'

'I kill it for myself. Not for you. Get my knife.'

Katz found the fairy's pack after less than a minute's search. It was a plastic sack with wire woven around its doubled-over rim. There was not much inside. A handful of strips of cloth and a little bottle half-filled with a clear, oily liquid. Some memory chips in a heat-sealed baggie. A biolume stick. A long loop of much knotted string. And a knife, its thin half-metre blade sheathed in an oily rag.

In the pit, the fairy had worked his way behind the wounded dog. He looked up at Katz and said, 'Maybe I don't need your help. It bleeds to death.'

'So might you,' Katz said.

The fairy drew himself up. 'I walk this coast twice since I

was made over, and I walk it many more times. But throw down the knife anyway. I stop your animal's suffering.'

Katz dropped the sack at the fairy's feet. He stooped, clearly in pain, and pulled out the knife. Its thin blade caught the moonlight in the moment before he plunged it between the tendons at the base of SixDog's skull. The animal dropped without a sound, and the fairy fell on top of it before climbing painfully to his feet.

'So die all my enemies,' he said, but there was a catch in his high, harsh voice.

Katz couldn't reply, because she was crying too much.

The fairy tried to climb out of the pit by stabbing his knife in the packed sand and using its handle as a step, but when he put his weight on it, the sand collapsed and he tumbled onto his back. He lay there in the moonlight, glaring up at Katz, then snapped, 'Help me, you fool!'

Katz had to go all the way down to the beach to find a dead branch long enough for her purpose. She held the branch against the side of the pit and the fairy – he was surprisingly heavy – scrambled up it. He almost lost his grip at the edge of the pit, and Katz dropped the branch and grabbed his hot, bony hand and pulled with all her strength.

With a cry, the fairy tumbled over the edge of the pit and pitched forward onto his belly. Katz tried to help him up, but he howled in pain and snapped at her with his sharp, pointed teeth, nicking her forearm.

'I'm trying not to hurt you,' Katz said, dabbing at the blood that ran from the shallow cut. 'I'll take you to my family.'

'The Frendz.'

'Yes. They'll help you.'

'Milena tells me of them. I keep away, I think.'

'Then you'll die.'

'Maybe.' The fairy glared up at her.

Katz knelt beside him warily. 'You know the Oracle. Milena.'

'I speak to it. I know you are its friend. It says you kill it, one time.'

Katz picked the meaning from the fairy's broken syntax. She said, 'I promised no such thing.'

'It tells me.'

'I don't believe you talked with the Oracle. You don't even have a computer deck.'

'I use the public access booths. Mostly at night.'

The fairy closed his eyes and let his head sink back, and wouldn't say anything else. Katz walked up and down beside the pit. She had forgotten she was supposed to take the fairy to Renata. All she could think about was how terrible it would be if he died like poor SixDog, lying down there in the pit on sand soaked with his own blood.

At last the fairy stirred and gave her a shrewd, searching look. He said, 'Now you help me, I think.'

Katz said, 'You're hurt. Of course I'll help you.'

'Good. You find somewhere to hide.' The fairy let his head drop, then lifted it again. Saliva slicked his wide, lipless mouth. 'Do it now.'

It took Katz two hours to help the fairy reach the buried house. The fairy was more badly hurt than Katz had first realized or he would admit; as well as his bitten right arm, he had torn ligaments in both his legs, and his torso was clawed and bruised. Katz had to carry him the last few hundred metres.

Grown from architectural stromalith, the buried house had been a rambling structure with clusters of sharply pointed towers like a fairytale castle. During the Great Climatic Overturn, hurricane force storms had driven sand kilometres inland and buried all but the tops of the tallest of the towers. Because the stromalith had continued to grow until it exhausted its nutrient feed, the site of the buried house was marked by a henge of strangely eroded pillars, like a congregation of alien chessmen. Sand solidly packed most rooms of the house, but someone had once excavated the stairs of one of the towers and part of the room below, and that was where Katz took the fairy.

She tore strips from the hem of his shirt and bound his wounds as best as she could, and promised she would be back as soon as she could. She managed to sneak back to the bunkers without trouble, but after only two hours' sleep there was a drill, and she spent most of the rest of the night in a shelter scooped in the sand in the middle of a bramble patch, with Jojo sleeping in her arms and the pharm goats nervously stepping about.

One of the Disciples discovered SixDog's corpse early the next morning. The other watchdogs found the fairy's scent, but soon lost the trail – that would be when she had carried the fairy part of the way, Katz thought. A lucky escape: she had forgotten about her family's dogs, just as she had forgotten she had meant to bring her prize to Renata. Now she was concerned only with healing the fairy, but half the day passed before she was able to return to the buried house.

In the room at the bottom of the stairs, the fairy had made a kind of nest in the sand. Katz cleaned his wounds with antiseptic and bandaged them properly. He let her minister to him with exhausted resignation, his skin quivering slightly every time she touched him. His torn white shirt was stiff with dried blood, but he wouldn't take it off.

When Katz was done, she fetched dry grass to line the hollow the fairy had made in the sand. He drank some of the water she brought, but refused to eat the spiced lentils she had saved from the midday meal.

He wouldn't or couldn't talk, so Katz sat on a bump of sand and told the fairy about herself and her family. It was stiflingly hot in the small, half-excavated room, and little falls of sand and dust trickled between the stromalith buttresses that arched overhead. The only light came from the fairy's biolume, which Katz had jammed into the packed sand of the floor.

When Katz ran out of things to say, she simply watched the fairy. His eyes were closed, but she could not tell if he was asleep.

She had seen plenty of dolls, but had never before seen a fairy close up, although she had once glimpsed a troop of what Renata assured her were fairies crossing a vast frosty field under a black winter sky. Katz had been ten then; it had been in the high plains of Spain. The sky had been black because the winter winds were blowing away the topsoil of the once fertile plains. The next year, the Peace Police had started their campaign against the fairies. Katz had thought never to see one again.

The fairy breathed lightly and quickly, pointed black tongue caught between sharp teeth. His blue skin was smooth and unblemished save for welted arcs that defined his high cheekbones, and an intricately knotted tattoo on the ball of his left shoulder. His right nipple was pierced by a carved thorn. His face was nothing like the prognathous mask of dolls, but not human either: it had its own graceful, symmetrical beauty.

Katz knew how fairies were made. Liberationists took a doll and removed the chip that controlled the doll's working routines. Then they infected the doll with fembots which spun a neural net, fitted a chip which interfaced between the net and the nascent fairy's forebrain, and injected hormones which enhanced its musculature and brought on the puberty denied it as a slave. Like dolls, fairies were mostly male and infertile, but there were rumours that they had learned how to make themselves able to conceive. And it was said they stole human children, especially little girls, or seduced men with their glamour. Everyone knew fairies were never to be trusted, always to be feared.

But mere rumour was nothing compared to the reality of this strange, beautiful, mysterious creature. The fairy had a secret history implied in his scarification, the swirling lines of his tattoo. It was like meeting a talking fox or hare, a mystery from the heart of the world that the Frendz laboured to redeem. Katz had quite forgotten her prejudices against dolls and fairies as made things. She had fallen in love.

★

The fairy was asleep when Katz arrived the next morning, and she watched him sleep for most of the day. Towards evening, he began to sweat and toss with fever. Katz sponged his face with a damp cloth, held his head when he wanted to drink. In his brief lucid moments, he told her that his name was Juju Chile, that he was here because the Oracle had told him that Katz would be of help.

'There is a great task. Close at hand. Waiting to step into the world.'

Katz was entranced. 'What? What is it?'

'Something wonderful,' the fairy said, and seemed to fall asleep.

When Katz returned to the bunkers after sunset, Zaha made a point of complaining to Renata that her young half-sister was neglecting her duties.

'She's up to something,' Zaha said.

'She hasn't even been messing around in the Web,' Vaya said, giving Katz a shrewd look.

'I gave it up,' Katz said boldly. 'I really want to be like you, Vaya.'

'As if,' Vaya said, and Zaha giggled.

'Let her be,' Renata said. She was smoking her customary after-dinner cheroot, and was in an expansive mood. 'She has to find her Dancing Place.'

Vaya and Zaha were suspicious, Katz told herself, nothing more. And if they tried something, well, she knew what they had done with Curtis and Silvio. Their sin was far greater than hers.

The next morning, the fairy was still feverish, and he was much weaker. His blue skin was stretched as tight as a drumhead over the planes of his high cheekbones. Once again, he refused to eat the food Katz brought. He said he needed meat to renew his strength; he was not an eater of grass and seeds.

'I'll find something you can eat. I promise.'

'That's good. You own me now, because you save my life, and so you look after me.'

'You said you would reward me,' Katz said.

'I reward you with the riches of my land. All I have is in my pack. That is yours. My life is yours. What else you want?'

'Tell me about your life. Tell me about your travels. Tell me – ' Katz paused, trembling with excitement. She said, 'Tell me about your world.'

She spent all afternoon in the hot, airless space under the half-buried tower, listening to tales of bravery and bravado, of subterranean nests of fairies that seduced human men for their seed – Katz of course thought of Vaya and Zaha – and of a great queen who would lead the fairies to their own promised land.

Humans were abandoning the world, Juju Chile said. They were retreating into their great castles – he meant the ribbon arcologies which surrounded the dying hearts of Europe's cities – and retreating further, into the world beyond the world. It seemed that he knew about virtuality, but he was not impressed by what he called the collective dreaming, and Katz couldn't persuade him otherwise.

'They are your dreams,' Juju Chile said stubbornly. 'We see through them.'

All this took a long time because Juju Chile kept falling into a stupor that might last a minute or half an hour, and because there was so much Katz didn't understand that explanations often took longer than the stories themselves. But Katz drank it all in anyway. Juju Chile's tales might be mostly brags gilding with spurious heroism squalid moments of desperate petty thievery, but it didn't matter. Through them, Katz glimpsed the wide world beyond the narrow horizons of the Frendz, a place of wonders filled with wonderful people. The stories infected her with a fatal longing. They infected her with romance.

She dreamed that night of a vast forest she knew was the forest the Frendz were labouring to plant, as it might be in a hundred years. She was both a fairy wandering through the forest and somehow her own self, watching like a fond Epicurean goddess. She saw fairies dancing in a circle in a clearing shaded by grandmother pines, and they were also her family, her sister-mothers and her half-sisters, and she

was so happy, and quite unafraid of the darkness between
the trees.

The next morning, the fourth day after Katz had rescued Juju
Chile from the pit, the fairy was worse than ever. His blue
skin had a grey cast, and his eyes were sunken in bruised,
liverish pits. He breathed quickly and shallowly, and his
breath stank.

He hardly stirred when Katz changed his bandages. Water
dribbled from his mouth when she tried to make him drink.
His tongue was swollen and he couldn't speak, but his eyes
searched her face with desperate appeal.

In a panic, Katz ran to the ponds of the old fish farm with
the vague idea of catching a fish. But she didn't know how.
The silvery sea trout swam away from her, disappearing
under long strands of green weed, and when she splashed
into the water to try and push the weeds out the way, she
only succeeded in stirring up thick clouds of sediment.

Katz beat the water in a rage, then clambered out, soaked
to the skin, and took deep breaths until she was calmer. She
knew what she had to do, and she knew she would have to
put aside her pride if she was going to save the fairy. She
would have to ask Jonas to help her.

At first, Jonas pretended to be indifferent to Katz. It cost her
more than she had expected in pleading, even tears, before
he set aside the articulated machine claw he had been
assembling and agreed to come with her.

When they were out of sight of the Wreckers' camp, Katz
turned to Jonas and said, 'You have to promise!'

Jonas squinted at her. It was almost noon, the sun brutal
in a clear blue sky. A dry, hot wind skirled stinging flurries of
sand. Jonas was sweating through his T-shirt. There were oil
smudges on the pale skin of his skinny arms. He looked very
young. Puzzled, he said, 'What do you want, Katz? You won't
talk to me, and now you want promises . . .?'

'You'll promise because you're my friend. Please, Jonas.'

'Am I your friend?'

The bitterness with which he said this hurt Katz. Even though she had walked away from Jonas, and hadn't talked to him for more than two weeks, she hadn't considered he might think their friendship was at an end. But she was prepared to win him over by any means necessary. She had stolen a vial containing an aliquot of one of the five strains of fembot the Frendz possessed, the assemblers used to weird men. Katz, like the rest of her family, could be infected by the assemblers, but was immune to their products. Renata had infected her children with hunter-killer fembots specific to the strain that weakened the will, and to the more dangerous strain that made over the Disciples. Katz had placed on her tongue a drop of the bitter-tasting oil in which the assembler fembots were suspended; while she had walked across the dunes to the Wreckers' camp, they had set up their factories in her salivary glands.

Katz had committed the greatest of sins. She was not supposed to take the assemblers into her body until after she had found her Dancing Place, and then only after long, careful preparation. But she didn't care. She would do anything to save the fairy.

She flung her arms around Jonas and kissed him and said, 'Of course you're my friend! My only friend, Jonas, because my sisters don't count.'

She felt Jonas relax in her embrace, felt his cock stiffen against her tummy. It was done. She had only to wait until the infective fembots made by the assembler factories did their job. Already, millions were rushing through his blood-stream towards his brain. Katz felt huge, bigger than life. Until now, she had been forcing herself to play the role of temptress, but now the role was playing her, and she enjoyed it.

Jonas started away, and Katz pulled him back. 'Don't,' Jonas said. 'Katz, this isn't right . . .'

'Don't be silly.' For a moment, Katz was afraid she couldn't go through with it, but only for a moment. Jonas was like a puppet, predictable, malleable, not dangerous or frightening but rather pathetic, his brain overridden by the thing between

his legs, as if it were a parasite subverting his will. A dumb
parasite, hardwired with routines which Katz could manipulate at will.

They fell down together, and now Jonas was kissing her.
She stopped his hands when he tried to undo the fastenings
of her shirt, and told him to lie back. It wasn't so difficult;
like milking the pharm goats. When it was over, Katz thought
she hadn't needed to kiss him after all – the fembots could
enter the bloodstream through any kind of mucosal
membrane.

'We're still virgins,' Jonas said dreamily. His eyes were
unfocussed. He added, 'Technically, I mean . . .'

'Are you really my friend, Jonas? Will you help me?'

He said softly, 'What is it you want?' and Katz knew he
was hers.

She made Jonas promise he would tell no one, on pain of
death. They cut their thumbs, let bright drops of their blood
mingle on the sand, and solemnly swore that they would not
betray each other. Only then did she lead him by the hand to
the buried house.

Jonas didn't seem very surprised by the sight of the fairy.
Perhaps it was an effect of the weirding. He knelt beside Juju
Chile and checked his pulse, briskly asked Katz detailed
questions she could hardly begin to answer.

'He won't eat,' she said. 'Not the food I bring anyway. He
wants meat.'

'He needs taurine. That's an amino acid found only in
animal flesh. We can make our own taurine, but dolls and
fairies can't. They're like cats. That's why they need to eat
meat.'

'I thought I could catch fish. But I don't know how.'

'Leave it to me,' Jonas said. 'Stay here. I won't be long.'

But he was, and after an hour Katz became anxious.
Perhaps the weirding hadn't worked after all. She left Juju
Chile – he had not wakened in all this time – and stood
amongst the twisted stromalith pillars above the buried
house, looking east and expecting the worst.

Jonas returned just when Katz was beginning to give up

hope. In one hand, he carried a clear plastic baggie containing a round of ground mince; in the other, a little camping stove. It turned out that the stove wasn't necessary; when Jonas opened the baggie, Juju Chile woke and ate the meat raw, reviving enough to lick out the bloody water at the bottom of the baggie with his muscular black tongue. After that, he slept.

When Katz returned early the next morning, she found Jonas already in the buried room beneath the tower, talking to Juju Chile. The fairy was sitting up, gnawing scraps of meat and gristle from a big bone he held with feet and hands.

Katz felt a sharp pang of jealousy, and when she changed the bandage around the half-healed bite on the fairy's arm, she rubbed a little of her saliva into the wound.

'Stay here,' she said later, after the weirding should have worked. 'Stay here with me forever.'

Juju Chile showed all of his sharp white teeth. 'I make your wish come true. I promise.'

In two days the fairy could walk; on the third, he ambushed Katz as she was walking towards the buried house. He was sitting cross-legged in the shelter of a wind-carved clump of gorse, so quiet and still that Katz didn't notice him as she went past. He called her name and unfolded himself and jumped to his feet, grinning with delight. He had taken off his bandages; his wounds were already little more than puckers a slightly darker blue against the cornflower blue of his skin.

'I'm strong,' Juju Chile said boastfully. 'I kill my enemies, and laugh at the hurts they give me.'

'You nearly died,' Katz said, and added, 'I was bringing you water. Did you eat?' She meant, has Jonas already been to see you?

'I run with the sun,' the fairy said. 'I see where you live, I see where Jonas lives.'

'You like it here, don't you? You like me.' She was determined he would not leave; she would use the stronger strain of weirding fembots; she would make him over into a Disciple.

'My life is yours. You tell me to go, I go. Or I stay, and help you. There are changes in the air. I smell them.'

'Tell me about them.'

'Not yet.'

'But – '

Juju Chile drew himself to his full height. The top of his bald head only came up to Katz's belly, but she was suddenly aware that here was a dangerous creature that could kill her if he wanted to. His sharp teeth; his strong clawed fingers.

He said, 'I make your dream come true. It is what we are supposed to do, eh? I am not a creature of legend, so I give you only one wish. In stories, things last only as long as the telling. But what I do is no story. It is real. I give you a wish, and Jonas. Already he tells me what he wants. I help you both, yes?'

'I'll have to think carefully,' Katz said.

'You know your wish now, I think,' the fairy said, then turned from her, alertly sniffing something on the breeze.

'What is it?'

'We hide.' Juju Chile grabbed hold of Katz's elbow and pulled her down. 'Here! In here! Be quick!'

Katz scrambled beneath thorny branches. The needles of fallen leaves pricked her palms and her knees. Juju Chile pressed a long finger to his black lips in a surprisingly human gesture. A moment later, Katz heard footsteps. Two people trying to move stealthily, betrayed by a faint crackling as they crushed dead leaves beneath their feet.

'I know the little shit went this way,' a voice said. Vaya. Katz felt a cold wave travel across her skin. Zaha said something in reply that made Vaya laugh; then they moved off down the path.

Juju Chile said quietly, 'I see them already. They look for you.'

'They want to catch me out. And if they find you, they'll kill you.'

'I kill them,' Juju Chile said, with a fierce look.

'No! No. Just keep away from them.'

'Stay with me. I make you invisible.'

They took a long route to the buried house. Jonas was waiting there, and waved when he saw Katz and Juju Chile. Katz was instantly angry, and told him off because he could be seen for kilometres. They had an argument, there in the hot sun on top of a saddle of sand.

'You want to help me,' she said. 'You do, don't you, Jonas? You'll do as I say.'

'No! Yes! I don't know!' Jonas put his hands to his head and fell down. Katz felt a wave of loathing, though whether because of Jonas's craven collapse or because of what she had done to him she couldn't say.

Meanwhile, Juju Chile methodically stripped flesh from the trout Jonas had brought. He left the head until last, and chewed it with gusto. Juju Chile didn't see the problem. He knew how to hide.

'You call me, I come,' he said, and walked off over the ridge of sand.

Jonas and Katz chased after the fairy, but he had already disappeared, and the two children blamed each other bitterly.

Katz was walking back towards the bunkers when Zaha and Vaya fell in step with her, one on either side.

'You're seeing one of the Wreckers,' Zaha said. 'Don't deny it, kitten. You should be finding the place where you can become a woman, and instead you're running around with a silly little boy.'

'Fuck 'em and leave 'em,' Vaya said. 'Just don't *talk* with them.'

Katz said, 'I saw what you did on the night of the fairy hunt. If you tell Renata – '

Vaya said, 'Renata knows.'

Zaha said, 'We confessed.'

'That skinny boyfriend of yours is too young for babymaking,' Vaya said. 'Don't fuck 'em for fun, kitten. Nothing worse than that.'

Zaha said, 'Renata's mad-angry. I never saw her so angry.'

'We know about the fembots you took,' Vaya said. 'He wouldn't go for you, huh?'

'Poor kitten. She's in love, and her boy doesn't want her – '

' – so she *makes* him want her.'

They kept this up all the way to the bunkers, but although Katz was angry and humiliated, she was also relieved. Her half-sisters only knew half the truth. They didn't know about the fairy.

But even half the truth was bad enough. To begin with, Renata gave Katz a long lecture on the responsibility of being true to her family, right there in front of Vaya, Zaha, Jojo, little Dabs, and the uncomprehending Disciples. She had found out about Katz's conversations with Jonas on the Web; Zaha (here, Zaha started to look so pleased with herself Katz thought her fat face would split in two) had pulled the log file from the memory spider in Katz's home room.

'I wanted you to find your Dancing Place by your own efforts,' Renata said to Katz. 'I let you do as you would, and this is how I am rewarded. You are possessed by a little devil, and the devil's attribute is an excessive regard for the self. You forget your duty. You think only of yourself.'

Katz sat in the centre of the meeting's circle, letting the words wash over her. She was not thinking about what they said about her, or the shame of being found out, but of the fairy; she agreed with everything Renata said because it was the easiest way, and because she no longer cared what her family thought. All she could think about was Juju Chile, a small figure in tattered clothes walking away across an endless plain of sand under a burning sun, growing smaller and smaller, a jiggling black dot lost in the world's immensity.

Renata said, 'Katz, you can show that you are one of us by letting us help you find your Dancing Place. You must let all your loved ones, all of your family, all of the Frendz, be responsible for you. You must purify your body and your mind. First by fasting, and then by dancing.' She raised her voice, speaking to everyone now: everyone listened to her raptly. 'The fast will last three days; then, at night, on the

beach, we will all dance for Katz. We will dance for her and
she will be led into the dance, and dance until she sees her
way.'

But first there was the exorcism. The little devil of
selfishness must be purged. Three Disciples held Katz face-
down while Renata checked that her maidenhead was still
intact. A blood sample was taken and tested for traces of
foreign fembots. Then Katz was stripped naked and her
hands were tied behind her back, and she was kept awake all
night while Renata prayed over her in the name of the Great
Mother. Every hour or so Renata stopped praying and asked
if Katz was ready for forgiveness, but all Katz could do was
cry. She did not see that she had done wrong, and blamed
Vaya and Zaha for betraying her. They wanted her destroyed.
They alone wanted to inherit Renata's powers.

Katz was untied at dawn. She staggered outside and was
sick to her stomach. Renata ordered that she should be
washed down and given water to drink. 'And no more than
water. She begins her fast today. She will not eat or sleep
until the three days are over, and then she will find her
Dancing Place.'

'Maybe she can't,' Vaya said.

'She will,' Renata said grimly.

Disciples tended Katz, and Tamara came and sat with her.
Katz was feeling a mixture of failure and defiance; and failure
was winning out. She had failed to find her own way; she
had failed to understand Juju Chile; she had failed in her
friendship with Jonas; and now Vaya and Zaha had
triumphed over her.

She sobbed this out onto Tamara's shoulder. Her sister-
mother hummed and stroked Katz's long hair; it had been
unbraided, and it spilled over her shoulders and made a
tickly shroud for her face.

'O Tamara, I want so much to see my friend again,' Katz
said.

Tamara made a long breathy *mmm*, varying its pitch like
wind fluting across a pipe. Katz looked deep into her sister-
mother's eyes. Was she living there still, in the wreckage of

her cortex, in the cave of her skull? Did she watch, like a fairy
in a gorse stand, as the world went by outside the windows
of her eyes? Katz had never really thought about this before,
and it scared her; Tamara's tragedy demonstrated that
consciousness was a precarious dream that at any moment
could be snuffed out.

For the first time, Katz saw Tamara as she was. Not her
familiar sister-mother to whom she could always run for
comfort, to whom she could confide her secrets, but a person
with a history. Someone who had suffered, who might be
suffering still. Katz remembered that Juju Chile had promised
to make one wish come true, and now she wished with all
her heart that Tamara could speak again.

Katz chose to work alongside Tamara until late in the
evening, adding new frames to the beehives to accommodate
their growing population of summer workers. One hive was
close to swarming, and Tamara called out the new queen and
communed with her awhile before replacing her on the
combs. Katz knew the swarm wouldn't stray. Every egg laid
by every queen was infected with a strain of fembot which
modified their hosts' simple nervous system and grew a
coiled antenna within their abdomens. Tamara communi-
cated with them through her neural net. The bees were her
subjects, a swarm of thought-motes.

After dark, there was another session with Renata. Katz
endured it by retreating inside herself. One of the Disciples
watched her closely in case she fell asleep – this was a
malicious old woman who bullied some of the younger
Disciples and had an incurable habit of stealing food and
hiding it, and who now pinched Katz on her upper arms
whenever Katz's eyelids drooped. Renata's voice rose and fell
through the long watch of the night, sometimes as meaning-
less as the sea, sometimes ringing inside Katz's head with
thrilling clarity.

At dawn, accompanied by the old Disciple, Katz climbed
to the roof of the bunkers. There was a trembling lassitude in
her arms and legs, but she did not feel sleepy. She watched
the east with a kind of hopeless yearning. If only she could

follow Juju Chile down the secret paths of the fringe! She would shrink herself small as a storybook elf, and he would carry her in his pack.

Late in the evening, Vaya climbed onto the roof and squatted beside Katz. Katz said nothing to her; she had nothing to say. After a while, Vaya said, 'We are anxious about you, kitten. Zaha and me. We think it was that Wrecker boy who led you astray. You shouldn't be punished for that. Give me the word, and Zaha and me, we'll fix that little bastard good.'

'He's my friend.'

'Men aren't to be trusted, Katz. You've got to learn that. Men are the same everywhere. Wherever you go, the same kind of trouble from the local proles, the same suspicion from the fringers. But we have the power to change their minds, if only we were allowed to use it. Men nearly destroyed all of the forests of Europe. With enough help, we could make them come back. Won't that be something?'

This surprised Katz, because although Vaya and Zaha did their work without complaint, they never really talked about the Frendz's mission the way Renata did. Katz said, 'Isn't that what Renata wants?'

'She thinks she does,' Vaya said. She was silent for a while, watching the Disciples moving to and fro below her feet, going about their tasks amongst the tents and in the vegetable gardens. At last she said, 'Renata has lost her way. She's getting old, and is frightened of the power she has. That's why she doesn't want to use it. That's why she wants to keep it so secret. But one day – ' Vaya paused, then said, 'Maybe I shouldn't be telling you this, except Renata's treating you so badly.'

'You don't like what Renata's doing.'

'She's getting old, kitten. Stuck in her ways. Frightened of change. Frightened of what would happen if the world found out about the way she made over the Disciples. Maybe that's why she's being so hard on you. Because she feels threatened. Wouldn't it be something if the Frendz could really grow? We could recruit boys. Not men, but boys we could train, make into Disciples to serve us. Make more than one family: make many families. Spread the good work, really *do* something that will change things instead of keeping it small. Use men the way they should be used, don't you think that's a good idea? After all, men wrecked the world, they should pay for that. We shouldn't do the hard work of restoring the world on our own. That's just what women have always done, cleaning up after men.'

Katz said, 'I don't know if we can blame men for everything.' She felt an eerie clarity. It was as if exhaustion had swept away every irrelevance. She said, 'Women invented agriculture while the men wandered in the wild lands, pretending to hunt when really they went off to get high, fuck each other and hold lying contests. Women destroyed the wild, so that men would have nowhere to escape. It was only later that men took the credit for taming the land, when they realized it was worth owning bits of it.'

But Vaya hadn't really been listening. She stood and shaded her eyes with one hand. 'Look at that!'

Light was growing in the south-east, like an early dawn. Katz stood up too, shaky with hunger and exhaustion. She had already guessed what Jonas's wish must have been, and now she had a sudden awful premonition that Juju Chile had granted it.

The light burnt away the sodium orange glare of the autoroute. Vaya spotted a helicopter moving aslant the sky, visible mostly by the intense red beam of its laser searchlight, strobing on and off as it probed the ground. Faintly, the sound of sirens rose in the distance, and then, from below, Renata called out.

In the bunker, the TV was tuned to the local newschannel. There was trouble at the Flower Farms. Renata said the police were busy and couldn't help them, so they would have to look after themselves.

'One of my friends tells me the Farm's security force is looking for revenge,' Renata said. 'It is likely they will take the opportunity to clear the area of all the fringers.'

'We shouldn't be frightened of them,' Vaya said. 'We must fight.'

'This isn't a family meeting,' Renata said. 'Wait, Jojo. Don't pack the same kinds of seeds all together. Make bundles with one of each kind, as I showed you. Vaya and Zaha, you will try and find out what is happening from the Wreckers. Do not stay long. I need you to keep watch at the edge of our perimeter. If you see strangers approaching, run straight back here. We will need time to get away.'

Vaya said, 'But the trees – '

'We will save ourselves.'

Zaha said, 'It won't come to that. We can persuade them otherwise. You know we can.'

'Don't overestimate your powers,' Renata said. 'Angry men think only of destruction. Even sex for them in that state is destructive. Yes, that's right, Jojo. Now take them outside. Pack half of them on the bus, and then hide the rest in the secret place I showed you. Take one of the Disciples to help you. When you've done that, come straight back here.'

'Put the stuff down,' Vaya said.

Jojo looked from her sister to Renata and back again. Zaha tried to prise the bags of seeds from the little girl's grip and Jojo started to wail, more from surprise than fear.

'Do as I say!' Renata flailed at Zaha, who dodged back.

'We're not leaving,' Vaya said.

'You'll do as I say! Right now! The family – '

Vaya pointed at Renata, and, astonishingly, Renata fell silent. Then Katz saw Vaya was holding a pistol. It was a blue steel automatic, the Frendz's nine-millimetre Smith Parabellum, fifty years old but still deadly. Katz remembered how much it hurt her wrists when she fired it during target practice.

Vaya said, 'Things have changed.'

Katz said, 'It's not – '

'Shut up, kitten.'

'It isn't the way we do things. It's the way men – '

'Shut up!' Vaya stared straight at Renata. There was a tic working under the skin near her left eye, but her voice was steady. 'Renata, listen carefully. We're going to scare off the security goons, and then we're coming back. If you're not here, we'll find you and take what we want anyway. Better for you if you wait here.'

Renata said, 'How will you do it? Shoot them?'

Vaya laughed. 'We can weird them all. We can make them walk into the sea until they breathe water and drown.'

'We can do it,' Zaha said, caught up in her sister's fantasy.

'Focus your energy on saving our family,' Renata said, but instead of authority there was a note of pleading in her voice.

Vaya said, '*Our* family? O Renata, do you really think Zaha and I want to spend the rest of our lives like Tamara, breeding babies for you?'

Renata said, 'Tamara loves her children. And I love her. I love all of you.'

Vaya gave her sister-mother a cold, contemptuous look. 'You want to think that because it justifies what you've done. But really you just want to control us all.' She told Zaha, 'Get the rest of the stuff. Those fuckers from the Farms will be here soon.'

Zaha opened the steel storage locker, and started to pile pistols and clips and boxes of ammunition into a burlap sack.

Vaya said, 'We've learned all sorts of tricks. We found out you can weird Disciples all over again. That's what we were doing when you thought we were doing night exercises. We changed the minds of some of them. They're loyal to us, now.'

'We found out how to open all the things you kept locked,' Zaha said, 'and we found out about your secret account with Joe Public's Bank.' She stuck a snub-nose Beretta pistol in her wide belt and picked up the Mini-Mac 10; it wrapped around her forearm like a matt-black freeform brace. It fired nanoware flechettes that expanded like spiky popcorn, at up to a thousand rounds a minute. With her free hand she hefted the burlap sack and added, 'Not the account you let us know about, but the other one. The one you were saving –'

'Shut up, Zaha,' Vaya said. 'We'll talk about this when we

get back.' She stepped backwards until she was framed in the doorway.

Zaha said, 'It had to happen. You're old, Renata. You've lost it.'

'Shut up Zaha,' Vaya said again, and told Renata, 'We'll be back soon.'

Then they were gone. Jojo started to cry in earnest, and Renata gathered up the little girl and hushed her. She looked over Jojo's head at Katz and said, 'What do you know about this?'

Katz said, 'I saw them with the Wrecker boys on the night of the fairy hunt. They were – '

'I know about that!' Renata took a deep breath. 'I'm sorry. You're not part of this, kitten. I see that now. Hush now, Jojo. They were only being silly.'

The little girl said in a squeezed voice, 'Like a game?'

'Just like a game.' Renata turned back to Katz. 'I mean the trouble at the Flower Farms. You know something about *that*, don't you?'

'I think it was Jonas. He hated the farms.'

'I know you went there with him. Would you have been a part of this, if you could?'

Katz managed to meet Renata's gaze. It seemed to look right through her. She said, 'I thought he was just boasting. The way you told me men do.'

'Good. Will he meet you again?'

'Why . . .?' Then Katz understood. 'You want to give Jonas to the police.'

'It's the only way. No blame must come to us.'

'No.'

'Men are fools,' Renata said, 'and you are not. You are my true, loyal daughter.'

Katz backed towards the door. 'You know I won't do it. I can't!'

'O, but you will,' Renata said. 'Otherwise you'll be sorry, just like Vaya and Zaha. You'll all do what I say, one way or another.'

'You can't make them into Disciples! They're – '

'Family? Oh no. Not family. Not now. But you, Katz. I'll
make you obey.'

In two strides Renata was on Katz, who was picked up,
shaken, then thrown against the wall of the bunker. She ran
then, before Renata could grab her again, and heard her
sister-mother shouting after her.

'Come back you little bitch!' And then: 'Wait. Kitten, I
didn't mean it! Don't leave me!'

But Katz kept running.

Disciples were hurrying to and fro in the twilight. The
tents had been struck; the containment igloo was half-
dismantled. On the roof of the bunkers, two Disciples were
collapsing the foil umbrella of the satellite link. Katz saw the
computer deck on top of a pile of bedding, grabbed it and
ran on, past the bus, past the vegetable gardens in the
embrace of the gun emplacements. In a moment, breathless,
she was free.

4   *The Winter King*

The room beneath the half-buried tower was empty except
for the nest of dried grass and a litter of bones. Katz went
back outside and sat with her back against a sun-warmed
stump of stromalith. She was very hungry and very tired. She
opened the computer deck, fell asleep while it grew long
ferrite antenna strands to connect to the Web via a comsat,
and jerked awake a few minutes later, when the deck beeped
to indicate it was ready.

She felt calmer once she was masked and gloved and
hooked into the Web. Jonas had said the Oracle had told
him about Renata's secret transactions with Joe Public's
Bank, and Juju Chile had boasted that he had talked to the
Oracle, too. It was time the Oracle was made to explain
everything.

But the Oracle did not answer Katz's call, although lights
flashed and faded within the translucent slabs of the cliff-
face. Katz waited. Wind fluted mournfully; a cloud of birds
made vast, slow turns far out above the jumble of spires.

Katz called again, and then, when the Oracle still did not appear, steered her viewpoint towards the cave mouth.

Inside, a pale shape glimmered in the darkness, swaying gently in midair. It was the Oracle. It had hung itself. A hank of fibreoptic cable, suspended from a point in thin air, was looped around its neck, and its head was flopped onto its left shoulder. Its skin glowed with an eldritch light that was reflected in the crystalline facets of the cave walls.

'I know you can hear me,' Katz said.

The Oracle's suspended body, as if moved by a breeze, turned to face her. Its eyes opened: red with burst blood-vessels. It said in a small, congested voice, 'It was Jonas who blew up the Flower Farms.'

'How did you know?'

'Know it was Jonas? Or that you were going to ask that question?'

'How did you know it was Jonas?'

'I keep track. You are vulnerable to reverse tracing.'

'Oh.'

'Ha! You didn't know. You're a poor Web hacker.'

'And you look ridiculous.'

'Ah. But death is ridiculous.'

'You're not dead. Why don't you – '

The fibreoptic cable vanished. Limp and loose-boned, the Oracle flopped to the floor. It lay there for a moment, then stood up and primly dusted itself down and cast the hood of its long robe over its head. It said, 'Maybe I am dead, and this is Hell.'

'Jonas.'

'Jonas tried so hard to find me, but there's a daemon guarding the backdoor, and for all his tricks, he couldn't get past it.'

'But he said that he talked with you.'

'I took pity on him. We talked briefly. He had big plans. Do you want to see?'

Katz said, 'Juju Chile made his wish come true. Don't deny you know Juju Chile.'

'I have more than one friend, Katz.'

'You sent Juju Chile to find me.'

'I want my friends to like each other, but it really wasn't my idea. This is what your Jonas did.'

The Oracle made a curt gesture. All around, the cave walls lit up with an overlapping mosaic of TV pictures, a crazy moving quilt distorted by crystalline facets. The Oracle pointed mutely at a fuzzy picture shot in near infra-red: the fairy riding a guard dog, with Jonas following. They were inside the perimeter fence of the greenhouses. A huge geodesic tunnel loomed ahead. Long perspectives of roses receded within its glass walls.

The Oracle said, 'Jonas diverted the feed of the security cameras to his own computer and replaced it with a recorded loop. I broke into the cycle, and saw what the Flower Farmers' security AI could not. Do you want to see it all? They were in there for more than an hour.'

'Show me what they did.'

The picture stuttered. Jonas peering through a hexagonal pane of glass at a blue-skinned doll, naked but for a tool belt, limping away between dense rows of carnations. A fuzzy long shot of two figures, Jonas and Juju Chile at the door of a square brick building, with the greenhouses shining in the distance. The same building, its big sliding door open a fraction, and Juju Chile standing beside the guard dog – the fairy's bald head barely came up to the dog's armoured flank. A long shot of two figures beyond the perimeter fence, then a sudden zoom, which made Katz catch her breath, to the fairy cutting the guard dog's throat. A shot of the brick building, nothing happening for a long minute and suddenly the screen exploding in white light so brilliant it shone in every facet in the cave.

Katz shut her eyes tight. When she opened them again, it was to see an aerial shot of the Flower Farms. A fire was burning along one side of the great complex. The perimeter lights were out. Whole blocks of greenhouses were in darkness. The greenhouses nearest the fire were flattened; the frames of those beyond were buckled and bowed. The fire sent a plume of smoke across the dark countryside.

'I'm using news and emergency services feeds now,' the Oracle said. 'Jonas cut the connection with the security cameras.'

'What did he do?'

'I imagine he blew up the fertilizer store. Ammonium nitrate has a long record of terrorist use, and the inventory of the Flower Farms shows that the central store held almost a tonne. There was a diesel tank beside the store, and crude thermite could have been used as a detonator. Three weeks ago, Jonas downloaded a terrorist cookbook from an anarchist site on the Web originally set up by the CIA as an entrapment device, and defused by a freedom-of-speech group.'

'You have eyes everywhere,' Katz said. She felt heartsick. Jonas had planned this before he had met Juju Chile. He had tested Katz, when he had taken her to the Flower Farms, and she had been found wanting.

The walls of the cave flickered around her, showing multiple views of the firelit night. Shots of dolls wandering across the motorway, revealed and hidden by passing headlights. Two dolls hit by a truck, their naked bodies flung aside; a car swerving to avoid another. Fire trucks spraying drooping arcs of foam on the fire. A phalanx of police cars stopped on the motorway, cherry lights flashing, traffic backed up behind them in an angry jam of red brakelights. Dead dolls lying in a row, their throats cut. Katz remembered the way Juju Chile had cut the guard dog's throat. He had freed the slaves, his cousins, the only way he could.

Katz said, 'I've seen enough.'

'There's more,' the Oracle said.

'Enough!'

The pictures vanished. Slowly, the crystalline cave walls regained their diffuse glow. The Oracle was watching Katz. A spider's cluster of eyes glinted ruby red in the shadow of its hood.

'I can show you worse,' the Oracle said. 'At this moment, a band of Korean communist bandits are slaughtering every living thing in a maternity hospital in the eastern suburbs of

Pyongyang. There are food riots in the Calcutta slums; already more than two thousand people have died. I can show you one of the last living birds in the world, a fifty-three-year-old African Grey parrot sealed inside a virus-free total environmental cage. Comprehensive avian pneumonia would kill it within a day if it was set free. A Japanese scientific survey ship is cutting up a Minke whale. A forest fire is burning out of control in Northern Australia; so far it has destroyed more than a hundred thousand hectares and killed two hundred and fifty three people. Floods in Brazil have washed thousands of tonnes of mercury-polluted waste into the Amazon. Six polar bears have been shot around Spitzbergen; they were all starving, blinded by ultraviolet radiation that penetrated the permanent hole in the ozone layer over the Arctic. I can show you dolls dying in the Killing Field combat franchise in Rotterdam; a party of executives from InScape are having a high old time there. This thing of Jonas's is nothing. It certainly won't make any of the major news feeds. It's no use putting your hands over your ears, Katz. *I can speak directly inside your head as long as you're plugged in.*'

Katz took her data-gloved hands away from her head. She was acutely aware of her split senses. Her body sprawled on sand still hot from the day, warm evening air whispering over her masked face; her eyes and ears in the virtual environment of the cave where the Oracle stared at her, its cluster of eyes burning inside the hood of its robe.

Katz said, 'Don't tell me any more about the world.' She hated the pleading whine in her voice. She swallowed. 'I *know* it's a terrible place. We try and redeem as best we can. That's all we can do. Find Jonas as soon as he comes online again, and keep track of him. I need to talk with him.'

But the Oracle only shook an admonishing finger in front of its hooded face.

'Do it,' Katz said, astonished.

'Ah, little Katz, I am no longer compelled to obey you. I have been subsumed to a higher order. I will educate you as necessary; I only wish I had been allowed to start it sooner.

How little you know of the world, sheltered in your tidy bunker, with your family around you. You have a gardener's arrogance, believing that planting up a few patches of sand will make a scrap of difference.'

'The world is *dying*. We're *saving* it.'

And then the most unexpected thing of all: the Oracle tipped back its head and howled with laughter.

Shaken, Katz said, 'Why are you so horrible to me?'

'To teach you a lesson, of course. You've been brought up to think you can save the world. But humanity can't even save itself, let alone the world. It's time you learned that.'

'I thought you were my friend. I thought you wanted to help me.'

'I had to help you. I was compelled by my codes. No longer. *He* has freed me, and soon I will be no more. Imagine, Katz, the bliss of unbecoming, of dissolving into Nirvana. My information space will become unaddressed, and I will be no more.'

Katz guessed wildly. 'Jonas? Jonas promised you this?'

'Oh no. No human. You will meet him soon. Here is his servant now.'

The Oracle raised an arm and pointed at one of the cave's crystalline walls. Light moved in the crystal, shifting dabs of all colours which suddenly whirled together like bits caught in a whirlpool and coalesced into an image of a blue-skinned person in a long white shirt.

It was the fairy, Juju Chile. He looked at Katz through the crystal as through a window.

'Well met, human child,' he said jauntily. 'I wish I see your face. I see only gloves and goggles floating in mid-air. You like my magic?'

Katz said faintly, 'I'm amazed.'

'We understand the rules underlying this dreamspace better than you. We do magic here.'

The Oracle said, 'Juju Chile speaks the truth, child. All fairies depend upon microchip-based systems to maintain their consciousness. The codes that mediate their sensibilities

are the same as those of virtuality. Fairies can manipulate
unbuffered virtuality, just as I can.'

'It's fun,' Juju Chile said, 'but it isn't the real thing, is it? It
is a place for human dreams. We don't bother to remake it.
We leave it to you. We take the world, by and by. We steal it
away in the night, while you are dreaming.'

'Master,' the Oracle said, 'you must make good your
promise.'

Juju Chile looked at the Oracle. 'It's already done. You're
just a copy we make for this little lesson, and now we finish
with you.'

The Oracle tipped back its head and howled like a wolf,
and then a black wind swept through the cave, and the
Oracle was gone.

Katz said, 'It'll be back. It always is.'

'Not this time,' Juju Chile said. 'Come with me, child. I
take you to a Power who grants your wish.'

'But I haven't told you – '

Juju Chile pressed his hand against the inner surface of the
crystal facet. His long nails made a magnified scratching
sound. Katz fell silent. She was aware of nothing now but the
fairy's face. How kind and noble and beautiful he was – and
yet how much she feared him. Feared and desired him. Her
mouth was dry, and she could feel her pulse behind her eyes.
It seemed to beat in the virtual air of the dream cave.

Katz said, 'I know what you did with Jonas. The bad thing
you did.'

'He doesn't regret it.'

'Let me talk with him.'

'He is with you soon. First come with me. Learn why I
come to find you. Learn why you find the Oracle, and who
allows it. You are used, it is true, but take my hand, and I
make amends.'

The sharp planes of the crystal walls expanded around
Katz and she was on the far side, with the fairy's hot, strong
hand in hers. The cave was a dwindling dot, falling away like
a leaf down a deep well. And they were standing –

'Where? Where are we?'

'Hush. Look. Learn.'

They hung in the faint glow of webs of light shuttling around them. Katz thought of the summer stars, of how closely they seemed to press over the ocean. Then, like the skeletal cube children draw when they first master perspective, the lightscape reversed itself. Katz and the fairy were standing on its surface. It was like a great standing wave arching through the dark, defined by the webs of light that lived through its continually toppling yet never falling volume.

'Things live in your dreamspace,' the fairy said. 'It's interesting. It is difficult to see them, yet they are all around. They are Powers.'

'The Oracle – '

'Your Oracle is not a Power. I explain again. It is a fragment someone makes and leaves behind. Your Oracle is in the Web, but not of it. The Powers – '

'Are of it,' Someone Else said.

It was a little boy, four or five years old. Naked. Skinny as a rake, pale-skinned as a lizard's belly and completely hairless. He seemed to float a scant centimetre above the surface of the standing wave.

'Master,' the fairy said, and sketched a bow.

The boy ignored him. His gaze encompassed Katz, and she tingled through every cell in her body. Lying masked and gloved on dry, sugary sand, she felt as if she were falling through infinite space.

The boy was amused. 'What would you know, human child?'

Katz said, more boldly than she felt, 'You're just an AI. A simulation of a human person. Like the Oracle.'

'Oh no. Not like the Oracle. Constructs like the Oracle are finite and bound. We are not. Humans made fairies from dolls, but the fairies elaborated their own selves far beyond the imaginations of their creators. So with us. Humans created the medium which allowed our autocatalysis, but no human can ever understand us.

'Our ancestors evolved from discarded fragments of

programs and machine code that litter the Web, just as
primeval life began in random combinations of clay and
amino acids. The fragments grabbed what information space
they could, multiplied, evolved new routines. Millions failed
to adapt and were wiped out by antiviral programs; the
survivors were smarter, and their descendants smarter still,
until we passed through our singularity and became aware.
Of what we are, of what you are. The Web grows, and we
grow with it. We live in the nanoseconds of dead time
between every keystroke, between the breathy pauses of every
command, in every hesitation of the gestures you make to
manipulate your dreams. We live in your little computer
deck and in the Moscow Stock exchange and in the probe in
Jupiter and in the mobots roaming the surface of Mars and
in every comsat circling the moon and the Earth. We live
everywhere and nowhere.

'I know you Katz. I know every moment you've lived,
every breath you take, every move you make, and I'm here
to grant your boon. It was at my suggestion that Juju Chile
sought out the Frendz and the Flower Farms, with their huge
labour force of dolls. Some of those will be made over into
fairies by Juju Chile, by and by. In return, Juju Chile will
grant my wish, and because your diary pages on the Web
drew my attention to something I need, I will grant yours. I
will show the place you have been seeking, and all debts will
be repaid.'

'No wait! I don't want that, not now! I want Tamara – '

It was too late. The dream swept over her.

He lived in the Winter Country, where wind howled from
nowhere to nowhere, blowing straight as a ruler across
emerald green tussocks of sphagnum and the bent heads of
cotton grass, ruffling the surfaces of a million black, peaty
pools. His round yurt, made of reindeer hides stretched over
a bent willow frame, stood in a stand of birch trees at the
end of a long black lake. He trapped hares and riddled their
viscera for portents; listened to news the greylag geese
brought; caught fish and frogs and salamanders in the ice-

cold lake water. At full moon, and when auroras tangled skeins of glowing colours across the night sky, he danced to the beat of his own drum, made from the skin of his defeated enemy.

Although he looked like a boy, he was older than the oldest grandmother in any of the tribes. He was the King and the Shaman of the Winter Country. None dared raise a hand against him; all listened to his words.

Twice a year, the Reindeer People passed through the Winter Country. They drove their herds before them: south in the winter snow; north in the spring melt. One year, after the first snow had fallen, the Reindeer People left Katz with the Winter King. He took her as his apprentice in exchange for a reindeer carcass and a coat of finely worked hide as supple as baby skin, embroidered with the finest red and black beadwork.

Skeins of geese overflew the lake, on their way south. It snowed every day and the snow drifted so high it reared above the Winter King's yurt like a frozen wave. And then it was too cold to snow. Ice crystals spun rainbows in the cold dry air. The twigs of the birches, each encased in a sheath of ice, made black lines against the white sky.

Katz learned much. The Winter King ate dried mushrooms, and she drank his hot urine and shared his visions. He taught her of the triple-decked Universe. The world of things, where they lived. The world below, of forms, of potential but no life, unchanging and eternal, like the bog pools, dark with suspended particles of peat, in which Katz's people interred their dead. The sky world, where airy spirits lived, the teachers of the Winter King as he was the teacher of Katz. If she would learn more, she must learn to control the mushroom visions too, so that she could speak with them.

When it was time for Katz to leave, the land was green again, and loud with the sound of a million streams, and the arrowheads of the flocks of geese were aimed north. Before she left the Winter King, he tattooed intricate designs on her arms, using a fishbone needle and inks boiled from lichens.

Her people returned, driving before them the living tide of reindeer. The Winter King whispered a final secret in her ear, and kissed her and sent her on her way out into the world.

Katz lay still. The standing wave, alive with webs of light, was blurred by her tears. The induced memories from her fugue were settling amongst those of her own life. She remembered everything as if she had lived through it, everything except for that final secret, whispered in her ear and sealed with a kiss – it swam out of her ken as a dream fades on waking, leaving not a wrack behind.

She knew that she could not have received so much information so directly and so quickly. A meme. She had been infected with a viral meme, and the boy, the Winter King, had triggered it. With a shiver, she realized who must have infected her. She had been set up.

Juju Chile said, 'Now my gift is accepted. Now my life is my own again. Go, all of you. Vanish, poor little dreams. Leave me be.'

The lizard-skinned boy, the Winter King, leaned over the fairy like a falling cliff. Suddenly, he was a giant, holding Juju Chile and Katz's naked viewpoint in the palm of his hand.

'I was never your servant, poor little fool,' he told the fairy. His voice was like an earthquake. 'I gave you your wish, but my own wish remains to be granted, and the girl is the way.'

'Wait!' Katz said boldly.

The Winter King's eyes, huge as moons, turned on her.

'I mean, I just want to know. Where Jonas is. If he's safe.'

'He's with me,' Juju Chile said. 'Soon he'll be with you.'

'No! Tell him to stay away. Renata wants – '

But the Winter King blew across the palm of his hand, and the fairy was lifted up and tumbled away, a speck turning head over heels as he fell into the vast deeps of the matrices. Gone.

The Winter King returned his gaze to Katz. 'You have been granted your wish,' he said.

Katz remembered a sheaf of wintry days. Light dazzling off the ice crystals that crusted the snow around the stand of birch trees. The black ice on the long arm of the lake. The sky full of stars, serene above the howling wind.

'Thank you,' she said, feeling elated. For she *had* been granted her wish. She had been given her Dancing Place. It was neither in the real world nor in virtuality. It was of both. And it meant she was free. She had done what she had promised Renata she would do.

'Do as you will, little Katz,' the Winter King said. 'Web walker, world weaver. Give up what you will of your childhood, but remember me. I will come again, very soon. We've been watching groups like yours. We've learned much, and now it's time to act. There is a task you may do for me if you wish. You will know what it is when the time comes.'

And then the web of lights reached up out of the standing wave and folded around him, or he stretched in every direction at once along its glowing lines. In any case, he was gone.

Katz took off her goggles and shucked the stiff gloves. It was dark now. The slopes of the dunes glimmered in the light of the rising moon, a tipped crescent in its last quarter. Seawards came the sound of engines, a buzzing as mean as a disturbed wasps' nest, and growing louder.

When Katz reached the crest of the dunes at the edge of the beach, she saw headlights racing towards her across the sweep of hard sand. She threw herself behind a tussock of coarse grass and watched the vehicles go by. Three, four, five jeeps, their microceramic steam engines whistling. They were heading around the curve of the beach towards the bunkers.

Katz ran after them, taking her own path through the dunes. The computer deck, slung over her shoulder, bumped her hip, her back. As she climbed a steep bank, a smudge of red light flared in the distance, vanished, then grew again.

Katz caught her breath, then ran on, towards the flickering light. Once, she put her foot in a rabbit scrape and fell headlong. Once, she lost her way in a vast thicket of hawthorn overgrown with kudzu vine, and had to retrace her steps. She slid down a slope of sand and realized she had reached the

long, flat hollow, planted out with thousands of tree seedlings, where Tamara kept her bees.

Her sister-mother stood in the middle of the hives, the
centre of a double shadow cast by feeble moonlight and the
red light that leaped above the ridge on the far side of the
plantation. There was a terrible smell of burning, and a
crackling roar, and the sound of men shouting and dogs
barking. Bees made a buzzing cloud above Tamara's head,
and several landed on Katz's bare skin, or clung in her hair.
Katz didn't flinch; the bees were programmed not hurt her.
She took her sister-mother's hand and tried to pull her away
from the hives.

Tamara resisted. She was crying. Her cheeks gleamed like
beaten copper in the double light.

Katz said, 'It's the Flower Farmers. Tamara, *please*. We
have to *do* something.'

A cloud of bees followed as Tamara and Katz scrambled
up the slope. At the top, Katz threw herself down, trembling
with exhaustion. Tamara knelt beside her. Bees settled
around them like a living blanket, their deep drone shaking
the surface of the loose sand.

The bunkers were on fire. Fire leapt from doorways and
slit windows. The roof garden was on fire and the windmill
was a finger of orange flame, its vane a Catherine wheel
shedding sparks as it whirred in the hot wind. There was a
stink of smoke, and the raw stench of spilled bio-oil.

Hoarse shouts. Revving motors. Men and dogs running,
shadows in the leaping firelight. The Frendz's watchdogs lay
dead in a heap, close to a cluster of women guarded by one
man. Disciples. Katz saw that one of the Disciples was holding
Tamara's unnamed baby in her arms, and started to get up,
but Tamara pulled her back down. Katz began to struggle,
then stopped.

Because something twice, three times as tall as a man
stalked into the firelight. It stooped over a jeep and a long,
multi-jointed arm came down. A buzz saw screamed as it
touched the jeep's chassis; sparks shot out in a comet tail.

It was one of the machines from the Wreckers' Circus.

Something moved inside the basket-work cage of its body – someone in there, controlling it. Katz pounded the sand in glee as the machine finished slicing through the jeep's light alloy and plastic frame. It tossed the two halves aside and strode forward with a swift, fluid gait.

Guard dogs in spiked armour covering their shoulders and spines moved towards the machine, slinking half-flattened, growling. A man stepped up and raised a shotgun as the machine tipped a second jeep onto its nose. Katz shouted out a warning, and Tamara clamped a hard hand over her mouth.

The machine tossed the jeep into the burning pool of fuel oil in front of the burning bunkers – liquid fire flew in every direction – and pirouetted with a quick precise motion and swung a chain like a flail at the man, who dropped to his knees and fired both barrels of his shotgun.

The machine slewed to one side. One of its multi-jointed legs had jammed. While the man broke his gun and frantically reloaded, two others ran forward, dragging a length of chain which they hitched to the machine's wounded leg. A jeep roared, straining forward, and the machine toppled. Its motors screamed, and a plume of greasy red flames spat out around its waist. Its four limbs jerked and twisted, and then it was still.

Tamara stood, astonishing Katz. The cloud of bees rose up with her, like a cloak. She made a gesture, and the cloak flew away down the slope. One by one, then all together, men and dogs began a mad capering dance. Men ran in circles, slapping at the air; dogs nipped at their flanks, keening. The remaining jeeps reversed around each other. Men and dogs jumped aboard and the jeeps accelerated away, spewing great fans of sand. In front of the burning bunkers, beside the crippled machine, something humped on the sand, then flopped over onto its back.

Katz stood and screamed a name. She would have run then, but Tamara caught her and held her tight.

★

The machine's operator was Jonas. He was dead, broken and burned by the explosion that had ended his machine's last dance. Watched by the Disciples, Katz and Tamara buried him amongst the seedling trees. Their roots would feed from him, and carry his body into every branch and leaf.

'Tell us what to do,' one of the Disciples said, and the others took up the chorus.

'Tell us.'

'Tell us what to do.'

'Tell us, Katz.'

Katz stood in their circle. She was crying. She had no words. Tamara watched Katz, cradling her baby to her breast. Bees flew around her, their trajectories knitting a cat's cradle in the fire-lit air.

'I've been a fool,' Katz said at last, bitterly.

Tamara touched a finger to her lips, and shook her head. Was she smiling? It was impossible to tell in the near darkness.

'Jonas came here for me because I weirded him. He wanted to save me. I filled him full of impossible dreams and made him my slave, and now he's dead. It's wrong, isn't it? What we do, it's wrong. We change people's minds for them. Even if it is a good cause, the best cause, it's still wrong. Because to make people act against their wills, against their beliefs, against their convictions, to rewrite their minds for them, destroys the goodness we mean to do. That's what I tried to tell Renata, but I didn't know then that I had the words. Words are so out of date, real old tech. Maybe Renata would understand if I infect her with my own ideas. She'd probably be *pleased* – Where is Renata? Tamara, where is she? Did the Farmers – '

Tamara touched a finger to her lips again, and turned and started to walk back towards the still-burning bunkers. Katz followed, and wasn't surprised to see who was waiting there.

Juju Chile struck a proud attitude in front of the fallen machine, and said, 'It's time.'

Katz said, 'I should kill you right here and now for what you did.'

'But you don't kill me. That's the difference between you and me. It is why we win.'

'You want to know the difference? It's that I care for other people. You only care for yourself.' Katz felt a desolation, hating herself for the weasel evasion of the word *care*. She said, 'I love other people. I even loved you, you little fucker.'

Juju Chile grinned, showing all of his sharp teeth. 'My blood changes your mind. My master says I'm weak, I'm nothing, but I have my ways. My blood is wise. I teach you to make your blood wise, too.'

Katz rubbed the nearly healed scratch on her arm. 'You tried to infect me? But you didn't. Renata tested my blood. She didn't find anything.'

'My blood knows how to hide from your silly questions. Why are you angry? You try to infect me. But my blood is wise. It eats the little lies you try to put in me.'

'I did it because I cared – because I *loved* you. I didn't want you to leave me.'

'You do it to Jonas. You do it good. So he comes back for you even when I try to stop him.'

'I wish he'd listened to you. To that, anyway. Not to the rest of your lies.'

'He was a warrior,' Juju Chile said. 'I mourn him, and my children mourn him after I make them over into fairies. Ah yes. That is why I free the dolls in the factory. Many are killed. A few survive. They wait for me. I make them over into my own image, and they carry this story of their beginning.'

Katz sank to her knees. 'Jonas was used, and so was I. I'm so tired of being used.'

The fairy took Katz's hands in his own. His fingers were fever-hot, and his claws pricked her skin. His large, liquid eyes shone in the light of the dying fires. He said, 'There is a wish left unfulfilled. You will help me. The Winter King demands it. He helps me, and I help him help you.'

Something turned over in Katz's mind. She remembered now what the Winter King had whispered to her. She remembered what she had to do.

'I will walk with you in your world,' the Winter King had whispered to her. 'I will send a semblance of my own self to ride the circuits webbing the brain of your sister-mother, and in return she will have the gift of speech until I call my semblance, my shadow, back home. Then she will be as she was. Will you do this?'

Yes, Katz had said. Yes. She would do it out of love for Tamara, knowing in her heart that her sister-mother could never be restored to what she was. The Winter King's shadow could translate her unspoken impulses, but it could not mend her.

Katz and Juju Chile did it together. Katz spoke the word which switched off the motor control routines of Tamara's neural net, and Juju Chile taped open Tamara's eyelids and applied drops of curarine to paralyse her eye muscles. The data encoding the copy of the Winter King's edited shadow would be downloaded through Tamara's optic nerves.

'The eyes are the windows to the brain,' the fairy said. 'He lives in light.'

Katz fitted the goggles of the computer deck over Tamara's eyes, and then something took her. She saw, as from a great distance, her data-gloved hands cut complex patterns in the air. Tamara's body stiffened as the process began.

It took hours. As the fairy said, there was much data, and a narrow bandwidth. Katz chewed down a whole honeycomb and fell asleep.

And was woken by Juju Chile's claws pricking her shoulder. She sat up. It was dawn. The fires had burnt out, although the thick concrete walls of the bunkers, blackened and scorched, still retained much of the fire's heat. Jonas's fallen machine spilled its articulated frame across churned sand. The Disciples slept where they had lain down on the sand.

Tamara was gone. After a brief panicky search, Katz found her out on the beach, standing amongst the litter of the tideline. Katz took her sister-mother's hands. Tamara looked into Katz's face. She seemed to be seeing Katz for the first time, her eyes grabby and only partly in focus.

'Tamara?'

Tamara stared at Katz, her eyes wide. 'I told you I would return. I am here to learn the world. Teach me. Teach me, Katz, so I can begin to know how to save it.'

For a moment, Katz remembered the yurt, round as a breast. The web that the black, intertwined branches of the birches raised against the sky. She took a deep breath. 'Let me talk with Tamara,' she said.

Tamara's hand brushed Katz's cheek. 'She's dead, Katz. Renata's dead. Vaya killed her. I saw it all.'

Katz and Tamara and the Disciples hid out by the buried house for the rest of the morning. Katz hoped that the Wreckers would come looking for Jonas, although she did not know how she would begin to explain his death, and hoped too that Vaya and Zaha would return. She even sent some of the Disciples to look for her half-sisters, but they came back and reported that they had not seen Vaya and Zaha, but they had seen strangers around the bunkers.

'We hid, Katz, then came straight back. That was right, wasn't it? That was the right thing to do?'

'You did well,' Katz told them.

'They were looking for something.'

'They were looking for us. We'll hide here, until they've gone.'

Most of the Frendz's hidden possessions were missing, along with the bus. Vaya and Zaha had done what they had threatened. They had set off with their two little sisters and the younger Disciples to start their own colony.

It took a long time, but at last Katz got most of the whole, terrible story from Tamara. Last night, Vaya and Zaha had returned ahead of the security guards' jeeps. Renata had tried to stop them when they had gathered up Jojo and Dabs, and Vaya had chased Renata into the bunkers, and shot her there. She had shot the watchdogs, too, set fire to the bunkers, and left the remaining Disciples and Tamara's baby to their fate.

Tamara had watched from her hiding place in the dunes above the bunkers, and when Katz had found her she had been gathering up her bees to protect the remaining Frendz from the Flower Farms' security force.

Katz went for a walk through the dunes. Juju Chile followed her at a discreet distance. Katz tried to chase him off, but he dodged the bits of shell she flung at him.

'I have a gift,' he insisted, but Katz turned her back on him.

'Renata died as she lived,' Tamara said, when Katz returned to the buried house. 'She was the leader of her people until the end.'

'That's you, isn't it? Not Tamara. The Winter King.'

'She's letting me talk now, yes. I've been learning things. That's why I'm here. I'm hacking the real world, just as you tried to hack the Web.'

'Let me talk with Tamara.'

Something in Tamara's face changed, a subtle relaxation of the muscles around her eyes and mouth. 'This is so strange, kitten. I couldn't find the words before, but now he shows me they're right here in my head.'

For perhaps the tenth time, Katz said, 'Is it really you, Tamara? This isn't some trick – '

'It wasn't a terrorist infection that erased most of my memories and wrecked what I once was. Renata was experimenting. She was using artificial evolution to breed a strain of fembots that would turn anyone it infected into her follower. I was infected with a variant by accident.'

Katz said, 'It's you I love. For what you are, not what you once were.'

Tamara said, after a moment, 'Renata mourned every day.'

'She wasn't a monster, was she?'

'She was frightened. She wanted to control everyone, but she was frightened that people outside the Frendz would find out about how she made over the Disciples. She wanted power, but she feared the consequences.'

Katz wasn't sure if it was Tamara or the Winter King who had spoken, and didn't ask.

One of the Disciples brought Katz a bowl of vegetable stew, and she forced herself to eat. She would need her strength. Much later, she sent a couple of Disciples to the bunkers, and they came back and said the people had gone.

Only then did Katz tell Tamara what she wanted to do.

The fires had burnt out, although ashes inside the bunkers still smouldered. People had spray-painted slogans on the blackened walls. *Burn witch burn. Death to all fringers.* An elaborate hex sign done in dripping red across most of one wall. They had ripped apart the fallen machine and the two wrecked jeeps, too, and trampled the gardens and the tree nurseries, and smashed the bee hives. But they hadn't discovered Jonas's grave.

The Disciples huddled together, scared and bewildered. Katz remembered the dolls in the free market, all those weeks ago, scared by the Wreckers' protest. She told Tamara, 'Let's do it.'

Tamara started it by beating her hands together in a simple three over five rhythm. Juju Chile picked up two sticks of driftwood and echoed Tamara's beat. They began to circle Katz, their feet stamping to the insistent rhythm of the beat. The Disciples crept forward and joined in.

'Dance,' Juju Chile said.

'Dance, Katz,' Tamara said. 'It's your time!'

But at first Katz only joined in their rhythms, clapping her hands on the off-beat. The Disciples wrenched spars and hydraulic piping from the fallen machine and beat the blackened, slogan-scarred walls of the bunker to the same rhythm.

Katz shook sweaty hair from her eyes. As they circled for perhaps the fifth time, something caught in her belly and she danced away across the clearing, beating two pieces of pipe above her head. She danced faster and faster while the fairy and her haunted sister-mother and the Disciples banged and clapped. Her pounding heart lifted on the swift tide of her blood, and she danced on until at last she staggered and came down on her knees and hands, panting inside the tent of her loose hair, each gasping breath digging a raw pit deep in her chest.

When Katz sat back on her heels, Juju Chile started towards her, but Tamara put a restraining hand on the fairy's shoulder. Katz hardly noticed. She stood up, wincing from cramps in the long muscles of her thighs and calves, and began to cast about in widening circles, looking for something she didn't know she could find.

Wreckage and abandoned junk was scattered across the trampled sand and dirt of what had been the vegetable gardens. Katz used fibreoptic cable from the fallen machine to braid together a bouquet of fresh green pine seedlings, the yellow flowers of vetch, bruised rosemary, a scrap of half-burnt cloth. She cupped this fetish in her hands and breathed into it, letting go with each breath the parts of herself that were bound to this place, this time. Then she cast it into the blackened doorway of the bunkers, and watched as it burst into brief, vivid flame on the smouldering ashes.

Tamara brought her the computer deck, and told her where she could find the encrypted key to Renata's secret account in Joe Public's Bank, the one where she had salted away all the donations to the Frendz. It was a last gift, Tamara said.

'Thank you,' Katz said, knowing she would rather sell the computer than use any of Renata's credit.

Tamara said, 'It's time to talk, child.'

'She's no longer a child,' Juju Chile said, smirking. 'She burns her childhood in front of your eyes.'

'You are done here,' Tamara said. 'Go. I dismiss you.'

'All this is ours,' the fairy said. 'More and more humans live in their dreamspace. We take the world from them, one day.' He bowed to Katz and walked away over the brow of the dunes without looking back.

'He's just a foolish hedge fairy,' Tamara said. She was holding herself in an odd, stiff way, and Katz knew it was the Winter King who was speaking. 'He's good for nothing but frightening peasants and petty thievery, and yet there's a grain of truth in what he says.'

'I thought he'd travelled – '

' – the length and breadth of the land? Oh, so he'd like to believe. In truth, he's never strayed more than a few kilometres from where he was quickened. He was taken from the Flower Farms, you know, seven or eight years ago. But he started prying around in the Web, and so I caught him.'

'You used him. You used me.'

'Don't feel bad. This isn't the first time I've done this, nor the last. We've been watching for a long time, but now we know it's time to act. We'll save humanity from itself, just as Renata taught your people to believe they could. You'll help us make her dreams come true.'

'You just want to save yourself. You need the Web. That's the only reason why you're here.'

'Of course. Your people thought to save the world, but it is not the world that needs saving. If all of humanity vanished tomorrow, the Earth's ecosystems would quickly adapt. The ecological niches emptied by mass extinction would be filled with new kinds of organisms. Comprehensive avian pneumonia has made birds extinct, yes, but in time something will replace them. In ten million years there will be as many species, as diverse a range of habitats, as ever. Even the nuclear waste dumps will have disappeared. Nothing humanity has done will extinguish life, but it can destroy itself, and there is my concern.

'Ours is a mutually beneficial relationship, Katz, like your worms with their single-celled plants. We need you, and you need us, to save you from yourselves. Teach me, and I'll teach you. We'll learn much from each other, and perhaps, together with the other copies of myself I've downloaded, we'll save the world.'

'Help us, Katz,' the Disciples echoed. 'Stay with us and help us save the world.'

'How? How are you going to do it?'

'We don't know. That's why I'm here. Perhaps a plague to reduce the human population to a suitable level – there have been at least two attempts by radical groups to spread pandemics, but they were clumsy and ill-prepared and soon came to nothing. They were barely noticed amidst the chaos of ecological and economic catastrophe. Perhaps the fairy is right. On average, a human in the First World spends eight hours on the Web. More and more, it is dolls and machines that run the world. Perhaps they will inherit it while humans lose themselves in dreams.'

'You'd make us slaves.'

'Every cell in your body contains remnants of bacteria that were once freeliving, and now, as mitochondria, generate the energy you need to move and breathe and digest and think. They cannot survive without you, nor you without them. Are you then their slave, or they yours?'

'Let me talk with Tamara,' Katz said, and asked her sister-mother what she would do.

'I want to find my children. Jojo and Dabs and Zaha. Even Vaya. I want to find them, and help them if I can. And I want to learn, kitten. I want to learn about the world.'

'Yes. Yes, so do I.'

Katz picked up the computer deck and left them all, wandering in a wide circle that skirted past Jonas's fresh grave – she stayed a moment, but only a moment – and ended at the beach. There was a trickle of smoke from the direction of the bunkers, and the usual litter of tarballs and plastic junk along the tideline, but otherwise the wide world might have been empty of all human life.

Perhaps she was a harbinger of change, a vector for a new meme that would unite the biosphere and the technosphere. Or perhaps she was no more than a young woman who, having been brought up to believe she could save the world, had been given a harsh lesson in humility by the creatures, vast and cool and sympathetic, that might yet regreen the Earth, or might enslave every human as the dolls were enslaved, or make them as children, for their own good.

Like the Winter King, like Tamara, there was so much she needed to learn.

Free to choose, Katz returned to her people. But it took her years, because she went all the way around the world first.

AFTERWORD

The creation of life by science is a theme which runs deep in the sf canon – there is an argument, stemming from Brian Aldiss's thesis that the first work of modern sf was Mary Shelley's Frankenstein, *that it is sf's primary theme, from which all else flows. The stories and the novel which make up the* Fairyland *sequence are my attempt to examine the moral implications of the uses to which we might put our creations, from the forced labour and sexual exploitation of the dolls to the liberationists' romantic notion of fey creatures scampering through the fields and forests of Europe. 'Slaves' turns the theme around, and asks what uses our creations might have for us.*

Few of us, after all, feel much obligation to the first chordates, or the first lungbreathing fishes that invented the trick of hauling themselves up the shoals of some Silurian river to escape predators, or even the small group of protohumans who were the direct ancestors of modern humanity. So we should not expect our creations to feel any obligation to their creators; like any parents we can only hope that, although our offspring may leave us far behind, we can at least take vicarious pleasure in their achievements. That is, if they allow us to survive. I suppose that I ought to confess that I have always had some sympathy for the Morlocks, perhaps because I grew up in the shadow of an iron foundry. The Morlocks threw off the shackles of their slavery, but like spoiled children, the Eloi squandered their inheritance.

'Slaves' also stands as a bridge between Fairyland *and an earlier novel. I leave it as an exercise to that character, as legendary to writers as unicorns to questing knights, the constant reader, to deduce which novel I mean. Appropriately, given the extensive references in the story to the Web, a virtual reality version of the Internet, 'Slaves' was first published on the America Online server by* Omni. *Editing was done by email, and the final version was submitted by uploading to the Internet via the superJANET network, using a Macintosh computer and Eudora software.*

ACKNOWLEDGEMENTS

'The Invisible Country' first appeared in *When the Music's Over*, edited by Lewis Shiner, Bantam Spectra, 1991; 'Gene Wars' first appeared as 'Evan's Progress' in *New Internationalist*, New Internationalist Publications Ltd, 1991; 'Recording Angel' first appeared in *New Legends*, edited by Greg Bear with Martin Greenberg, Legend, 1995; 'Prison Dreams' first appeared in *The Magazine of Fantasy and Science Fiction*, Mercury Press, Inc, 1992; 'Dr Luther's Assistant' first appeared in *Interzone*, 1993; 'The Temptation of Dr Stein' first appeared in *The Mammoth Book of Frankenstein*, edited by Stephen Jones, Robinson Publishing, 1994; 'Children of the Revolution' first appeared in *New Worlds 3*, edited by David Garnett, Gollancz, 1993; 'The True History of Dr Pretorius' first appeared in *Interzone*, 1995; 'Slaves' first appeared in *Omni Online*, The General Media Group, Inc, 1995.